NIGHTHAWK'S
TURMOIL

LEE WILLIAMS

LW PUBLISHING ENTERPRISES
WESTMONT, IL

ACKNOWLEDGMENTS

To THE MEN AND WOMEN in law enforcement who unknowingly contributed to this story and all the first responders who sacrifice their safety to make our daily existence possible. I addition I would like to thank the members of the Room Seven writers' group including Pat Camalliere, Luisa Buehler, Pam Holman, Rod Brandon, Jon Payne and the late Frederick Meek. Without their patience and constructive criticism this novel would not exist. Finally, to my significant other, Debbie Geary, for expanding my consciousness of a woman's thought process in my attempt to write from the perspective of a female protagonist.

CHAPTER 1

Courtroom 2502
Dirksen Federal Building
219 S. Dearborn, Chicago, IL
Monday, December 6, 2004
11:00 a.m.

HIS BLACK SKIN AND ORANGE jumpsuit made him look like most defendants that appeared in federal court. He was not sitting on the bench today, deciding someone's fate, but instead found himself escorted to the lectern by two U.S. Marshals. Federal judge Robert Carlton contemplated the plea he was about to make. It would shock everyone, especially his wife, IRS Special Agent Gloria Nighthawk, and his son Darius. Gloria was responsible for his indictment.

Carlton stood to the left of Todd Jeffreys and Phillip Tunney, the assistant U.S. attorneys. Jeffreys was white and ten years out of Harvard. Tunney was African American, a solid Midwesterner from the University of Wisconsin.

Carlton faced Judge Peterson, the only other Black man who wore a robe in this district. On the wall behind the judge was the seal of the United States District Court for the Northern Judicial District of

Illinois, beneath which Carlton himself had presided for fourteen years.

"Mr. Carlton, I understand you have reached an agreement with the U.S. Attorney's office not to go to trial and have decided to plead guilty to all the charges filed against you," Judge Peterson said. "This includes those on which you were most recently arraigned, obstruction of justice and theft of government property, as well as the original charges of money laundering and conspiracy to defraud the government. Is that your intention today?"

Carlton glanced around the courtroom. The jury box was empty now, but if he didn't plead guilty there soon would be twelve men and women seated in it who would decide his future. He would have little more than a week to persuade them that he had not sold his judgeship to a gangbanger. Was it possible to convince total strangers that his character was above reproach when ninety percent of the time at trial was spent introducing the prosecution's incriminating evidence?

His gaze shifted to the prosecution table, where IRS Special Agent Lauren Ashberry and FBI Special Agent Anthony Fanelli sat alongside the prosecutors. Lauren had been trained by Judge Carlton's wife. The young blonde agent was sure to report every move he made back to Gloria, and she would advise Lauren on countermoves. Gray-haired Fanelli, toying with a pen, was one half of U.S. Attorney Jeffreys's private investigative arm. Fanelli and his cohort, Wayne Axelrod, would leave no stone unturned unless it hurt the prosecution's case.

Carlton looked past them, over the rows of newspaper reporters, television anchors, and court buffs waiting to hear how he had betrayed the trust that the people of this jurisdiction put in him. His gaze reached the last row of benches in the courtroom, where his son Darius sat. Tears welled in Carlton's eyes at the thought of what he had put the boy through.

"Mr. Carlton, I asked you a question. Are you pleading guilty?" Judge Peterson said. His deep voice filled the courtroom.

Carlton returned his focus to the judge. "Your honor, I realize that I previously advised you I intended to plead guilty. But in my heart, I know I'm innocent. So today I'm changing my plea to not guilty on all charges. I will be representing myself."

Fanelli slammed his pen on the table, then stared at Ashberry, shook his head, and mumbled several words. The only one loud enough to be heard was, "Nighthawk."

Jeffreys spoke up. "Your honor, this comes as a complete surprise to us. Based on Mr. Carlton's word, we have stopped preparing for trial and devoted our resources to other cases. Obviously, his word carries no weight."

"Mr. Carlton, you have the right to change your plea. However, at this late date I must give the government adequate time to prepare for your trial," the judge said as he paged through his calendar. "Based on what I had been advised regarding your plea, I have accorded today and the ensuing week to another trial. My next opening would be Monday, February fourteenth, 2005."

Fanelli leered at Lauren, sending a message that was meant for her partner.

The judge nodded to Jeffreys. "Does that fit into your schedule?"

"Your honor, whatever date you pick, this office will be ready to prosecute this case to the fullest extent." Jeffreys's eyes went from Judge Peterson to Carlton. "I anticipate you will keep Carlton incarcerated. Considering that he was surveilling a principal witness in this case and carrying a firearm he had withheld from evidence in another case, the prosecutor's office believes him a threat to public safety."

Peterson nodded. "The court agrees. Therefore, Mr. Carlton, you will remain incarcerated at the Metropolitan Correctional Center until trial is held and a verdict has been returned. If found guilty, you will remain in the custody of the MCC until sentencing."

"Your honor, that will impose a serious hardship on the preparation of my defense—"

Jeffreys gripped the lectern. "Your honor, there's no way you can allow this man his freedom so he can go hunting witnesses. Bad enough the key witness was murdered by the defendant's wife—"

The judge cut him off. "I understand that matter is still under investigation. Before you jump to conclusions, Mr. Jeffreys, why don't you let me rule."

"Sorry, your honor." Jeffreys took a step back. Carlton smirked and folded his arms across his chest.

The judge continued speaking. "Mr. Carlton can use the library and meeting facilities at the correctional center to prepare his defense."

Carlton's arms fell to his sides. "Your honor, we all know it can take hours for someone to gain access to an inmate. If there's a lockdown, even longer. How can I arrange for assistance in preparing my defense under those conditions?"

"Mr. Carlton let's give this a try. If you have any complaints, you know where to reach me. Next case."

Carlton held up his index finger. "Your honor, may I have one minute to see my son? I'm locked up in security and it's very hard to get a visit."

"Very well." Peterson beckoned to the marshals and conveyed the order. They escorted Carlton to the door on the side of the courtroom next to the holding cell, and one of them patted Darius down before allowing the boy to move forward.

Carlton embraced his son. Darius stood rigid, not hugging back. He was seventeen, an inch shorter than his father at six feet six, with the same slender build and coffee color. "I couldn't plead guilty," Carlton whispered, then stepped away enough to look Darius in the face. "Jeffreys is going to ask the court to sentence me to twenty years. If you had done what I said, this would be all over."

"You were wrong to get me involved," Darius whispered back. "Mom said I did the right thing."

The marshals let Darius and his father share one more embrace and then took Carlton into the holding cell. Darius's last view of his father was of handcuffs being slapped on his wrists.

The prosecution team entered Jeffreys's office. Lauren sat in one of the four chairs that circled Jeffreys's desk and prepared to take notes. Fanelli sat in the chair farthest away from Lauren. Tunney and Wayne Axelrod, Fanelli's partner, joined the meeting and filled in the empty seats.

Already, Lauren could feel an "us against IRS" mood.

"I told Nighthawk he wouldn't plead guilty." Fanelli glanced at Lauren as he tossed his notebook to the floor.

"Lauren, I don't want to put you in a difficult position." Jeffreys walked to his desk, past his Harvard Law School diploma, photos of his wife and two daughters, and pictures of Attorney General John Ashcroft and President George W. Bush and eased into his chair. "I know Gloria is your partner and you have a great deal of respect for her, and you should. From what I've heard, she's had an outstanding career. But there are some things we must discuss about the direction of this case that could create a conflict for you."

Lauren crossed her legs. She was overmatched against the prosecutors and senior FBI agents but determined to hold her own. "Mr. Jeffreys, I don't think it's fair to exclude anyone from our office from a meeting regarding any trial strategy that directly affects CID and one of its agents."

Jeffreys continued as if she hadn't spoken. "It could also destroy your relationship with her. So right now, I think it's best if you return to your office. I promise you, at the right time we will advise you and your management of whatever direction we feel is best for this case."

She knew what was coming but had only one card to play. "Then I'll have to advise my office that this meeting is being held to develop strategy for the Carlton trial without a representative from CID."

"I understand, Lauren. Rest assured, we will cooperate fully with your chief, and you, and any other CID personnel," Jeffreys said.

They all looked at her, clearly waiting. Lauren slammed her notebook shut, got up, and left the office. *Damn…they're going to indict Gloria.*

"I told Nighthawk he wouldn't plead guilty," Fanelli groused, again. "'Oh no,' she said, 'he promised.' Bullshit. The only way to get the truth is to indict Nighthawk." He leaned forward in his chair. "She whacked McElroy, our only good witness. What did you expect her to do when he was going to put her husband away for years?"

Tunney looked at the floor, took a deep breath and exhaled, then raised his eyes again. "We can't jump to conclusions about what happened and why. We have to give this some serious thought, figure out what's best. Should we offer her immunity? How would that look in the eyes of the jury, giving immunity to a federal agent? That's an admission she's withholding evidence or would otherwise testify falsely, which would affect her credibility as a witness."

Fanelli raised his arm. "Why don't we drag her in here, Mirandize her, and see what she says?"

Jeffreys broke in. "Do we know for a fact she's withholding evidence? Isn't it possible that what she said is the truth? She went to the West Side after she read the FBI informant's report."

Fanelli smirked. "Yeah, and showed up just in time to kill McElroy."

"We can't overreact. We have no evidence besides what common sense may tell us that this was an unusual confluence of events." Jeffreys pointed at Axelrod and Fanelli. "I want you two to interview the responding police officers and see if they observed or suspected anything. I think it's the same two officers that took her statement. Nighthawk has an excellent reputation in this office, and I don't intend to ruin it without a damned good reason." He reached for a pen and tapped it several times against his desktop. "However, if she is withholding anything, she'll have to pay the price just like anyone else."

CHAPTER 2

CID-IRS Office
Kluczynski Federal Building
230 S. Dearborn, Chicago, IL
Monday, December 6, 2004
12:30 p.m.

SEATED AT HER DESK, SPECIAL Agent Gloria Nighthawk wondered what was taking so long. *Robert pleads guilty, the judge reviews the charges and accepts the plea, and they set a date for sentencing.* She glanced at the photos of her son Darius and daughter Adsila on her credenza. So far, there'd been no mention of Darius being at the scene of the shooting. *He's safe. Time to move on with life as best we can.*

Abruptly, the office door flew open. Lauren rushed in, caught Gloria's eye, and jerked her head toward the office of their supervisor, Special Agent Tom Stephens.

Gloria got up and met Lauren, and the two of them walked into Stephens's office. Gloria closed the door behind them. Stephens leaned back, resting his elbows on the arms of his chair. His belly covered his belt. "What happened?"

"Trouble." Lauren filled them in on Carlton's change of plea and the new trial date.

Stephens shifted his gaze to Gloria. "Why do you think he's pleading not guilty?"

Gloria took a deep breath and blew it out. "I have no idea." That wasn't true, though. She knew what her husband was thinking. He could threaten to make a statement to the prosecutors that his earlier plea was made under duress, giving them the testimony that would make her a defendant and implicate Darius. She could envision Fanelli and Axelrod pressuring Darius about the night McElroy died. Could he hold up?

Lauren briefly touched Gloria's hand. "Darius was in the courtroom. The judge let him visit with his father for a minute."

Gloria bowed her head, her chin dropping to her chest. "I can't believe this."

"There's more." Lauren gazed at the floor and then at Gloria. "Jeffreys made me leave the meeting after the plea hearing. He said it was a potential conflict, that it could destroy my relationship with you and affect the direction of the case. He said he would keep CID informed, but right now it means only Fanelli and Axelrod are on the case and it worries me…what direction they might go in."

"Direction of the case? I don't like the sound of that." Gloria swallowed, imagining the feel of handcuffs on her wrists.

"We don't have many options. It's the U.S. Attorney's call. I'll advise the chief," Stephens said. He nodded toward the door — a signal for them to leave — and picked up the phone.

CHAPTER 3

Courtroom 2502
Dirksen Federal Building
Monday, December 6, 2004
1:00 p.m.

DARIUS RETURNED TO HIS SEAT in the back of the courtroom, dazed at the turn of events. In his father's eyes he knew he would always be a failure. His father's words echoed through his mind: *If you had done what I said this would all be over.* Darius was supposed to kill the dope dealer, McElroy, but at the last second he couldn't pull the trigger.

The door to the lockup clicked shut, as if sealing his father's fate. Robert Carlton was unlikely to be a free man again. Darius sighed, overwhelmed by the massive courtroom with its thirty-foot ceilings. His father was doomed, and it was Darius's fault. The presumption of a defendant's innocence was bull, his father had said, the government's burden of proof a fable. The real burden was on the defendant to convince twelve ordinary men and women of his innocence.

The main attraction gone, the press scurried like lemmings to the next free show in another courtroom. Darius picked up his parka, laid it over his lap, and rested his elbows on his knees with his head in his hands. Time slipped by as a parade of other defendants, their lawyers and prosecutors sidled up to the lectern. It was white noise to Darius. His thoughts circled in his mind as he tried to figure out what he owed his father and what could be done about it now. *If I testify for my dad and the truth comes out, then I destroy my mother. Either way, I destroy my family.*

After a while, the noise around him lessened. He straightened slowly. Judge Peterson wasn't seated up front at the bench anymore, and a court security guard in a blue blazer approached. "Son, it's 2:30. You've got to leave the courtroom now. Court is done for the day and I'm locking it up."

Darius stood and nodded. He shuffled out of the courtroom and down some hallways, exited the federal building on Dearborn, and headed south and then east on Jackson Boulevard. Wandering aimlessly, he crossed Michigan Avenue and tramped through Grant Park. The wind swirled out of the east through the naked trees. Darius crossed Lake Shore Drive onto the cement walkway that bordered Lake Michigan. In the summer, halyards clanged against the masts of sailboats, but on this December day the wind whipped up whitecaps. Waves crashed over the wall, spraying Darius. He rounded the walkway as he approached the south side of Monroe Harbor. The wind turned out of the north, and waves began rolling the length of the harbor. They called him toward the lake.

He moved closer to it. The waves cascaded over his shoes and soaked his pants knee high. One slip and he could escape the despair of betraying his father, rid himself of the fear of ruining his mother's life. The pain wouldn't last long. After the initial shock of the ice-cold water, he would quickly go numb. The waves crashed harder. He felt drawn to the lake. It would be as pain free as possible. An alternative to the curse he was living under. The guilt of betraying his parents gave him no choice.

He inched closer, the toes of his shoes over the edge of the cement wall. The north wind buffeted him. He slipped, twisting to his left. He fell hard onto the cement, balancing on the edge. His right knee hung over the wall, in the icy water. His fingers grasped for traction. He pushed himself up and rolled onto his back.

For a few seconds, all Darius could do was stare up at the gray sky. Then he righted himself, pushing onto his hands and knees. He looked at his soaked pants and cursed, disgusted that he hadn't done what he should have. In his father's eyes, it would be one more example of his cowardice. He stood, turned his back on the lake and stumbled up the stairs heading toward the Shedd Aquarium. From there, he wandered back to the Loop.

After a time, he found himself on Clark Street standing in front of Stebbins, the bar where he'd met his father after the arraignment. It was the day his father told him they were going to celebrate his rite of passage by getting drunk together.

Darius grabbed the door handle and pulled it open. He paused, undecided on entering.

"Come the fuck in or leave," someone yelled.

He let the door close and headed south on Clark. Thoughts of the days right after the arraignment crossed his mind. The day his father planted the seed. His father had woken him in the wee hours of the morning and told him what he needed Darius to do. "I'm innocent," he'd said, and then told Darius that killing McElroy was the only way to ensure his freedom.

Darius kept trudging south, crossing over to State Street. Staring at his feet as he mindlessly kept putting one in front of the other, his hands buried in the pockets of his parka.

Dusk settled in as the December wind chilled his soul. His posture sagged, neck bent low as he sloshed through dirty snow. He saw no solution that could help both of his parents. His mind went numb looking for an answer where none existed.

He crossed 35th Street and gazed at the hulking group of high-rises known as the Robert Taylor Homes, a notorious gang-infested, low-income housing project. Each of the twenty-six buildings stood sixteen stories high, with chain link fences on the catwalks locking in the inhabitants. Shadows of people hustled between the buildings. Others lurked near the doorways, controlling who could enter or leave.

"Yo, boy. Nice coat you got. Nice and warm, I bet."

Darius halted as a tall boy stepped into his path. He was almost as tall as Darius. The boy tugged on Darius's sleeve.

Darius attempted to walk around him. Then two others showed up, blocking the sidewalk. One of the new arrivals pulled down the zipper on Darius's parka. The other, along with the first boy, slid the coat off his shoulders.

Darius just stood there, dressed in one of his father's three-piece suits.

The one who'd unzipped the parka grinned. "Holy shit, look at this pretty boy. Hey, Blood. This boy and you jus' about the same size. Why don't you take his rags? He ain't gonna need them anymore."

"Yeah, Shorty. They be looking good on me." The tall boy, Blood, reached for Darius's lapel. Darius jerked his shoulder away.

Blood pulled out a switchblade, then flipped the knife from one hand to the other. "You gonna make me cut that off you? I have to mess it up, might as well toss you and the threads in the garbage."

Darius's heart pounded in his chest. He tried to come on strong, but the words stuttered out. "My…my father's…a judge. You better back off. Let…let me go and I won't say anything."

Swift footfalls sounded behind him. Then a voice: "What the fuck you doing?"

Suddenly looking nervous, Blood and his homies backed away. "Nothin'," Blood said. "Jus' seeing if this boy wants to buy some weed or toot."

"That his coat?"

Blood handed the parka back to Darius. The newcomer moved into view. "Now get the fuck out of here," he said.

Darius shrugged his parka back on and looked at his rescuer. The man was dressed in black and had a diamond stud in his front tooth. "Thanks. I thought they were going to kill me."

"Punks don't think twice 'bout killing. They don't realize it's bad for business. Draws too much heat. What you doing here anyway?"

The reply stumbled out of Darius's mouth. "I…was walking home. Just…had a bad day. A lot on my mind."

"What gots you down so bad?"

He couldn't tell it. But this stranger on the street seemed to care. "Family problems. Everything turning south. No matter what I do, I'll make it worse."

"You need something get your mind off your troubles." The man reached into his black leather coat. "Here, take this." He handed Darius a couple of small plastic bags filled with brown powder. "Help you forget about bad days. Make you feel good."

"What is it?"

"A little smack. Good stuff. You don't have to shoot it in your arm. Just rub it on your gums or snort it."

Darius nodded and slid the bags into the pocket of his suit jacket. "Thanks. Thanks for helping me out."

"No problem. Anybody give you trouble, tell 'em you're with Marvin. No one will bother you." The man walked off toward the nearest building, 3904. The two gangbangers guarding the entrance opened the double doors for him as if he was royalty. Darius watched as he disappeared inside.

CHAPTER 4

Carlton/Nighthawk Residence,
Bronzeville, Chicago, IL
Monday, December 6, 2004
4:30 p.m.

DARIUS LET HIMSELF INTO THE house and plodded up the stairs to his bedroom. His mother called out to him from the kitchen: "Hi honey, we're making soup. Want some?"

He ignored her. His thoughts were consumed with his failure to protect his father's future. A future that now looked like Robert Carlton could die in a federal penitentiary before ever again seeing the light of day.

Darius pushed his bedroom door open, went in, and closed it behind him. He dropped his parka to the floor and collapsed in bed, the damp legs of his father's three-piece suit clinging to his calves. He reached into the jacket pocket and pulled out one of the dime bags Marvin had given him. He battled temptation as he recalled the pusher's words. *A little smack. Good stuff, you don't have to shoot it in your arm. Just rub it on your gums or snort it.*

He shoved the bag back in his pocket and rolled on his side. *If I'd had the courage to do what I should've, there wouldn't have been a witness against my father, and my mother could have walked away. It's my fault.*

Darius remembered how his hand shook when he pointed the pistol at McElroy. He'd tried to pull the trigger, but his finger froze.

Then his mother yelled, "Get down!" And Darius listened to her like a little boy hiding behind his mother's apron. He dove to the curb, hearing the shots fired from her pistol that should have come from his.

He rolled onto his back. His eyes flooded with tears that streaked down his cheeks. He fished into the suit coat pocket again, pulled out a bag of the powder, and tugged at the seal, breaking it open. Again, Marvin's words came back to him. *Help you forget about bad days. Make you feel good.*

He shoved his index finger in his mouth to moisten it, then pulled it out. He looked at his finger, felt it cooling as the saliva evaporated. He repeated the action, this time rolling his wet finger in the plastic bag. The brown powder stuck to his skin.

He gazed at it, knowing he was about to change his life. His hand started shaking just like it had when he aimed the pistol at McElroy. But this time he would have the courage to do it.

He thrust his finger in his mouth, rubbing the powder against his gums, and waited. Where was the euphoria? He lay there for several minutes. The miracle drug was not delivering. Then it crept up on him—a nice feeling, chilled, happy, mellow. He felt love all over. His eyelids grew heavy. They slowly closed, and he drifted off to peace and contentment.

A light knock on the door. His mother's voice. "Honey, I've got homemade chicken soup. Can I come in?"

———

"Huh," was the only response from inside Darius's room. Gloria entered, the soup bowl balanced in one hand, and saw Darius lying in bed. He was still wearing his father's suit. The trouser legs were damp up to the knees.

She placed the bowl of soup on the nightstand, sat on the corner of the bed, and rested her hand on his forehead. "You feel warm. Are you okay?"

He rolled on his side, away from her.

"Baby, why don't you have some soup." She moved her hand to his calf. "Your suit is wet. Take it off and get under the covers."

"I'm not hungry. I just want to sleep." He sounded shaky, his voice lacking its usual energy.

"Have you had anything to eat?"

"I said I'm not hungry."

Gloria clenched her jaw but kept her tone calm. "Okay, baby. I'll check on you later." She stood, pulled a blanket over him, and left the room, closing the door on the way out.

In the hallway, she leaned her back against the wall and hung her head. She wished she knew the right words to say to Darius. She knew teenage sons grow distant from their mothers. Gaps develop. But her involvement in the indictment and arrest of his father had created a chasm, and she had no idea how to bridge it. She dragged her sleeve across her face, wiping away a tear.

CHAPTER 5

CID-IRS Office
Kluczynski Federal Building
Tuesday, December 7, 2004
8:30 a.m.

AFTER WORKING WITH GLORIA FOR six months as a special agent, Lauren Ashberry knew what it meant when her partner jerked her head toward the heating vent next to Gloria's desk. She took her usual seat there, finding the heat welcome as it seeped into her legs. "Remember Marvin told us about that janitor, Wilson?" Gloria asked. "McElroy used the guy as another straw purchaser for cars from Henderson's."

"Yeah. We had to leave for Iraq, never got a chance to talk to Wilson."

"Our memo wasn't turned over in discovery," Gloria said. "No one knows about Wilson except us."

"You want to talk to him now?"

"Exactly."

"What if Wilson tells us about other vehicles McElroy purchased under his name?"

"We corroborate the testimony if we can and turn it over to Jeffreys. I checked our memo. There's no school on Franklin, but there is a Franklin Elementary on Evergreen just west of LaSalle, in the same area Marvin was talking about. I'm betting that's where he meant."

They entered the school at 9:00 and went to the administrative office, where they introduced themselves and presented their identification to the clerk at the front desk. The clerk was fiftyish, slender and wore thick glasses. The name plate near her read *Cheryl Archibald*.

"We need to meet with an employee of the school," Gloria said.

"You'll have to get permission from the principal."

"That's fine. Can we speak with him?"

"He's not in."

"When do you expect him?"

"He floats around. He makes his own schedule."

Gloria slowly drew in a breath and released it. "What if you need to talk to him?"

"He calls in…sometimes."

Lauren glanced at the name plate. "Mrs. Archibald, we can't wait around for the principal to show up or call in."

"We only need to talk to Reginald Wilson for a few minutes. He's not in any trouble. We just need to verify some information," Gloria said.

"Mr. Wilson? Why didn't you say so. Him, I can tell you about."

"Good. I assume he's working today?"

"No, he's not. That's why I can tell you about him. He's no longer an employee. He was caught smoking marijuana on school grounds. We can't have that kind of behavior here."

"Certainly not. We must protect our schoolchildren from that kind of influence," Gloria said seriously. "Do you have an address for him?"

"I have his termination file right here, as a matter of fact." Mrs. Archibald snagged a manila folder from one end of the counter, opened it, and ran her finger down the first page. "Let's see. Here it is — 3904 South State Street, Apartment 404." She glanced up at them, her expression somber. "I don't think you ladies should go there by yourselves. That's the Robert Taylor housing project."

Robert Taylor Homes
South State Street
Tuesday, December 7, 2004
9:30 a.m.

Half an hour later, Gloria pulled the Blazer into the parking lot of the high-rise with 3904 on the front. Brown weeds escaped from between cracks in the asphalt amid the slushy snow.

Lauren bit her lip. "Maybe that Archibald woman was right. We should have backup."

Gloria shrugged. "We'll be okay. This is the best time to go into the projects. Before it gets too active."

They got out of the SUV and headed toward the entrance. Two young Black men stood on each side of the double doors, which were painted with gang graffiti. Above the doors, about ten feet up, was a six-sided star with the letter G on one side and D on the other — Gangster Disciple turf.

"You sure this is a good idea?" Lauren murmured.

Gloria slid her a glance. "You've got to act like you own the place."

They reached the doors, and one of the men eyed Lauren up and down. "Yo, sweet stuff. You want a guided tour of the premises?"

Gloria pulled her jacket back, showing her belt badge and holstered Sig.

"Whoa, it the *po*-lice," the man said as he opened the door and bowed, allowing them entrance.

They passed through the doors and headed to the stairwell. Gloria figured other eyes would pick them up as soon as they reached their destination; it wasn't just her badge and gun that had gotten them past the sentries. "They say never take the elevators. You never know what you'll see when the doors open—like a Mac-10," she said.

Lauren gave a nervous smile. "I'm glad we're only going to the fourth floor."

They climbed four flights, huffing slightly at the top of the last one. Gloria hesitated at the interior door to the hallway but opened it at Lauren's nod. A few loiterers were visible at both ends of the corridor, apparently waiting for them. The gangbangers wore baggy jeans hanging around their hips, sweatshirts, and do-rags. Not one of them looked more than sixteen.

"You think the boys at the door sent a message up to see where we were heading?" Lauren asked.

"Wouldn't surprise me." Gloria eyed the apartment doors as they proceeded down the hall. The numbers were scribbled on with magic marker in different colors. Number 404 was red. Music came from inside the apartment: Alicia Keys' song, "You Don't Know My Name".

"You ready?" Gloria asked.

Lauren gave her a thumbs-up and knocked. There was no response. Gloria waited ten seconds, then pounded on the door with her fist. "Chicago P.D." The music stopped, and they heard footsteps rushing toward the door. The man that opened it was a light skinned African-American, about thirty-five years old, five foot seven and slender. He wore a black sweatshirt and sweatpants.

"Are you Reginald Wilson?" Gloria asked.

"Why you want to know?"

Gloria flashed her badge and identification. "We're IRS special agents, Mr. Wilson. We need to ask you a few questions."

Wilson looked up and down the hallway, eyeing the boys there. "About what?"

"We'd rather not talk out here. Can we come in?"

His hand fluttered to his lips. "Uh . . ."

"Either that, or you can come downtown with us. Your choice."

He nodded and stepped back, allowing them inside.

The temperature in the two-bedroom apartment was only slightly warmer than the outside air. Gloria glanced around, sizing up the place. A blanket tossed over the sofa and a pillow on one end made it clear where Wilson slept. Across from the sofa was a twenty-inch television on a milk crate, and next to it a CD player. On the kitchen table were a pack of Marlboros, a Bic lighter, a box of Cocoa Puffs sitting next to a bowl, and a black cat licking the residue of milk.

"Sheba, get off the table," Wilson ordered. The cat looked at him lazily, then lowered its head for a few more licks at the bowl. He shooed the cat away, put the bowl in the sink and the cereal box on the kitchen counter. "Okay if we sit here?"

"Sure." Gloria grabbed a chair, and Lauren did the same. "I'm Agent Nighthawk, and this is Agent Ashberry," Gloria said as they sat and Lauren pulled out a small notepad. "We want to ask you about some cars that were purchased in your name."

Wilson cleared his throat. "These cars. They have to do with Spencer McElroy?"

"That's right, Reginald. Why don't you tell us about them?"

He rubbed a hand over his lips. "Is he, is he dead? I heard he was dead."

Gloria sat straighter. "Yes. He's dead." *I'm the one that shot him, but you don't need to know that.*

"'Cause that's the only way I talk about him. Him being dead."

"Okay. Tell us about the cars."

"There be three. I don't remember the dates. A Cadillac DeVille, a SRX, and a BMW 500."

"Where were they purchased from?"

"I don't know. He brought the paperwork to the school and had me sign for the cars. He was supposed to pay me $300 for each car.

The S.O.B. gave me $100 and that was it. McElroy, he ain't the kind of guy you argued with."

"How did you know McElroy?"

"We went to Marshall High together. So, we hung for a while. Stuff like that."

"Was that the extent of your relationship with him?"

"Like I say. We hung out, cars and stuff."

"You didn't pay any of your own money toward any of those cars?" Lauren asked.

"No, ma'am. He was supposed to pay me."

"You said 'stuff'. What do you mean, stuff?" Gloria asked.

Wilson moistened his lips. "You said he's dead, right? I mean, gone forever and forever."

"Definitely dead and gone." A memory flashed through Gloria's brain, McElroy firing toward Darius and her squeezing the trigger.

Wilson grabbed the pack of Marlboros, tapped a smoke out and stuck it between his lips. He lit it with the Bic and took a deep breath. "He'd kill me for sure, but it don't make no difference now."

"What doesn't make a difference?"

"His baby momma. Tamika. She really my baby momma."

Gloria stiffened. She reached to twist her wedding ring, but it wasn't there anymore. "You're saying Tamika's baby girl isn't McElroy's. That you're the father?"

He took a long drag on his smoke and nodded. "Yeah. He kill me for sure."

Lost for words, she couldn't come up with the next question. Lauren filled in. "How long have you been in a relationship with Tamika?"

"Couple of years. She liked his money, but she loved me." He took another drag on his smoke and tapped the ashes into his palm.

"She ever tell you what they were doing with his money?' Lauren asked.

"What you mean?"

"Like, was there anyone else McElroy was using to hide it?"

Wilson looked thoughtful for a moment. "She told me they bought some buildings and cars under her mama's name, Shiquita DuBonnet. That they were fucking with her old man. That guy that's a federal judge. Carlton. Tamika made up some bullshit story that Carlton told them to do that. She was getting even 'cause her mother killed herself when Carlton wouldn't marry her. Didn't want to divorce his wife, I guess."

Lauren rested her pen on her notepad. Heart racing, feeling dazed, Gloria briefly caught her partner's eye.

Lauren lifted her pen. "When did Tamika tell you this? That she lied about Judge Carlton's involvement?"

"I don't remember the last time. I haven't seen her for a while. Say a couple of months ago."

"The last time? How often did she mention it?"

"It came up a few times when we were together. Usually when she was pissed at McElroy. When she thought he was messing around, so she figured it was all right for her to mess around. She'd call me, and we'd meet at a motel. Usually that one on 59th and King Drive."

"Did you book the rooms under your name or hers?"

He snickered. "Shit, ain't nobody use their real names."

"What names did you use?"

He shook his head. "I don't remember exactly." He glanced up at the ceiling, as if jogging his memory. "I like cars. One time, I used Nick Cadillac. Another time, Joe Mercedes. The motel people don't care as long as you give them cash."

"You ever pay with a credit card?"

"Me?" He laughed. "I don't have no credit cards. Tamika had one. Don't remember she ever used it at the motel. They don't like credit cards."

"You remember any of the dates when you two were at the motel?"

"McElroy went to Mississippi right after Christmas to visit his mother. I met Tamika at the motel a day or two after."

"Did you get a copy of the motel bill?"

"Nah. You pay cash, there ain't no bill."

Gloria broke in. "Let me ask you one more time. Tamika was upset because her mother committed suicide when Judge Carlton refused to divorce his wife and marry her. So, Tamika invented the story that Judge Carlton told them to buy cars and real estate under Tamika's mother's name—Shiquita DuBonnet?"

"Yeah, that's what she told me. Said her mother took a bunch of pills and killed herself."

Gloria pushed her chair away from the kitchen table and stood. "Thanks, Reginald. We might have to come back if we have follow-up questions, but I think we're done for now." *I'm done for sure when we tell the U.S. Attorney.*

They left Wilson's apartment and headed down the stairs. "What are you going to do?" Lauren asked.

"There's no option. We have to tell the prosecutors."

"Fanelli's going to think this is proof of a conspiracy between you and your husband. First you kill the principal witness against him in the money laundering scheme and then you come up with a witness to refute Tamika's testimony."

"But Tamika had motivation to lie. You heard it, same as I did." Gloria shook her head. Now she had to face the reality that the case she'd developed against her husband was based on that lie. Why couldn't she have seen it? The acts he took out of fear of a long jail sentence—the pistol he stole from evidence, his arrest for stalking McElroy—none of it would have occurred if Robert had never been charged with the original violations. Guilt washed over her, more intense than any she had ever experienced. Why had it been impossible for her to believe her husband's innocence? Had she wanted him to be guilty? How could she have made such an error in judgement? Was it a way to justify a divorce to their children? The thought that she might have stooped so low made her shudder.

The cold air outside felt like a slap in the face. They crossed the parking lot and got into the Blazer. Gloria started the engine and backed out of the parking space, her mind still full of what Wilson had said.

"Stop!" Lauren yelled.

"What?" Gloria snapped.

Lauren pointed at the sidewalk fifty yards away. "Isn't that Marvin, pushing some kid around?

Gloria stopped the SUV and looked. Lauren was right—there was Marvin Bailey, her informant, shoving a teenage boy and yelling something unintelligible at him. "I can't deal with this now. We'll ask about it the next time we meet him."

She took her foot off the brake and finished backing out, then pulled out of the parking lot. "We've got to go straight to the prosecutors. The longer we delay, the more it's going to look like we made it up." She could guess how Jeffreys and Tunney would take the exculpatory evidence eliminating the major charges against her husband. The case—*her* case—was falling apart. Now she had to weigh what it could cost her. Fanelli already thought she'd shot McElroy to protect Robert. If he could convince the prosecutors of that, at the very least her career was over. At worst, she was headed to jail.

CHAPTER 6

U.S. Attorney's Office
Dirksen Federal Building
Tuesday, December 7, 2004
11:00 a.m.

"I DON'T FUCKING BELIEVE IT," Fanelli said, pacing across Todd Jeffreys's office. Gloria and Lauren had gone there as soon as they left the housing project, to advise the U.S. attorney of Reginald Wilson's statement. "First you kill McElroy, and then you come up with this bullshit story—"

Gloria pointed her finger at him. "Listen, Fanelli, I'm getting tired of your bull. I didn't put your informant's memo in discovery. That was someone else's oversight. Then you go ahead and indict my husband and arrest him without consulting us. We never advised anyone that our investigation was complete. There was no reason you had to move quickly. You could have waited until we got back from Iraq. You just wanted to steal the case because he's a federal judge!"

Fanelli slammed his fist on Jeffreys's desk. "We don't have to steal—"

Jeffreys raised both hands. "Hold on, both of you. This is what needs to happen." He turned to Lauren. "You already have a relationship with Wilson. You and Axelrod go back out and interview him again. Let's make sure his testimony is one hundred percent accurate." His gaze shifted to Gloria. "Get whatever corroborating information and documents you can. I'm not implying that Wilson's testimony is false, is that clear? We're just dotting the I's and crossing the T's. Then we'll meet again and decide where we go from there."

"I want to interview him," Fanelli said.

Gloria turned on him. "You don't think we know how to interview—"

Jeffreys interrupted. "You're not going, Anthony. There's no need to pour more gas on the fire. I'm certain Wilson's testimony is accurate, as Gloria described. But with the defendant a federal judge, and us now possibly having to reduce the charges filed against him, I'll have to explain that to the attorney general in Washington."

Buoyed by Jeffreys's apparent support, Gloria crossed her arms and stared Fanelli down.

⁎ ⁎ ⁎

The next morning, Lauren met with Gloria, Tom Stephens, and Jeffreys in the assistant U.S. attorney's office. "Wayne went through the rough draft of our memo with Wilson, line by line," Lauren said. "Wilson didn't make a single change, except to add one more name he might have used to book a room at the motel—Dickie Dodge. Wayne is going through the motel records to see if they can find anything. He's been there before. He said he doesn't expect there to be any records."

Stephens looked at Gloria. "Are there any other contacts that you think need to be made to wrap up the case regarding your husband?"

With effort, Gloria focused her thoughts. "Just corroborating the remaining cars Wilson was a nominee for. At least one of them was purchased from Henderson's, the dealership we have under investigation. We've got that deal jacket. The other two, we'll have to get a chain of title on. That might take a week or more."

"Okay, so it's just a question of contacting the dealership and reviewing the paperwork. Would you review the documents, and if that's it, give them to Lauren so she and Wayne can use them for one last contact with Wilson?"

"Sure."

"All right, we're all involved in this together. Let's work like a team." Jeffreys picked up the phone, signifying the end of the meeting. "I'll let Phil Tunney know about recent developments. Lauren, get back to me when you and Gloria have the additional records. Let me know when you and Wayne have contacted Wilson. Oh, and one more thing. From now on, Agent Fanelli will only have contact with me on this case."

Lauren smiled at that, and Gloria allowed herself to feel a small breath of relief. It wasn't every day an FBI agent got sent to a back seat on a case. Maybe the worst scenario wouldn't happen to her.

Columbus Park, West Side
Wednesday, December 8, 2004
2:00 p.m.

Gloria drove the SUV westbound in light traffic on the Eisenhower Expressway. They exited north on Austin Boulevard and turned east on Jackson.

"There's his car." Lauren pointed at the yellow Cadillac with the cracked passenger side taillight.

Gloria parked behind the Caddy. Marvin got out and strolled back to the SUV. He opened the rear passenger door and climbed in. "Hello, ladies."

"What's new, Marvin?" Gloria asked.

"Got something really big for you. I'm already setting it up."

"What's that?"

"Ran into this guy. Babatunde. He drives a taxi. Sells dime bags out of his cab."

Gloria shrugged and stared out the front window. "Dime bags doesn't sound like much."

"'Cept this guy got connections to the biggest money launderer for the Nigerian heroin dealers. That should be worth a fat payday for Marvin. You know how dangerous this is? This money man, he's a player."

Gloria turned to face Marvin again. "What's his name?"

"I don't know yet, but I'm sure Babatunde will tell me. I'll just keep on working him. Matter of days he be tellin' Marvin everything." Marvin pointed his thumb at his own chest. "This worth some big money."

Gloria sighed. "You know how it works. I can't get you anything until you get me a name and other stuff, like who this person is laundering money for. You find that out and we'll see."

"Man, a little flash money would help. Make Babatunde think I'm a player, too. He more likely to give me the guy's name."

"I need more solid information before I can give you any cash. What did you mean, you're already setting it up?"

"I told Babatunde you're big time, got a lot of cash needs moving. Told him you're an Indian. Didn't you say you're Apache or Sioux or something? Ain't too many Indian heroin dealers."

"Marvin! You can't do that. If this money launderer is for real, the plan to set up an undercover agent has to be made very carefully."

Marvin waved his hand. "Ah, you could do it. Smart lady like you."

She gritted her teeth. "Marvin, you never do something like this unless I specifically tell you to. You understand?"

He shrugged. "Didn't mean to piss you off. But you're smart. You could do it."

As if she needed more complications in her life right now. "There's something else we need to talk about. Saw you at Robert Taylor Homes the other day. You don't live there, do you?"

Marvin narrowed his eyes. "No. No, ma'am. Why you asking?"

"It looked like you were pushing around some young boy."

"Oh, that." Marvin grinned. "You don't have to worry about it. I'm a sub on a CHA contract. I told you about my painting jobs, remember? I caught that homie stealing my paint. You can't let them boys get away with that. That's all it was."

"Okay. Like I said, I can't get you any money yet. But if you learn more about this money launderer, that would be good. And don't be telling anyone I'm a heroin dealer, or I have lots of cash, or anything like that. Got it?"

"Yes, ma'am. Marvin got it." He got out of the SUV. The rear door clunked shut behind him.

Lauren looked at Gloria and laughed. "You're Sonny Crockett, *Miami Vice*."

Gloria chuckled. "Ha, that makes you Tubs."

CHAPTER 7

Robert Taylor Homes, Chicago, IL
Thursday, December 9, 2004
4:30 p.m.

DARIUS APPROACHED THE PROJECTS FROM the east as the sun settled behind the buildings, casting tall shadows that lurked across the patches of snow and brown weeds.

He wore jeans and the black hoodie his father had given him to use on the night he'd failed to kill Spencer McElroy. Today, he was changing his life. No more basketball, though he knew some people once considered him one of the better high school players in the city. His father had convinced him he was a step too slow to drive to the basket and didn't have the range to can three-pointers. There was no future in it. The words had cut deep. Darius was a failure there, too. Time away from the hardwood would be better spent.

His wet boots sloshed through the melting snow as he neared the 3904 building. Two familiar figures moved toward him—Blood and Shorty. As was their duty, they stopped him.

"You ain't from around here. What you want, nigger?" Blood said. He wore a black leather jacket frayed at the sleeves and gloves with the fingertips cut off. Darius knew why. Easier to slip his finger onto a trigger.

Darius pulled his hoodie down. "I'm Marvin's friend from the other day. Don't you remember me?"

Shorty tilted his head. "That's Three-piece, Blood. The homie that wore the suit."

Blood nodded. "So, what you doing here? Stay away. I don't want to see you around here again." He jabbed Darius's shoulder.

Heart pounding, Darius smashed a right hook into Blood's left cheek and sent him tumbling to the ground. A pistol fell from Blood's waistband and skittered across the dirt and snow.

Darius picked up the gun. A Ruger LCR. He turned it over, looking at it. He'd never seen one with a shrouded hammer. Temptation hit, and he pointed the pistol at Blood's head. He didn't feel nervous, like the first time when he aimed the gun at McElroy. *I can do this.*

"Shit, man. You ain't got to be like that," Shorty said. He sounded worried. *Good*, Darius thought. It occurred to him that there might be another time, another place when he would need this strange-looking gun. He slid the pistol into the pocket of his hoodie.

Shorty bent over, grasped Blood's elbow, and helped him to his feet. He brushed the snow off Blood's jacket.

"I don't have time for you low-lifes. Where's Marvin? I need to talk to him." Darius raised his chin. He had no reason to fear these boys. He had demonstrated his superiority. They might be street creatures, but they were not as physically fit as he was from hours of running across the basketball court and lifting weights, and certainly not as smart. He had read Machiavelli's *The Prince* and Sun Tzu's *Art of War*. Their education probably hadn't passed a rapper's CD jacket.

Blood held his hand to his jaw and moaned. Shorty let go of him. "Follow me."

Shorty led the way, Blood second in his groggy state. Darius tugged his hood over his head again and brought up the rear. He slipped his hands into the pockets of his hoodie, his right hand gaining a firm grip on the pistol.

The shadow of the hood covered Darius's face as they reached the entrance of the 3904 building. The two boys monitoring the front door had seen the brief struggle that left Blood prone on the sidewalk. They opened the double doors, allowing the threesome to enter.

The hallway inside was filled with people. Music blasted from a boombox. Kanye West sang, *how do you console my mom or give her life support. Telling her, her son's on life support?* A crowd of young girls spun around to the music, mouthing the words, gyrating their hips. Men hung near the walls—glassy eyed, nodding their heads, salivating over the women.

Shorty pushed through the crowd and pulled open a door marked *Building Manager.* Inside, off a short hallway, were two offices. The first one was occupied by a heavy-set Black woman, pounding on an adding machine. Her desk was piled high with folders and invoices. A phone rang. She ignored it and the call went to the answering machine. She glanced up at the boys, stuck her hand into a bag of caramel corn, and filled her mouth, nodding as they passed her.

In the second office, Marvin sat at a clean desk. Two ladies stood in front of him. They wore blue jackets, with *Tenant Patrol* stenciled on the back in white lettering. Marvin walked around his desk, withdrew a wad of cash from his pocket, peeled off a few bills, and handed them to the ladies. "This oughta buy plenty of snacks for the after-school program," he said.

One of the ladies stroked his forearm. "Thank you, Marvin."

He gave her a kiss on the cheek, then kissed the other one. "You sweethearts come see Marvin anytime. Gots to take care of the kids."

The ladies backed out of the office, their faces aglow with wide smiles. One of the ladies looked at Darius as they passed him. "Marvin's such a good man."

Darius didn't know about that, or care. He followed Shorty and Blood into the office.

Marvin looked at Blood, whose cheek was swollen and beginning to discolor. He nodded at the door and Shorty closed it. "What the fuck happened to you?" Marvin asked.

Blood hung his head and nodded toward Darius. "He hit me."

Darius pulled down his hood. Marvin raised his thick eyebrows. "You're the boy from a couple days ago—the suit. What the fuck are you doing back here?"

"I want to talk to you about some things."

"I'm busy, boy. People always asking for favors. Those ladies just hit me for a couple hundred." He held his head high as he walked back to his desk, sat down, and perched his feet on the desktop. "So, what you want?"

"Like I said. Need to talk to you." Darius glanced at Shorty and Blood, then gestured at the door.

Marvin waved a hand. "All three of you get the fuck out of here. Ain't got time for teenage bullshit."

Shorty and Blood scurried out. Darius didn't. He closed the door and then stood facing Marvin, alone.

"Didn't you fuckin' hear me?" Marvin banged his fist on the desk. "Get the fuck out!"

"I can help you. Give me ten bags. I can sell them in a day."

"Bullshit, nigger. I gave you a couple of bags to get you through a bad time. That was it. I don't run no charity."

"I know a lot of rich kids. You could expand your market beyond your ghetto customers."

"Hah—expand my market." Marvin was mocking him now. "You think you're a smart boy. Don't you?"

Darius thought fast. "What do you gots to lose?" he said, imitating Marvin's way of talking. "I can put cash in your pocket."

"Why you care about that?"

He'd thought about this the whole way over. "'Cause you helped me out. A man settles his debts."

The sneer faded from Marvin's face. "How old are you?"

"Twenty. Why?"

Marvin got out of his chair, walked around his desk, and grabbed Darius by the shirt collar. "First of all. Don't you ever fuckin' lie to me."

Darius looked down and licked his lips. "Seventeen," he mumbled.

Marvin let go of him. "You think you know this business? You don't know shit."

Darius raised his head. "I can do this."

"Who you gonna sell to?"

"I have a lot of rich friends. They like the stuff, just like ghetto people do. But they can pay more per bag and buy more quantity." *Put him on defense now.* "That is, if your quality is good."

Marvin took a deep breath. "My quality? You fuckin' nigger. Question my shit. Just as good as anybody else's. All right, I'll front you ten bags to see how you do. These are dime bags, so if you got rich buyers, they should pay more than a dime. You got two days. You be back here Saturday, or you be in trouble."

Darius slipped his hands in his pockets, gripped the pistol again. *Got my foot in the door.* "No problem."

"Gimme your cell. What's your number?"

Darius recited it as he handed his phone over. Marvin set the cell on the desk, then put the number in his contact list under Suit and dialed it. Darius's phone rang. Marvin grinned, snatched it up, and slammed it back in Darius's hand. "Testing you. Wait here."

Marvin left the office. He returned a few minutes later with a brown paper sandwich bag. Eyes narrowed, he shoved the bag at Darius. "Saturday or else!"

Darius folded both hands around the bag. It was his future.

Chapter 8

GLORIA DROVE WEST ON THE Eisenhower Expressway, heading for Jackson Boulevard to meet Marvin. Riding in the passenger seat, Lauren turned to face her. "I didn't want to say anything in the office…"

Anxiety stirred in Gloria's stomach. "About what?"

"We had a meeting with the Chief, Stephens, and me, I mean. Because this is such a sensitive matter, your husband being a federal judge, they want us to clear everything through the Chief—"

"And?"

"About Tamika and Reginald Wilson. Axelrod and I interviewed them last night." Lauren fell silent, staring out at the traffic ahead of them.

It was an effort for Gloria not to snap, to keep her tone easy. "Well, don't stop there. What did she say?"

"First, the Chief is backing you all the way. He specifically wanted me to tell you that." Lauren paused. "As far as Tamika, it's not good. She retracted her statement."

Yeah, the chief is backing me until the shit hits the fan. Gloria slammed a palm against the steering wheel. "Damn. Makes me look like a total incompetent."

"It happened to us, not just you. You take what a witness says and run with it. It was believable. This could have happened to anyone."

"Yeah, but I'm the lead agent and it was my husband she was testifying about. Makes it look like I wanted to hear what she was saying." Gloria broke off, wondering. "Maybe I did?"

"Tamika even admitted that Reginald Wilson was the father of her baby, just like he told us. I guess what difference does it make with McElroy dead?"

"Yeah. I wonder how many times Fanelli has tried to convince Jeffreys to charge me on something. And Wilson, what did he say?"

"His testimony was the same. It corroborated Tamika's."

"So, will Tamika be charged with making a false statement?"

"They don't have a choice. Her lie was the entire basis for the FBI arresting Carlton."

"And I was the basis for getting that false information," Gloria muttered as she rubbed the back of her neck.

The ride went quiet as Gloria pulled the Blazer off the Eisenhower and onto Jackson Boulevard. A few minutes later, she parked behind Marvin's yellow Cadillac. The first fairway paralleled the street and was blanketed with a light snow.

"Marvin told me he had more information about the money launderer," Gloria said.

Lauren nodded. Through the windshield, they saw Marvin leave the Cadillac. "Okay, Crockett. Here you go."

Gloria watched her informant approaching. Marvin wore a black stocking cap pulled down to his bushy eyebrows, a black leather hip length coat, and black slacks. He opened the Blazer's back door and slid onto the seat, then rubbed his hands together. "Damn cold out there. Makes you want to go someplace warm."

Gloria thought about Iraq. *I've had enough with warm places.* "It's not that bad. I like the cold. Just wait until the end of January and the beginning of February."

Marvin laughed. "By then you might find yourself in Nigeria."

Gloria faced Marvin and pointed a finger at him. "Not so funny. What did I tell you about not making any kind of commitments?"

Marvin held his palms up. "Marvin didn't say nothin' to nobody. Jus' kidding you."

Gloria shook her head. "What did you find out about this money launderer?"

"He a she. Her name is Uka Kafi. Babatunde said she handles a lot of cash money."

Lauren opened her notepad and clicked her pen. "How does she wash it?"

"Don't know. You smart. You can find out."

"Where does she work out of?" Gloria asked.

"She's got an office at Clark and Lawrence. I checked it out. That's a big Nigerian neighborhood. She sells car insurance to all the Nigerians."

Gloria nodded. "Okay. You stay away from there unless I tell you to go there. You understand, Marvin? You don't go near that place unless I say so."

"Marvin got it. Only trying to help."

"How can we get an introduction?"

"Babatunde knows her. He's seen people drop off cash."

"So why would he cooperate? How do we get him to introduce an undercover agent?"

Marvin glanced down at the floor, then up at Gloria. "Marvin told him about you and all the cash you holding."

Gloria sighed. They were back to the "Indian drug dealer" story. "How many times did you tell Babatunde this?"

Marvin shrugged. "A few."

"What *exactly* did you tell him?"

"I told him Marvin works for you."

"And what does Marvin do for me?"

"Marvin picks up your cash and takes it to your banker."

"How much?"

"Marvin don't know."

She pursed her lips. "I'm getting tired of pulling teeth. Tell me the whole story."

He shrugged. "Told Baba I pick up duffel bags full of cash for you. Don't know how much is in 'em. But the banker went missing a few days ago. Word on the street is, he got caught stealing somebody's money and you ain't got no one to go to now."

"Huh. That's a pretty good cover story. "Do you know if Babatunde talked to Uka about me?"

Marvin shrugged again. "Not sure."

"Okay. At this point, if you talk to him, don't ask about that. Don't say anything about me unless he brings it up. If he does, just say I haven't found anyone to take my banker's place. You got that?"

"Sure. Don't talk to Baba unless he brings you up and don't go past Uka's business."

"Good. I'll be in touch."

"What about me? Should be big money in this for Marvin. You check with your boss?"

"I'll do that. First chance."

Marvin sighed. "Told you before, this shit's dangerous. Baba said one of Uka's brothers killed some guy over drugs."

"How do you know so much about Uka?"

"From Baba. Everything I got is from him."

"Okay." Gloria nodded toward the Blazer's door. "We're done for now. I'll be in touch."

"All right." Marvin opened the door, pulled his collar up, slid out, and strolled back to his Caddy.

Lauren closed her notepad. "Looks like you're in business, Crockett."

CHAPTER 9

Carlton/Nighthawk Residence, Bronzeville
Saturday, December 11, 2004
10:00 a.m.

GLORIA SIPPED HER MORNING COFFEE as her children went their separate ways, Adsila to gymnastics and Darius to basketball practice. *A little time for peace and quiet.* She unfolded the *Tribune* and scanned the headlines. The usual political bullshit, nothing to hold her interest.

She set her cup down and flipped to the sports page. Northwestern had lost another game, falling to two and four for the season. *The Bears play Jacksonville tomorrow. They're five and seven.* She shook her head. *What a bunch of losers.*

She opened the Lifestyle section. It had an article about women balancing careers and family. *This is a subject I could use some help in.* She folded the paper in half and started reading. Seconds later, the phone rang.

She recognized the number and picked it up. "Hi, Coach. How are you?"

"I'm good." Coach Netti ran the varsity basketball team. "I was wondering how Darius is feeling?"

Confused, she stammered out, "Um, Darius is good." Half an hour ago, her son had told her he was going to practice. Clearly, he hadn't shown up. Where was he?

"He hasn't come to practice all week," the coach said. "I know he's got a lot on his plate now. I just want to help him anyway I can."

"I'll try his cell. If you hear from him, please call me." Gloria hung up before Coach Netti could reply. *He must wonder what kind of mother I am. Darius plays hooky all week and I didn't know.* Her jaw set. *I'll bet his father has something to do with this. He's probably got Darius working on his defense.*

Gloria called Darius's cell.

Darius walked into Marvin's office and closed the door. He yanked $200 in small bills out of his pants pocket and fanned it across Marvin's desk like a blackjack dealer feathering the cards. His phone rang. He pulled it out of his jeans pocket and looked at the caller ID. *Mom.* He hit the decline button.

Marvin picked up the cash and counted it. "You did good, boy. So, what do you want to do? Make this a regular thing?"

Before Darius could answer, his phone rang again.

Marvin grinned. "You a busy boy."

Darius glanced at the caller ID. *Mom* flashed across the screen again. He shook his head and hit the decline button. "They can wait."

"Yeah, if it's some bitch, always make 'em wait. You don't want 'em thinking you'll jump every time they call." Marvin leaned back in his chair. "So, Saturday night is usually a good night for selling shit. You want some stuff?"

"Yeah. How about twenty bags?"

"That's good. Build up gradual. That'll work. Wait here." Marvin got up and left the office, closing the door behind him.

Darius sat in the chair in front of Marvin's desk. He felt drained, a little jittery. He was starting to know what that meant. But he just needed a dime bag every once in a while. Just to get him through his dad's trial. After that, he'd leave all this behind him. Focus on school again and basketball, maybe. He could make a name for himself in the summer leagues and get a scholarship. In the meantime, he'd get free smack and some spending cash. He was too smart to end up being a junkie.

Ten minutes later, Marvin returned with a brown paper bag and a handful of bills. "Here's twenty dime bags. Bring the cash back Monday. And here's fifty bucks for you."

Darius took them both, stuffed the cash in his shirt pocket and stashed the paper bag inside his parka. He'd made a good deal. *Kept a bag for myself, and twenty bucks. With Marvin's fifty, not bad for a couple of hours' work.*

He left the office and the 3904 building. As he ambled down the sidewalk, his phone rang again. He dug it out of his coat pocket and glanced at the display. He couldn't avoid her forever. He touched accept and brought the cell phone to his ear. "Hi, Mom."

"Darius, where are you?"

She sounded angry. He hesitated, biting his lip.

She rushed to the next question. "When were you going to tell me you quit the team? Are you helping your father?"

"Yeah. It's something I have to do, no matter what the outcome. I'd never be able to forgive myself if I didn't." Lying to his mother was a new experience. He wasn't comfortable with it. But what could he tell her? "I'm at the DePaul law library. I just stepped out to take your call." His chin quivered.

"Honey." The anger was gone from her voice, and he felt even worse as he plodded through the snow. But what choice did he have? "I'm so sorry you're involved in this predicament. You can't forsake your future for something your father did. That's his responsibility. This is your senior year. There's so much riding on you getting a basketball scholarship."

"I know, Mom. But I need to be there for him. I can always play in a summer league. Lots of guys get scholarships that way, or I can try out as a walk-on."

"Darius, I hope you know what you're doing. I can't come between you and your father. I understand that. Just, be careful."

Through a hole he'd cut in the parka's left pocket, he pressed the lunch bag securing the heroin against his stomach. "I will, Mom. I promise. I'll be really careful."

CHAPTER *10*

CID-IRS Office
Kluczynski Federal Building
Monday, December 13, 2004
8:00 a.m.

SEATED AT HER DESK, GLORIA scanned Lauren's notes from their meeting with Marvin. "We have to find evidence that Uka Kafi is predisposed to laundering money before we can initiate an undercover investigation. I'll draft a memo of Marvin's statement. In the meantime, I want you to run Uka Kafi through TECS," she said, referring to the Treasury Enforcement Communication System. "Check for currency transaction and suspicious activity reports, foreign bank accounts, 8300 forms, and Customs monetary information reports. Look for anything under the last name Kafi. She might have relatives involved in the business. After that, we'll check with DEA and Customs."

"I'm on it," Lauren said, and went off to get started.

An hour later, she returned with several pages of computer printouts. "The first thing I did was check with the Secretary of State's office. Uka Kafi is a registered insurance agent, her business incorporated in 1996 under the name of Uka's Auto Insurance at the location on the North Side that Marvin gave us.

"There was only one CTR under her name. It was for a $15,000 cash deposit back in 1999, made to her business account at BCD National Bank. The cash was a mixture of small bills and hundreds. The bank is located next to her insurance business."

"Maybe she got smart and started using someone else's accounts," Gloria said. "One CTR is better than none. I called one of my contacts at DEA, Mike Greely. He's expecting us. Mike's not your typical buy and bust guy. He's willing to work long-term conspiracy cases. We worked an international cocaine case a few years ago. Ended up convicting ten of eleven defendants. Four of them were major drug dealers. The eleventh defendant was just a mope who unknowingly off-loaded 2,500 kilos of cocaine from a truck, concealed in boxes of plantains. He ran out of the courtroom as soon the not guilty verdict was read."

Lauren laughed. "He was probably worried that the Colombians thought he cut a deal, or the G would indict him on some other charge."

Gloria slipped on a black ski jacket and Lauren a beige double-breasted trench coat, and they headed across the street to the DEA offices in the Dirksen Federal Building. The receptionist recognized Gloria and paged Mike Greely. He met them a few minutes later, and they followed him back to his desk.

"I checked NADDIS," he said, meaning the Narcotics and Dangerous Drugs Information System. "There are quite a few references to the Kafi family. They have a long history of dealing heroin, but there's not much on their cousin Uka." He gestured toward a file folder on the desktop. "The DEA sixes are here. Have at it."

"Thanks, Mike." Gloria picked up the folder. "We owe you."

Back at the IRS office, Gloria and Lauren spent the next hour reviewing the DEA reports. Three of the four Kafi brothers had arrests for sale of heroin and had served time in federal penitentiaries. That gave Uka Kafi a source for illicit funds her family members would want transported to Nigeria or laundered for use domestically.

Gloria felt the thrill of the chase. Each step was bringing the undercover investigation closer to a reality.

Robert Taylor Homes
Monday, December 13, 2004
4:00 p.m.

Darius trudged through the snow toward the 3904 building. His pocket was full of cash, and he intended to cement his relationship with Marvin. He approached the front doors. The two boys on guard gave him a nod, and he entered with little fanfare. The usual crowd lingered in the lobby. Kanye West bellowed from a boombox. Girls gyrated their hips to the music. Men leaned against the walls, enjoying the entertainment.

Darius went through the door marked *Building Manager*. The manager herself sat at her desk with an old-fashioned phone receiver against her ear, mumbling into it: "Uh-huh, uh-huh." The other phone lines blinked like a slot machine when somebody won the jackpot. Her desk overflowed with repair orders for apartments. A bag of Cheetos near one of the paper piles fell over, and a handful of them rolled across her desk. She picked the Cheetos up one at a time and tossed them in her mouth. Darius nodded at her in passing, and she returned the favor.

He stepped up to the closed door of Marvin's office and knocked on the glass panel. He could only see a corner of Marvin's desk, couldn't tell if the dealer was seated behind it. "It's me, Suit." The name Marvin used for him on his contact list.

Marvin's reply, muffled, came through the door. "I'm busy. Come back in half an hour."

Darius walked back to the foyer and found a spot against the wall. He got into the flow of the music, nodding his head with the beat. A while later, maybe fifteen minutes, a girl moved toward him, her hips swaying, and grabbed his hands. She wore a red top, tight across her chest, and matching leggings. "Come on. Dance with me, tall boy."

"I can't. Waiting on Marvin."

"Oh, you one of his boys? Ain't seen you around here before."

"I don't live here."

She moved closer, inches from him. "Why don't you take that coat off. You mus' be getting hot." She smiled, snapped a piece of Juicy Fruit in her mouth. She pulled down the zipper on his parka and placed her hand against his heart. "So, where's you live?"

Just then, Darius saw a man leave the management office. He was burly, his head shaved, and he wore a brown leather flight jacket a shade lighter than his skin. Handcuffs dangled from his belt, and a revolver was holstered on his hip. *Security? Cop?* Darius pushed the girl away. "I got to go."

He walked to Marvin's office, saw the door was open. He entered and closed it behind him.

Marvin was sitting at his desk. He had a black eye and held a napkin to his nose. He briefly pulled it away and scowled at the blood on it. "What the fuck do you want?"

"You told me to come back today with your money." Darius laid $340 on Marvin's desk.

Marvin threw the napkin into a trash can and counted the bills. He picked up five twenties and pushed them toward Darius. "Here, take that and get out of my sight."

Darius grabbed the cash and stood there.

"Didn't you hear me?" Marvin's nostrils flared, and he waved his hand at Darius. "Get the fuck out of here!"

"That guy punch you in the nose? The one who just left?"

Marvin shook his head. "You real smart. How'd you figure that out."

"He had a gun and handcuffs. Is he a cop?"

"You don't want to know. Didn't I tell you to get the fuck out of here?"

"What about next week? Can do more than twenty bags."

"Damn it, boy. Can't you see this a dirty business? You get in front of it like me, there's always somebody sucking the life out of you."

"My face isn't out front." Darius paused. He knew the answer to his next question but wanted to hear it from Marvin. "You paying the cop?"

"How you think we stay in business. Everybody wants their share."

Darius took a step toward him. "You need someone you can trust…like me. I can handle more for you, and you won't be so stressed out."

Marvin pressed his lips together. "You want to do more? I got just the job for you. Follow me." He stood abruptly and stalked out of his office, crashed through the crowd in the foyer, and headed for the stairwell. Darius trailed in his wake, and they marched up to the third floor. Marvin strode down the hall to Apartment 304, unlocked the door, pushed Darius inside ahead of him, and locked the door again behind them.

Darius looked around. The apartment was empty of furniture except for a table twelve feet long, a fluorescent light hanging above it. Around the table sat four women who ranged in age from forty to fifty. They were naked except for panties, their jowls baggy, breasts droopy, arms flabby and thighs heavy. No danger of an overseer trading smack for sex. But what really caught Darius's eye was the powder on the table. Lots of it.

Marvin pointed at the nearest two women. "They're emptying kilo packages of smack and cutting it with whatever we can find.

Sometimes we use mannitol, sometimes powdered milk, sometimes quinine. They cut it. The next two bitches bag it, two grams a bag. You got to keep an eye on them, make sure they don't slip any bags into their panties. But you can work here, and your face don't show. Got to watch the inventory. Count the bags. You don't give any out except to me or on my say-so."

"How come you don't have anyone watching them now?"

"The previous boy was helping himself to product. Serious violation. He's no longer available." Marvin watched Darius for a moment, as if waiting for his reaction. Darius shrugged. Marvin gave a small nod, like he'd passed some test. "Every time you got a thousand bags ready to go, you page me and enter that number, 1,000. I'll be by to pick them up shortly. You got that?"

"No problem. But I got to be in school during the week."

"That's fine. You start work at 4:00 every day. A couple of hours is all you got to do. But you got to move to a different apartment every week, ten days or so. Otherwise, some fool with a gun will be hunting to rip you off." Marvin's mouth twisted into a grin. "That good for you?"

"I can do that. How much will you pay me?"

"Give you $250 a week."

Darius laughed. "How about profit sharing?"

Marvin gave him a long stare. "You better be making fun, or you end up like the last boy."

CHAPTER 11

Offices of U.S. Customs
610 S. Canal, Chicago, IL
Tuesday, December 14, 2004
11:00 a.m.

SPECIAL AGENT DAVID LOPEZ WAS waiting for Gloria in the outer lobby of U.S. Customs. She nodded at him in greeting, then got right to it. "Thanks for the call. You said you have something interesting for me?"

"I think you'll like this. Come back to my office," Lopez said.

She followed him, weaving through a haphazard maze of hallways. Her mind briefly drifted, savoring Fanelli's fall from grace in Jeffreys's eyes. The FBI *had* screwed up, arresting Robert so fast, and the prosecutor was finally realizing it. *If no one's listening to Fanelli anymore, maybe that'll keep me out of a jail cell.*

They reached Lopez's office, and he sat behind his government-gray desk. Gloria took the only chair in front of it. Because of his senior status, Lopez had landed one of the few offices with a window, even if it only overlooked the back end of the customs office parking lot. She glanced over her shoulder at the agency's fleet of cars. "Nice view."

Lopez laughed. "You take what you can get." He opened a drawer, pulled out a folder, and laid it in front of Gloria. "Take a look at these."

She opened the folder. Inside was a slender envelope, the thin cardboard kind, addressed to Uka Kafi's insurance business. The return address was from somewhere in Nigeria. "Our guys intercepted that, found a pair of fraudulent passports inside," Lopez told her. "Go ahead and take a look."

She dumped the contents of the envelope onto his desk. The passports bore photographs of the same subject, but two different names: Abadi Ademela and Dele Kehinde. She looked up at Lopez, unable to hide a smile. "This is unbelievable. It'll definitely help us with probable cause for a search warrant."

"I knew you'd be happy to see these." He dug in another drawer and pulled out a one-page form. "You can have them. I've got copies made for our file. Just sign the receipt for chain of custody."

"Thanks, Dave." Gloria signed for the passports, tucked them back in their envelope, and left.

Back in her own office, she had Lauren run Ademela and Kehinde through TECS. Ademela was a blank, but a CTR in Kehinde's name turned up, for a $12,000 cash deposit on December 14, 2001, and a cash withdrawal of that amount just a few days later at a bank in the northern suburbs. *I bet those funds had something to do with Uka Kafi.*

At her request, Lauren pulled the rap sheets of the Kafi brothers' arrests by the Chicago Police Department. "Bright Kafi was previously convicted of heroin trafficking, and served three years of a five-year sentence," Lauren said, one hip propped against the side of Gloria's desk. "He was released from the Pontiac Correctional facility in 2001."

"Anything on Kehinde?"

Lauren nodded. "Kehinde has an outstanding warrant for credit card fraud, issued in January 2002."

Gloria sat back in her chair. "That's interesting. Looks like the Kafi organization is diversified. Who knows what else they may be involved in, aside from heroin and credit card fraud." She blew out a breath. "I'll start drafting an undercover request. We're going to need way more than the $10,000 we can get from our office. National should give us more."

"How much more?"

"I'm thinking a hundred and fifty grand."

Lauren's eyes widened. "That's a lot of money."

"Well, if my man Marvin is picking up duffel bags of cash for me, we can't show up with small change."

"What about the FBI?"

"What about them?"

Lauren pushed her blonde hair out of her face. "We checked with DEA, Customs, and CPD. Don't you think we should check with the FBI?"

Gloria narrowed her eyes. "You want to call your friend Fanelli, go ahead."

Lauren frowned. "He's not my friend. It just seems like a logical thing to do."

"So do it if you want to. I'm drafting the request. I think we have enough to show that the Kafi family is heavily involved in the heroin trade and that Uka is predisposed to laundering the proceeds."

"Okay, if you think we can get the UC investigation approved, let's go with it."

"In the meantime, I want you to request tax returns filed by Uka and any of her family members. While we're waiting for the request to be approved, let's run a surveillance of Uka's business." Gloria looked up from her computer. "There's one other thing we'll need."

"What's that?"

"An undercover agent. For this type of assignment, we have to get an agent that's been through the undercover school. The national office will assign one. I'll do the UC work with him and you can be the contact agent."

"What's a contact agent do?"

"Manage the administrative chores. Track the cash we're laundering, determine where it's deposited and when it shows up in our undercover accounts, and generally help in the investigative decision-making process."

"Contact agent," Lauren said with a grin. "I can do that."

Their secretary, June, waddled over to Gloria's desk. "I have a telephone message for Lauren, from U.S. Attorney Jeffreys. They're having a meeting at ten tomorrow morning regarding the charges against Judge Carlton. Mr. Jeffreys would like both of you to come."

"Thanks, June." Lauren glanced at Gloria.

Gloria folded her arms across her chest. "This has to be about reducing the charges against him." *Surprised I got an invite. I wonder why?*

CHAPTER *12*

U.S. Attorney's Office
Dirksen Federal Building
Wednesday, December 15, 2004
10:00 a.m.

GLORIA AND LAUREN STOOD IN front of the door to Jeffreys's office. Lauren shrugged, as if to say *are we going in or not?* Gloria could feel the tension emanating through the door. She knew Fanelli would play his blame game. "Might as well get it over with," Gloria murmured.

Lauren opened the door, and they stepped inside. They were the last to arrive, judging from the two remaining empty chairs centered in front of Jeffreys's desk. Fanelli leaned over and muttered something to Axelrod, who raised his eyebrows but said nothing. Second chair Phillip Tunney stood to greet Gloria and Lauren. They exchanged hellos, and the two women sat down.

Jeffreys looked professional as always. Today he wore a dark blue suit and a red and gray striped tie in a tight Windsor knot. "You're all aware that Tamika Carlton recanted her testimony," he said, "so the money laundering and conspiracy charges against Judge Carlton will have to be withdrawn. The remaining charges, obstruction of justice and theft of government property, are still supported by the evidence we have."

Fanelli spoke up. "This guy is crooked. We can't have anyone like him sitting on the federal bench. Can't you get a motion limiting what he can present to the jury? If Carlton can't bring up the dropped charges…" the FBI agent paused and stared at Gloria, "then you won't have to be concerned about them."

"No judge will rule in our favor on such a motion," Jeffreys said.

Fanelli shook his head. "Whole damn thing was a colossal fuck-up. We talked to the cops who arrested Carlton the night of the shooting, and —"

Gloria broke in. "I know. Officer Fuelling called me. Told me as far as they were concerned, it was a good shoot. And that's true. You shouldn't have jumped the gun arresting my husband." She couldn't withhold her feelings any longer. In her mind, it was the FBI that fucked up. "If you'd waited for me to return from Iraq, we'd have contacted Reginald Wilson then, found out his testimony conflicted with Tamika's, and resolved the situation before you got the indictment. And none of what's going on now ever would have happened." Her own sense of guilt still troubled her, but damned if she'd let Fanelli see it.

"Cool it, both of you. This isn't about attaching blame to anyone. It's about deciding what's best to do now." Jeffreys rose, walked around his desk, and leaned against the front of it. He liked to be close to the people he was talking to, Gloria recalled. Especially if he considered them his allies. As Jeffreys focused on her, she tightened her lips, trying to suppress her growing dislike of Fanelli. Everything the man said carried the innuendo of *it's not my fault, it's yours.*

Jeffreys spread his palms wide. "We have to revise the charges against Judge Carlton. It does open a potential defense: would he have committed those offenses if he had not been charged with the crimes in the original indictment? There's an extra burden on us to prove his willfulness and intent. Any comments or ideas?"

Tunney shook his head. "With Carlton's record of service to the community as a prosecutor, defense attorney and judge, we have a high bar to reach. He'll tell the jury he was misguided by the false charges the government brought against him. He'll claim he was entrapped, that he saw his years of service rewarded by the prospect of twenty years in jail. What would any reasonable man do?"

They all looked at Tunney for the answer, and he gave it. "We have to up the charge and supersede with a new indictment for a violation of Title 18, Section 1512."

Lauren tilted her head. "Section 1512?"

Tunney rolled his sleeves up to his elbows. "Carlton was out there that night for one reason and one reason only — to kill Spencer McElroy. Section 1512 is interfering with witness testimony in a criminal case. For Carlton, it's attempted murder, and he's looking at twenty years. If he's willing to plead, we can offer him a max of ten years."

"Yeah." Fanelli clapped his hands. "Why didn't you guys think of that before?"

Jeffreys nodded. "With the money laundering charges, he was looking at twenty years maximum for each count. We drop those, it becomes a simpler case but not necessarily an easier one." He caught Gloria's eye. "You'll be the core of it. What do you think?"

Gloria gazed down at the floor, recalling with dread the day she'd interviewed Tamika. The trial would be won or lost on her testimony…and testimony from Darius, if her husband dared to call him as a witness. She shook her head no…but said, "It's the right thing to do. God knows I wasn't out there to shoot McElroy."

Fanelli shook his head. "To kill him, you mean?"

Gloria glared at him. "I guess you'll have it your way, Fanelli. You'll get to see if I can hold up while my husband cross-examines me. That's what you want, isn't it?"

"All right, you two," Jeffreys said. "This isn't a battle of who's right or who's wrong. We need to do the right thing for the case.

Carlton is in the marshals' lockup now. Once we're finished here, he'll be brought down to my office and advised of our position, and the new charge. We have to deal directly with him since he's representing himself."

"That's why we all have to be on the same ground," Tunney added. "You can be sure that if we keep the remaining charges instead of superseding, Carlton will file a motion to have them dismissed before the trial starts. If they haven't been discharged at that time, he'll move for a directed verdict of acquittal from Judge Peterson after we present our case, and if Peterson is sympathetic to his motions—"

"Figures he would be, since he's the only other Black judge." Fanelli glanced around at the others, who stared back at him. "I'm just saying."

Jeffreys fixed his gaze on Fanelli. In a slow, steady voice, he said, "I'm confident that any decision Judge Peterson makes will be based on the rule of law."

Fanelli scoffed. "Sometimes he makes his own rules."

Jeffreys looked at him a second or two longer, then pointedly turned to Gloria. "You've been quiet. Tell me what you think."

Gloria wrinkled her brow. Her gaze travelled from Fanelli, to Axelrod, to Tunney, to Lauren and then to Jeffreys. *If the charges revolving around Tamika's lie are dropped, what are the chances Robert will call Darius as a witness?* She had no idea. Her mouth felt dry as she answered. "I'm trying to take an impartial look at the facts, keep my personal feelings out of it." She paused. *Surely Robert won't put his own son in jeopardy.* "He did break the law, and we have an obligation to prosecute." She exhaled loudly. "We should go ahead with the case."

Jeffreys nodded. "I appreciate your honesty and professionalism. We'll proceed with 1512. Fanelli and Axelrod can get Carlton from lockup. Gloria, I'm sure you agree it's in your best interest to return to your office. Lauren can brief you on the results of this meeting later."

Gloria stood. "Thanks, Todd." She nodded at the others and walked out. *Robert, you better keep your word. Don't hurt our son! You'll be a sorry S.O.B. if you do.*

Thirty minutes later, Fanelli and Axelrod brought Judge Carlton into Jeffrey's office. He wore an orange jumpsuit and his hands were cuffed behind his back. The FBI agents closed the door.

"You can take the cuffs off," Jeffreys said.

Fanelli unlocked the cuffs and slipped them in his belt.

Jeffreys pointed to an empty chair in front of him and looked Carlton in the eye. "Sit down, Judge."

Rubbing his wrist, Carlton sat. "Is it necessary to tighten these damn cuffs so much?"

No one answered him. Fanelli smirked as the FBI agents sat on either side of Carlton. Lauren sat next to Axelrod, Tunney to her right.

Jeffreys cleared his throat. "Judge, there's been some changes in your case. We're dropping the money laundering and conspiracy charges. Your daughter Tamika recanted her statement and we've corroborated her new testimony with another witness."

"About time justice is served." Carlton gave a toothy smile. "So I'm being released today?"

Jeffreys steepled his hands. "You're on the court call this afternoon. Your release is up to Judge Peterson, but we'll be superseding with a new charge. Violation of Title 18, Section 1512."

Carlton shot out of his chair. "What the fuck. That's ridiculous. You think I was out there to kill McElroy?"

Fanelli and Axelrod stood. Carlton got the message and sat back down. Jeffreys went on as if Carlton hadn't spoken. "You'll be indicted tomorrow on the new charge, and your trial is still February fourteenth."

"That's bull and you know it! Maybe I was out there to protect McElroy from someone that might do him harm. I'm not saying another word." Carlton folded his arms and his nostrils flared. "You can take me back to the lockup. Wait, is my wife here? I was hoping she would be. She needs to apologize for all the crap she's put me through—"

Lauren glared at him. "Gloria was doing her job, and she did it well."

Carlton snorted. "She's got you hoodwinked. My wife will make an interesting witness for the defense. You can be damn sure I'll waive marital privilege. And my daughter, Tamika, I assume you'll charge her with perjury. Quite a collection of witnesses." He stood, eyeing the FBI agents, and put his hands together behind his back. "Take me back to the lockup now." He cocked his head at Jeffreys and Tunney. "Gentlemen, I'll see you in court. Good luck, you'll need it."

Fanelli smiled as he snapped the handcuffs back on Carlton's wrists. He and Axelrod grasped Carlton's elbows, ready to lead him out of the office when Carlton looked over his shoulder at Jeffreys. "Hopefully, you have enough common sense to drop the new charge. I know how much you guys hate to lose." He laughed menacingly as he stepped through the doorway and into the hall.

CHAPTER *13*

Courtroom 2502
Dirksen Federal Building
Wednesday, December 15, 2004
1:00 p.m.

T WO U.S. MARSHALS ESCORTED ROBERT Carlton to the lectern in Judge Peterson's courtroom. The assistant U.S. attorneys, Jeffreys and Tunney, were there already, waiting.

Jeffreys stepped up to the lectern. "Your Honor, based on new witness testimony and a recantation, today we are eliminating counts one and two from the original indictment, money laundering and conspiracy. Counts three and four, obstruction of justice and theft of government property, still stand. We intend to add a Title 18-1512 charge, and also to charge the recanting witness, Tamika Carlton, with making a false statement to federal agents in violation of Title 18, Section 1001. These changes will shorten the time we'll need to prosecute from a week to two or three days." Jeffreys stepped back.

Judge Peterson flipped through the pages of the indictment, then focused his gaze on the defendant. "Mr. Carlton, does this affect your plea?"

Carlton smirked. "No, your honor. This is a reflection of the weakness of the government's case. I was advised of the dropped charges and the new charge in a meeting with Mr. Jeffreys and his team of FBI and IRS agents earlier today. In fact, I intend to file a motion today if possible, or whenever I'm returned to MCC, asking that in all future communication until the end of this trial, I be referred to by my title, either Judge Carlton or the honorable Judge Carlton. I want the jury to understand that if this government can indict me, none of us are safe from the abusive tactics the prosecutors have stooped to in this case—even using loved ones, like my wife, against me."

Jeffreys stepped up to the lectern. "Your honor, Mr. Carlton is grandstanding for the media. If this is any indication of the defense he intends to present, he's making an attempt to disqualify the jury by appealing to its emotions and ignoring the law."

Carlton pointed a finger at Jeffreys. "Ignoring the law. If the government knew the law, I wouldn't be here today."

Judge Peterson banged his gavel. "From this point on, the defendant will be referred to as Judge Carlton in all future motions, direct and cross examinations, opening and closing arguments and any other form of communication during this trial. However, Judge Carlton, I must warn you that if you decide to proceed with a jury trial, some members of the jury may view the use of your title as a negative. If that is your wish, I will rule in advance in your favor. But I will not allow my courtroom to become a zoo with the two of you hurling accusations and shouting at each other. Is that understood?"

"Yes, your honor." Jeffreys stepped away from the lectern.

Carlton gripped it with both hands. "Thank you, your honor. You can count on me to respect this court and give it the decorum it deserves. You have spent many years sitting in the same chair I have, and you understand the heavy responsibility that goes—"

Jeffreys strode to the lectern again, bumping Carlton to the side. "Your honor, Carlton—Judge Carlton—is practicing his opening argument. I respect how precious the court's limited time is—"

"Your honor, I was just expressing my gratitude to—"

Judge Peterson banged his gavel again. "Order in the court! If this keeps up, I'll find both of you in contempt. Is that understood?"

Jeffreys lowered his head. "Yes, your honor."

Carlton stood his ground. "Thank you, your honor, for being firm. You're right. We need to treat this matter with the respect our system of justice deserves, that has separated this country from anarchy." He cleared his throat. "I have one more important matter before the court today. Since the government has seen fit to drop most of the charges, I feel it is appropriate that I be released on my own recognizance."

Judge Peterson gave a slight nod. "What's the government's position?"

Jeffreys got the message. "We won't object to Judge Carlton's release on an O.R. bond."

"So ordered. I expect to see you gentlemen on February fourteenth and to conduct this trial in an orderly fashion." He eyed Judge Carlton. "One last question for you. How many days do you expect your defense will take?"

"A day, two at the most." Carlton crossed his arms and smiled. "I do plan on some lengthy cross-examination, so the government's witnesses may be on the stand for extended periods of time."

The marshals approached Carlton. He looked to the rear of the courtroom and saw Darius seated in the last row. That was a surprise. "Your honor, can I have a word with my son?"

Judge Peterson nodded. One of the marshals walked over to Darius and spoke briefly to him, then escorted him to his father's side and gave him a quick pat down. "Clean," the marshal said.

"Can we have a moment alone?" Carlton asked.

The marshals stepped away. Carlton embraced his son. "Don't go home," he said, low in Darius's ear. "Meet me at the hotel. We're going to win this case. Make the government look like fools, and your mother too."

The boy nodded and smiled. Carlton kissed Darius's cheek, then glanced at the marshals. "I'm ready now."

They moved up to flank him, and he headed back to the lockup. *But not for long.*

CHAPTER 14

Columbus Park, West Side
Monday, December 20, 2004
2:00 p.m.

GLORIA AND LAUREN WAITED IN the Blazer, in the usual spot near Columbus Park. "Stephens approved $1,000 for Marvin, with more down the road if he can pull off an introduction to Uka Kafi," Gloria said. The cash was in a thick envelope, tucked in her purse.

"You did a good sales job on the boss." Lauren unbuckled her seat belt and leaned against the passenger door.

"There's hope for him." Gloria laughed. "He's learning what you have to do to make a case. We get the intro and give Kafi the initial cash to launder from our undercover account. We'll find out what account she used, then subpoena her bank and see how much money has gone through it over the last couple of years."

"Where's our undercover account?"

"The national office gave us one in Switzerland."

"With all the tax cheats. That's funny." Lauren shook her head. "Aren't you concerned that her bank would notify her of the subpoena?"

"They don't get the subpoena until we have a few transactions with her. Then we serve it with a nondisclosure letter and stress that they're forbidden to contact the account holders."

"What if they do?"

"Then they're in contempt of the grand jury and could be indicted for obstruction. Since I'm doing the undercover, I can't be involved in any field work. You'll have to serve the subpoenas. Make an issue of the nondisclosure order when you do, so they won't dare notify Kafi."

A late model red Cadillac pulled in front of their black Blazer. Marvin got out and stomped through the six-inch deep snow toward the SUV.

"Looks like Marvin's got a new ride. Life must be good," Lauren said, jotting down his license plate number on her notepad.

Marvin opened the rear door, kicked the snow off his boots, and slid into the back seat. "What's up, ladies?"

"Got a new Cad?" Lauren asked.

"Nah, mine's in the shop. Borrowed a friend's."

"We've got the undercover case approved," Gloria said. "But we'll need a little extra help this time."

He wrinkled his brow as he unbuttoned his black leather coat and leaned toward Gloria. "What you want Marvin to do?"

"Get Baba to introduce us to Uka."

"What you mean, us?"

"Me. And you."

Marvin fell back against the seat. "Whoa, that's never how we worked."

"Unless you can think of another way, I don't see how else to do it."

"You can't pay Marvin enough to do that. No ma'am, no way, no how." He waved his hands in front of him, palms down, timed perfectly with each phrase.

"The boss gave me a nice amount of cash to make it worthwhile."

"Yeah? How much?"

"A grand, for starters." Gloria opened her purse and pulled ten Benjamins out of the envelope nestled there, fanning the bills like a poker hand.

Marvin shook his head. "Ain't enough."

"I can get more. And once you introduce me, you're out of the picture."

Marvin extended his hands, palms up. "How much more?"

"It depends how the case goes. I can put you in for a twenty-five percent award."

Marvin shook his head and laughed. "Twenty-five percent of nothin' is nothin'."

"If she's a bigtime money launderer, it could be a lot of cash. If we seize a million, say, you'd get $250,000."

Marvin raised his eyebrows. "That's…a lot of money."

"You said you told Baba that you pick up duffel bags full of cash for me. Did he tell Uka that?"

Marvin looked away. "I believe he did."

The look-away bothered her. "What do you mean, you believe he did? Either he did, or he didn't."

"He told Marvin he was talking you up."

"All right. So, she's expecting that kind of cash from me. If she can handle that amount, she must have washed a lot before."

Marvin's expression suggested he was doing the math. He grabbed the door handle. "I'll talk to Baba, find out what he told her."

Gloria held up her hand. "One more thing."

Marvin frowned. "What?"

"You've got to wear a wire."

"Oh shit, you crazy? I can't do that."

"A quarter-million dollars, Marvin," Lauren said.

He crossed his arms. "You gonna put the cash in my casket? That'll look real pretty. Then everybody will know I was a snitch."

Gloria hastened to reassure him. "Look, we'll take it one step at a time. You meet with Baba and find out what he told Uka. That ought to be a two-minute conversation, at most. What's the best way to get in touch with him?"

Marvin laced his fingers together and looked down at the floor.

"A quarter-million," Lauren reminded him.

Marvin licked his lips. "What if Baba didn't tell her anything?"

Eyes narrowed, Gloria pointed a finger at him. "You said he did."

"That's what he told me, but I don't know for sure."

"Okay. This is what you do. You talk with him and beat around the bush. Bring it up and see what he says. Like I said, it's a two-minute conversation. Now how do you get in touch with him?"

"I call him, and we meet. He works a lot in Broadview and Maywood. So, if I'm out that way on a painting job I'll give him a call."

"That'll work. What's his number?"

Marvin pulled out his cell phone, checked his contact list, and gave them the number.

"Good. I've got a tape recorder here." Gloria fished a microphone from a mini-digital voice recorder out of the glove compartment, along with a roll of tape. "Let's call him now." She grabbed Marvin's phone and taped the mic, no bigger than a Bic lighter, onto its face. "This'll record both ends of your conversation."

Again, Marvin looked away from Gloria. "I can't do it now."

Gloria leaned toward him. "Why not?"

"Marvin's got to think about it."

"You don't have to meet him. Just call him. Mention me in vague terms, like you know that lady I told you about, that I pick up things for. She was wondering if you talked to Uka about her. If she could meet with her? That's all you have to say," Gloria told him. "You do it now, you get a thousand bucks for a phone call. Easiest money you ever made."

Marvin rubbed his hands down his pants legs. "You pushing hard."

Gloria waved the cash in his face, nodding to Marvin. He reached for it and stashed it in his pocket.

"Hit Baba's number," Lauren said.

Marvin exhaled loudly and tapped the cell phone keyboard. The phone rang several times before someone answered—a high, squeaky voice with a Nigerian accent. "Yo, my main man. How you doing?"

"Marvin's good, Baba. How you?"

"Slow day. You know, it snows a little and people don't want to go out."

"Yeah, I'm just sitting around. Doin' a little painting but not real busy. You know that lady I was telling you about? The one I pick up things for sometimes?"

"Yeah, how she doing?"

"She good, real good. But she needs some help. That insurance lady you told me about. Did you tell her about my lady friend?"

"Yeah."

"You think we could put the two of them together? I'm sure my lady friend would give you a good tip if you could do that?"

"I don't know. Maybe. I'm gonna be up to Uka's office the Monday after Christmas to pay my insurance. I can talk to her then."

"Thanks, Baba. I'll give you a call." Marvin hung up, exhaled a heavy sigh, and leaned back against the seat.

Gloria smiled at him. "Good job, Marvin. See, that wasn't so hard. We'll have to get together the day after Christmas to tape your next call. Did I have your consent to record the call you just made?"

"Yeah, yeah, yeah." Marvin scrubbed his hand over his face. "Why me? Why me?"

"Two hundred fifty thousand reasons," Lauren said.

CHAPTER 15

Carlton/Nighthawk Residence, Bronzeville
Saturday, Christmas Day, 2004

GLORIA AND ADSILA HAD DECORATED the tree the day before while listening to Nat King Cole's Christmas album. His version of "White Christmas" was Gloria's favorite. Three wrapped gifts sat under the tree. One each from Gloria to Darius and Adsila, and one from Adsila to Gloria. Nothing at all like prior years, when the area under the tree was filled with gifts up to the bottom branches and the kids hung their favorite ornament. Gloria remembered their hands cradling the delicate sphere of translucent glass that contained a photo of two African-American children, except this year it was only two hands instead of four, and Gloria's and Adsila's eyes had welled with tears.

Christmas morning, Gloria found the ornament under the tree, shattered to pieces. She fell to her knees, thinking *no, no.* She refused to attach any significance to the broken ornament. But the longer she looked at it, the more she wondered if it was a portent of the future. The scattered pieces that her life had become.

She moved the presents to one side and carefully swept up the shards of glass. Her heart ached. She couldn't help but think the fragments symbolized every significant relationship in her life she'd had a hand in destroying. Her parents' murder in the Oklahoma City bombing, Jim Abbott killed in Iraq, the abortion of their child, the death of her marriage to Robert, and now her estrangement from her son. Was she going to lose him too?

She'd hoped to clear up the remnants of the ornament before Adsila came down. Too late, she heard her daughter's footsteps on the stairs, then padding up and halting just behind her. "What happened, Mom?"

Gloria's chin quivered. "I guess we didn't hang the ornament securely."

"Oh no, that was my favorite! The one with the little boy and girl inside." Adsila sighed as she moved into view. "You always told us that was Darius and me."

Gloria stared down at the remaining debris while Adsila knelt beside her. "Don't let it get you down, Mom. It's only an ornament. It can be replaced. Why don't you call Darius this morning? I'm sure he wants to hear from you."

Gloria looked into Adsila's eyes, hoping her daughter was right. But the heavy feeling in her chest made her doubt it. "I don't know if he'll answer me. Why don't you try? He'll answer if he sees your caller ID." Gloria glanced at her watch. "It's only 7:15. Let's have breakfast first and then call him. He should be up by then."

In the kitchen, Gloria whipped four eggs in a bowl and fried bacon while Adsila made toast. The sense of doing something together as a family, even if it was only half of them, filled her with love as they stood beside one another at the stove. It was good to feel the connection when everything else was being ripped apart. "The eggs are almost ready. Do you want onions in them?"

Adsila's smile faded. "Darius is the one who likes onions and is the bacon eater."

Gloria rested her hand on Adsila's shoulder. "Force of habit, I guess. I love you, honey, and I miss him terribly."

Adsila looked up from the toaster. "I love you too, Mom."

After breakfast, Gloria and Adsila washed the dishes. Gloria was afraid to ask the questions on her mind, but she worked up the courage. "Have you seen much of Darius at school?" She eyed her daughter closely, searching for any positive sign.

Adsila shook her head. "Hardly at all. Once in while I see him when he's leaving, but he's rushing out and doesn't even notice me. One time I saw him getting into a yellow Cadillac."

Gloria froze, gripping the edge of the kitchen counter. *Yellow Cadillac. No…it must be a coincidence.* "What's he doing with his time these days? I mean, he doesn't practice with the team anymore."

"I don't know." Adsila picked up a juice glass and slowly dried it. "Mom, are he and Dad going to live away from us until the trial is over? And what happens if Dad…if Dad is convicted?"

"If he's convicted, he'll go to jail." Gloria put her arm around Adsila's shoulders and pulled her close, so she couldn't see her mother's eyes tear up. The guilt felt like an anvil in her chest. Was she wrong to have pursued the case against her husband? She could have buried it at the very beginning when she first recognized his signatures on the money orders, and no one would ever have known.

"For how long?" Adsila pressed her lips together. "And what about Darius? Will he come back home to live with us if Dad goes to jail?"

Gloria exhaled, let go of Adsila, and rubbed her forearm over her eyes. "I don't know what his sentence would be. If he's found guilty the prosecutors, the probation department, and your father, since he's representing himself, will make recommendations."

"And Darius? Will he come home?"

"He'll have to. He's only seventeen. He can't live on his own." Gloria wondered how that would work.

"Will you…" Adsila paused, as if unable to get the words out. "Will you and Dad ever get back together?"

The question just deepened Gloria's pain. She sniffled and choked down a sob. "I don't know." She leaned back, as if creating space between her and the mere mention of her husband. In the back of her mind, she knew there was no hope. Especially after he'd tried to get Darius to kill Spencer McElroy. But she could never tell Adsila that.

They moved to the living room and sat on the sofa. Adsila called Darius from her cell phone and put the call on speaker. Gloria listened intently, hoping to hear a sign that her son was open to talking to her.

"Hi, bro, merry Christmas!"

"Same to you, sis."

"Are you coming over to visit? There's a gift under the tree for you."

"I don't know."

Adsila took a deep breath and exhaled loudly. "Darius, how can you not come over to see Mom? It's Christmas."

"We have a lot of things to do—"

Gloria whispered, "Ask him to call me."

"Please call Mom," Adsila said in a hushed tone.

His tone was cool, distant. "Sorry, I'm busy. I've been working after school trying to make a little money. I really feel like I need to spend my time with Dad. Who knows what will happen to him in the future?" Abruptly, he ended the call.

Adsila dropped her hands to her sides and shook her head.

Gloria's chin trembled. *I've lost him.*

CHAPTER 16

Broadway Avenue, North Side, Chicago, IL
Monday, December 27, 2004
8:00 a.m.

AGENT LUIS GARCIA PARKED THE beige surveillance van on the west side of the 4800 block of north Broadway, a block from Uka Kafi's storefront insurance office. The bland work vehicle had a faded magnetic sign on its door that read *Ace Plumbing*. Garcia eased out of the driver's seat and crept through the narrow interior doorway to join Agent Steve Edwards in the back of the van.

Edwards turned on the directional camcorders concealed in the PVC pipes mounted on the van's roof. Kafi's storefront came into focus on the monitors, one close-up and the other wide angle.

Edwards radioed Lauren Ashberry. "206, be advised we're in place just north of the location, across the street from it. The cameras are activated."

"All right, 143. We're on the subject's condo, 147 and 212 are with me in separate vehicles. We'll advise you of any activity."

"10-4," Edwards responded.

Time dragged on. After a while, Edwards turned in his chair and faced Garcia. "Lauren has worked a lot with Gloria Nighthawk."

"Yeah, Nighthawk's really done a lot for Lauren's career."

Edwards folded his arms across his chest. "You were out of town last September, right? I mean, for Jim Abbott's funeral?"

"Yeah, sorry I missed it."

"It was strange." Edwards leaned against the shelving unit that held the two-way radio and recording equipment.

Garcia furrowed his eyebrows. "What do you mean?"

"Well, when they were carrying Abbott's casket out of the church, his wife was about to enter the limo and she does an about-face, scanning the people standing on the steps. Her eyes lock onto someone and she moves away from her kids and marches toward the crowd. They parted like she was Moses stepping into the Red Sea. She walks right up to Gloria, face to face, inches apart."

"So? Abbott and Gloria worked together. His wife probably knew her better than anyone else from the office."

"Yeah, but it was weird." Edwards laughed. "Gave me the feeling her and Abbott did more than work together. I bet—"

"Cut the bullshit. Gloria's one of the best agents we have. I'd trust her in any situation, and I'm sure Jim's wife had no problems with them working together. Gloria always helped anyone she worked with. Ask Lauren."

"Yeah, Gloria takes care of those she likes, but if you're not on that list, don't ask her for anything."

"Steve, no one's obligated to show you how to do the job. It's up to you to use your initiative. But I'm sure if you had any questions, Gloria would give you a straight answer and there's probably no one better to ask."

"Yeah, sure." He folded his arms and turned away from Garcia, facing the monitors.

The small talk lagged after that. At 9:00 a.m. Lauren radioed: "All units, the subject just left her condo. I've got the eyeball. She should be at the storefront in ten to fifteen minutes. She's driving a late model black Mercedes Benz E500." The license plate number followed. "She's dark skinned, tall, about forty years old, wearing a black overcoat unbuttoned, over an African outfit; a green and gold headdress and matching dress. It won't be hard to pick her out."

Ten minutes later, the Mercedes drove into view. Lauren and the two agents with her followed behind. The Mercedes parked in front of Uka's Auto Insurance. Uka Kafi exited the car, walked to the front door of her business, unlocked it, and entered. Before long a neon sign flashed *OPEN* and the interior lights went on. Fifteen minutes after that, three African-American males entered the office. Two of them wore knee length dark green overcoats, white collars from dress shirts peeking out above, ties hanging down. They both carried briefcases. The third wore a waist-length black leather coat and black slacks.

"I got all of them on video," Edwards said.

Garcia nodded but didn't say a word.

For the next hour and a half, no one else entered or left the business. Edwards leaned back in his chair and kicked his feet up on the edge of the shelf holding the two-way radio. "This is the part of surveillances I hate — boring. Is Gloria going to be out here?"

"Nope, she's undercover, so she can't be in the field. Can't risk getting burned."

"I didn't know she was an undercover agent."

"She's only done local stuff. It was her informant that initially gave her the tip about this set-up, so she's working with the CI to get an introduction to Kafi."

Edwards opened his mouth, stopped short of saying anything, and then picked up the two-way microphone. "A taxi just parked behind Kafi's Benz. The cab driver is getting out…he's entering Kafi's business. He's wearing jeans and a tan ski jacket. He's short, slender, and dark skinned. Got him on video." He scrawled on his notepad the time the individual went inside: 11:15 a.m.

Lauren's voice sounded over the radio. "212, see if you can take the cab driver when he leaves the place."

"10-4," Wilson responded.

Edwards gave the surveillance units the cab's number. He kept watching for another couple of minutes, then broadcast again. "The cab driver's leaving Kafi's and he's carrying a briefcase." Edwards jotted down the cabbie's time of departure, 11:25 a.m.

"10-4, we've got him," Lauren said. "He's on foot heading north, on the same side of the street as Kafi's." A pause, maybe two minutes long. "He just entered the bank on the corner. 212, can you get inside the bank and see what he's doing?"

Another three minutes crawled by. The agent entered the bank. A few minutes later the cab driver left, briefcase in hand. He returned to Kafi's office.

Wilson radioed them. "I didn't see our guy until he walked out from a private office. Name on the door is Nelson Adabayo. Looks like they've got a private banker."

"So, what else is new?" Edwards muttered. Garcia chuckled.

At 11:45, the cab driver left Kafi's without the briefcase, entered his cab, and drove off. Edwards relayed the observation. "147, follow the cab," Lauren ordered.

Someone banged on the side of the van. It sounded like thunder. "What the hell?" Edwards said. He and Garcia drew their Sig Sauer semi-autos and braced themselves against the walls.

"We're sitting ducks if some asshole decides to start shooting." Garcia checked the monitors. "Damn. Whoever's out there is too close. Can't see a thing."

The banging came again, louder and harder. The van rocked sideways on its shocks. Garcia held on to his chair as it crashed against the wall.

Edwards grabbed his mic. "206, we've got company. Somebody's banging on the van, sidewalk side."

"Are you okay?" Lauren radioed back.

"I can hear you in there," a husky male voice yelled. "Chicago P.D. Come out with your hands up!"

Edwards's forehead was moist with sweat. "It's the CPD. We'll see what's going on."

Garcia shook his head as he holstered his Sig. "You stay here. I'll get out and give them a cover story." He pulled his sweatshirt over his weapon, then crawled through the interior door of the van, slid over the passenger's seat, opened the door, and stepped onto the sidewalk. Two men awaited him there, guns drawn. "You guys CPD?" he asked, careful to keep his hands in view.

"You fuckin' hard of hearing?" The speaker was a Black man with a burly build and a shaved head. He wore a brown leather bomber jacket and a CPD badge hanging on a chain around his neck, and he was pointing a Glock 19 at Garcia. "We're with the Tac Unit. I'm Jefferson." He nodded at his partner. "He's Pipowski." The second cop was white, slender, mid-thirties. A cigarette dangled from his lips, and he covered the van door with a chrome-plated .357 Magnum. "What're you motherfuckers doing here?" Jefferson demanded as he lowered his pistol to his side.

Garcia shrugged. "Goddamn piece of shit van stalled. Costing me a fortune."

The white cop—Pipowski—holstered his .351 revolver. "We got a call about a suspicious vehicle. How long you been sitting here?"

Garcia shrugged again. "Not sure exactly. I wasn't watching the time."

Jefferson scowled. "Get this van outta here!"

"No problem. I think the engine was flooded. It should start now," Garcia said. "Thanks, officers—"

"We see you guys around here again, you'll be in deep shit," Jefferson said.

Garcia's eyes widened. He climbed into the driver's seat and cranked the ignition, then rolled down the window. "It seems okay now." He waved to the cops as he pulled away from the curb.

In the back of the van, Edwards radioed Lauren. "206, we just got burned by a tac unit. Suggest we break off the surveillance for today."

"10-4. There's a coffee shop on Clark, about 5500 north. Let's meet there."

Edwards turned the two-way off, then left the rear compartment and got into the passenger seat. "Jesus Christ, we're lucky they didn't empty their pistols on us. You ever met those cops before?"

Garcia headed north on Clark. "A salt and pepper combo, Jefferson and Pipowski. I've met a lot of cops. Don't recall them." He let another block go by in silence, then said, "Listen. When we meet up with the others, keep your fucking opinions about Gloria to yourself."

"Sure, you bet," Edwards muttered.

At the coffee shop, they joined Lauren and the other two agents, Kozlowksi and Wilson, and debriefed each other on the surveillance.

"That's one of the downsides of the van. If you're stuck in it when gangbangers decide to start shooting, you're dead meat," Garcia said. He glanced at Edwards, who said nothing.

"Did you get the cops' names?" Lauren asked.

Garcia nodded. "The Black guy was Jefferson and the white one was Pipowski. Said they were with the Tac Unit."

"Any sign that any of Kafi's people were paying attention to what was going on?"

"Didn't see anything to indicate that. The cops said the call was anonymous, but you never know. Could have been Kafi, could be cops are just too curious or worse." Garcia raised his coffee cup. "Let's hope it was just a coincidence."

CHAPTER 17

GLORIA SAT IN THE BLACK Blazer, accompanied by rookie Special Agent Craig Holcomb. He wore a navy sport coat and matching tie over a white shirt, gray slacks, and black horn-rimmed glasses. They were parked on Jackson Boulevard, waiting for Marvin. She had contacted her CI immediately after Lauren called and told her an individual matching Baba's description had been to Uka's, left with a briefcase, and gone to a nearby bank.

Fifteen minutes later, Marvin's yellow Caddy went past, and he parked in front of them.

"That's him." Gloria nodded at the car. Her stomach roiled at the thought that Marvin could be picking up Darius in it. She jotted down Marvin's license plate number on a notepad. Maybe it wasn't so, but if it was, nothing mattered more than protecting her son, even if he was estranged from her.

A warm Christmas Day had melted most of the snow. Gloria calmed herself as she watched Marvin stroll down the sidewalk to the Blazer. By the time he got in the back seat, she figured she could trust herself to sound normal. "Marvin, this is Special Agent Holcomb. Lauren is on another assignment at the moment."

Marvin nodded at Holcomb.

"Have you talked to Baba or Uka since we last met?" Gloria asked.

Marvin shook his head. "You told me not to."

"Good. We have to document any conversations between you and Baba, or Uka, or anyone else that might have anything to do with this case, so it's best to limit your contacts with them."

Marvin frowned. "Document?"

"Tape them, like when you talked with Baba last Thursday. You remember you told Baba you would call him today, to see if he talked to Uka about meeting me and my associate. He told you he had to see her to pay his car insurance."

"Yeah, I remember. What if he says he hasn't seen her?"

Here was a way to test Baba's veracity...*and Marvin's,* Gloria thought. "Let's call and find out. Give me your phone."

Marvin handed his phone over. Holcomb gave her the mini-mic, and she taped it to the speaker. "You know the number of his cab?" She didn't mention the surveillance—better Marvin didn't know about it—but corroborating information was always good.

"No, I never noticed."

"What's he look like?"

"He's a little guy. I'd say about five feet six. Can't be more than 120 pounds. Darker than me."

That description matched the one Lauren had given her. Gloria turned on the mic and read the preamble into the phone. "Do we have your permission to record the telephone conversation you're about to have with Babatunde Okoye today, December twenty-seventh, 2004, at 1:20 p.m.?"

Marvin nodded.

Gloria gritted her teeth. "Marvin, you have to say yes or no."

He avoided eye contact, looking up at the roof of the car instead. "Yeah, yeah, yeah."

"Okay. Pull up Baba's number and hit it."

Marvin glanced at Holcomb and then at Gloria. She mouthed the words, *two hundred fifty thousand dollars.* He hit Baba's number.

Baba picked up on the fourth ring. "Hey, my main man. What you doing?"

"Always keeping busy, hustling here and hustling there."

"Good man. Always good to be busy."

Marvin nodded. "You told me you were seeing that lady to pay for your insurance. You know, the one I'm trying to arrange for my lady friend to meet."

"Yeah, yeah. I talked with her earlier today."

"Did you tell her about my friend?" Marvin glanced at Gloria. "The one that's lookin' for a new banker?"

"Yeah, yeah. She said she don't like doin' business with people she don't know."

"Baba, you been knowing me for a long time. I wouldn't do you wrong."

"We good, but what can I say? *She* don't know you, or your lady friend."

"Did you tell her you been knowing me for years?"

"No, no. I didn't say that, exactly."

"So tell her. Tell her you trust me. I wouldn't do you bad, you know that."

"I guess I can. She's a smart lady. I can't promise you she'll change her mind."

"Just try it. My lady told me she'd pay you good for putting her together with yours."

"Yeah, yeah. I try, my friend. I got to go now. I got a fare to pick up. We'll talk in a few days."

"Okay, Baba. Don't forget, you'll get a nice tip."

"How much? Gas is expensive."

Marvin glanced at Gloria. She held up two fingers.

"At least two bills. That'll buy a lot of gas."

"I'll try. I got to pick up my fare. Talk to you in a couple of days."

"Okay, thanks, Baba."

Marvin clicked off, and Gloria dictated the post-amble: "The call with Baba ended at 1:25 p.m. on December twenty-seventh, 2004." She turned off the tape recorder and exhaled. "We need this to work out. You've got to make this happen."

"I'm trying. You heard." Marvin splayed his hands out to his sides. "What else can I do?"

"We might have to send you in to meet Uka on your own before she's willing to meet with me."

Marvin shook his head. "Shit, man. That was never the way we worked before."

"Sometimes you've got to try a different way. Could be well worth it for you."

Marvin rolled his eyes. "Or maybe not."

Gloria glared at him. "Or maybe yes. We're getting together in a few days to call Baba again, no matter what." She wasn't sure if her anger stemmed from her need to move the case along, or her fear that her informant might be involving her son in something that could have a terrible outcome. For a moment, she felt tempted to confront him about it, but that would be stupid. She needed Marvin, couldn't cut him loose yet even if she wanted to. Realizing how little control she had over events only added to her frustration.

Marvin nodded and got out of the Blazer. Gloria watched him return to the yellow Cadillac. Her hand tightened on her Sig Sauer. If Marvin was messing with Darius, this could explode in many ways.

Belatedly, she noticed Holcomb's gaze. He was focused on her white-knuckled grip on her pistol. She eased it and slid her hand down her pants leg. *I've got to surveil Darius, find out if he's somehow gotten tied up with Marvin.* The only place she felt certain of finding him was right after school. She couldn't use the Blazer; Marvin and Darius would both recognize it. "Craig, what G car are you driving?"

"A Nissan Maxima. Why?"

"I've got a couple of spots I've been checking out. But I think I might have burned my Blazer. Would you mind switching cars for a few days?"

"No, that would be fine. I could go with you if you want?"

Gloria turned to face him. "No, that's all right. I'm trying to keep down the time I charge to this project. You know how Stephens is about charging hours to case development."

Holcomb took off his eyeglasses and cleaned them with his tie. "Gloria, you seem kind of intense about this. I can bury my time on some other case too."

"Thanks for the offer. I don't want to teach you my bad habits. Stephens wouldn't appreciate that." She turned away from him and faced the windshield. "At this point, I can manage it on my own."

Holcomb's shoulders slumped, "Okay. I guess we can go back to the garage and switch now, if that works for you."

"Great." Gloria fired up the SUV and pulled away. As they headed back downtown, her mind was focused on Marvin's yellow Cadillac. She knew Darius would be off from school until after Christmas break. She would look for him the first Monday back.

CHAPTER *18*

Whitney Young High School
211 S. Laflin, Chicago, IL
Monday, January 3, 2005
3:00 p.m.

GLORIA FOUND A PARKING PLACE on Adams Street east of the school's main exit. She hoped the Nissan Maxima she'd borrowed from Agent Holcomb would help conceal her identity, not only from Darius, but also from Adsila and Marvin, if in fact her informant had been picking up her son. If that was true, where was he taking Darius?

She slumped down in the driver's seat, pulled a wide-brimmed hat low on her head, and waited. She reached to twist her wedding ring, but it wasn't on her finger. Old habits died hard. *How can it be that I'm surveilling my seventeen-year-old son?* Her stomach churned.

Fifteen minutes later she saw Darius exit the building. He wasn't hard to spot; not many students stood six feet, six inches. He was looking up and down the street, as if for his ride. *If it's a yellow Cadillac, let it be someone besides Marvin.* Maybe Robert had traded in his Lexus. That must be it. More minutes passed, seeming like hours as one car after another pulled up to the curb and kids hustled into them. But there was no Cadillac to be seen, yellow or otherwise.

A red 5.0 Mustang came roaring past Gloria and screeched to a halt at the school entrance. Darius darted for the car and got in. It squealed away from the school, leaving skid marks on the street. Gloria floored the Maxima in pursuit.

The Mustang sped south on Ashland, veering in and out of traffic. Gloria followed, torn between trying not to get burned and not losing them. They went east onto the Eisenhower Expressway, then south on the Dan Ryan, and exited at 35th Street. The Mustang roared through a red light at 35th and headed further east over the Ryan. Stopped at the same light, Gloria clenched the steering wheel and searched for an opening into the eastbound traffic. Finally, she found one. She gunned the Nissan through the intersection and saw the Mustang turn south on Federal Street, a block ahead of her.

Gloria punched the accelerator. The Nissan veered in front of an eighteen-wheeler. The truck's brakes screeched and its horn blasted as she cut in front of it and headed south on Federal. The high-rises of the Robert Taylor Homes loomed up ahead. She slowed, looking for the red Mustang in the parking lots. What in God's name was Darius doing here, and with who?

Nothing in the first lot. She cruised past the second lot, shaking her head. "Maybe he didn't stop here," she muttered, and hit the accelerator. The Nissan picked up speed as she cruised past the third lot.

There it was, the red Mustang. She slammed the brakes, then pulled into the lot and parked on the opposite side, facing the low-slung car. The driver and Darius were gone. She jotted down the plate number and picked up the microphone to call it in, then stopped herself. What if the Mustang was registered to Darius? If she called in the plate number, there would be a record on the radio log. Gloria set the mic down and waited, not exactly sure what she would do if Darius returned to the car. There was no way Darius and his father were living in the projects, so why was he here?

Better make sure she had the right vehicle. She exited the Nissan and pulled her jacket collar up as she walked across the lot. The asphalt was cracked and veined with dead weeds. Litter blew across the pavement. She reached the Mustang and felt the hood. It was still warm. She looked at the sign posted nearby. Bent and mangled, it read *Parking for Residents Of 3904 Building Only.*

She returned to the Nissan, waited for ten minutes, and then decided to leave—wanting to know what her son was doing here but afraid of what she might learn.

⸻

The usual hangers-on crowded the foyer of 3904, dancing as rap music blasted through the room. The aroma of weed filled the air.

Halfway up the stairwell, Darius halted. "I left my calculator in the car. What apartment is Marvin using to cut the shit?"

"They moved it this weekend. It's in 604 now," Shorty said. "What you need a calculator for? You just trying to look smarter than the rest of us."

"I am smarter than the rest of you. I'm giving Marvin the best profit he ever had. That's why I need the calculator. I'll meet you on six."

Darius hurried down the stairs and back through the foyer. He left the building and headed to the parking lot. As he rounded the corner of the building, he froze in his tracks, then skirted back out of sight and pressed himself against the wall. Someone was standing by Shorty's car. His heart raced. What was the guy doing? He peered around the corner again for a split second and saw him place a hand on the Mustang's hood. The guy's face was hidden by a wide-brimmed hat and the raised collar of a tactical field jacket. *Got to be a cop.*

Darius risked another look and saw him walking back to a Nissan Maxima. *Fuck the calculator. We've got to move the shit.* He turned and ran back to the building, hurried through the crowd in the foyer pushing people out of his way, got into the elevator. Two girls were in it. He shoved them out—"Get out of here. I'm in a hurry"—and hit the button for the sixth floor.

When the doors opened, Darius hustled out of the elevator and down the hall to 604. He knocked with the coded entry—three times, pause, and twice more. "Shorty, open the fucking door," he yelled. He heard the deadbolt click and leaned his shoulder into the door, pushing Shorty against the wall.

"What's your fucking problem?" Shorty bellowed.

Darius slammed the door shut and turned the deadbolt. The nearly empty room held the usual pair of six-foot tables set end to end, with four women wearing only panties working at it. Two were cutting heroin, the other two bagging eighths of a gram into small plastic bags. He ignored them and grabbed Shorty by the collar of his tee shirt. "I saw a cop in the parking lot, checking out your car. We've got to close this place down and move the shit out of here, now!"

"What the fuck you talking about?"

"You heard me. Do it. If they raid us, we could lose a whole kilo, not to mention getting thrown in jail."

Shorty smoothed his wrinkled shirt. "You better be right, or Marvin will be pissed."

"Better to be safe. Losing a day of mixing is better than losing everything. Shut it down," Darius said.

Shorty turned toward the women. "Bitches, get the fuck out of here. Move your asses!"

The women rushed to the corner of the room where their clothes were piled. They quickly pulled on sweatshirts and sweatpants and then raced out the door.

Shorty moved to the table and swept fifty finished baggies into a gym bag. Darius sealed the larger bag that held most of the remaining kilo with duct tape and dropped it into a backpack.

"Where do we go now?" Shorty asked.

"There's got to be another vacant apartment we can put this stuff in."

"Yeah. Most of them on the eighth floor are empty."

Darius held the backpack out to Shorty. "You take these up to eight. I'll go down to the property manager and get a key."

Shorty pushed the backpack away. "I don't want to take this stuff. My luck, I'll be stuck up by some homie looking for a new backpack and then Marvin will say I ripped him off."

Darius shoved the pack into his arms. "Just fucking do it! Take the stairs. It'll be safer." He ducked out of the apartment, not waiting to see if Shorty obeyed orders, and ran for the elevator.

A few minutes later, he met Shorty on the eighth floor and unlocked the door to Unit 810. Inside, Shorty dropped the gym bag and backpack to the floor. "Go get the women," Darius said. Shorty nodded and left. It took them a while to round the women up, but eventually Shorty ushered them into the new workplace. They quickly stripped down and started mixing and bagging again.

Forty-five minutes from when he'd first spotted the cop, Darius leaned against the door of Unit 810, exhaled in relief, and texted Marvin — *911, 5-0, 5-0.*

Gloria raised Agent Holcomb on the two-way radio and agreed to meet him in Oak Park at 4:00, in the shopping center parking lot east of Harlem and south of Lake Street. As she headed toward her destination, her thoughts wandered from Darius to the money laundering case. Nothing she could do about Darius at the moment, but the case was something she could control. *I've got to try a different approach. If Baba is going to the bank for Kafi, she must trust him.* She ran through options as she drove, testing, discarding. Slowly, a plan took shape.

When she got to the lot, Holcomb was waiting for her. She parked next to the black Blazer and popped the Nissan's trunk, then got out, took off the tactical field jacket and wide-brimmed hat, and tossed them in it. A navy North Face ski jacket lay in the trunk; she snatched it out and slipped into it, then got into the Blazer and brushed her fingers through her hair. Holcomb had already moved from the driver's seat to the passenger side.

"We'll take this car to meet Marvin," Gloria said. "When we finish with him, we can come back here." She hesitated, then plunged on. "I'd like to use your car for a few more days, if you don't mind?"

"No, that's fine. I really appreciate you taking me to work with your CI. It's a new experience for me. Like I said, if you need any help on that case development project you're working on, I'm available."

"I appreciate the offer, Craig. But not quite yet." Gloria started the Blazer, left the lot, and slipped smoothly into traffic.

Columbus Park was a little more than a mile away. As usual, Marvin's yellow Cadillac was parked on Jackson, and she pulled the Blazer up behind it. She needed to focus on the Uka Kafi case, but thoughts of Darius kept creeping into her mind. The image of him in the red Mustang. Gloria inhaled and blew out a deep breath, trying to gain control as she watched Marvin exit his car. He reached the SUV, got into the back seat, and slammed the door shut.

Marvin nodded at Holcomb, then focused on Gloria. "What's up?"

"Have you heard from Baba yet?"

Marvin rubbed the back of his neck. "No. You told me not to make any contact on my own." His cell phone buzzed. He pulled it out and looked at the screen.

"That Baba?" Gloria asked.

"Nah. Text." He seemed agitated.

"Everything okay?"

Marvin drew a deep breath. "You know I got this painting business. Some people that work for me are fucking up."

"Sorry to hear that. It's not easy to get good help. We're in a situation where we can help each other. I want you to call Baba again."

"He probably hasn't seen that lady since the last time I talked to him."

"You're probably right, but we've got to force the issue a little. You still have the grand I gave you?"

"Most of it. Why?"

"Here's what I want you to do. Take $200 and give it to Baba. Tell him it's his tip from me. Tell him I'm trusting him to go back to the lady and say he's known you for years, you're a standup guy, and you've known *me* for years. I understand her position, and I'm willing to do our first transaction with her dealing directly with Baba and you."

Marvin jerked his head back. "That grand is Marvin's. You got all the cash in the world."

"I'll pay you back when I get more. I've never shorted you."

"Why you got to use my money?"

"I want to get this moving. I don't want to go through the" — she paused, glancing at Holcomb — "the trouble of trying to explain this to my boss."

"Shit, man. Marvin's got to get burned *and* pay for the G." He shook his head. "Who ever heard of shit like that?"

"You want to turn your back on $250,000? Remember that?"

He nodded and clasped his fingers together. "Yeah, yeah."

"Okay. Call Baba." Gloria hooked up the recorder to Marvin's phone and read the preamble into it, then handed it back to him.

He tapped out Baba's number. "Hey, Baba, it's me."

"What's up?"

"My lady friend gave me the tip to give to you."

"Didn't you tell her Kafi doesn't want to do business with someone she doesn't know?"

"Yeah, but you were good enough to ask, so she just want to show you that she a lady of her word."

"That's a nice lady. How much?"

Marvin held up two fingers, as if he was talking to Baba face to face. "Two bills. Just like she said."

"I can use the money. When can we meet?"

"Where are you?"

"I'm in Broadview."

"I'm heading out to the West Side. How about on Jackson east of Austin, by the golf course? I'll be in my yellow Caddy."

"I can be there in fifteen minutes," Baba said.

"All right, see you then." Marvin terminated the call and looked at Gloria. "Marvin did good. Right?"

"Marvin did good. When Baba comes to get his tip, you ask him about delivering my cash to Uka Kafi. I'm going to give you the tape recorder. All you have to do is press this button when you meet." She tapped it lightly. "Ask him to check with her. Say you'll go with Baba to make the drop-off. We'll be parked on the side street, behind the golf course starter's building." She handed Marvin the recorder. "Remember…$250,000. That's what you're looking at when everything's done."

"Uh-huh." Marvin stashed the tape recorder in the pocket of his black leather coat and got out of the SUV.

As he returned to his car, Gloria pulled out and headed east a hundred yards on Jackson, then turned south on Menard and parked the Blazer behind the starter's cabin for the golf course. She and Holcomb had a clear view of Marvin's Cadillac from here. She kept her eyes glued to it as she fought a battle within her. *He's being as cooperative as I could ask. I can't imagine he has anything to do with Darius.*

Fifteen minutes later, a cab parked behind Marvin's car. A Black male matching Baba's description exited the cab and entered the Cadillac's passenger side. Through the car's rear window, Gloria could just see the two men slapping their hands together.

***

"Hey, my man. Good to see you," Marvin said. He'd turned the recorder on as soon as Baba pulled up.

"Good to see you too," Baba said.

"Look what I got for you." Marvin slid ten twenty-dollar bills across the seat.

"Thank you, thank you." Baba nodded as he picked them up. "That's real nice of your lady friend."

"I got an idea, Baba. How long you been knowing this lady, Uka?"

"Since I got in the country. Over ten years. Been buying my insurance from her for a long time, and sometimes she asks me to do a favor. You know, deliver a package for one of her cousins. Shit like that."

"I been knowing you for what? Five years at least."

"That sounds about right."

"She pay you extra for those deliveries?"

"Oh, yeah. She's good to me. Sometimes she doesn't charge me for insurance."

Marvin nodded. "That's good. That's the way it should be. You do a favor for her; she does one for you."

Baba reached for the door handle. "Thanks again for the cash. I gotta run."

Shit. "Wait a second. I got a favor to ask you. You said your lady doesn't do business with people she don't know. How about we do this? You tell her you and me been knowing each other for five years. I go with you to meet your lady, and I'll bring some cash for her to take care of for my lady friend. If things work out, if everybody's happy, then they can do business. If not, your lady never has to meet my lady."

Baba settled back, looking sideways at Marvin. "I can do that, but I don't know if she'll go for it."

"Just tell her we've been knowing each other five years and she can make a lot of money. If she goes for it, you can make some extra too."

"Can't hurt to ask." Baba yanked the handle, opening the door a crack. "Okay, my man. I'll let you know." He stepped out and headed back to his cab.

Marvin reached into his pocket and shut off the tape recorder. "If I get fucked up, it ain't gonna just be me."

Chapter 19

Robert Taylor Homes
Monday, January 3, 2005
6:00 p.m.

MARVIN PUSHED HIS WAY THROUGH the hangers-on in the foyer and hurried to his office. He slammed the door shut and texted Darius. Ten minutes later, Darius stepped into the office and closed the door behind him.

Marvin glared at him. "What the fuck is going on?"

Darius told Marvin the whole story. How he'd started back to Shorty's car to get his calculator and saw the cop checking out the Mustang. That he ordered Shorty to close down Unit 604 because he feared the police were going to raid it, got another apartment, and resumed the operation there.

Marvin shook his head. "Things like this aren't supposed to happen." He pinched his lips together. *I'm paying that tac cop, Jefferson, for protection.* "What did the fuckin' cop look like?"

"I didn't get a good look at him. I only saw him for a second. Didn't want him to see me."

Marvin slammed his fist on his desk. "Answer my fucking question, damn it."

Darius jerked back. "He was wearing a military jacket, like a combat jacket, and a floppy hat. Couldn't see his face. He wasn't too big…could've been a woman."

Marvin's eyes narrowed. "Why you think it was a cop?"

Darius shrugged. "Who else would be checking out Shorty's car?"

"What you mean, checking out his car?"

Darius stretched out his arm. "The cop extended his hand and felt the hood. Checking to see if the engine was warm, I guess. Maybe he was watching us."

Marvin nodded. A thinker, this kid. "Tell Shorty to shitcan that car. Park it somewhere with the keys in it. No more red Mustangs. Get some car that won't draw attention." He jerked his head toward the door. "You can get out of here now."

The boy nodded and started to leave. Marvin unlocked a lower desk drawer, opened it, and looked at the mess of $100 bills inside. "Wait a second." Gently, he shut the drawer. "You did good, Darius. And you're smarter than the rest of these fuckups. I want you to come with me tonight. Meet me at 7:00, at the drugstore across the street."

"Where're we going?"

I'll tell you when I decide for sure I trust you enough. "You'll find out when we get there. Don't be late."

Darius shrugged. "Sure. See you at 7:00." He walked out of the office.

Marvin went to the door and locked it, then picked up his land line and dialed a number. "Hi, Mama. Okay if I stop by in twenty minutes? No, sorry, Mama. I ain't got time for dinner. Just have to stop by for some business."

He hung up, then grabbed handfuls of the hundreds from the drawer and piled them on his desk in stacks of ten. He swept up the eight stacks, rubber banded five in one pile, the remaining three in another, and slipped them into the pockets of his black leather jacket. He needed another $50,000 and knew where to get it. He locked the drawer again, then left his office and walked down the short hall, nodding in passing to the property manager, Ruby Anderson, as she filled her mouth with a handful of caramel corn. Marvin supplied her with it and other snacks on a regular basis.

The foyer was filled with the usual comings and goings. Marvin pressed his way through to the elevators and headed up to the tenth floor. He stepped out of the elevator, went to Unit 1018, and knocked.

A soft, gentle voice responded: "Hello?"

"Mama, it's Marvin."

He heard the clicks of three deadbolt locks, and then the door opened. An elderly lady stood there, slender and just under five feet tall, in a blue dress, her silver hair in a short afro. Her eyes still sparkled despite her age, and she and Marvin hugged each other. A black and tan tabby brushed against Marvin's legs. Beatrice Moore was like a mother to Marvin, a child of foster homes who'd never known his parents. Mama was one of the few people Marvin felt he could trust.

He stepped away from Beatrice and picked up the cat. "How's my little Bailey? I know you like to dance." He held the cat against his chest and did a two-step, humming a tune as he crossed the threshold. He pushed the door closed with his foot and locked the deadbolts. The cat sprang to the floor.

Beatrice took his hand and led him toward the sofa, and they sat. Next to the sofa was a recliner with handmade doilies on the head and arm rests. Centered in front of the recliner was a large flat-screen TV mounted on the wall and a VCR in a stand under the TV. "I know you said you can't stay to eat, but why don't you let me make you a sandwich?" Beatrice said.

Marvin glanced at his Rolex. "I really can't stay long. I'm meeting a young man in a few minutes."

"That's too bad. I enjoy talking with you." Beatrice tilted her head down.

Marvin sat up straighter. "Is everything okay? Have the boys been dropping off the rent money? You got enough food?"

"Oh, yes. The boys have been very good. Shorty is a nice young man and very respectful."

"Good, good. You let me know if there's anything you need?"

She smiled. "Everything is fine, Marvin. Thank you for being so kind."

Marvin let go of her hand and stood. "My associate will be waiting for me. I better get what I came for." He headed down a hallway to the second bedroom. Shelves lined one wall, filled with books by James Baldwin, Toni Morrison and others, plus record albums and CDs ranging from Nat King Cole to Placido Domingo, a turntable, and a CD player.

He sat in a love seat next to what looked like an end table covered by a tablecloth. He pulled the cloth off, revealing a safe twenty-five inches high and eighteen inches wide. He spun the dial to the left, then the right, then back again and pushed the handle down, opening the door.

He took a black bag from the safe, then reached in again for stacks of cash wrapped in $5,000 bundles. He counted them as he placed them in the bag, until he reached $45,000. Then he pulled the $3,000 bundle out of his pocket, loosened the rubber band, and added $2,000 more from the safe before wrapping the bundle again and shoving it in the bag. "Fifty grand," he murmured.

He removed one last item from the safe, a Walther PPK semi-auto, and stuck it in his waistband. He closed the safe, locked it, and draped the cloth back in place. As he stood, his knees cracked. *Getting too old for this.* Maybe his load could be lightened, if Darius could be trusted. That thought made him smile as he headed out of the bedroom. *Let's see what that boy is made of.*

CHAPTER 20

3600 South State Street, Chicago, IL
Monday, January 3, 2005
7:00 p.m.

DARIUS ARRIVED TEN MINUTES EARLY and waited just inside the entrance to the drugstore. He could feel the chill coming through the front door. The temperature had dropped to 25 degrees and it was only going to get colder. Snow had begun to fall. Shortly after 7:00, a green 2000 Honda Accord pulled up to the curb and the driver honked the horn.

Darius stepped up to the store's front door and peered through the window. The Honda wasn't familiar to him. He rubbed his hand across the glass, wiping away condensation from his breath as he tried to see who the driver was. The horn blasted again. It had to be Marvin.

Darius pulled up the hood of his parka and hurried from the storefront to the street. The snow was heavier now, pushed by a chilling wind that blew from the north. As he grabbed the Honda's door handle, he noticed a Crown Vic parked two spaces behind.

He opened the door and slid into the passenger seat. "Never seen this car before."

"You might never see it again. Just like the red Mustang." Marvin stepped on the accelerator and pulled away from the curb.

Darius glanced in the sideview mirror in time to see the Crown Vic pull out behind them. "I think there's a cop car following us."

"Don't worry about him."

Darius nodded. "That the guy who punched you in the nose?"

Marvin's grip tightened on the steering wheel. "Don't be too smart for your own good."

They rode north on State Street in silence, letting the tension ease for a few minutes as they passed rib joints with greasy smoke exhaling from the rooftops and strip clubs advertising *Girls, Girls.*

"Where are we going?" Darius asked.

"You're a smart boy." Marvin glanced at him. "That's why you're here. You're smart and I can trust you, right?"

"Yeah, sure. I've done right by you. Haven't I?"

Marvin turned west onto Cermak Road. "You have, especially with that cop in the parking lot earlier today." He leaned forward, reached between his legs, grabbed a small black bag, and set it on Darius's lap.

Darius sat back in his seat. "What's this?"

"Open it."

Darius pulled the zipper. "What the…" He shoved his hand in the bag, rustling his fingers through the bills. "These are all hundreds." He looked at Marvin. "How much?"

"Fifty grand."

"What for?"

"It's an opportunity for you. You can make more money. But it's more responsibility."

Darius zipped the bag shut and gazed straight ahead.

Marvin eyed him. "You in or out? I need to know."

"Exactly what do you want me to do?"

Marvin turned north on Racine. Neon lights burned in the windows of buildings they passed, advertising taquerias and currency exchanges. He pulled into a parking spot, and the Crown Vic nosed up behind them. "I'm planning on you meeting my connect. Taking over this part of the operation. All you have to do is deliver the fifty grand to him, pick up the package, and bring it back to the stash pad."

Darius looked over his shoulder at the Crown Vic. "He be following me each time?"

"That's how he earns his money."

"When do I have to tell you if I'm in or out?"

"When?" Marvin laughed. "Now!"

Darius let loose of the bag and jammed his hands into his coat pockets. His voice trembled. "What if…what if I don't think this is a good idea?"

Marvin's expression hardened and his nostrils flared. "You think you're too fucking good for this?"

"No, man. It's not that. I just never thought you'd ask me to help you like this."

Abruptly, Marvin laughed. "You know what, young blood? You'll be fine. And you'll have lived life to the max. Not sitting in the back seat, getting old and pissed off as the world keeps turning, leaving you behind. You got choices to make. Good ones."

Darius thought about it. Here was an opportunity to break away from all the rules that controlled his life, and his parents' lives. What the hell, even they had a fucked-up vision of right and wrong. His mother was responsible for his father being indicted. Wasn't she supposed to be loyal? As for his father, had he not followed the oath he took when he became a prosecutor and a judge, was he lying about his guilt, or had he been falsely accused because of Darius' mother?

They really piss me off. He clenched his hands around the money bag. He needed to be loyal to himself, not to those rules that even his self-righteous parents violated. He needed to live each day, learn the day's lessons, and not count on tomorrow. He responded with a slow nod. "How much does this pay?"

"A grand per trip."

"Let's do it."

Marvin pulled into traffic again, still heading north on Racine. A few minutes later, he turned right onto Blue Island and then onto a short driveway leading to a dilapidated warehouse. The warehouse door was covered in purple and yellow gang graffiti. It creaked upward, revealing a Mexican man standing next to a rusting 1998 Chevrolet Cavalier spotted with gray primer. The man wore jeans and a faded brown leather jacket. He was short, paunchy, with thinning salt and pepper hair.

Marvin pulled the Honda into the warehouse. The door lowered with a thud. He glanced at Darius. "Put the bag on the floor of the car and come with me."

Darius did as he was told. They got out of the Honda and approached the man. Marvin halted and stood face to face with him, Darius standing behind Marvin's right shoulder.

Perspiration rolled down Darius's neck and his heart pounded in his throat. He glanced away from the Mexican man and looked for exits, just in case he had to make a quick escape. Marvin and the Mexican were talking, the conversation unintelligible to Darius. He felt like he was frozen in time, watching a scene from a movie. He saw the Mexican go to the Honda and pull the black bag out of the car. The man counted the bundles of cash, placing them on the hood.

"There's only ten. There should be twelve." He pulled a large revolver out of his waistband. "You get me two more."

"No, no, Miguel." Marvin waved his finger. "This is what Alejandro and I agreed to."

Miguel waved the pistol. "I set the price. Not that fool."

Marvin spread his palms. "Let's split the difference. I'll get another five."

"Okay, but the boy stays here." Miguel had a licentious look in his eyes.

Darius shook his head vigorously, his lips trembling.

"No, no, Marvin's word is good. We're going now. I'll get the extra five the next time we meet."

Miguel locked eyes with Marvin. They stared each other down, while Darius perspired even more. Then Miguel nodded, dug in his pants pocket, and tossed something small at Marvin. A car key.

Marvin caught it. He pointed at the Chevy and popped the trunk. Darius could see something inside. Then he felt Marvin tug at his sleeve. "You got this? You know what we're doing?"

Darius fought down his fear. "Uh?"

Marvin shook his head. "The product is in the trunk. We leave the Honda here and take the Chevy."

"I'm going with you, right? I can do that?"

Marvin handed Darius the key. "You drive."

Darius went to the Chevy and got in the driver's seat. Marvin closed the trunk and slid in on the passenger's side. The warehouse door scraped open, and Darius backed the Chevy out. As they left the driveway and turned onto Blue Island, the Crown Vic eased into traffic and followed them.

Darius gripped the wheel hard as he drove. "That guy was nuts. What were you going to do if he wouldn't let me go?"

Marvin reached behind himself, pulled the Walther PPK from his waistband, and flashed it in Darius's face.

One-handed, Darius took the pistol from Marvin and cradled it as if embracing a newborn puppy.

CHAPTER 21

CID-IRS Office
Kluczynski Federal Building
Tuesday, January 4, 2005
10:00 a.m.

GLORIA SAT AT HER DESK, counting the holes in the acoustic ceiling tiles while she waited for Lauren to return from the trial-prep meeting with the U.S. Attorney's office. She wondered if Robert might change his plea to guilty to avoid exposing Darius's involvement in what happened to Spencer McElroy. She prayed to God, who she seldom sought out, that somehow Robert would be a man and protect their son.

Her mind drifted back to Darius's childhood, moments of innocence and love. The day he was born and she held that beautiful baby against her breast. He was so tiny, so vulnerable. She and Robert had cherished many years watching Darius grow into a young man. They'd sat in the bleachers as he learned to play basketball in grammar school, and now he was passing up a chance for a college scholarship. Her mind jerked back to a few days ago when she trailed Darius to the housing project. Something dark and sorrowful scuttled in her chest and she wondered what grief the future might hold.

The office door clicked shut, and Gloria glanced over to see Lauren headed her way. Lauren wore a St. Laurent navy suit, appropriate for her meeting with Todd Jeffreys and his second chair, Phil Tunney. Lauren reached her, sat next to Gloria, and dropped a yellow legal pad on the desk. A list of names graced it, in Lauren's neat handwriting.

"What's this?" Gloria asked.

"Those are the people your husband intends to call as witnesses."

Gloria picked up the pad and read Lauren's notes. *Darius Carlton, Gloria Nighthawk, Tamika Carlton.* She slapped the pad back down. "That son of a bitch."

Lauren cleared her throat. "He advised the U.S. Attorney that he'll probably testify, too."

Gloria shook her head. "What is the motha…trying to do?"

"What do you mean?"

Gloria clenched a fist on her desk. "I can see he wants revenge against me because he blames me for his indictment. But how can he put our son and his daughter in the middle of this? They don't deserve that." *Not even Tamika, whose lie set this whole thing going.* "Can't the prosecutor make a motion limiting them from being called? How do Jeffreys and Tunney plan on cross-examining them?" Her nostrils flared. "I won't allow Darius to be subjected to this. He's supposed to testify as his father's witness, and then the prosecutors will try to make a liar out of him. For Christ's sake, he's seventeen years old. He'll be scarred for life. What if they trip him up, are they going to charge him with perjury?"

Her thoughts raced on into things she couldn't say. *What if he admits on the stand that he was going to kill McElroy? Will they charge him? Do I become part of that alleged conspiracy because I'm the one who killed McElroy and hid Darius?* She jerked upright, sending her chair crashing into the cubicle behind her. "I've got to get out of here."

"Where are you going?" Lauren grabbed her legal pad and followed Gloria out the door.

"I need to get my mind off the trial. Let's go talk to Marvin. The national office approved an initial $15,000 to launder through Uka. She'll have to structure the deposits to evade reporting requirements because it's over $10,000 and that'll make it a violation." As they hurried out of the secure area toward the bank of elevators, Gloria pulled out her cell phone. "This will just be the first transaction, and all the money will be deposited back into our undercover account except for her fees."

An elevator dinged and the doors opened. She hit Marvin's contact number and stepped through. The elevator closed and started down.

Marvin answered as they neared the first floor. "Yeah?"

"Meet us in the usual place in thirty minutes." The elevator doors opened again. Gloria charged across the lobby and out the exit to Federal Street, then hurried down the sidewalk toward the parking garage, Lauren a step behind her.

"I'm in the middle of a job. I just can't get up and leave."

"Do it, Marvin. It's time." They reached the garage and she hustled up the stairs to the second level.

"Why now?"

"Because I said so."

"Jesus, Marvin can't jump just 'cause that's what you want."

"Be there, or I'll come looking for you." She reached the Blazer, got into the driver's seat, and slammed the car door shut. "You don't want me looking for you."

"Okay. Gimme forty minutes. I've got to come from the South Side."

She turned on the ignition as Lauren hopped in on the passenger side. "See you in forty."

Columbus Park, West Side
Tuesday, January 4, 2005
11:00 a.m.

Gloria parked the Blazer in the usual place on Jackson. Marvin arrived ten minutes later and parked his yellow Cadillac in front of them. He trudged through the ankle-deep snow and hopped into the Blazer's back seat. "What's up?"

"I've got the money to launder through Uka. I want it done Friday. That'll give us some time to make arrangements with Baba and Uka if we need it," Gloria said.

"How you think this will go down? We still don't know if she'll go along."

Gloria looked Marvin in the eyes. "She'll do it once we put the cash in front of her. How many people turn away money when a pile of it is sitting in front of them?"

Marvin shook his head. "It can happen. From what Baba said, she seems pretty uptight. You heard him on the tape."

"Give it your best to make it happen. Call Baba and tell him to meet you at Uka's office on Friday. Any time that's good for him. Say your lady friend has a pile of cash building up and she wants to give Uka a small amount to see how it goes. If it works out, you can tell her we've got six figures waiting to be washed."

Marvin rubbed the back of his neck. "Yeah, but what if…"

"I don't want to hear no what ifs." She lowered her chin, looking down at him. "Tell her I paid my old guy seven percent but I'm willing to go to ten for her because I've got to get the cash out of the country to Switzerland. Holding it is too dangerous. You can tell Baba if Uka goes ahead with the deal, he'll get a bonus."

Marvin nodded. "Switzerland, isn't that where all the mob guys send their money? You're making it look for real."

While they were talking, Lauren had set up Marvin's phone with the tape recorder. She held the phone up. "You ready?"

He sighed. "Yeah. Say the usual stuff you got to."

The call went like Gloria wanted, Marvin sticking to the script she'd laid out. After some persuading, Baba agreed to a Friday meet at 11:00 a.m. and gave the street address for Uka's Auto Insurance at Clark and Lawrence. "Nice work," Gloria said after the call ended. She ignored the little voice in her head that said she was making another error in judgment, pushing too hard and putting her CI too much at risk. "I'll meet you here at nine on Friday, give us time to get everything set up."

CHAPTER 22

Columbus Park, West Side
Friday, January 7, 2005
9:00 a.m.

GLORIA GLANCED AT HER CASIO watch. It was 9:15. "Where the hell is he?"

"He's only fifteen minutes late. Take it easy," Lauren said.

"Don't tell me to take it easy." Gloria shook her head. "I've been through this before. You haven't. There are a lot of moving parts in an undercover investigation. You can't have an informant running amuck setting his own schedule. We're trying to get people to do things, and we're two to three people away from them."

"I'm just saying I know your husband's trial is only a few weeks away, and I can understand that's putting a lot of pressure on you and your family."

"I can handle it." Gloria's knuckles whitened as she gripped the steering wheel tighter. "Don't be telling me what I need to be concerned about. I can take care of my family. That's my business. You need to focus on this case."

They sat in silence for ten minutes, letting their mutual anger simmer.

Gloria pressed her lips together. "I'm sorry. I know you mean well, and you're right. The pressure is getting to me. Something happened the other day that I don't understand, and it scares me."

Lauren faced her. "I've tried to be the best partner I could for you. You taught me how important it is to be able to trust each other, have each other's back, and I've been there for it all. What happened that has you so worried?"

Gloria's voice wavered. "I…I have no idea where Darius is living or what he's doing. I thought he was with his father at the hotel where Robert is staying, but I'm not sure anymore. Adsila told me she saw Darius getting picked up after school in a yellow Cadillac. So—if you can believe it—I surveilled my own son. Some kid driving a red Mustang picked him up after school on Monday. I trailed the car, lost them, then spotted it parked in a lot at the Robert Taylor Homes. The car was empty by the time I got there. What the hell is he doing in the projects?" Gloria crossed her arms. "The Mustang was registered to some seventy-year-old lady, Beatrice Moore. Can't believe she'd own a red Mustang. She's got to be fronting for somebody."

"The yellow Cadillac," Lauren said. "You don't think it was Marvin's?"

"Probably not. I mean, there must be five hundred yellow Cadillacs in Chicago. What's the chance?"

Lauren pulled down the sun visor and checked her reflection in the mirror. "The only time Darius saw me was four months ago, when you received that award for killing the insurgents in Iraq. I'm sure he won't remember what I look like. I can help you surveil him."

"I don't know. In a way I want to know what's going on, and in a way I don't." She broke off as Marvin's Caddy pulled in front of the SUV. "Here's Marvin now. We'll talk about it later."

Marvin parked and got out, walked to the Blazer, and took his usual position in the back seat. "Today's the day," he said reluctantly.

"Are you ready, Marvin?" Lauren asked.

Marvin shook his head. "Do I have a choice?"

Gloria leaned toward him. "Of course, and you're choosing to do the right thing."

"Whatever." He exhaled. "Just tell me what I need to do to get ready."

Lauren lifted a brown briefcase from the floor and set it on her lap. "This is the case you'll carry into the meeting with Uka and Baba. There's three bundles of $100 bills in it, five grand in each bundle." She handed the case to Marvin. "The name of the Swiss bank and the account number are on a sheet of paper wrapped around one of the bundles."

"The recorder is hidden in a false wall of the briefcase, and there are several hidden microphones built into the sides," Gloria said. "Once we turn on the recorder, it's voice actuated. That means it automatically records all conversations. You must be careful what you say. You can't threaten Uka in any way. Do you understand? This is important!"

Marvin nodded. "Yeah, don't threaten nobody."

"Another thing. There's a transmitter built into the briefcase, so we'll hear what's being said. If anything happens that makes you feel like you're in danger, use the code phrase 'hot dog.' Lauren will come in and get you. That's only for emergencies, though. What's the code?"

"Hot dog."

Gloria nodded and sat back. Lauren showed Marvin a fountain pen. "This is a digital recorder. I'll give it to you before you go in. Don't go off telling stories, like you know who killed President Kennedy. We don't want anything like that on tape."

Marvin tugged on his chin. "Wasn't that that guy Oswald? Anyway, I got it. Don't make up no stories."

Gloria broke in again. "Remember what I told you about how much we're willing to pay her to wash our money? Seven percent. If she wants more, negotiate. If you agree too easily to a higher rate, she'll think this is a sting. But don't go higher than ten percent and don't use the word launder. That sounds like a government agent."

"Got it. Go for seven but not more than ten."

"One last thing." Gloria paused to let what she was going to say sink in. "You have to tell her that all this money I have is from selling heroin."

Marvin dragged his hand across his lips. He looked worried, and she wanted to say something, but just then his cell phone rang. He looked at the caller ID. "It's Baba."

"Don't answer it. Let him leave a message. We'll have you call him right back," Gloria said. "Why is he calling you?"

"I don't know."

Was Baba not going to be available? Was he refusing to contact Uka? Was the case going down before it even got started? No, she couldn't let herself think that. It was the pressure, the damned pressure of everything.

She eyed Marvin's phone. The screen said VOICE MAIL.

"Play the message and don't delete it," Lauren said.

Marvin tapped in his password. Then Baba's voice sounded in the SUV. "Hey, my man. I talked to Miss Uka this morning. She won't be back in her office till 3:00. So if you want to meet me there then, let me know? I talked you up like you said, so we'll see if she'll help your lady. You should know Miss Uka is very smart. She was a high priestess in the Yoruba tribe in Nigeria. You must treat her with respect. She has special powers. She put a curse on a man who cheated her out of some money. His eyes turned yellow, he lost weight, and he died. Talk to you later."

"That sounds promising," Lauren said.

Marvin clutched at his throat. "Marvin don't want no curse."

Gloria frowned. "If you don't believe in that stuff, nothing will happen to you."

They taped Marvin's return call confirming a 3:00 meeting. Sweat beaded on his forehead as he talked. *Best get his mind back on practical things, not stuck on mythical curses*, Gloria thought as he signed off. "All right, Marvin. Let's go over everything we talked about a few more times so you've got it cold," she said.

Marvin swallowed as he dragged his sleeve across his brow. "Marvin won't look good with yellow eyes."

CHAPTER 23

Two blocks west of Uka's Auto Insurance, Chicago, IL
Friday, January 7, 2005
2:40 p.m.

GLORIA SAT IN THE SURVEILLANCE van with her CI and two fellow IRS agents, Luis Garcia and Steve Edwards. "All right we've gone over everything several times now. Do you have any questions, Marvin?"

Marvin shook his head. "I'm good."

"Baba's cab and Uka's Mercedes are parked in front of the business, so I'm assuming they're waiting for you. I'll walk you to your car and activate the monitoring system. Once you're in the car, don't play the radio. That'll activate the battery and it's only good for three hours."

Gloria and Marvin got out of the van and went to his Cadillac. "Are you ready?" Gloria asked.

"Ready as I'm going to be."

She nodded, then took a fountain pen from her jacket pocket and held it up. "This is Special Agent Nighthawk activating an electronic monitoring system." She gave the rest of the preamble—date, time, place, and parties involved—and then watched as he got in and pulled away. Gloria returned to the van, where she joined Garcia and Edwards in listening to the two-way radio.

A few minutes later, Agent Wilson's voice came over the line. "The CI just parked his vehicle and entered the business."

They waited. The next voice was Baba's, and then Marvin's.

"Hey, my man, how're you doing?"

"Good. You, bro?"

"Come here and sit down."

Sound of chairs sliding across the floor.

Baba spoke again. *"Miss Uka is on the telephone. She'll come get us when she finishes the call. You see these men here? They all rent desks from her. Tama buys and sells used cars, Zalan has a towing company, and Chinwe sells tires. Ah, here she comes."*

The sound of chairs sliding back.

"Miss Uka, it's an honor and pleasure to meet you. Baba has told me so much about you," Marvin said.

Miss Uka's voice was rich and low, her Nigerian accent slight. *"Thank you, Marvin. Baba has told me quite a bit about you, too. Come with me to my office where we can talk privately."*

Shuffling feet, a door opening and closing. Then more chairs skidding across the floor.

"So, Marvin, what can I do for you?" Miss Uka asked.

"I'm sure Baba told you the situation my lady friend is in. She has a lot of cash from her business and her banker isn't around anymore. I used to take the cash to him, but he's disappeared."

"What do you mean, disappeared?"

"We don't know what happened to him. He's gone."

"Sounds like he was pilfering someone's money."

"No. We never heard anything like that," Marvin said.

"How long was he working for your lady?"

"A couple of years. I'd bring him the money in a green garbage bag. No one ever stopped me. They just thought I was a homeless man carting my belongings around." Marvin laughed.

Uka's voice cooled slightly. *"I am sure Baba told you I only work with people I know. I do not know you or your lady friend. Therefore, I cannot help you."*

Agent Edwards crossed his arms and leaned back in his chair. "Looks like this isn't going down." He kicked his feet up onto the table holding the two-way.

Gloria cocked her head at him, catching Garcia's eye. *What's his story?*

Agent Garcia gave him a long stare. "Don't rush to judgement. It's early in the conversation."

Gloria held up a hand. Marvin was speaking. *"Miss Uka, please think about this. You know Baba and I have been friends for years…well, more than friends. I'm sure you know he sells dime bags out of his cab to make ends meet when things are tight. He has a wife and a little boy to take care of."*

"But we are not discussing that, are we?" Miss Uka, still cool. Wary.

Gloria pursed her lips. "Shit, she's smart. Not saying a thing I can use to prove she knows the source of the money."

Marvin again: *"I've helped Baba whenever I can. I front the heroin to him, so he doesn't even have to pay for it until he sells it."*

"How kind of you. But that has nothing to do with me."

Edwards scowled. "Why's your CI keep talking about drug dealing? Is he in that line?"

Gloria shook her head. "That's got to be bullshit. He keeps on saying that, he's talking himself into a guilty plea. I told him not to make up any stories, goddamn it."

"No, but the bags I front to Baba I get from my lady," Marvin said.

"That helps," Garcia said. "Not good enough, but we're heading in the right direction."

"You're right, that's not good enough," Edwards muttered. When Gloria shot him a sharp look, he shrugged. "I'm just saying."

Miss Uka's answer was a shade chillier. *"Once again, that has nothing to do with me. Why are you telling me this?"*

Gloria squirmed in her chair. "Come on, Marvin. Show her the money!"

"If you could just please help out my lady. She's afraid someone will cut her if they know she's holding cash. Let me show you." Thump of the briefcase on a desk, the click of clasps opening. *"She's given me a small amount for you to take care of for her, along with her bank account in Switzerland. See, here's the number."*

Silence. Nerves taut, Gloria counted seconds.

"How much is she willing to pay?" Miss Uka asked.

"Seven percent."

"That wouldn't be worth my trouble."

A second's pause. Then soft thumps, blocks of bills being tossed back into the briefcase, the briefcase slamming shut.

"Sounds like this is over," Edwards said. Inwardly, Gloria cursed. Too soon.

"How much would make it worth your trouble?" Marvin asked.

"Twenty percent."

"My lady paid five to the other guy. Can't you go lower?"

"Fifteen percent," Miss Uka said.

"That's three times more than she was paying before."

"I do an excellent job of protecting the money, sending it through various financial institutions before it gets to her account."

Gloria clapped her hands. "Now we got her. Take the cash, Uka."

"Could you do ten percent?" Marvin asked.

"Twelve is my bottom." Miss Uka paused. *"It seems you have nowhere else to go?"*

Marvin sighed. *"She won't be happy with me. She'll tell me I was stupid."*

"Marvin, don't blow the deal. Do it for twelve," Gloria said softly. They waited.

"Twelve is it for this installment," Uka said. *"But if you come back with more, I will do ten."*

Clicks as the briefcase opened. A few seconds of silence, then it shut. "That's good. Thank you, Miss Uka."

Gloria let out a breath. "Marvin, you're my hero."

Garcia laughed. "She's negotiating her way right into jail. What do you think of that, Edwards?"

"Yeah, that was great." The agent's feet dropped to the floor. A minute or so later, Agent Wilson reported Marvin leaving the business.

Gloria left the van and waited outside it for Marvin. He parked his Cadillac behind the van and rolled down his window.

"Good job," she told him as he handed over the briefcase and fountain pen. "Now we wait for the money to hit our account before you go back to see Uka again."

He looked startled. "Again? Marvin don't want no yellow eyes."

"Don't worry about that. I told you — if you don't believe, nothing bad will happen."

Back in the van, Gloria broadcast on the two-way to all units. "Let's meet at the Golden Nugget. It's about a mile south of here on Clark. Coffee and snacks on me."

They gathered in a corner booth away from other patrons.

"Thanks for all your help. This was a good start," Gloria said.

Garcia nodded. "Things went well."

An anorexic-looking waitress in a baggy black uniform stopped at their table and took orders for coffee, Cokes, and apple pie for Wilson, Garcia, Lauren, and Gloria. Edwards one-upped everyone and ordered cherry pie ala mode with a donut chaser.

After the waitress left, Wilson said, "We got a lead on the banker Baba met with."

Edwards folded his arms over his paunch. "It's only fifteen grand. That'll get you probation on the sentencing guidelines."

Gloria narrowed her eyes at him. *He's been putting down every move I've made on the case.* "Steve, this was our first transaction. Our introduction to Uka. It went well, and we'll do more. Once we find out which bank accounts she used to launder our money, we'll subpoena them and find a lot more cash she's washing for other people."

The waitress returned and laid the beverages, pie slices, and Edwards's donut on the table, then moved off. Edwards shrugged and dug his spoon into his cherry pie ala mode. A dollop of vanilla ice cream dribbled onto his lap. "Maybe…could be?"

Gloria's yearning to be the best she could be had always brought praise from her fellow agents. What was Edwards's issue? Did he just not like her? That shouldn't make a difference, though. Her coworkers' respect was more important than being liked. Still, it bothered her that Edwards apparently wasn't on board.

"Let's move on," Gloria said. "Everyone give your notes to Lauren. She'll prepare the memorandum of surveillance. Lauren, try to knock the memo out over the weekend so everyone can review it first thing Monday morning and give you any changes."

The agents ripped their notes from their memo pads and slid them across the table. Lauren gathered them up, rescuing Edwards's notes from a splash of coffee. She blotted the paper with her napkin, shook her head, and gave him a wink.

That bothered Gloria, too. She knew management thought highly of Edwards and was grooming him for the fast track. He could be her next manager. Maybe she *had* lost a step. Twenty-five years on the job could take it out of you. This last year had been full of turmoil. Her husband's indictment and arrest, Jim Abbott's murder in Iraq, the abortion, her son's estrangement. She had to pull herself together. *I need to focus. I need to get this case done.*

"One more thing, Lauren." Gloria sipped her coffee. "Call the national office when we get back and let them know we delivered the cash to Uka. We need confirmation that the money was deposited and Uka didn't rip us off."

Edwards ate his last bite of pie. "The N.O. is closed already. It's an hour later in D.C."

Gloria's lips pursed. "I know that, Steve. Lauren can leave a voicemail. I want them advised immediately so we can stay on top of this. We have to find out what accounts Uka used as soon as we can." Gloria's chair screeched across the floor as she stood. Her eyes danced across each agent, stopping at Edwards. "Meeting's over. Everyone have a good weekend."

Gloria walked alone from the diner to her car, feeling more unsettled than she should. Was this what burnout looked like? She could work seven more years before she had to retire, but she was eligible now. Did she have enough gas in the tank to deal with the drama?

Maybe she should look at her life in a new way. Darius was seventeen and Adsila fourteen. With all the recent turns of events, they needed her now more than ever.

CHAPTER 24

GLORIA WAITED AT HER DESK for Lauren to come in. Questions charged through her mind. Had anyone from the national office spoken to Lauren yet? Hopefully, they'd gotten the message about the cash delivery to Uka.

A half-hour dragged by before Lauren strolled in. Before she could take her coat off, Gloria stood and waved her over. "Any feedback from national?"

Lauren shook her head. "Not a word."

"You gave them your cell number?"

"Of course."

Gloria glanced over at Edwards. The *Sun-Times* lay flat on his desk. His head was down like he was reading the paper, but Gloria could tell he was listening to their conversation.

Gloria nodded at an empty chair nearby. Lauren pulled it over and sat next to her. "It's after 9:30 in D.C.," Gloria said. "Give them another call. Someone's got to be there."

Lauren took a deep breath and exhaled. "Let me get a cup of coffee first."

Jesus Christ, make the fucking phone call. Gloria didn't say it, just watched as Lauren stopped by her own desk, shrugged out of her coat and draped it over her chair, and strolled to the coffee pot in its cubbyhole about twenty feet away.

Edwards joined her. They engaged in conversation as they filled their cups. Gloria was sure he knew exactly what he was doing, aggravating her. He and Lauren sipped their coffees, then topped them off, talking the whole time.

Gloria rose from her chair and marched to the coffee area. "Edwards, if you're not busy, you can go back and read your paper some more. Lauren's got plenty to do!"

"I told you, I'll call them," Lauren said. "Give me a minute."

Edwards smirked. "Sorry. I don't want to get in the way of your case."

He moved away from the coffee station. Gloria stalked back to her desk. She watched Lauren stroll to her own desk, dig her cell phone out of her purse, and make the call. It was a brief conversation.

Lauren clicked off and took a sip of coffee, then ambled back over to Gloria. "No one answered. I left another voicemail. As soon as I hear from them, I'll let you know."

"Thanks." She knew she sounded curt, but she couldn't help it. She glanced over her shoulder and saw Edwards turn the page of his newspaper.

Lauren leaned forward and said in a low tone, "You don't have to micro-manage me. I think you should know that by now."

Gloria took refuge in procedure. "You know management won't approve another payment to Uka until we know for certain that she forwarded the funds to our undercover account."

"I do know that. Like I said, as soon as I hear from the N.O., I'll let you know." Lauren turned on her heels and marched back to her desk.

Gloria kept an eye on Lauren for the rest of the morning. At 11:30, Lauren slipped her overcoat on and headed out of the secured area to the bank of public elevators. *I'll take her to lunch, make peace with her.* Gloria shrugged into her North Face ski jacket and followed.

She entered the public area as the doors of an elevator were closing. Through the narrowing gap, she saw Lauren and Edwards standing together. Edwards leaned into Lauren, and she laughed. Gloria froze in her tracks. *My partner and my antagonist. God help me.*

Robert Taylor Homes
Monday, January 10, 2005
4:30 p.m.

Darius entered Unit 510, the new mixing house this week. There were only a few ounces of heroin left to cut and bag. Four women sat at the long table, busy at their tasks. Darius spent a minute watching them, and then someone pounded on the door. "It's Marvin. let me in."

Darius flipped open the three deadbolt locks. The mostly naked women kept working, not missing a beat. Marvin entered the apartment, and Darius locked the door again.

Marvin looked at the small amount of heroin left to be processed. Anger flared in his eyes. "Why didn't you tell me you're down to just this little bit?"

"I told you Friday we were down to less than a half kilo. You know how fast it goes over the weekend."

Marvin set his hands on his hips. "You gotta go get some more, tonight."

Darius frowned. "Go to that Mexican guy? He said you shorted him five grand."

"I'll get the cash. Meet me in front of the pharmacy in half an hour."

"You want me to leave the ladies all alone?"

"No, call Shorty. Get his ass up here and then you meet me. Don't be late. I'll call the Mexican and set it up."

"What if he gives me shit, like last time? Wanting me to hang around. I think he's gay."

Marvin laughed. "I know he is. Do what you like, or what you have to do. Just don't shoot the motherfucker until you get my smack."

◆

Pharmacy, across from Robert Taylor Homes
5:15 p.m.

Darius ran through sleet and snow, across State Street to where Marvin was parked in a gray1998 Hyundai Elantra. Darius yanked the car door open and plopped into the passenger seat. He was breathing heavily.

Marvin glared at him. "Where the fuck you been?"

Darius shook his head. "I couldn't get ahold of Shorty."

"So, you got me sitting out here with a garbage bag holding sixty grand in the back seat. What if some fucker tried to rip me off?"

"I'm sorry, man. I couldn't leave until Shorty showed up."

"You motherfuckers." Marvin waved a hand. "I should get rid of all you useless pieces of shit."

Darius splayed his palms. "Come on, man. I've done right by you. I'll prove it. I'll do this for free, just to show my loyalty."

Marvin gave him a calculating look, then killed the engine and handed him the key. "Don't fuck this up."

Darius looked at the fogging windshield. "Where'd you get this piece of junk?"

"Shut up and do what you're told."

"The Honda was better. Where is it?"

"Why're you asking so many fucking questions?" Marvin threw open the door and stormed out of the car, pulling up the collar of his black leather jacket as he hurried across State Street, back to the projects.

Darius slid into the driver's seat and locked the doors. He took off a glove, wiped the moisture off the windshield, and started the car. The wipers swept across the glass, piling snow at the base of the windshield. He reached under his parka and steadied the Walter PPK 380 Marvin had given him after they first met the Mexican. "I'm not gonna put up with any crap from that fag."

He reached into the back seat, lifted the green garbage bag and hauled it over onto the passenger seat. He untied the loops securing the bag and spread the top open, then gazed at twelve bundles of $100 bills. Some quick math told him each bundle was $5,000. He put the car in gear and fishtailed away from the curb, heading north on State Street. A Crown Vic parked behind him turned on its headlights and followed him. *The cop,* Darius thought.

He followed Marvin's original route, heading west on Cermak, north on Racine, and finally northeast on Blue Island. A block south of the warehouse, the emergency lights in the Crown Vic's grill started flashing. *What the hell?*

He pulled to the side of the street. The Crown Vic parked behind him. In his sideview mirror, Darius saw a white man get out of the car and pull a revolver from a holster. Panic dried his mouth. He reached into the garbage bag, grabbed a handful of bundles, and tossed them on the floor under the dashboard.

The cop drew even with the Honda. A cigarette dangled from his lips, and a CPD badge hung from a chain around his neck over the outside of his ski jacket. He tapped the barrel of his chrome-plated .357 Magnum against the driver's side window. "Roll your fucking window down."

Darius complied. His breath fogged in the freezing air. "What's up, officer?"

The cop waved the pistol in Darius's face. "You got something that belongs to me."

"What're you talking about?"

"Don't act stupid."

Darius frowned, playing tough. "You know who this belongs to?"

"Yeah, not you and not him. It belongs to me, shitface!"

Darius tensed. "This is Marvin's. You don't let me deliver it, he's gonna be out of business."

"Too fucking bad. Give me the bag." The cop jabbed the Magnum against Darius's cheek and pulled the hammer back. "I don't want to have to call in a police shooting."

Cold sweat broke out on Darius's forehead. He pressed an elbow against his side and felt the Walther 380. But the massive pistol the cop held was denting his cheek, and he knew he didn't have any options. He picked up the bag and handed it through the window. "What do I tell Marvin?"

The cop laughed. "Tell him his insurance premium went up." He holstered his pistol and sauntered back to his car, got in. The emergency lights went off and he drove away.

Darius leaned forward, resting his head against the steering wheel, his chest expanding and contracting with each breath. *What do I tell Marvin? What if he doesn't believe me?* He remembered the dealer glaring at him, all pissed off at Darius because he'd had a hard time tracking Shorty down. Mad over something that wasn't Darius's fault. Sending him back, alone, to that crazy Mexican in the first place. *Fuck him!* He looked at the bundles of cash on the floor. Three of them, $15,000.

I'm not going to get killed for that fucker. That's my money now.

CHAPTER 25

Robert Taylor Homes
Monday, January 10, 2005
6:30 p.m.

DARIUS RUSHED PAST THE PROJECT manager's office, opened the door to Marvin's, and charged in. Marvin was seated at his desk, Shorty standing next to him. On the desk were piles of street money — singles, fives, tens, and twenties.

Marvin glared up at him. "Don't just jump in here, boy. Can't you see we're busy? What's wrong with you? Close the fucking door."

Darius closed it and nodded at Marvin. "I've got to talk to you. Alone."

Marvin shook his head. "What'd you fuck up now?" He waved a hand at Shorty. "Give us ten minutes."

Darius stood there, one arm holding the opposite elbow. He'd stuffed the $15,000 in his coat, $5,000 in each side pocket and the remaining $5,000 in the inside pocket. There was no place else to hide it, and he couldn't leave the cash in the car. What if Marvin wanted the key back right away? He gazed at the floor as Shorty left the office. At the sound of the door closing, he looked up and saw Marvin staring at him. Could he see the bulges in Darius's pockets? *Does he know I'm about to tell my biggest lie ever?*

"What happened?" Marvin nodded at the bruise on Darius's cheek and laughed. "The Mexican poke you with a pipe?"

Darius hadn't even felt the pain from where the cop's pistol had pressed. He raised his hand to his face and felt the swelling. "He took it. He took it all."

"He's supposed to. Did you get the smack?"

Darius shook his head. "I'm not talking about the Mexican. I never got there. The cop took the cash."

Marvin's eyes widened. "What the fuck are you talking about?"

Darius told Marvin what happened.

"Son of a bitch. A white cop took all my money? What did he look like?"

"He was thin and smoking a cigarette. He had a chrome-plated pistol. That's what he jabbed me with." Darius rubbed the bruise again. *How I said it made it sound real, like the cop took all the money.* "He was driving that Crown Vic."

"That's Pipowski. Gotta be. Jefferson must have told him we were going to make a pickup." Marvin slammed his fist on his desk and the piles of cash scattered. "I'll kill that motherfucker!"

"Maybe you should talk to the Black cop. Maybe he'll get the money back for you." As soon as he said it, Darius realized he'd made a mistake. *If those cops give Marvin the money back, there'll only be forty-five grand.* He rubbed the back of his neck and let out a deep exhale, picturing himself lying at the bottom of the Chicago River.

"He'd never have the balls to take the cash from me." Marvin's brow furrowed and his eyes narrowed. "Can't send a boy to do a man's job. I'll take care of this." He jerked a finger toward the door. "Get the fuck outta here."

Darius left the office, not sure if he had screwed himself. If the cops said Pipowski only took $45,000, how could he convince Marvin they were lying?

***

Marvin grabbed a burner phone out of a desk drawer and called the Mexican. "There's been an accident. My boy can't make it tonight. I'll make other arrangements with you." He killed the call and texted *111* to Jefferson, a prearranged code to meet at the Shedd Aquarium parking lot in an hour.

By 7:30, he was there waiting for Jefferson. As the temperature dropped, the sleet turned to heavy snow. Ten minutes later, the Crown Vic pulled into the lot and its headlights flashed through the thickly falling flakes.

Marvin left the Hyundai. He yanked his stocking cap down over his ears, pulled the collar of his leather coat up, and hurried to the cop's car, quickly got in and slammed the door shut.

"This is my fuckin' day off. You better have a good reason to get me out on a shitty night like this," Jefferson said.

"I got sixty thousand reasons." Marvin folded his arms across his chest. "You talk to your fuckin' partner?"

"Talk to him all the time. Get to the point?"

"He's trying to fuck up my business. You guys supposed to be runnin' security for me, but he stopped my boy on the way to the Mexican and ripped me off."

"Son of a bitch." Jefferson laughed. "I'll talk to Pipowski tomorrow. The vig on his juice is making him stupid. I know he owes his bookie, and you don't want to mess with a mob guy. How much did he grab?"

Marvin glared at Jefferson. "Sixty thousand. Cop or no cop, I can't let nobody rip me just 'cause he's got a personal problem."

"Marvin, you better settle down. Nobody's gonna hurt one of my brothers in blue. You better hope he didn't put that money on a long shot. Got to get back to my shagger before she passes out from drinking all the Dom Perignon. I'll call you when I find something out."

"I need the cash. The Mexican was waiting for it, and I don't have any product left."

"I'm sure you've got more than sixty g's laying around. Do your deal, and if you're lucky I'll get some cash back for you tomorrow…that is, if Pipowski didn't blow it all." Jefferson jerked his head toward the passenger door. "Now get outta of here."

The door creaked open and Marvin got out, into the swirling snow.

Whitney Young High School
Tuesday, January 11, 2005
9:00 a.m.

Darius waited in the hallway outside of Adsila's advanced placement chemistry class. There she was, hurrying up just before the classroom doors were about to close. "Adsila," he called out.

She blinked as if she didn't recognize him. "It's been a long time since we talked. You must need something."

"I know. I'm sorry. I'm so focused on helping Dad, it's hard for me to think of anything else."

"I'm glad to chat with you, but my class is starting in about two minutes and this is the toughest class on my schedule."

Darius laughed. "I know, and you can't risk not getting an A, Miss Perfect."

"Well, I need higher than a four-point GPA if I want to get into an Ivy League school. I better get in class." She grabbed the door handle.

Darius put his hand over hers. "Wait just a second. I need you to hold something for me. But you can't tell anyone, especially Mom or Dad."

"What is it, and why can't I tell anyone?"

"It's money I got from…" He swallowed. "An AAU basketball coach who wants me to play for him this summer. If anyone finds out, I'll lose all my college eligibility."

"Why can't Mom or Dad know?"

He thought fast. "Dad's so jammed up, if the government found out he was concealing this, they'd use it against him. The same goes for Mom. She can't be involved in anything that even looks like it might not be right. The money's for us, for our family, in case Dad goes away."

She bit her lip. "Can't you hide it somewhere else?"

"Please, Adsila. You're the only one I can trust." Darius held out a lunch-sized paper bag.

Adsila grabbed it, stuffed it in her backpack, and rushed into her class.

CID-IRS Office
Tuesday, January 11, 2005
11:00 a.m.

Lauren's cell phone rang. Area code 202…finally, the national office was returning her phone call. "Special Agent Lauren Ashberry," she answered.

"This is Robert Jamison, undercover coordinator. I'm calling regarding your Swiss account."

"Good, we've been waiting to hear. Have the funds been deposited?"

"I'm afraid I've got some bad news for you," Jamison said.

"Don't tell me Uka absconded with the money."

"Not that. Someone made a mistake when they gave you this account. It was closed eight years ago."

"Shit, how the hell could that happen?"

"I don't know. I emailed you a new account number. It's in the Bahamas."

Lauren shook her head. "If the funds we gave her bounce because you gave us a closed account, the agent's and the informant's lives could be on the line. All we asked for was an active account, and you couldn't even do that."

"What can I say? We screwed up. All I can tell you is, the Bahamian account is active. Good luck. I hope we didn't hurt your case." The phone went silent.

Lauren resisted the impulse to slam the phone down. She could see the credibility of the undercover operation crumbling. She settled for shoving the phone a few inches away, then opened her email and printed out the details on the new undercover account. She walked to the printer and retrieved the copy, then took a deep breath and headed toward Gloria's desk. Gloria had been so uptight lately, and Lauren sensed an explosion coming.

CHAPTER 26

CID-IRS Office
Kluczynski Federal Building
Tuesday, January 11, 2005
11:10 a.m.

GLORIA'S STOMACH CHURNED WITH NERVOUS tension. She couldn't do anything on Uka's case until the national office confirmed the deposit of the undercover funds, and her husband's trial was only a month away. And Darius—she still had no idea what to do about him.

She glanced up as Lauren reached her desk and laid a printout on it. Lauren's clenched jaw said it wasn't good news. Gloria frowned. "What's this?"

Lauren pursed her lips. "The national office fucked up. The Swiss account they gave us was closed eight years ago."

Gloria picked up the printout and read it. "If this is your idea of a joke, it's not funny."

"Not in a thousand years would I ever—"

"Those fucking idiots. All they have to do is shuffle paper around, and they can't even do that right." Fuming, Gloria stood. "Did you tell Stephens?"

"No, you're the first one—"

Gloria stalked past Lauren, heading to their supervisor's office. The chief, Tony Spagnola, was sitting in the chair in front of Stephens's desk. "Sorry to interrupt, but I'm glad you're here, Chief. Those imbeciles at national really fucked up this time. The account they gave us for the undercover operation was closed eight years ago."

The chief's eyes narrowed. "I can't believe that. Who told you?"

Gloria looked at Lauren, who'd followed her in, and cocked her head.

Lauren swallowed. "Robert Jamison, the undercover coordinator."

"Bobby? I can't believe he'd make a screwup like that. What did he tell you, Ashberry?"

"Just that the account was closed and here's the new one."

"I'll call him as soon as I get back to my office, find out what happened." The chief rose from his chair, with a look at Stephens. "Give me a memo documenting all your contacts with the national office regarding the undercover account. We can't have screwups like this interfering with cases. And keep me posted on your next move."

After he left, returning to management's domain on the twenty-eighth floor, Stephens nodded toward both empty chairs in front of his desk. Gloria sat in the one the chief had vacated, Lauren claiming the other. "So, tell me what you're thinking, Nighthawk," Stephens said.

"I think the best thing is for me to go in and talk to Uka myself. I'm supposed to be a big-time heroin dealer, so I'll give her a cover story. It's logical that it would come from me. Who else would know about the bank accounts?"

Stephens looked doubtful. "You sure? You have enough going on with your husband's trial coming up."

Anger flared, and she throttled it back down. He wasn't wrong. But he didn't understand how badly she needed to do this, get this damned case right. "I can handle it." She took a deep breath, aware he wouldn't like her next suggestion. "I just got off the phone with one of my buddies from DEA. They seized $100,000 in small bills, street money, from a dealer last night. I know you don't want to hear this, Tom, but I've had situations in the past when DEA let us use seized cash as flash money."

"You want to borrow a hundred grand from DEA?" Stephens shook his head. "I don't think so. We definitely have to put it in writing, and even then, I doubt the chief would approve it."

"We've done it before. The chief doesn't have to know about it. DEA gets their cash back as soon as we're done. If they're willing to go along with it, why not? We have a chance to nail this lady. I bet once we subpoena her bank accounts, we'll see she's been laundering a lot of cash for drug dealers. We flip her and make more cases." *The magic words — more cases, that'll whet his appetite.*

"What about the memo the chief wants?"

"You do it. I don't have time to write anything. I've got to call Marvin, tell him we had a problem and we have to come up with a cover story. We've got to do this today to make it real. He doesn't need to know all the details. We walk into Uka's place with a large amount of cash, especially in small bills, that'll build up my credibility with her. I'll tell Uka my partner closed the account for security purposes, that he does it on a regular basis. She'll relate to that."

"You can't just have your CI go in, like you've been doing?"

Gloria glanced at her watch. She had to set the wheels in motion to get this done today, and here she was wasting time explaining. "Marvin wouldn't be in a position to know the account was closed. The only people who'd know that would be high up in my organization—me and my imaginary partner." She leaned toward her boss, pressing her case. "It's the only way we have a chance to make this work. If we show up empty-handed, at best Uka will just give us our first $15,000 back and walk away. If that happens, we're done."

Reluctantly, Stephens nodded. "Check with DEA and make sure they're up for this. If they give you the green light, I'll run it past the chief. And for God's sake, make sure you have plenty of backup. Be safe."

"You sure you want to tell the chief?"

"Yes, I think we need his backing."

Grow some, Gloria thought. "That's your call."

"DEA gets an easy stat too," Lauren said.

Gloria eyed her. *Spoken like a future manager.*

⬥

Shedd Aquarium, Chicago
Tuesday, January 11, 2005
Noon

Marvin parked the Hyundai in the aquarium lot. It had taken him an hour to drive here after getting the 111 text on his burner phone. *That's got to be good news,* he'd thought. *Jefferson got my cash from Pipowski.*

He was waiting for Jefferson when his cell phone rang. The caller ID was blocked. Cautiously, he answered anyway. "Yeah?"

"It's Gloria."

Marvin shifted in his seat. "What's up?"

"We need to meet. Right now."

He saw Jefferson's Crown Vic pull in and park thirty feet in front of him. "I'm kind of busy. Can't meet you right now."

"Meet me up by Uka's, where we parked before, on Glenwood north of Wilson. I'll be there in half an hour."

Marvin thumped the steering wheel with his palm. "You can't expect Marvin to drop everything on a moment's notice."

She sounded sharp, angry. "We've got to meet with Uka today, or the whole thing goes down the drain."

"Why? What happened?"

"You don't need to know. The only thing you need to do is meet me."

The Crown Vic's headlights flickered. "Come on. Marvin can't just leave right now."

"I've got some flash money to show her, to cement the deal. You want any of that reward we talked about, you better be there. Thirty minutes."

"Give me an hour." *$250,000 when they bust Uka, plus whatever I get from Jefferson. This could be a good day.* Marvin heard the Crown Vic's horn blast. He saw Jefferson get out, holding up a paper bag. "I'll be there as soon as I can." Marvin killed the call, then hustled out of the Hyundai and into Jefferson's car. "How much you got for me?" he asked the cop.

Jefferson tossed the bag onto Marvin's lap. "Thirty grand."

"Shit, that fool owed his bookie thirty?" Marvin shook his head.

"I don't know. He paid what he had to. This is what's left. Whatever, you're lucky you got that. You owe me, big time. Another day and it probably would've all been gone." Jefferson nodded toward the passenger door. "I got things to do. I'm on duty."

Marvin stepped out of the Crown Vic and watched Jefferson squeal away. *Darius, you owe me thirty big ones.*

He gave it a few moments' thought, then got into his Caddy and drove to Darius's school. Stopped at a red light not far from it, he sent Darius a text: *Meet me on Laflin in ten minutes.*

Darius was standing on the street when Marvin pulled up to the curb. The boy hopped into the Hyundai. "I can't believe you're driving this junk."

"Listen, smartass." Marvin pointed at Darius. "You fuckin' owe me thirty grand for your fuckup." He pulled away from the curb, heading back to the Robert Taylor Homes.

Darius sucked in a quick breath. Unless he was misreading Marvin, the man didn't know he'd pocketed $15,000 from the cash meant for the Mexican. "How am I supposed to get thirty grand?"

"I've made arrangements. You and Shorty gonna head up to New Town. Take the Honda and park on Marine Drive around Foster. You know where that is?"

"Yeah."

"Make sure you're strapped."

Darius swallowed. "Pistols?"

"Yeah, pistols. You still got the one I gave you?"

"Yeah, yeah I do."

"Tell Shorty to bring his and a couple of ski masks. I'll drop you off at the projects to meet him. Call him now and get your asses up there on Foster. This could go quick."

Darius called Shorty on his cell and arranged to meet. He ended the call and faced Marvin. "What're we going to do?"

"Some guy is dropping off a lot of cash to some woman at her insurance company. She's Nigerian, wears fancy African clothes." Marvin scribbled Uka's address on a scrap of paper and gave it to Darius. "Should be easy pickings."

"What do you know about the place?" Darius rubbed the bruise on his face from Pipowski's pistol. It still hurt. "Does anyone there have guns?"

They'd reached the projects. Marvin pulled into the parking lot of the 3904 building and saw Shorty sitting in the Honda. "I don't know. I doubt it. It's time for you to man up. When you fuck up big time like you did, you have to take a risk to make it right. I got some place to be. If it's a go, I'll send you a text saying just that—*GO*. If it isn't, I'll send *NO*." He was running short on time to meet Gloria. He gave Darius a hard stare. "Get the fuck outta the car."

Darius scrambled out of the Hyundai.

CID-IRS Office
Kluczynski Federal Building
Tuesday, January 11, 2005
1:10 p.m.

GLORIA HUSTLED OUT OF STEPHENS'S office, Lauren trailing close behind. "Get the agents together and brief them on the surveillance," Gloria told her. "Try to get the same guys we had last time; they'll be familiar with everything. I've got to meet with the tech agent to see what we can do to monitor the meeting."

"I'm on it," Lauren said, and headed toward her desk to make some calls.

Gloria went down to the fifteenth floor, where the secured room was. A steel door protected the interior from any unwanted intruder. She pressed the intercom mounted next to the door.

"Yes?"

"Bill, it's Gloria Nighthawk, I need to see you right away."

A series of locks clicked and the door opened. Special Agent Bill Wilmon, the regional tech specialist for the last ten years, towered over Gloria. His thick wire-rimmed glasses slid down his pug nose. "One of my favorite customers. What's up?"

"I'm sorry to do this to you," Gloria said as they stepped into the room. Wilmon closed the door, and they headed to his desk in the center of his office. Each wall was lined with steel shelves from floor to ceiling, filled with equipment. Crammed next to his desk was a worktable covered with various devices, soldering irons, amp meters, and other items unknown to Gloria. "I've got an undercover meeting in an hour with a money launderer and I need to get wired."

"Some things never change. I'm sorry, my last monitoring set went out the door an hour ago."

Gloria frowned. "I've got to have some way to record this meeting. I'm going in with a hundred grand in flash money that I have to return to DEA right after. Can't take the chance something might go wrong when we don't have solid proof documenting the cash."

Bill's eyebrows rose. "Give me the Cliff's notes version of what's going on."

The words came out in a rush, which happened when she was nervous. "I'm meeting with a CI and the target. The CI has met the target once, but this is my first time. I'll be taking flash money to entice her." She shook her head. "Can we get monitoring equipment from another regional office?"

"We could, but it wouldn't be delivered here before tomorrow, and that's assuming it's available. What's the chance of the bad guys checking the briefcase or patting you down?"

Gloria exhaled. "She probably will. She's leery of meeting people she doesn't know. The CI dropped off fifteen grand with her last Friday that she was going to launder for us, but the national office screwed up and gave us a closed account." She shook her head. "Idiots."

"Even if we had equipment, it sounds like wiring you or a briefcase up isn't an option." Wilmon rummaged through one of his shelving units and came up with a rectangular box the size of his hand. "I've got this, but it's never been field tested. It works in my office." He opened the box and handed Gloria a pair of black horn-rimmed glasses.

Gloria slid them on. "Kind of heavy."

"They're brand new. They've got a built-in transmitter. Never been used in a real-life situation. It's all I've got for you. They cost five grand, so make sure you bring them back."

"Thanks, Bill." Gloria gave him an impish smile. "How do I look?"

He laughed. "Smarter than normal. Before you leave, let me charge the battery and check the transmitting frequency."

Gloria gave him the glasses back, and he attached a device to the rear of the earpiece.

After a few minutes he returned the glasses to her. "If you want to monitor the transmissions, you can only do it on Channel Two. The battery is fully charged. It's good for two hours, with a range of approximately five hundred feet. If the battery gets low or there's a malfunction, you'll hear a soft humming from the earpiece. No one should be able to hear it but you. If that happens, take the glasses off and fold in the earpieces. In thirty seconds, the system should reboot and you're good to go." He dropped an inventory receipt and a pen in front of Gloria. "Sign here. Just so you know, we have payroll deductions for lost equipment."

"Thanks, smartass." She headed back to the sixteenth floor, wearing glasses for the first time in her life.

Fifteen minutes later, Gloria and Lauren met with DEA agents Mike Grobski and Paul Manker in Tom Stephens' office. Grobski and Manker each held a green garbage bag containing seven pounds of cash, $50,000 in a variety of singles, fives, tens, twenties, and fifties. The bills were fresh off the streets. Many had been folded, some rolled so they could be used to snort whatever was the customers' pleasure. The cash was wrapped in rubber bands, mostly in bundles of $5,000 each, with the dollar amount written across the face of the bill on top of each stack.

Gloria signed the chain of custody receipt.

"Good luck," Grobski said. "Hope you nail the lady."

"Thanks. Can you guys wait ten minutes? I've got to change into my successful drug dealer outfit, and Lauren and I would appreciate an escort to the garage, if you have the time." *And a little added security might prevent a rip-off before we even get started.*

She left Stephens's office, stopped briefly by her desk to pull a bag of carefully chosen clothing from her bottom desk drawer, and ducked into the women's room, where she changed out of her casual street attire into a black designer suit with a white high-neck blouse and black Stuart Weitzman boots. The boots, blouse and suit had been seized some time back and put into their stash of undercover assets. She supplemented her look with her own fox fur coat and a few more assets borrowed from undercover inventory: a gold Cartier watch, a matching necklace, dangling gold bracelets, earrings, and a Gucci bag.

After she returned to the office, the DEA agents escorted her and Lauren to the federal garage. "The others are in place at Uka's business," Lauren told her as they got into the black Blazer and headed out. "Her Mercedes is parked in front of her insurance company."

A nervous energy skittered through Gloria as they rode toward the meeting—a weird combination of excitement, anticipation, and fear. It was that feeling of assuming someone else's identity and being able to make another person believe it was real.

Before long, Lauren pulled the black Blazer to the curb on Ravenswood north of Foster, behind Marvin's yellow Cadillac. Gloria grabbed the garbage bags and got out, hurried with them to the Cadillac, and opened the back door. She set the bags on the rear seat. "All the players have seen your car, so let's use it."

Marvin was staring at her. "You look different," he said.

She pointed at the glasses. "Getting old, just got these."

He nodded. "Makes you look smart."

"How did I look before?"

"You always look smart. But before, it was just street smart. Now Marvin thinks you look smart-smart."

"I hope it's smart enough." She closed the door and got into the Caddy on the front passenger side. "So, this is what I'm going to tell Uka. My partner, who you don't know, closed the Swiss bank account you gave her Friday. He always closes accounts and opens new ones so the wrong people won't figure out what's going on. She should be able to relate to that. To show her I've got an ongoing business, I've brought a hundred grand in street money that you and I collected from our people over the weekend. The cash is in those two garbage bags."

"Holy shit, a hundred grand. Can I see it?"

"Take a look. I don't want you to act like you haven't seen it before, since you would have helped collect it."

Marvin leaned over the front seat and untied each bag in turn, running his hands through the stacks. "Marvin likes this. Cash is cool. Marvin will apply for this job."

The glint in his eyes gave her a moment's pause. "Don't go too crazy over the money. It's not yours and has to go back where it came from.

Marvin retied the bags and nodded. "Yeah, it's got to go back. Yeah." He gave Gloria a sidelong glance and his lips froze, not quite hiding a smirk.

"Let's go see Uka," Gloria said. "And by the way, I'm Gloria Nightingale for the rest of the day. Can you remember that?"

He smiled. "Marvin likes that, Miss Nightingale."

CHAPTER 28

Uka's Auto Insurance
Lawrence and Clark
Tuesday, January 11, 2005
2:30 p.m.

GLORIA STEPPED OUT OF THE Cadillac. Marvin followed, toting the two garbage bags. She paused as they approached the front door, letting Marvin scoot in front of her to open it. Marvin nodded approval. "A queen of the city shouldn't open a door for herself."

He pulled the door open, and Gloria flowed into the insurance office. The clicking of her boot heels drew the attention of the three men already there, seated at their desks. The first two were on their phones, and there was a momentary pause in their conversations as they stared at her.

The third man stood and approached Gloria and Marvin. He was dark skinned, tall and slim, and wore a multi-colored kufi hat and a hip length blue and red dashiki shirt. He tipped his head at Gloria as if bowing to royalty. "My name is Kunta Tama, may I be of service?"

Gloria returned the nod. "Thank you, Mr. Tama. Is Miss Kafi available?"

He interlaced his fingers. They were long and slender with three gold rings. "She's in her office. Let me see if she's available. Can I tell her who's calling?"

Gloria turned to Marvin. "This is my associate. Miss Kafi met him previously. My name is Gloria Nightingale. I have not had the pleasure of meeting Miss Kafi yet."

Tama raised his hand, index finger pointed toward the ceiling. "One second." He turned and walked toward a door behind the open space with the desks—Uka's inner office, Gloria guessed. There was a supple nature to his stride, suggesting confidence. He tapped lightly on the door and waited a moment, then opened it, entered, and closed it behind him. Gloria heard the back and forth of conversation but couldn't make out what was being said. A few minutes later, Tama walked back out and approached Gloria again. "I'm afraid Miss Kafi is very busy, and apparently you don't have an appointment."

"That's true, Mr. Tama. I don't have an appointment. But Miss Kafi had an agreement with my associate"—she pointed at Marvin—"and unfortunately, something has come up that will affect her ability to complete her end of it. I thought it would be best if I personally explained the circumstances to Miss Kafi. Why don't you try asking her again?"

Tama cleared his throat and nodded. He returned to Uka Kafi's door, knocked, and entered. Their conversation this time lasted longer, but again Gloria couldn't hear what they said.

This time, when Tama returned, he had a different answer. Standing very close to Gloria, he said in a soft tone, "You may meet with her, but you and your associate must be searched first."

Gloria shrugged. "I have nothing to hide, and neither does Marvin." Her glasses slipped down her nose. She pushed them up with her index finger.

Tama nodded. "Please follow me." He led them to Uka's office, knocked once more, and pushed the door open. Gloria entered, followed by Marvin with the bags and then Tama.

Seated in a rattan chair behind a desk with a black onyx top was Uka Kafi. Her skin was as dark as her desk and contrasted with the bright green and gold of her dress and headpiece. The office was crowded with more rattan chairs in front of the desk, a black leather sofa, and a mahogany credenza against a side wall. The credenza was topped with statues of elephants and naked men and women carved in ebony in various seductive poses. The walls were covered with African art, the subjects in their native clothing.

Uka Kafi stood. Narrow eyed, lips pressed together, she did not offer her hand. She nodded sharply at Tama, who moved close to Gloria and eyed her fox fur coat. "Maybe you can drape it over the chair?"

"Of course." Gloria slipped out of the coat and laid it over the back of the rattan chair closest to her. "As I said, we have nothing to hide. But I do understand taking precautions."

Uka smiled without warmth. "You needn't be concerned with Tama's touch. I'm sure he will get more pleasure from checking Marvin than you."

Gloria kept quiet, refusing to rise to the bait. She felt Tama's fingers gently caressing her back, then moving around to her chest, and finally down her thighs. When he stepped away from her, Gloria glanced at Uka. "I hope that satisfies you."

Tama turned to face Marvin, whose brow furrowed. "Come on, Marvin didn't have to do this last Friday."

"We've come one step further than we did that day," Uka said.

Gloria gave him a stern look, playing her role. "Marvin, assume the position."

Marvin shook his head but set down the garbage bags and placed his hands on Uka's desk. Tama did a thorough examination, then smiled. "He's clean."

"Good." Uka returned to her seat behind her desk. "What is the nature of your visit?"

Gloria sat in one of the matching chairs in front. Marvin moved to stand behind her, the two garbage bags in his grip again. Tama, she noticed, took a similar stance behind Uka. "In our business, we don't always get to know the people we deal with. It's very unusual for me to conduct business with another woman. I hope our relationship can be long and mutually profitable."

Uka leaned forward and steepled her fingers. "I'm sure you have been told that I don't do business with people I don't know. That is a long-standing policy of mine and has brought me a successful career."

"Yes, I've been told that." Gloria rested an elbow on the arm of the chair. "Our situation is a little different, though. I've already entrusted you with a small amount of cash, based on your relationship with Baba and his relationship with Marvin. I've known Marvin for many years, and he has known Baba for over five years."

"Baba can be very convincing when he wants to be."

"Let me explain what brings me to you. My partner ended the relationship we had with the Swiss bank where you were meant to deposit the funds Marvin gave you. It's my partner's long-standing policy to periodically terminate banking relationships, for security reasons. I'm sure you can appreciate that. Unfortunately, the account you have for me is no longer valid. I have a new account in the Bahamas to give you instead." Gloria took a folded paper from her suit pocket and laid it on Uka's desk. "The account name is Gottlieb Reinsurance, a common industry in the Bahamas. It should blend in nicely with local practices."

Uka shook her head. "You did not come here today just for this. Otherwise, your associate would not have brought those." She nodded toward the garbage bags, still tight in Marvin's grip.

Marvin raised the bags. "Let Marvin show 'em what's in these."

Gloria eyed Uka. "If you don't mind, I'd like Marvin to place the bags on your desk and open them so you can inspect the contents." *She won't be able to resist a hundred grand.*

Uka nodded. Marvin stepped forward and hefted the bags onto the desktop, untied the straps, and pulled the bags open, revealing the cash.

Gloria spread her hands, palms up. "This represents some of my proceeds from the weekend. It's $100,000 and it doesn't represent all my cash flow. If we do business together, you can expect this much on a weekly basis."

Uka looked impressed, or at least Gloria thought so. The woman was so guarded, it was hard to read her expressions. "That would be welcome," she said, and Gloria felt a little thrill of triumph.

A quiet humming distracted her, and she realized it was coming from the glasses. She took them off, folded the earpieces in, and placed them on Uka's desk by the bags. "New glasses, they don't fit right." She rubbed her nose. *I hope the monitoring is working.* "Are we good?"

Uka stood, reached across her desk, extended her hand. "We're good."

They shook hands. Everything was perfect—until Uka went on talking. "I'll do the $100,000 too, at seven percent." She tied the garbage bags closed and swept them off her desk onto the floor.

What the fuck? Gloria hadn't expected this, couldn't lose DEA's flash money. "Oh—I didn't know you'd offer to do that. Are you sure you can handle that much?"

"Of course. It will take me about a week, but the amount will not pose a problem. I will notify you once I have processed the funds, and of course you will see when the money is deposited to your account." Uka smiled, a shark-like expression. "I'm looking forward to a long successful relationship."

Shit. How do I salvage this? She couldn't think of a way. Awkwardly, she fished in her handbag for a business card and laid it on Uka's desk. The card bore her undercover name and cell phone number. "I look forward to hearing from you."

Tama ushered them out. As Gloria and Marvin left the insurance office, her mind wrestled with how to tell DEA that their street money was about to be laundered. *Calm down. Everything will work out. I can give it back to DEA after Uka does her thing.*

A few steps from the Cadillac, Marvin slowed. He had his phone out and was texting someone. "Who're you texting?"

Marvin cocked his head. "CHA manager about a paintin' job." He tucked the phone in his pocket and opened the passenger door for her. "Get on in, Miss Nightingale. I'll drive us back to the meeting place."

CHAPTER 29

Far North Side of Chicago
Tuesday, January 11, 2005
3:00 p.m.

DARIUS WAS IN THE DRIVER'S seat of the Honda, parked a block north of Foster on Marine Drive. In the left pocket of his parka, he grasped his cell phone, and in the right pocket the Walther PPK Marvin had given him. His stomach churned as he waited for the text from Marvin. Hoping it wouldn't be GO.

Shorty was in the passenger seat, toying with a snub-nose Colt .38. "What if a cop comes by and sees you playing with that?" Darius snapped. "Put the gun in your pocket."

"Let some trigger-happy cop try. I'll shoot the motherfucker." Shorty opened the cylinder and gave it a spin.

"Sure, you will. And then we'll be two more dead homies." Darius clenched his teeth. "Put the fucking pistol in your pocket or I'll take it away from you."

Shorty shoved the .38 in the pocket of his black leather coat. "Calm down, man. If I knew you was gonna be so uptight, I would've told Marvin to have somebody else come with me."

"You didn't have a choice. Marvin asked me first. You're second chair."

Shorty frowned. "What's that mean, second chair?"

"Never fuckin' mind. Why don't you play with that old laptop I gave you?" Darius was confident he had cleared his hard drive. He pulled a dime bag out of his pocket and opened it, licked his forefinger, dipped it into the bag, and rubbed the powder on his gums. He felt more like a gangbanger than a prospective college student. "Better get chilled to do the job."

Shorty had grabbed Darius's Gateway laptop off the car seat and was messing with it. He closed the computer, laid it on the floor, and pulled a small bag of coke out of his jacket pocket. He tapped the coke onto the back of his hand and snorted it.

A gust of wind from the northeast sent a chill through the leaky windows of the Honda. The sun was setting behind the high rises on the west side of Marine Drive, casting long shadows across the street. Darius pulled the lever on the side of his seat, lowered the back, and stretched his long legs across the floor. "You know why we're doing this?"

Shorty rubbed his palms together, trying to warm them. "Some cash we're supposed to rip."

"Yeah, but that's not *why*."

Shorty's eyebrows squished together. "What you mean?"

"The *why* is, one of the cops Marvin pays for protection ripped sixty g's off me. So, my punishment is, I've got to rip off some bitch. You get to come along."

"Shit, if he ripped you, why I got to be here?"

Darius thought, *Marvin must have figured out I ripped some of his money before the cop took it.* "I don't know. Maybe he doesn't trust me to give him all the cash we get from this bitch."

Shorty shook his head violently. "Fuck, man. I'm puttin' my ass on the line just as much as you. We should get a fair share."

That made sense. Why hadn't he thought of it? "Yeah, you're right. I say we each get a quarter and Marvin gets the rest."

"How much we rippin'?"

Darius shrugged. "I don't know. He didn't say. All I know is that I'm not going to shoot someone for money and turn it all over to Marvin."

"I don't give a shit about shootin' somebody." Shorty pointed his hand straight ahead, shaping it like a pistol. "I'll shoot anybody that needs shootin'."

The phone vibrated in Darius's palm. He straightened his seat, lifted his cell out of his pocket, and looked at the text message. "Fuck it. We got to go." His muscles tensed and he held out the phone so Shorty could see the text. Darius swallowed. The heroin was supposed to help him settle down, but he felt jumpy, perspiration beading on his forehead.

He made a U-turn on Marine Drive and headed south to Lawrence and then west. After ten blocks, he turned south on Clark. The sign over a storefront on the east side of the street read *Uka's Automobile Insurance*. He pulled the Honda into a spot across from Uka's and killed the engine. He lifted the Walther out of his pocket, ejected the magazine, and made sure it was full. He slammed it back into the grip, pulled the slide back, let it go, and chambered a round. "I'm ready. Make sure you're loaded."

Shorty spun his snub-nose's cylinder open, eyed the six bullets, and flicked his wrist, slamming the cylinder closed.

<hr>

Lauren terminated the surveillance and waited for Gloria and Marvin at the rendezvous location, a few blocks away on Ravenswood north of Foster. She watched from the black Blazer as Marvin parked his Cadillac, and he and Gloria had a brief conversation. Then Gloria got out of the Cadillac and joined Lauren in the SUV. They watched Marvin drive away.

Lauren caught Gloria's eye. "What do you think?"

"It went well." Gloria laughed. "That is, if DEA doesn't mind getting their money laundered."

"God, she took it? All of it?"

"Didn't you hear it on the monitor?"

Lauren shook her head. "Everything came through fine except for the last few minutes. The reception was crackling a lot."

"Shit." Gloria pressed her hands to her face, then searched the pockets of her fur coat and suit pants. "I don't fucking believe it. I left the glasses in Uka's office."

"Jesus. What should we do?"

My second big screwup of the day. There can't be a third. "I've got to get them. Park the Blazer a block south of her business, and I'll run in."

⌄

Darius received a second text from Marvin. One hundred G's, in two green garbage bags in the lady's office in the back.

"What'd he text now?" Shorty asked.

Shorty doesn't need to know how much is there. "Don't wait, he says. They might move the cash."

He and Shorty piled out of the Honda, pulling their ski masks down over their faces, and ran across Clark Street. "Cash is in the back office. I'll go get it. If there's anyone in the front room, you stay there and cover them."

Darius yanked open the door of Uka's Auto Insurance. It slammed into the plate glass window, cracking it with a loud boom. The sound jolted the three men seated at their desks inside. Shorty rushed in, pointing his snub-nose revolver at them, aiming from one to the next and then the third. "All right, motherfuckers! Don't do anything stupid and maybe you won't die."

Darius ran to the rear office door, shoved it open and barreled inside. A woman was in there, standing at a desk. She was tall and dark, wearing green and gold. He felt her eyes burning into him.

"Don't be stupid, young man. You take this money, it will not end well for you," the woman warned. "These people don't play."

Darius felt like a gangbanger in a video. Like this was happening to someone else. He pulled the hammer back on the Walther. "If you want to see tomorrow, don't fuckin' mess with me." The two garbage bags were on the floor in front of the desk. He darted forward and grabbed them and then ran out, shouting at Shorty: "Let's get out of here."

Shorty fired three warning shots over the heads of the men. "Don't be stupid fuckers."

They ran out of the place and across the street, stripped off their ski masks, jumped into the Honda, and peeled away.

Gloria hopped out of the Blazer and hurried up Clark Street toward Uka's. She was fifty feet from the door when she saw two young men rush out, the taller one hauling two green garbage bags. She automatically reached for her sidearm, then remembered she wasn't carrying. Half a second later, she recognized the tall man's familiar gait. She'd seen it a thousand times, loping across a basketball court. "Darius. No, no." Gloria watched her son strip off his ski mask and toss it into the rear of a beaten-up Honda. Her heart raced as she held her trembling hands in front of her face and stumbled into a storefront window, almost knocking herself to the sidewalk.

CHAPTER 30

Uka's Auto Insurance
Tuesday, January 11, 2005
3:30 p.m.

GLORIA TURNED AWAY FROM THE storefront window. She watched the Honda head north to Lawrence, then turn east out of sight. Her pulse pounded in her throat. How could she bury what she had seen, pretend it hadn't happened, break all the rules she lived by, and still work this case? *What do I do now? Go to Uka's to get the glasses? Go back to Lauren and tell her I just saw Darius ripping off our undercover funds?* The scattered pieces of her life were burning a hole in her heart.

She knew Bill Wilmon wanted those glasses back. If she returned to the SUV and got Lauren to come with her, she'd have an armed agent as backup. But then she'd have to explain a new face. *Not a good idea.* Nor was abandoning the glasses, even though she didn't like the risk of walking back into Uka's place mere minutes after the robbery at gunpoint. Gloria steadied herself and headed toward Uka's office, her mind racing. *What the hell do I tell her?*

Approaching the insurance company's front door, Gloria noticed the crack in the pane. Inside, she saw Uka and the three men. The tension on their faces was clear. Tama was holding Uka's arms, trying to talk her down. Uka shook her head, pulled away from his grip, and pointed at the wall behind them.

Gloria took a deep breath and exhaled, trying to calm her nerves. She entered the office, halted and stared around, wide eyed, as if she had no idea what just went down. "What's going on?"

Uka turned and jabbed her finger at Gloria. "You trying to get us killed?"

Gloria shook her head. "I don't know what you're talking about."

"Two men came and stole your money. They shot at us," Tama shouted. "We're lucky to be alive."

Gloria pressed a hand to her mouth. "Oh, my God. Is everyone all right? I'm so sorry, I had no idea —"

"They came minutes after you left." Uka waved her arms, her nostrils flaring. "They must have been watching you. You didn't notice anyone?"

"We're very careful. You've got to be when you're carrying that much cash. We circled the block several times, looking for anything suspicious. No one caught our attention."

Uka's eyes narrowed. "Where is Marvin?"

Gloria felt uneasy. *I'd like to know that, too.* "He dropped me off at my car."

"We're lucky they didn't kill us." Uka pointed at the wall behind her. "Look at the bullet holes."

Could they identify Darius, even masked as he was? "You said two men? What did they look like?"

"One was tall. The other was short," Tama said. "They wore ski masks, black sweatshirts, and gloves. The shirts were plain, no writing or anything on them."

Relief swept through Gloria. A description that general meant Darius was safe. *Now I've got to save the case.* She approached Uka. "If you had anything to do with this…" Uka said.

"I didn't. I'm going to find out who the fuck was behind this. Believe me. When I get my money back, I'll come see you again and —"

Hands on her hips, Uka snapped, "God, you must be kidding. I don't ever want to see you again." She pointed at the door. "Get out!"

Gloria didn't move. "Look, this never happened to me before. I'll sort it out. Things can still work for both of us. You can make some good money."

Uka's gaze sharpened and she cocked her head. "Why did you come back, anyway?"

"I think I left my glasses on your desk. Do you mind if I check your office?"

"You stay here. I'll look." Uka marched into her office. She returned a minute later, carrying the glasses. "Here they are." She extended her hand, and Gloria took them.

"Thank you." Gloria held Uka's hard, judgmental gaze. "Do you think I would have returned here if I knew you were going to be robbed?"

Uka's stony expression eased a fraction. "I suppose that doesn't make sense. This has never happened to you before?"

"Never." *Because I'm usually the one packing.* "Let's not lose this opportunity for a good deal for both of us."

"How is this a good opportunity for me? I don't want anyone pointing guns at us."

"I'm sorry that happened. I'm willing to pay a higher fee for your services."

"How much higher?"

"We had agreed on seven percent. I'll pay you eight."

Uka gave a caustic laugh. "Ten, or just go away."

Gloria paused, as if giving it some thought, although she knew there was no alternative. "Okay, okay. Ten it is.

"You better look for a leak in your organization. To time this so tight, someone had to know we were meeting." Uka stepped closer to her. "I promise you, if this ever happens again, the results will be different. All of my men will have weapons."

Gloria stood her ground. "If I find out I have a problem, I'll fix it."

"All right. Go now."

"That's best, yes. I've got a lot to do."

She left the insurance office and hustled toward the end of the block, where Lauren waited in the Blazer. *I have to protect Darius. He wouldn't have done this on his own. Someone must have forced him into it. Maybe his father? What do I tell Lauren?*

She reached the SUV and hopped in. "Make a U-turn. I don't want to go past the business and risk any of them seeing me in this car."

"Okay." Lauren started the Blazer and turned around, heading south on Clark Street. "Everything all right? You look frazzled."

"No, everything is not goddamn all right." With effort, she reined in her temper. How much had Lauren seen of the robbery? *I have to test her, partner or not.* "Did you see anyone leaving Uka's?"

"No, I was on my cell phone. Why?"

Talking with lover boy Edwards when she should've been providing security for me? Lucky me. "Uka said they were ripped off by a couple of guys wearing masks and waving pistols."

"What the fuck? Do you believe her?"

"I don't know what to believe just yet. Whoever did it fired a few rounds at them, but no one was hurt. I saw the bullet holes in the back wall."

"How would anyone know you were meeting her with a boatload of cash? That's too much of a coincidence."

"I know. I'll have to tell Stephens and then DEA." Gloria shook her head. "They're going to be really pissed. We'll never get money from them again. After that, we talk to Marvin."

"Marvin and Baba are the only outsiders who knew what was going on. Do you think your cover is blown?" Lauren asked.

"No, I think it's still good. Uka upped her fee to ten percent. Assuming I can get more cash, I have to get back to her soon before she gets cold feet."

Lauren steered the Blazer around a corner. "The reason I was on my cell. I got a call from Stephens. You're in for a hell of a week. Your husband's trial has been moved up from February to this Thursday, January thirteenth. The congressman's trial that was supposed to start Wednesday isn't. He's pleading guilty."

Gloria swallowed and stared at the floor of the SUV. *The next time I see Darius, he'll be on the witness stand testifying for his father.*

⌄

Darius headed south on Lake Shore Drive. "We've got to stop someplace to split the cash."

"Ah, man. I don't know," Shorty said.

"You talk big, but you're scared of Marvin."

"It ain't right. Marvin's done a lot for me—"

"Yeah, like got you into drugs and dealing. Good chance you'll go to jail if you're not killed by a homie or some cop."

"What the fuck you talkin' about!" Spit flew from Shorty's mouth. "You doin' anything different than me?"

The truth hit Darius hard as he sat there, his hands wrapped tight around the steering wheel. He was no different than Shorty. Maybe one small step behind him, but that step could come quick.

He was Shorty in the making. Even beyond that. He could see himself taking over for Marvin. Moving up to pushing weight—kilos, multi-kilos. But what were the odds on the outcome being any different? Darius knew he would most likely end up in jail, or worse. The smack wasn't working like it used to. He might have to jab a needle in his arm, become a junkie, and see how dark his world would turn.

He exhaled slowly. His grip on the steering wheel lightened up. It was decision time—maybe take a step in a different direction.

"Yeah, I hear you, Shorty. We'll do it your way. We'll give all the cash to Marvin."

Marvin waited in his office, seated at his desk and checking his watch every five minutes. What was taking Darius and Shorty so long to get back to the projects? Twenty minutes later, the boys rolled in, each of them holding a green garbage bag. They closed the door and tossed the bags on the desk.

Marvin stood and gestured at the door. "Lock the fuckin' thing." He leaned over the bags, untied them, and spread them open. "Look at this. All bundled and marked." He fished a bundle out, then another. "Looks like each one is five grand. You did good, Darius. You don't owe me anymore." He sat back down and waved a hand at them. "You guys can go. Hold up, what the fuck is that?" He pointed at a narrow case Shorty held under his arm.

Shorty grinned. "Darius gave me his old laptop computer. He said I've got a knack for this."

"Yeah, sure." A wide grin swept across Marvin's face as he closed up the garbage bags. "I'll talk to you later. I got to take care of these."

***

Shorty followed Darius out of Marvin's office. The door shut and the lock clicked behind them. "I'm getting out of here," Darius said.

Shorty gave him a raised eyebrow and a *see what I'm doing* look. "I'm going to hang here for a while and play with the laptop."

"That's a good way to learn. It's got a few years on it, but it's good enough for you. See you." Darius waved as he walked away.

There was a chair outside of Marvin's office. Shorty sat down, set the computer on his knees, opened it, and turned it on. He punched the keys with one finger and fumbled across the touchpad as he surfed from one website to another, stumbling across porn and then onto a sports page from the *Chicago Tribune*. There was a photograph on it, of Darius with a lady and some girl. Shorty frowned at the photo. The date on it was a year ago. It must be left over from the computer's memory.

He read the caption under the photograph. *Darius Carlton, congratulated by his mother and sister after leading his team in scoring in the 2003 city league championship game.*

The door lock clicked and Marvin stepped out, carrying the garbage bags. "Hey, look at this," Shorty said. "We've got a star."

Marvin's eyebrows furled. "What're you talking about?"

"Here." Shorty pointed at the laptop screen. "Look."

Marvin leaned over him and looked at the picture. He dropped the two bags. "Holy fuck."

CHAPTER 31

Tuesday, January 11, 2005
4:40 p.m.

GLORIA SAT IN THE PASSENGER seat as Lauren drove the Blazer south on Lake Shore Drive, heading back to the federal building. The sun sank behind the buildings, darkening the sky. Dirty snow covered the city streets. Dread weighed on Gloria as she contemplated who she should talk to first—Stephens or DEA—about the total failure of her investigation. What could be worse than having her undercover funds stolen? Her cell phone rang, and the caller ID flashed. Marvin.

She jerked the phone to her mouth and snapped, "What?"

"Marvin's got something for you."

Gloria guessed what his answer would be, but hoped she was wrong. "What's that?"

"Two garbage bags."

She felt a sensation in her gut like a flame burning through a sheet of paper. "What the fuck are you doing with those?"

"Marvin's saving your ass."

She struggled to contain her growing anger. *You son of a bitch.* "You get those bags right up to where we met this afternoon,

Ravenswood north of Foster. We'll be waiting for you. Do you understand?"

"You should be happy Marvin called. I didn't have to."

"Be there in a half-hour!" *Or your sorry ass will regret this day forever.* She killed the call and looked at Lauren. "Go back to where we met with Marvin earlier. I'll tell the surveillance team to go back to Uka's business."

She made the call, brief and terse, as Lauren turned off Lake Shore Drive at Belmont and headed north on Clark. "What did Marvin want?"

Cell phone resting in her lap, Gloria stared straight ahead. "He said he's got the garbage bags."

"That son of a bitch!" Lauren punched the gas, cutting in front of a school bus. The driver blasted his horn. "Marvin must have set you up."

Gloria's response came out in a sharp staccato beat. "Don't you think that thought occurred to me?"

Lauren flinched and swallowed, backing down. "So, uh…how do you want to handle this?"

"Take the bags to Uka and get the case back on track."

"And what about Marvin?"

"I don't know. I might shoot him." She laughed, trying to lighten the situation, but deep inside there was some truth to what she'd said. If Marvin was fucking with Darius, Gloria would have little trouble putting a target on his kill zone.

They reached Foster, and Lauren parked the Blazer. "The van won't be set up to monitor a call until they find a parking spot within five hundred feet of the business. You going to wait to call Uka?"

"No. I don't want to give her any chance to change her mind." Gloria pulled a microphone out of the glove box and taped it to the mouthpiece of her phone, then hit speed dial.

A deep voice sounded in the SUV. "Uka's Auto Insurance, Tama speaking."

"Tama, it's Gloria Nightingale. Listen, everything's been resolved. I need to meet with Uka right away."

"Hold on."

Gloria waited, trying to anticipate every response Uka might make. She couldn't screw up this second chance.

Uka came on the line. "I'm surprised to hear from you so soon," she said, sounding pleased.

Gloria closed her eyes and nodded, even though the woman couldn't see her. "Whenever issues come up, I try to handle things immediately. The problem we discussed earlier has been eliminated and won't present itself again." *Let Uka think whatever she wants about what that means.*

"Fine, you can't let something like that go on. So, what now?"

"I'll have the bags back in a short while. I'd like to finish what we started earlier and deliver them to you."

"When?"

"Fifteen, maybe thirty minutes."

"All right. See you then."

Gloria killed the call, then looked at Lauren. "Don't say anything to anyone about Marvin being involved in the robbery. Until we know for certain, we can't let even a rumor get out. It'd fuck up this case, big time." Gloria swallowed. *And it would tie Darius to Marvin.*

Minutes later, Marvin's yellow Cadillac pulled up on Ravenswood behind the Blazer. He got out empty-handed, strolled over to the SUV, and climbed into the back.

Gloria's heart raced. She felt ready to explode but took a deep breath, trying to control her emotions. "Where's the bags?"

"I left them in the Caddy. Figured we'd be taking my car to see Uka."

She didn't know how much longer she could contain herself. The thought of Marvin using Darius to rip off the target of her undercover operation was fanning the embers of her anger to white hot. She took another deep breath. "Let's go, then. I want to check the bags before we head to Uka's."

They left the Blazer and plowed toward the Cadillac through the ankle-deep snow. Marvin unlocked the doors and slid into the driver's seat. The bags were on the floor of the front passenger side. Gloria slid into the passenger seat, arranging her legs and feet around the bags. She untied them and counted the bundles of money. All of it was there.

She glared at Marvin. "How long have you been fucking with my son?"

He exhaled and shook his head. "I didn't know he was your boy until a half-hour ago. He gave his old computer to a homie. Homie was playing with it by my office and pulled up a photo of you, your son, and your daughter from some basketball game a year ago and—"

Gloria grabbed Marvin by the collar of his black leather coat and jerked him over the console between the car seats. "How did this fucking start?"

"Let go of me." He looked shocked and a little scared.

She eased her grip, but only a bit. "Talk first."

"Around the holidays. He was walking by Robert Taylor Homes and got in a fight with a couple bangers. He was in a bad way. He wasn't beat up. Just messed up in his head. Something about his old man. I got him a dime bag of smack to mellow him out."

Gloria pushed Marvin away and jabbed her hands in the pockets of the fox fur coat. "Shit, he's using?"

Marvin bobbed his head from side to side. "I don't know how much or how often."

"What else has he been doing?"

"I don't know. Hanging around the projects, I guess." Marvin looked down. "He's a lot different than the regular homies. He's smart. He talks like an educated guy, like a lawyer. We had a relationship."

"A relationship?" Gloria felt her world crumbling. "What the fuck does that mean?"

"He'd do things for me, run errands."

"Don't fuck around, Marvin. I need to know exactly what Darius was involved in."

He folded his arms across his chest. "Marvin's done a lot for you. Been doing a lot for a couple of years now. Don't forget that."

"Don't fucking bullshit me. You didn't do anything for free. You got paid and you knew what you were getting into."

"So, I'm just a snitch to you. Use me up and throw me away."

"Give me a break. You're a grown man. Darius is just a boy. You were using him for God knows what. Tell me everything."

"You gonna grant me, what's that lawyer's word? Immunity?"

Gloria hesitated. She didn't have legal authority for that. She could tell him he had street immunity, though. That wasn't legal, but no prosecutor would ever charge him if she said that magic word.

Her thoughts went back to last October, when she'd hidden Darius in the back of the Blazer after she killed the dope dealer, McElroy. *I can only protect Darius if I know what he's done.*

She cleared her throat and nodded. "Yeah, immunity." *From the law…but not from me, you son of a bitch.*

CHAPTER 32

Uka's Auto Insurance
Tuesday, January 11, 2005
5:15 p.m.

MARVIN PARKED HIS YELLOW CADILLAC behind Uka's Mercedes. "Don't fuck this up," Gloria murmured to him as they got out. He didn't answer, just nodded. As they approached the insurance company, she slipped on the special glasses to record the upcoming conversations. The big crack in the door's glass pane was still there.

Gloria twisted the knob, but the door didn't open. Standing behind it was one of Uka's employees…the one named Zalan, she thought. His muscular arms stressed the sleeves of his untucked white shirt. She knocked on the glass. Zalan's eyes drilled into hers before he unlocked the deadbolt and opened the door. As she passed him, she noticed a bulge on his right hip under his shirt.

She stepped past him into the office, followed by Marvin carrying the garbage bags. Zalan closed the door behind them and re-locked the deadbolt.

Kunta Tama rose from his desk and greeted them halfway down the aisle. "Follow me," he said, and sauntered to Uka's office door. Gloria spotted the knob of a pistol grip at his waist, under his blue and red dashiki shirt. *It didn't take long for them to learn the Chicago way – everyone has a gun.* The third man slammed his desk drawer shut and she saw him jab a pistol beneath his belt.

Tama tapped on the door, then pushed it open. Gloria and Marvin followed him into Uka's office and he closed the door behind them.

Uka sat in her chair as if she were African royalty. She said nothing, just rested her elbows on the onyx desktop and steepled her hands together. Tama moved behind her desk and stood at her side.

"It looks like your men are prepared to go to war," Gloria said.

Uka opened her hands briefly and steepled them again. "Fortunately, in this city it's not hard to buy guns. We will never go through an experience like that again without being able to protect ourselves."

Gloria sat in a rattan chair in front of Uka. "No one can fault you for that."

Tama cocked his head. "You're walking around with all this money. Don't you have protection?"

"We left our weapons in the car. Didn't think we'd need them coming in here, especially after what happened."

Uka was gazing at Marvin. "He's still with you I see."

In a voice strong enough to cover her lie, Gloria said, "He was not the problem."

Uka pushed her chair back and crossed her legs. "I'll take your word for that and hope that you resolved the issue, like you said."

Gloria held Uka's gaze. "Everything has been resolved." Looking into someone's eyes and lying was a skill she was perfecting.

Uka nodded. "Good. Just to remind you, the terms of our agreement have been revised. It's now ten percent for each transaction."

"Yes, we agreed to that." Gloria nodded. "But let's consider going back to the original rate of seven percent if the volume of cash increases."

"We'll see, but it would have to be a substantial increase."

Gloria nodded to Marvin. He approached Tama and handed him the bags. Tama placed them on the floor next to Uka's desk, untied them, and took a few minutes to count the number of bundles.

Gloria looked around Uka's office. "That's quite a collection of African artifacts you have."

"I go back to Nigeria at least once a year." She spread her arms. "Everything you see, I bought there, even this desk. It was handmade for me by a member of my congregation."

"Congregation?"

Uka raised her chin and straightened her shoulders. "Yes. I am a high priestess of the Yoruba religion. Its history dates back over one thousand years." Uka shifted her gaze to Marvin. "I caution you that it is decreed that once a priest is ordained, they have the power to cast spells."

Marvin's brow furrowed and he gave Gloria a worried glance.

"It's all good." Tama turned to face Uka. "Twenty bundles. A hundred thousand."

"You'll let me know when you've finished managing my money?" Gloria said.

"Of course. It will take a week to ten days before the money hits your account, in the form of bank wires from various entities. Too large an amount at once attracts…unwanted attention."

"I'll wait to hear from you and then we can discuss future business." Gloria rose from her chair and nodded a goodbye to Uka. Picking up his cue, Marvin opened Uka's office door. Gloria exited, followed by Marvin and Tama.

In the outer room, Zalan rose from his desk and walked to the front door. He raised his shirt and lifted a Colt .38 from its holster. Taking no chances, Gloria figured. Holding the pistol at his right hip, Zalan turned the deadbolt with his left hand and opened the door, then nodded toward the gap. Gloria got the message: exit fast. As soon as she and Marvin were over the threshold, the door chunked shut and the deadbolt clicked behind them.

They returned to the Cadillac and Marvin pulled onto Clark Street. He turned at Foster and headed west.

"Pull over here," Gloria ordered.

"Don't you want to meet up with Lauren?"

"Fuck it, Marvin. I said pull over."

"No problem." Marvin shrugged and pulled into a parking spot on Wolcott Avenue.

"I want you to arrange for me and Darius to meet."

Marvin extended his hands, palms up. "Can't you just call him?"

"He won't answer."

"Why not?"

"That's none of your business." She leaned toward him. "But first, tell me about your 'relationship' with my son."

Marvin hesitated, then shrugged. "I see him around the projects. Sometimes I pay him for painting an apartment or cleaning a place out. Some of those tenants are pigs."

"You have him do anything illegal?"

He shook his head. "I pay him in cash. It's off the books."

Her breath came faster, fueled by repressed anger. "I don't give a fuck about that. Nothing worse than getting cash for painting and cleaning apartments?"

Marvin rubbed a hand over his lips. "No, that's it."

She inquired again, making a point of it. "Nothing else?"

"Nope."

"You said you gave him heroin the first time you met him. Is he using?"

"Marvin don't know what he does when I'm not around."

Her voice wavered. "Damn it, if you know, just tell me!"

"Marvin *don't* know. Swear to God."

"Why am I having such a hard time believing you?"

"You're a cop. That's how you guys are."

"You'd better be telling me the truth. Where will Darius be tonight? You going to see him or talk to him?" She watched his eyes, looking for any movement that might indicate he was withholding something. If he was lying, he was good at it. Of course, he had years of experience when it came to concealing the truth.

"Marvin don't know for sure." His eyes flicked to the left.

"Don't lie to me!"

Marvin nodded, didn't say another word.

"You bring him to me, tonight. I'll meet you at the Shedd Aquarium parking lot at 8:00. That's twenty minutes from Robert Taylor. An easy drive. You got that?"

He swallowed. "What if Marvin can't find him?"

Gloria glanced at her watch. "You've got more than an hour and a half. I'll be waiting for you. Don't tell him you're bringing him to me, and don't fuck with me on this." She leaned back in the passenger seat. "Now, let's go meet up with Lauren."

CHAPTER 33

DARIUS SAT IN FRONT OF the television, watching a rerun of *Lost* and devouring a beef sandwich he had picked up on his way here from the projects.

His father walked into their hotel suite. "What are you munching on?"

Darius wiped a napkin across his face. "A beef from Al's on Taylor Street."

"Why didn't you call me? That would have hit the spot."

"Sorry, Dad. I didn't know if you'd be here. You're spending a lot of time at the law library." He felt guilty at what he was about to say, but it was time to head back down to the projects for his night's work. If the prosecutors found out he was involved in drug dealing, they would find a way to use it against his father, either at trial or for sure during sentencing if his father was found guilty. "I'll be leaving soon. I've got a workout with an AAU team. If I make the team, there's a good chance I can get a scholarship in the fall."

"How're workouts going?"

"Great. I sunk fifteen three-pointers in a row yesterday." Another lie; he hadn't touched a basketball in a month.

His father smiled. "That's a step in the right direction. But I know you can do even better if you keep at it. Anyone there that can measure your body mass index? It should be in the single digits with someone your age and height. Guys like Luol Deng and Ben Gordon are probably under five percent. You keep eating beefs with all that gravy and…" He paused, shaking his head. "Is that mozzarella on it?" He set his hands on his hips and exhaled. "You can't be eating that and expect to stay in competitive shape."

Darius laid the second half of the sandwich on the coffee table. The words stung, and his appetite was gone. "No, Dad. There's no one who measures BIM at the AAU team."

"BMI, son." His father shook his head. "Why don't you try asking the coach? He might know someone who can do it. It would be for the benefit of the whole team, not just you. I'm sure there are a few guys who could stand to drop a little weight." He pointed at the half-eaten sandwich. "Do you mind if I finish that?"

"No, go ahead. I'm full. I better go. I don't want to be late."

His father picked up the sandwich and took a bite. "These are good. Come here."

Reluctantly, Darius approached him. His father put his arm around Darius's shoulders. "Don't forget, my trial starts Wednesday. Jury selection and the prosecution case could be over by week's end, which means I may need you to testify on Friday. We can talk about that in more detail later, but I wanted to remind you." He gave Darius a gentle shake and released him. "Now get out of here and show that coach everything you learned from your old man. Keep working hard and one day you'll be able to fill my shoes."

"Sure, Dad." Darius slipped on his parka and dragged himself out of the hotel, struggling with what their 'talk' might involve and how he would have to cope with it. He felt like he had never pleased the man, no matter how hard he tried. In the past few months, their relationship had gotten worse.

His breath fogged in the cold night air as he jogged down South Michigan Avenue. What had he learned from his old man? *Lying,* he thought. This trial would require him to lie not only about his activities with Marvin, but also about what happened on that night in October with McElroy. He'd have to fall on the sword for his father, testify that he found in the courtroom the pistol his father gave him. He'd have to say he intended to kill McElroy to save his father from being convicted. There was no way around it. His father's innocence depended on the effectiveness of Darius's testimony. Only the better he testified, the more it would implicate his mother. Her being at the crime scene that night was the only way to explain Darius's disappearance from it. How would this affect her? His stomach roiled. Should he lie for his father? How could his father ask him to? That couldn't be right, could it?

Marvin had never hidden anything from him. They were honest with each other…well, mostly. With Marvin, Darius had crossed a thin line between right and wrong, but Marvin never hid that from him. Darius knew what that line was and crossed it knowingly. Marvin had taught him things, given him responsibilities, trusted him not to mess up. His father had never done that, for as long as Darius could remember.

Their whole relationship was built on lies. A lie that started twenty years ago before Darius was even born, his father concealing an illegitimate daughter from Darius's mother. A lie carried on until just a few days ago, when his father told him the truth about Tamika. Darius wondered how many more lies there were.

He slowed as he neared the Robert Taylor Homes. It could be dangerous running in the 'hood. Around here, it was a given that a kid was running away from something—most likely the cops. He strolled to the 3904 building and stopped in the crowded lobby, braced his hands on his knees for a minute, and then headed for the stairwell. He charged up the stairway to the fourth floor, stopping to blow out a series of short breaths to gain control of his wind. He knew Shorty would be waiting impatiently for him to take over the cutting and bagging operation.

He went to Unit 403 and knocked on the door, a double knock three times. "Yo Shorty, it's me." Three deadbolts clicked and the door opened.

Shorty extended his closed fist. Darius tapped his hand on top of it. "Yo, man, how's it going?" Shorty said.

"Can't complain. How 'bout you?"

"Mos' def good." Shorty flashed a roll of greenbacks in his free hand, a smile on his face.

It was always the same setup, fluorescent lights hanging from the ceiling and two four-by-six tables set end to end, the women at one of them cutting and mixing a kilo of brown Mexican heroin while the others at the next table portioned the cut heroin into dime bags. Tonight, they were cutting it with baking soda. Marvin Gaye's song "Trouble Man" rose from a CD player — *I didn't make it, sugar, playing by the rules.*

Shorty bent over, stashed his roll in his sock, and left the apartment. Darius locked the door. The women kept working, not paying him any mind. He tossed his parka over the back of the worn recliner, seated himself in it between the cardboard-covered windows. He kicked back, lowering the chair into a horizontal position. The music set a mood and he let himself drift with it, not thinking.

About 7:30, the kilo was wiped out, the dime bags were filled, and the ladies were slipping into their sweats. Darius roused himself from the chair and escorted them to the turoor, locking it behind them. In the empty apartment, he turned up the volume on the CD player. Chaka Khan's sexy voice sang out: *I feel for you, I think I love you.*

Darius grabbed a dime bag and fell back into the recliner. He ripped the bag open. Rubbing the stuff on his gums wasn't giving the same effect as it used to, so he'd started snorting the powder. He knew that with the high, everything would make perfect sense and he would find himself at peace with his life—even with his father. It worried him, how long snorting smack would work. He tried to forget what he knew: a junkie's need for the poison was always increasing. With each hit they needed it more often and stronger. Darius's appetite for heroin was growing and his willpower was weakening, but he couldn't see himself ever plunging a needle into his arm and watching his blood spurt from the injection. *I can stop before it gets that bad.*

Darius ripped the bag a little more and poured the powder on the back of his hand. He lifted it to his nose, pressed a finger against one nostril and inhaled, then closed his eyes and pushed the recliner back. Ten minutes gradually rolled by and he felt hazy, but not the usual warm glow. He needed more.

Another snort might do it. He opened his eyes and stared at the torn baggie. What if it didn't? What if hazy was the best snorting could do for him?

Anxiety poked through the muddled feeling. He needed the high. He couldn't go on without it, not tonight.

He glanced around the room and saw a junkie's paraphernalia lying on the floor in the corner. Bic lighter, spoon, water bottle, stretch band, syringe. The sight made him laugh a little. *Where would we be if we didn't have a drug fiend to test this shit.*

He stared for a while at the syringe and the other items. Then he rolled out of the recliner, grabbed another bag from the table, stumbled across the room, and collapsed in the junkie's corner. He had seen this act before. He could do it. *I'm no coward.*

He rolled up his sleeve, wrapped the band around his bicep and flicked his finger a couple of times against the muscle. A blood vessel popped up like it had been anticipating this moment.

Darius ripped the baggie open and poured the smack onto the spoon, then added a splash of water. He flicked the Bic lighter and held the flame under the spoon until the mixture started to bubble. He laid the spoon on the floor, grabbed the syringe, and slipped the tip of the needle into the heroin. Slowly he pulled back the plunger, filling the syringe.

He remembered that junkies always pointed the syringe toward the ceiling and tapped it with their finger to get rid of any air bubbles as they squeezed a few drops out. Easy enough to do. He watched the drops of heroin slide down the sides of the syringe.

Darius licked his lips, knowing the moment he had been waiting for was now. He plunged the needle into his bulging blood vessel and pulled the plunger back, watching his blood trickle into the syringe. Then he pushed the plunger down.

He could feel the heroin rushing through his veins. His head fell back against the wall and his mouth hung open. He was in ecstasy, as if he'd ventured from a chilled room and stepped into the comfort of a warm bath. Life was worth living again, and everything else was unimportant.

His cell phone rang. His eyes opened, barely. He lay there with the needle protruding from his arm as a word dragged out of his mouth: "Whaaat?"

Down in the lobby of 3904, Marvin flinched at the sound of Darius's slurred voice. "It's Marvin," he growled into the phone. "I need you to come with me."

"Go away. Leave me the fuck alone."

"Now, you gotta come, now!"

The phone went quiet.

Marvin swore under his breath and looked at Shorty. "Shit, he turned the phone off. Come on." *I'm fucked. I have to take him to meet Gloria and he's stoned.* He dashed for the stairwell, Shorty following behind.

On the fourth floor, Marvin and Shorty rushed to Unit 403 and double-knocked on the door three times. No one answered. "Shorty, unlock the door. The kid's turning into a fuckin' stone junkie."

"Let him sleep it off," Shorty said. "Where he gotta be that's so important?"

"Never you fuckin' mind." Marvin pointed at the door. "Unlock it."

Shorty inserted the keys one at a time into the three deadbolt locks and pushed the door open. Marvin rushed in. Darius lay in a drug stupor in the corner of the room. The CD played Curtis Mayfield's *"Freddie's Dead – That's What I Said"*.

"Yank that needle out of his arm and help me get him up," Marvin ordered. "Then help me take him to my car."

Shorty shrugged. "Don't know why we can't just leave him be. Let him be high."

Marvin shoved Shorty toward the corner. "Get over there. Just do what I fuckin' say, damn it."

They lifted Darius, managed to slide his arms into the sleeves of the parka and the hood over his head. "What the fuck you doing?" Darius muttered. "Leave me alone." He shook his head as he slumped back down to the floor.

They hauled him upright again. It felt like they were lifting dead weight. "Come on. I gotta take him outta here," Marvin ordered. He thought of the immunity Gloria had given him. *This better not fuck me up.*

With Darius's arms across their shoulders, their own bodies bracing him up, they walked him out of the apartment with his feet shuffling under him. Shorty locked the door and they went down the elevator and through the lobby, getting a lot of stares as they pushed through the nightly crowd. Outside, the wind pushed them along toward Marvin's Cadillac. Marvin tossed Shorty the key so the boy could open up, and they dropped Darius into the back seat. Marvin covered him with a blanket and closed the door.

Shorty stood next to the car. "Where're you taking him?"

"Where else, to see his mommy."

"Yeah, sure. He musta really pissed you off. I mean, you're not going to…" Shorty gestured as if squeezing a trigger.

"Marvin goin' to do what he has to do." He glanced at his watch. 8:10 p.m. So, he'd be a little late, but he figured it wouldn't matter. *She'd wait all night to see her boy.*

CHAPTER 34

Shedd Aquarium Parking Lot
Tuesday, January 11, 2005
8:30 p.m.

THE NIGHT WAS LIT BY only a quarter moon and the temperature was freezing. The cityscape glowed and the reflections of tall buildings danced across Lake Michigan. Gloria fought the impulse to leave. It felt like she'd been here for hours, though only half of one had elapsed, and with every passing minute it seemed more unlikely she would see her son tonight. Or maybe ever. She sighed. Was Darius so upset with her that he would refuse any attempt to mend their relationship? She glanced at her watch. Marvin was late, but she had to give him every chance to bring Darius to her.

She picked up her cell phone to call Marvin when she heard the sound of gravel crunching under the weight of a car. She looked up and saw the familiar yellow Cadillac, but there was only the silhouette of Marvin in the driver's seat.

"Damn it, where's Darius?" She slammed the steering wheel with her fist.

Marvin pulled up parallel to Gloria's side of the Blazer, and they rolled down their windows. "Where's my son?" Gloria demanded.

Marvin nodded toward the back seat.

Gloria piled out of her car and hastened to the rear passenger door of the Cadillac. She yanked the door open and climbed over the limp body, lifting the blanket from his face. *Darius.* She checked his neck for a pulse and felt the slow beat, as if he were sedated. "What have you done to him?"

Marvin licked his lips. "He's coming down from a high."

Her eyes blazed with anger. "How could you let this happen?"

He looked at her over his shoulder. "Marvin couldn't stop him. He likes the drugs since the first time. He blamed his old man."

"We've got to take him to an ER. I'm not waiting a minute."

"Where?"

"Go up the Drive to Northwestern." She lifted her son's head and slid onto the seat beneath him, cradling his body, then leaned out and pulled the door shut. "Go, now!"

CHAPTER 35

Wilton Hotel
Wednesday, January 12, 2005
9:00 a.m.

After working on his case into the wee hours of the morning, Judge Carlton slept in. When he finally woke, he stretched his arms and legs to the length and width of the king-size mattress. With a hearty yawn, he thought of his son. Be nice to have breakfast with him, hear how last night's practice session went. He threw his legs over the mattress, got out of bed, and went to Darius's bedroom. He opened the door a crack, soft-stepped in, and raised the curtains. The sun blasted into the quiet room.

His eyes darted to the bed. The pillows had no indentations, and the bedspread lay smooth across the taut sheets. Had Darius gone home with someone? He knew the AAU teams attracted sports groupies, and some of the women weren't shy about approaching the players afterward. "My boy had an overnighter. Maybe she's got a place of her own." The judge laughed. *He found himself a shagger.*

He returned to his bedroom, picked up his cell phone, and hit Darius's number. The call went to voicemail. The judge laughed again. "Congrats, son. I'm sure you had a memorable experience. I've got a meeting with the damn prosecutors at 11:00. Call me when you get a chance. I'd like to hear about your night and discuss what I mentioned to you yesterday. Remember, I might need you by Friday. See you later."

At 10:55 he walked into the lobby of the U.S. Attorney's Office on the fifth floor of the Dirksen Federal Building. A bulletproof sheet of glass covered the east side of the lobby, protecting the three administrative aides. Carlton laid his black wool overcoat across the row of visitors' chairs and introduced himself to the clerk sitting behind the protective barrier. She handed him a nametag. He printed his name on it and stuck it on his dark gray pinstripe suit. Placing his black leather briefcase on the empty chair next to him, he waited while she called the assistant U.S. Attorney. He watched her hang up the phone and mumble a few words to her coworker. There was no doubt in his mind that he, the indicted federal judge, was the topic of conversation.

At 11:15 the door to the inner sanctum opened. FBI agent Wayne Axelrod leaned against it. The judge nodded in acknowledgment, picked up his overcoat and briefcase, and glanced at his Rolex. "You're late," he said as he entered the long narrow hallway. Axelrod did not reply.

They passed the first five offices filled with administrative personnel, followed by row after row of newer prosecuting attorneys. With each step down the hall, Carlton's anger grew as he contemplated the upcoming meeting. By the time they rounded the corner and approached the office of Assistant U.S. Attorney Todd Jeffreys, Carlton felt ready to explode.

The usual suspects were all there, Carlton thought grimly as he stepped over the threshold. Seated to Jeffreys's right was second chair Phillip Tunney, and next to him, Lauren Ashberry. Agent Anthony Fanelli sat to the left, joined by Axelrod. The sun that had shone through the windows dimmed as clouds covered it, turning the office a shade of gray.

Carlton laid his coat over the back of the chair directly in front of Jeffreys's desk and sat down. On the wall behind the prosecutor were his diplomas from Brown University and Harvard Law School. *Typical white boy who was cradled through the Ivy League by his wealthy father. This boy from the streets of Chicago will chew him up in the courtroom.* The credenza sported the usual array of family photos and politically correct pictures of Jeffreys shaking hands with President Bush and Attorney General Ashcroft.

"Good morning, Carlton," Jeffreys said.

Carlton flexed his fingers and closed them into a tight ball. "It's *Judge* Carlton to you. Now shall we get on with this?"

Jeffreys scooted his chair closer to his desk. "Unless you have any motions that require a continuance, your trial starts tomorrow—"

"Come on, Jeffreys." The judge's gaze ran across everyone's faces, centering on Jeffreys last. He felt like he was witnessing his executioners. A guilty verdict could bring a ten-year sentence. He had to take command of this meeting. His hands flew into the air. "You can dispense with the formalities and get down to business. I expect you have a final plea offer to make, because if there's one thing I know about your office, you don't like to lose, and you realize you're encountering a much greater risk in my case than you normally do."

Jeffreys shook his head. "We're ready to go to trial and looking forward to a successful prosecution. At this late date, our policy is to not negotiate any plea agreement. But you know that already."

Damn. Jeffreys was calling his bluff. Ten years of his life were at risk. *Can I rely on Darius? Can I count on my son to lie for me?* He felt like a spike was being driven into his forehead. He rubbed his temples with his forefinger and thumb. He needed his son now, and the kid was out sowing his wild oats. "I would like to make a phone call."

"Sure," Jeffreys said. "If you want some privacy, you can use the office next to mine. It's vacant."

Carlton nodded. He stood and walked into the vacant office, taking his briefcase with him, and closed the door. He fished his cell phone from the inside pocket of his suit coat and paced across the floor as he hit the speed dial for Darius. "Come on, son, answer."

The call went to voicemail again. Carlton cleared his throat. "Darius, this is extremely important. I must talk to you about Friday. About your testimony. Please call me immediately!" He ended the message, then ambled to the desk and sat in the chair behind it. Outside, the winter sky was turning darker as the sun drifted behind the federal building.

His phone rang. He hit the receive button. "Darius—"

"If your new car warranty is expiring—"

He slammed the phone down. "Son of a bitch. Fucking robocall." He rubbed his sweaty palms down his pants legs. "Where are you, Darius?"

He exhaled and pushed away from the desk. *Got to keep my composure. Be confident. Can't let them see any weakness.* He stood, straightened his tie, and headed back to Jeffreys's office. Walking in, he noticed that his overcoat was positioned differently on the chair back than when he'd left it. "Did someone search my coat?"

Fanelli smirked.

"I don't believe you guys. You better believe I'll tell the judge about this illegal warrantless search."

Fanelli laughed and crossed his legs. "I think you're getting paranoid."

Carlton shook his head. "Let's get back to why we're here. First, I have a motion for a bench trial." He set his briefcase on the chair seat, opened it and pulled the document out, and flipped it onto Jeffreys's desk.

Jeffreys picked it up and fingered through the pages. "We'll go over it this afternoon. If we don't have any objections, we won't contest it."

"I'm sure you'll find it fulfills all the requirements."

Jeffreys shrugged, clearly unimpressed. "Is there anything else?"

Carlton clenched his jaw. *What if I can't find Darius? I've got to play every card I have.* "Yes. I'm putting you on notice that I will consider a guilty plea to a reasonable misdemeanor in place of the charged felonies and with no recommendation from the government in regard to incarceration."

Jeffreys actually chuckled at that. "Thank you for offering. But, like I said, it's the policy of this office not to negotiate any pleas this close to a trial. If you want to make a blind guilty plea to the existing charges, that would be fine. But of course, we reserve the right to make a recommendation at sentencing. I don't recall any prior conversations regarding your plea, but if you believe we had any, they are now off the table." Jeffreys folded his arms and leaned back.

"I'll…I'll see you in court." Carlton stood, feeling his heart thudding in his chest. He slowly picked up his overcoat and briefcase.

Jeffreys nodded. "Agent Axelrod, escort Judge Carlton the to lobby."

The FBI agent didn't say a thing on the way down, just kept that damned smirk on his face. As Carlton left the building, the wind gusted out of the north and a slushy rain started falling. He raised the collar of his overcoat. He felt the chill in his bones, more than just a response to the weather. *What if Darius is sick or hurt? Maybe that's why he's not returning my calls.*

He pulled his phone out of his pocket and looked at it, but there were no missed calls or messages. *That boy better have a damn good reason.*

CHAPTER 36

Courtroom 2502
Dirksen Federal Building
Thursday, January 13, 2005
Noon

JUDGE ROBERT CARLTON ENTERED THE courtroom wearing a tailor-made charcoal grey suit, crisp white shirt, and a silver tie. The prosecutors were already seated at their table on the right side of the courtroom, along with Fanelli and Lauren Ashberry. They all wore suits as well, none as nice as Carlton's except for Ashberry, who wore a dark green Armani and an open-collar shirt with narrow green vertical pinstripes. Next to the table was their trial cart with a half dozen legal-sized files, a semi-auto Beretta 92FS wrapped in red evidence tape, and an empty magazine capable of holding seventeen rounds.

The gallery was filled with television and newspaper reporters, courtroom buffs, and young prosecutors wanting to see their boss at work. As Carlton passed the throng, he heard a murmur from one of the reporters: "It isn't every day a federal judge will be trading in his black robe for an orange jumpsuit."

Carlton stopped and glared at the reporter, who shrugged in response.

He took his seat at the defense table on the left side of the courtroom, feeling like all eyes were upon him. He opened his briefcase and attempted to block the prosecution team's line of vision, but there were too many of them. He swiveled in his chair and focused on the plaque mounted high above the trial judge's seat. The gold emblem Carlton himself had sat in front of for more than a decade—the bald eagle fronted by the colonial flag, circled by the words *United States District Court Northern District of Illinois*. The ceiling loomed thirty feet above him, yet it and the dark walnut walls seemed to be closing in. How different it felt to be seated at the defense table. He was now the target of the U.S. government. Despite his towering frame, he suddenly felt small. He was the prey looking down the lion's jaws.

Judge Peterson entered the courtroom. His black robe flowed behind him as he quickly moved to his chair.

"All rise, this court is now in session," the court security officer chanted.

There was a rumble of noise as everyone rose from their seats.

Judge Peterson sat, and the crowd followed suit.

Before proceeding, Peterson adjusted his tortoise-shell glasses. His thinning gray hair looked extra neat, as if he'd had a fresh cut since the last time Carlton had appeared before him. "We are scheduled to commence with the trial of Judge Robert Carlton this morning. Is the prosecution ready?"

Jeffreys stood. "Yes, your honor."

"And the defense?"

Carlton stood. "Yes, your honor. I'm prepared to defend myself against these baseless allegations."

Judge Peterson raised his voice slightly, for the benefit of the media people and spectators. "The prosecutor and the defense have agreed to a bench trial. If there are no other matters, let's proceed. Mr. Jeffreys you may present your opening arguments."

Jeffreys approached the podium, carrying the pistol wrapped in red evidence tape. "Thank you, your honor. I'll make a short presentation. Our witnesses will prove that during a trial this past summer in Judge Carlton's courtroom, this pistol," he lifted it and waved it in the air, "went missing." He placed the pistol on the podium.

"The pistol was not found, even after a diligent search of the courtroom and the ATF secured evidence room. The only logical conclusion is that someone stole it, sometime between the end of the trial and delivery to the evidence room. The one thing we know for sure is that on October twenty-third, 2004, Judge Carlton was arrested in possession of this firearm as he approached the key witness against him, convicted drug dealer Spencer McElroy, who was prepared to testify against Judge Carlton for conspiring to launder the drug dealer's funds. This is the basis for the first charge of unlawful possession of a firearm. It cannot be contested that Judge Carlton had possession of this Beretta, and this fact will be corroborated by the testimony of other law enforcement officers."

He paused briefly for effect, then went on. "The October incident occurred in Lawndale, one of the most dangerous areas of the city, where McElroy was allegedly picking up illicit cash from his ghetto heroin ring. You will hear from Judge Carlton's wife, IRS Special Agent Gloria Nighthawk, that she feared for McElroy's well-being. In a turn of events that may seem surreal, she ended up killing McElroy in self-defense, thereby saving Judge Carlton the trouble of having to kill McElroy himself."

Jeffreys clenched the Beretta in his hand again and turned to Carlton. "Judge Carlton brought this pistol with him that night because he was out to kill McElroy." He turned back to face Judge Peterson. "That is the evidence in support of Title 18, USC 1512, tampering with a witness by preventing him from testifying. At the end of the evidence, we will ask the court to reach a verdict of guilty."

Brief silence fell as Jeffreys returned to his chair at the prosecution table. Judge Peterson looked at Carlton, who drew a quick breath. "Your honor, I'll reserve my opening statement. I want to start cross-examining the government's witnesses immediately to prove how preposterous this case is."

Judge Peterson nodded. "That is your right. The government can call their first witness.

The second chair, Phillip Tunney, stood. "Your honor, the government calls ATF Special Agent William Joseph Rockford."

Rockford approached the witness stand. His paisley tie sagged a quarter inch below the collar of his green shirt. The court security officer swore him in and Rockford sat down.

Tunney approached the podium. "What is your full name and occupation?"

"My name is Billy Joe Rockford and I'm a supervisory special agent with Alcohol, Tobacco and Firearms," Rockford said, with a noticeable Southern twang.

Tunney shifted from one leg to the other. "Agent Rockford, can you tell us about your career?"

"Yes, sir. I was hired after getting my degree in criminal justice from Strayer College in North Carolina."

"So, you were hired right out of college by ATF."

"Yes, sir. The only job I've ever had. Well, besides working on my father's tobacco farm."

"Where were you assigned?"

"Initially I was assigned to Montgomery, Alabama for two years. Then I transferred to Atlanta, Georgia. After three years there I was promoted to my current position as a supervisory special agent here in Chicago."

"So, you were the supervisor during a trial in front of Judge Carlton in June 2004."

Rockford nodded. "Yes, sir."

"Can you tell us about that trial? Who were the defendants, what were they charged with, and what was the outcome?"

"It was a case involving a bunch of Black gangbangers from the West Side. They were dealing crack and selling guns." Rockford braced himself with his right arm and sat erect, body language that showed he was proud of his accomplishments. "There were eleven defendants and everyone was found guilty on all counts."

"At the end of trial, did you come to learn there was an issue with one of the trial exhibits?"

"Yes."

"And what was that?"

Rockford exhaled audibly. "Well, there was a pistol, a Beretta semi-auto, that went missing."

"What do you mean, it 'went missing'?"

"After the trial was over, we went through the list of seized weapons, and the pistol was not in the inventory. We checked the serial number, BER431605, against the number on all the seized weapons. It's the same number. Same weapon."

"Did you check to see if the pistol might have been misplaced?"

"Yes, we went through all the weapons taken from the gangbangers and then we went through all the boxes stored in our secured evidence room. The pistol wasn't anywhere."

"Did you search Judge Carlton's courtroom?"

"Yes, but the pistol wasn't there, either."

"Did you ask Judge Carlton if he knew the whereabouts of the pistol?"

Rockford folded his hands in front of him. "Yes. Shortly after the trial ended, my chief sent him a letter. Because he's a federal judge we thought it was appropriate that the chief communicate with him directly."

Tunney nodded. "What was Judge Carlton's response?"

"The chief said the judge told him he never saw the gun."

"One last question. Are you aware that this 'missing' semi-auto Beretta was seized from Judge Carlton on October twenty-first, 2004?"

Carlton rose from his chair. "Objection! This witness has no personal knowledge of who had possession of the pistol."

"Sustained," Judge Peterson said.

"No further questions." Tunney returned to the prosecution table.

"The witness is yours Judge Carlton," Judge Peterson said.

Carlton stepped to the podium. He flipped through the pages of a yellow legal pad, laid it down, and folded his arms across his chest. *I won't give him the dignity of using his name.* "Agent, how long have you been employed by the ATF?"

"Eight years, sir."

"You sound like a Southern boy. Where was your initial assignment?"

Jeffreys rose from his chair at the prosecution table. "Your honor, these questions regarding Agent Rockford's background have been asked and answered."

Judge Peterson nodded. "Judge Carlton, please try not to duplicate the prosecutor's direct examination. And I remind you that this is a bench trial."

"Yes, your honor." Carlton took a step toward the judge, then turned and pointed at Jeffreys and Tunney. "But I assure you, I intend to bring out this agent's background in a slightly different light than the prosecution."

Judge Peterson looked at the witness. "You may answer the question."

Rockford glanced past Carlton and caught Tunney's eye. *Checking in,* Carlton thought. *Wants to know if it's okay to do as he was just damn well told.*

The disrespect irritated him. He returned to the podium, picked up his legal pad, and slammed it down. "You heard Judge Peterson. Answer the question. It's not a hard one."

Jeffreys rose again. "Your honor, Mr. Carlton just started his cross and already he's badgering the witness."

Judge Peterson cleared his throat. "I will not have this trial become a battle of egos between the defense and the prosecution—"

Carlton put his hands on his hips. "Your honor, you ruled before this trial started that I'm to be referred to as Judge Carlton throughout. The prosecution just violated that."

Judge Peterson held up his hands, palms out. His horn-rimmed glasses slid down his nose, and he pushed them up. "Judge Carlton, I realize you are in a difficult position and I'm willing to give you some leeway in defending yourself. However, you of all people know you must respect the court and reflect the appropriate demeanor in presenting your defense."

Carlton took a step back. "I apologize to you and the court if I have in any way disrespected this institution that I owe so much to. But everything that has ever meant anything to me is at stake. I'm defending myself against a case that was developed by my wife and then taken over by the FBI with trumped-up charges that could destroy everything I have worked for—my marriage, my relationship with my children, my career, and not least, my reputation."

Tunney stood this time. "Your honor, he had the opportunity to make an opening argument and chose not to. Unless this is it, Judge Carlton?"

"Gentlemen, let's stop this bickering," Peterson rumbled. He nodded at Carlton. "Resume your cross-examination."

Carlton returned to the podium and fixed his gaze on Agent Rockford. "Let's talk about the trial that was in front of me in June of last year. You referred to the defendants in that case as 'a group of Black gangbangers from the West Side.' What were the ages of these *Black* miscreants?"

Rockford's lips thinned at the emphasis. "A couple of them were eighteen, the rest were in their mid-twenties, a few in their thirties."

"Remind us of the charges again?"

"There were several, including narcotics distribution and weapon charges."

"How many guns were seized?"

"Approximately thirty weapons, several pistols, AK-47s, and a few sawed-off shotguns."

"And I believe you told us all eleven defendants were found guilty on all counts. So, would you say that was a successful prosecution?'

Rockford held his chin high and shoulders back. "Yes sir, I would."

"Did the defendants file any appeals?"

"Not that I'm aware of."

"These *Black* gangbangers as you called them." Carlton glanced at Judge Peterson. "In what section of the city did they sell their drugs and guns?"

"In Lawndale. Like I said before."

"A high crime area, wouldn't you say?"

"Yes, lots of shooting, drive-bys. You name it."

His next question might prompt an objection, but he risked it. "Would you ever consider going to Lawndale unarmed?" He glanced at Jeffreys, who remained silent.

"Are you kidding?" Rockford shook his head. "Never!"

"Let's move on to the missing Beretta. What happened to it?"

Rockford flicked a hand. "Nobody knows. It was either lost or stolen."

"Or it could have fallen out of the evidence cart and lain under the prosecutors' table."

"We checked the courtroom and it wasn't there. But like I said, that was a couple of days after the trial."

"So maybe it was misplaced in your evidence locker. You said you searched, but how do you know if someone found it on the floor of your evidence room, didn't know what case it belonged to, and stashed it in the wrong box? After all, the case against the Black gangbangers was successfully prosecuted, so you would never need the Beretta again."

"No, I'm pretty sure that's not what happened. We went through all the boxes and couldn't find it anywhere."

"How many boxes of evidence are stored in the secured lockers?"

"Just those for current investigations and ongoing trials."

"How many evidence boxes would that be?"

"Well over a hundred. After a trial ends, the seized weapons are destroyed and the boxes are sent to storage."

Jeffreys stood. "Your honor, I object. We know where the Beretta ended up. It was in Judge Carlton's possession when he was arrested."

"Judge, I may have had the weapon in my possession, but the prosecutor has no idea how it got there or why. I have a right to develop that point."

Judge Peterson exhaled. "Objection overruled. You may continue."

Carlton smirked at Jeffreys. "So, there's hundreds of cases being investigated or on trial, and I guess that means several hundred evidence boxes that you looked through. Did you personally check all those boxes?"

"No."

"I see. Who did check all those hundreds of boxes?"

"The agent who assisted the prosecutors during the trial."

"Who was that?"

"Agent Maurice Spencer."

Carlton held his hands out, a look of disbelief on his face. "He's the only one that went through all those hundreds of boxes?"

Rockford shrugged. "Probably had some clerks assist him."

"Let me ask you this. Is Agent Spencer still with the ATF?"

Rockford glanced at Jeffreys and swallowed. He moistened his lips as he returned his gaze to Carlton.

Carlton tapped his fingers on the podium. "Are you going to answer the question?"

Rockford looked to Jeffreys again, then pursed his lips. "Agent Spencer was fired."

Carlton moved squarely in front of the witness stand. "Fired? Why was he fired?"

Again, Rockford looked to the prosecutors' table, but no help was coming.

"I'll repeat the question in case you didn't understand it," Carlton said. "Why was he fired?"

"He had a relationship with a defendant's wife."

"What?" Carlton slammed his fist on the podium, then jerked his head toward Jeffreys. "This is a blatant violation of discovery. I never received any documents indicating Spencer was terminated, let alone for what cause."

Judge Peterson gave Jeffreys a hard look. "What's the story here?"

Jeffreys stood. A pink flush had crept into his cheeks. "Your honor, Spencer's termination had nothing to do with this case or the missing pistol. In fact, it was after the trial in Judge Carlton's courtroom that Spencer's relationship with this woman occurred."

Judge Peterson pointed a finger at him. "I don't care when it occurred, I want a copy of this agent's personnel file delivered to Judge Carlton today. Am I understood?"

"Yes, your honor. We'll have Agent Rockford personally deliver it to Judge Carlton. But the only address we have for him is a mail drop. We don't know where he's residing."

"Do you care to give the prosecutor your address?"

Carlton shook his head. "No, your honor. The mail drop will be fine."

"You may continue with your cross-examination." Judge Peterson exhaled a sigh of disbelief and leaned back in his chair.

"One last question, Agent. You don't know how many hands that Beretta passed through before it got into my possession nearly five months later? It could have been any number of people, isn't that correct?"

"Yes, sir."

"No further questions." Carlton picked up his legal tablet and returned to the defense table.

Judge Peterson looked at the prosecutors. "Any redirect?"

Tunney got up and returned to the podium. "Just one question, your honor. Agent Rockford, from your knowledge of this case, who had possession of this pistol in the early hours of October twenty-first, 2004?"

Carlton's eyes blazed. He shot to his feet. "I object. Tunney's trying to sneak this in again!"

"Objection sustained." Judge Peterson's brow furrowed. Tunney sat down. Peterson gestured toward Carlton. "Any recross for this witness?"

Carlton remained standing by the defense table. "You have no personal knowledge that the Beretta was ever in my possession, do you, Agent?"

"No, sir."

"No further questions." Carlton sat back down, with a nod at the prosecutors. *I beat their asses on this one.*

"Agent Rockford, you may stand down," Peterson said.

Rockford stepped down from the witness stand, looking relieved that his part was over. He barreled down the aisle past the gallery and out of the courtroom.

Peterson looked at Jeffreys. "You may call your next witness."

Jeffreys rose. "The government calls Gloria Nighthawk."

CHAPTER 37

Courtroom 2502
Dirksen Federal Building
Thursday, January 13, 2005
3:00 p.m.

A CLAMOR AROSE FROM THE gallery. Many there wanted to lay eyes on this woman, the wife of the defendant, who would lay out the government's case against her own husband. They'd come for that, and to watch her husband cross-examine her.

Carlton swiftly rose to his feet. "Your honor, I object to any testimony from this witness, based on my previously submitted motion that her testimony would violate marital privilege."

"So noted. My earlier ruling stands: Agent Nighthawk's testimony will be limited to subjects that do not violate your privilege. If her testimony crosses that line, you may object." Peterson stared down at the prosecutor. "Be careful, Mr. Jeffreys. I won't hesitate to rule a mistrial if you step wrong."

Carlton sat down, a smug smile on his face.

Gloria approached the witness stand. She had dressed conservatively in a black suit, matching pumps, and a white blouse. She was aware that she looked like she was attending a funeral and felt like it was for her marriage. *I've testified at least fifty times over the years. This is just one more. Stay calm.* She took the stand and was sworn in.

Jeffreys stood at the podium, flipping through his notes. "For the record, you're the wife of the defendant, Judge Carlton?"

Gloria's eyes shifted to Robert. She knew she was fooling herself if she thought this would be like the other times she had testified. This was going to get very personal. She wondered what had happened to their marriage. In the beginning, their love seemed so strong and she felt so safe. When had it shifted to this malaise? How long had his secrets undermined their relationship? How many were there that she didn't even know? And what about her secrets? Now their relationship had been reduced to fire, and the flames were about to have gas thrown on them. She went to her old nervous habit, twisting the wedding band on her finger, but it wasn't there. "Yes, sir. He's my husband."

"Now I want to get into how this investigation of Judge Carlton started. You initially contacted a witness by the name of Tamika Carlton."

"Yes."

"What was the reason for contacting her?"

"She was the girlfriend of Spencer McElroy. He was alleged to be affiliated with a gang involved in mortgage fraud, based on a tip from an informant."

"Was this informant reliable?"

"Yes. I have received credible information from him on numerous occasions for a period of approximately five years."

"How was this interview set up?"

"On October eighth of last year, we surveilled McElroy away from his residence at 400 E. Randolph, and once we ascertained that he would be away for a period of time, we returned to the residence to interview Miss Carlton."

"Did you know at the time that she was Judge Carlton's daughter?"

"No, I didn't."

"When and how did you meet her that day?"

"I gained access to a parking garage on the lower level of their residence, and she walked up to me as I was checking a Porsche 911 that was registered in the name of a woman who turned out to be her deceased mother."

"Did you interview Miss Carlton in the garage?"

"No. We went up to their condo on the twenty-eighth floor and conducted the interview in the living room."

"Were you accompanied by another agent?"

"Yes." Gloria nodded at Lauren, seated with the prosecutors. "Agent Ashberry."

"What was the name of Miss Carlton's deceased mother?"

"Shiquita Dubonnet."

"Did you have any knowledge of Shiquita Dubonnet prior to the interview?"

"Based on leads we received from the informant, we knew that several vehicles and a six-flat had been purchased under the name Shiquita Dubonnet, which we corroborated through vehicle titles and Cook County real estate records. But we had no prior knowledge regarding Ms. Dubonnet's relationship to Tamika Carlton, or my husband. Based on what we did know, it appeared there might be a money laundering conspiracy."

Jeffreys glanced at the judge. "Your honor, may I approach the witness?"

Judge Peterson waved his arm. "Go ahead."

Jeffreys briefly stepped back toward the table, picked up the deal jacket for the Porsche from Lauren, and handed it to Gloria. "This is the file you obtained from the dealership. Can you read off the date when Ms. Dubonnet allegedly purchased the Porsche?"

Gloria paged through the file. "The bill of sale reflects that she purchased the vehicle on July fourteenth, 2002."

He took the file back and handed her a certified copy of Shiquita Dubonnet's death certificate. "What date is reflected as the day she passed?"

"April seventh, 1997."

"So, Miss Dubonnet allegedly purchased the Porsche almost five years after she died?"

"Obviously, she didn't. They used Tamika's mother as a nominee to conceal the true ownership of the car, and the purchase. According to the deal jacket, the purchase price of $50,000 was paid in full with cash. A copy of a driver's license in the deal jacket had Shiquita Dubonnet's name on it, but the photo was Tamika Carlton."

"Were other vehicles purchased using Ms. Dubonnet's name?"

"Yes. There were two Bentleys, one of which was traded on the later purchase, a Ford van, and a Chevy Impala, plus the Porsche."

"And these vehicles were all purchased after the date of Ms. Dubonnet's death?"

"Yes."

Carlton stood. "Your honor, to save the court's time I'll stipulate to these transactions and we can get on with the case. The transactions have nothing to do with me and I want this trial to be over as soon as possible so I can get back to my life as I once knew it."

Jeffreys nodded. "Your honor, Miss Dubonnet's name was also used to purchase a six-flat on the South Side—"

"I'll stipulate to that too," Carlton said, shaking his head. He returned to his seat and shoved the tablet he had been taking notes on across the table.

Jeffreys grabbed the files documenting the additional purchases from the trial cart and handed them to Lauren Ashberry, then returned his attention to Gloria. "Okay, now at some point during your interview of Tamika Carlton, she left the living room and returned with some records. What were those?"

"When she returned, she had numerous money orders that she handed to me. They were all payable to Tamika Carlton in the amount of $500 and dated the beginning of each month. The first few money orders didn't list a remitter, but then I saw several of them with my husband's name listed. It was his signature. I know it well."

"Did you have any previous knowledge that Judge Carlton was purchasing money orders payable to Tamika Carlton?"

Gloria shook her head, with a harsh glance at Robert. "No. No, I had no idea."

"Did Miss Carlton explain why he was sending her the money orders?"

"She didn't identify him as her father at first. She said he was her mother's attorney and had advised Shiquita Dubonnet to take a guilty plea on a federal charge, which resulted in her getting a one-year sentence. As a result, Tamika was born in a federal penitentiary. When Ms. Dubonnet was released, she tried to renew her relationship with Robert but he refused to do so. She subsequently committed suicide. Tamika blamed Robert for her mother's death."

"What was the purpose of the checks?"

Gloria's stomach knotted. "Tamika gave birth to a baby girl, and Robert was trying to gain favor with Tamika so she would let him see his granddaughter."

"Why do you think Judge Carlton refused to at least recognize his relationship with Shiquita Dubonnet?"

Gloria paused. *That sneaky unfaithful S.O.B.* "Because he was married to me."

A murmur went through the gallery.

Jeffreys paused, letting the reaction to Gloria's response fill the courtroom. "This interview with Tamika Carlton took place what day of the week?"

"A Friday."

"After you finished the interview, did you have any contact with your husband, Judge Carlton?"

"I wasn't sure what to do. I needed time to think things over. I was shocked that he had kept his relationship with Shiquita

Dubonnet hidden from me, along with the fact that he had fathered a daughter so many years ago."

"I can understand that."

Carlton stood. "I object to the prosecutor's remark regarding his opinion about my wife's personal feelings toward me."

"I apologize and I withdraw the remark," Jeffreys said, turning away from Carlton to hide the smirk on his face.

Judge Peterson gave him a stern look. "Let's avoid any questions regarding the witness's feelings toward Judge Carlton."

"Yes, your honor." Jeffreys continued with his direct examination. "Did you have any contact with Judge Carlton after interviewing Tamika Carlton on October eighth?"

"I tried calling him a couple of times that weekend and left messages. He didn't return my calls, and he didn't come home the entire weekend; I didn't know where he was."

"What did you do next?"

"When I arrived in the office on Monday, the first thing I did was meet with Agent Ashberry and our supervisor, Tom Stephens, to advise him about our interview of Miss Carlton and the nature of her testimony against my husband."

"As a result of that meeting, what actions were taken?"

"Stephens called our chief to inform him that Tamika had implicated my husband in a potential money laundering conspiracy. Because of my husband's position as a federal judge, the chief called your office."

"What happened after that?"

"I subsequently received an assignment in Iraq to trace Saddam Hussein's assets. It was my second assignment there. I had an earlier assignment from June through September of last year."

"While you were in Iraq did anything happen on your husband's case?"

"Yes, you explained to me that it was not appropriate for your office to be in possession of allegations against a sitting federal judge knowing that he would be hearing evidence in any ongoing trial. Therefore, it was necessary to move on his case. On October fifteenth, 2004, you and the FBI executed a search warrant on our residence and arrested my husband."

"Had you had any contact with him between the interview of Tamika Carlton and that day?"

"No. I was in Iraq when he was arrested. I immediately made arrangements to come back home because I was concerned about my children. I arrived in Chicago on Sunday, October seventeenth."

"When is the next time you saw your husband?"

Gloria shook her head. "About 4:00 a.m. on Saturday, October twenty-third."

Jeffreys leaned forward, resting his elbows on the podium. "What were the circumstances surrounding this encounter?"

She drew in a breath. "Your office sent a package containing the discovery for my husband's case to our home. My daughter had received the package and opened it. When I arrived home later, the documents were spread across the kitchen island. I went through them and found an FBI report documenting a statement from an informant that Spencer McElroy regularly collected cash from his drug operation at Hainey's Bar on the West Side at approximately 4:00 a.m."

"Go on."

"I couldn't sleep. I just felt something bad was going to happen. I called Agent Ashberry and we talked, but I couldn't shake the feeling. About 3:00 a.m., I got up and drove out to the West Side."

"To Hainey's Bar?"

"Yes."

"What did you observe when you got there?"

She laced her fingers together. Her palms were sweating. "I saw McElroy arrive in a car that wasn't one of the vehicles we previously discussed. He entered the bar and a few minutes later he left, carrying a paper bag. As he crossed the street and approached his vehicle, I saw another individual moving up the sidewalk on the opposite side of McElroy's car. That individual pulled out a pistol and pointed it at McElroy but didn't fire. McElroy pulled out his own pistol and fired numerous shots in the direction of the individual. I pulled out my service pistol and shot McElroy twice, stopping him from being a threat to me or anyone else."

Jeffreys nodded slowly. The courtroom had gone dead quiet. "What did you do next?"

"I went to the unidentified individual. He was stooped down behind the fender of McElroy's car. He was wearing a black hoodie pulled over his head. I saw a pistol in his hand, so I pointed my service weapon at him and ordered him to drop the gun, which he did. He stood up and lowered the hood, and I recognized my husband. We did not have a pistol in our home, aside from my service-issued Sig Sauer, so I arrested him for illegal possession of a firearm."

"Did McElroy survive?"

"No. Unfortunately, my shots killed him."

"No further questions, your honor." Jeffreys returned to his seat. Gloria braced herself.

Judge Peterson looked at his watch. "Gentlemen, it's 4:30 and I suspect that Judge Carlton's cross-examination of Ms. Nighthawk will take a while. I suggest we start with it first thing tomorrow morning. Is that agreeable to both of you?"

Jeffreys nodded. "Yes, your honor."

Carlton stood, his eyes narrowed to mean slits. "Yes, sir. That will give me even more time to prepare."

Gloria felt Judge Peterson's gaze on her. "Ms. Nighthawk, you may step down, but I want to remind you that your testimony is not completed, so it would be inappropriate for you to confer with the prosecution or the defense until you're finished."

"I understand, Judge." Gloria stepped down from the witness stand. As she neared the defense table, her husband looked down and rested a hand against his forehead as if he were studying his notes.

Gloria paused briefly, but he didn't say a word or look up. Not even to ask where Darius was.

What a coward, she thought. *Will he try to get Darius on the stand?* She thought of her son in the ER, what he'd done to himself that put him there, and why. *Damn well not, if he knows what's good for him.*

CHAPTER 38

Courtroom 2502
Dirksen Federal Building
Friday, January 14, 2005
9:30 a.m.

GLORIA STOOD BEHIND THE PROSECUTION table, waiting to return to the witness stand. She could feel her husband's eyes drilling into her and she clenched her fists but refused to look in his direction.

Judge Peterson entered the courtroom. Gloria glanced over her shoulder and saw the gallery was full. *Everyone's here to see the S.O.B. cross-examine me.*

The judge directed his attention to the attorneys. "Are there any matters that need to be handled before we call Ms. Nighthawk to the stand?"

Jeffreys stood. "No, your honor."

Carlton swiveled in his chair and snapped his legal pad down on the table. "No, your honor. I'm definitely ready!"

Judge Peterson's gaze turned to Gloria. "Ms. Nighthawk, you may take the witness stand."

She moved forward and climbed the short steps to the hot seat. "I'll remind you that you're still under oath," Peterson said as she sat down.

Gloria nodded. "Yes, Judge." Her heart was pounding and her face was surely a map of tension, anticipating her husband's questions about Darius.

Peterson nodded at Carlton. "You may start your cross-examination."

Carlton approached the podium and smirked. "Hello, dear."

Gloria thought, *You ass.*

Jeffreys stood, fast. "Your honor?"

Judge Peterson glowered at Carlton. "Let's keep this professional as much as possible."

Carlton nodded. "All right. Agent Nighthawk, let's talk first about those $500 money orders I gave to my daughter, Tamika. During the course of your investigation, were you able to make any connection between them and any other financial transactions conducted by Spencer McElroy and/or Tamika Carlton, and me?"

"No, I was not," Gloria said.

Carlton extended his hands outward. "There was no connection to any money laundering scheme?"

Gloria leaned forward, locking eyes with her husband. "I can't say if there was or if there wasn't, only that we weren't able to prove it."

His jaw tightened for half a second, and she felt a brief sense of satisfaction. "Did you find any connection to the various cars McElroy purchased? The Porsche, the Bentleys, and the other vehicles you mentioned yesterday."

All right, if you want to play this game, I'll give you what we've got. "Only that Tamika Carlton initially said *you* were the one who advised her and McElroy to use her mother's name to purchase the cars and the six-flat."

"But she subsequently recanted her testimony. Isn't that correct?"

She didn't want to answer that, but she had no choice. "Yes."

"So, initially she was lying, making a false statement to you, a federal agent."

Gloria sat silent in the witness chair.

"Well, do you have an opinion about that?"

Gloria folded her arms across her chest. "I didn't respond to your previous statement because you didn't ask me a question."

"I just did. Do you have an opinion about Tamika recanting her initial statement to you and your notetaker?" Carlton said, pointing to Lauren. "And even though Tamika violated Title 18, Section 1001 by lying to you, the U.S. Attorney's office is not going to prosecute her?"

"I don't know. That's up to the U.S. Attorney's office."

Carlton rested his hands on his hips. "Apparently the only purpose for my purchasing those money orders was a failed attempt to convince Tamika to let me see my granddaughter."

"I don't have any personal knowledge of that." Gloria shook her head. "You never, not once during our entire marriage, mentioned to me Tamika's mother, Tamika, your granddaughter, or the money orders."

The gallery's murmur filled the courtroom.

Judge Peterson slammed his gavel on the sounding block. "Order in the court. We'll have none of this."

"Let me repeat that," Carlton said. "You have no personal or professional knowledge regarding these money orders other than my failed attempt to build a relationship with my granddaughter?"

"No," Gloria said through clenched teeth.

"Thank you. I didn't think I was going to get that out of you."

Jeffreys stood. "Objection, your honor. It's inappropriate for the defense to comment on the nature of a witness's testimony."

"Sustained. Judge Carlton's remark will be stricken from the record."

Carlton took a step closer to the witness stand. "Let's move on to the Friday night before you killed Spencer McElroy. You mentioned that you read an FBI memo documenting an informant's statement that McElroy went to this bar called Hainey's to pick up cash from his drug operation."

Gloria scrunched back in her chair, her stomach roiling. *Don't bring up Darius. Don't.* "Yes, it was an FBI 302 report."

"Why was this report delivered to you?"

"I answered that question yesterday."

"Answer it again."

She reached for the absent wedding ring, pinched her finger where it should have been. "The U.S. Attorney's office mailed the discovery on your case to our home address by mistake. They subsequently had a duplicate copy delivered to a mail drop you were using."

"So, you illegally opened mail addressed to me?"

"No. Our daughter, Adsila, opened it. She went through the pages, and left them scattered across the kitchen island. That's where they were when I got home later and realized what had happened."

Carlton turned to the judge. "Your honor, this constitutes an illegal search. Certainly, I have a reasonable expectation of privacy that mail addressed to me is not to be read by law enforcement. My wife is a federal agent, and she is the one responsible for the initiation of this witch hunt."

Jeffreys rose from his chair. "Judge, first of all, this package was delivered intact to the only address my secretary had at the time. As soon as we discovered that Judge Carlton wanted his mail sent to a mail drop, we arranged a separate delivery so he would have it same day if he chose to pick it up. Secondly, it was his daughter who received the package and opened it, not Agent Nighthawk. So, these documents were left in plain view. The transmittal letter we sent with the second package to the mail drop indicated that the same materials were initially sent to his home. As far as we know, Judge Carlton made no attempt to secure the initial package. Finally, Agent Nighthawk is a member of the investigative team and would've had access to this information, including the FBI 302 report, regardless."

Judge Peterson nodded. "It seems like the government's efforts to comply with its discovery responsibilities were not the problem here. They arranged for delivery to each address they had for you, Judge Carlton. If you weren't there to retrieve the documents, it's not the government's fault, and if those documents were opened by an innocent third party, I don't believe you would have a reasonable expectation of privacy. Those documents are admissible. You may continue."

Gloria saw Carlton glance at his watch and then look around the courtroom. She guessed he was looking for Darius. But Darius was in rehab and couldn't leave. Carlton bit his lip, then paged through his notes for several seconds. Gloria knew he was trying to buy time, hoping his son would arrive. He *would* have put Darius on the stand if he could. He looked at her, and for a moment she felt dizzy with anger. "So why on earth would you get up in the wee hours of the morning and drive to one of the most dangerous parts of the city?"

She knew she was taking too long to answer. She thought, *what would be a good reason?* but couldn't find one. When she finally spoke, her voice wavered. "It was a gut reaction, instinct. Something just told me to get out there."

"Do you often call on your instincts?"

"When it happens, it hap—" Gloria froze, staring over Carlton's shoulder. Darius was outside the courtroom doors, peering through the glass. *What is he doing here?*

She saw Carlton glance at the doors. He looked back at her and smiled. "No further questions for *this* witness, your honor."

Judge Peterson looked at Jeffreys. "Any redirect?"

"No, Judge."

Peterson swiveled his chair toward Gloria. "Miss Nighthawk, you may stand down."

Gloria stumbled away from the witness box and rushed out of the courtroom.

Jeffrey stood behind the prosecution table and announced, "The government rests."

CHAPTER 39

Courtroom 2502
Dirksen Federal Building
Friday, January 14, 2005
10:00 a.m.

GLORIA SHOVED THE COURTROOM DOOR open and rushed to Darius. She studied his face, then wrapped her arms around him and squeezed with every ounce of her strength. "Honey, why are you here? You can't leave rehab. They won't let you back in." Her eyes flooded with tears.

She stepped back and looked at him. He wore an old gray hoodie and matching sweatpants that looked slept-in, and his old Air Jordans. She knew he had sneaked out of rehab.

Darius frowned as he pulled a rumpled Kleenex from the pocket of his hoodie and wiped his nose. "Mom, I promised Dad I'd be here on Friday to testify."

Gloria put one hand on the back of his neck and pulled him down to eye level. She felt the sweat on his neck while she gazed into his eyes. His pupils were the size of pinpoints. She knew he had been using. She pulled his head down to her mouth and whispered, "Daruis, are you okay?"

He trembled and spoke softly. "I'm ready, Mom. I'll do my best, do what I can."

"Think about your future. You must be very careful what you say. You can't admit to being there the night I shot McElroy. You have to protect yourself. I wish you hadn't come but you're here and he saw you. I only have a few moments to talk to you. So here it is. Your father's a desperate man. He's not the man we once knew. He'll put himself first and you'll be in the back of his mind, if at all—"

The courtroom doors burst open and Carlton rushed to step between Gloria and Darius. "My son. I knew I could rely on you." He snaked his left arm around Darius's shoulders and herded him into the courtroom.

⸺

"Sit here." Carlton pointed at the chair next to his at the defense table. "We only have a few minutes before the judge will tell me to start my defense. You're it, Darius. I'll run you though the trial of the gangbangers. The one where you found the pistol and we'll go from there. Follow my lead. You'll know where I'm going by my questions. I'm counting on you. Okay, you got it?"

Darius nodded and wiped the sleeve of his hoodie under his nose.

Judge Peterson returned from his chambers.

"Court is now in session," the court security officer announced.

"Judge Carlton, are you ready to commence your defense?"

"Yes, your honor." Carlton stood, his chin held high and shoulders back, buoyed by the knowledge that his son would save him. "I call Darius Carlton to the stand."

Darius lumbered to the stand and was sworn in.

"Are you all right, young man?" Judge Peterson asked.

Darius straightened up in the witness chair, held his hand to his mouth, and cleared his throat. "Yes, Judge."

Judge Peterson let out a sigh. "If your witness is ready, you may proceed."

Carlton skimmed his fingertips along his jawline and smiled at Darius. "Good morning. Can you advise the court of the nature of our relationship?"

"I'm your son," Darius sniffled.

"On a regular basis, have you attended trials that I have been involved in as a prosecuting attorney, defense attorney, and judge?"

"Yes. I'd like to become a lawyer."

"Good, son. I'm sure you'll be a very good one. In the summer of 2004, did you attend a trial that was heard in my courtroom involving a drug and guns case against a West Side gang?"

Darius blinked. "Yes."

Carlton glanced down at a paper on the table, a copy of the indictment from the gang case. "Included among various charges were the illegal possession of some thirty-odd weapons?"

"I don't recall the number of guns. If you say so, that must be right."

"Darius, the number of weapons I just read was from the indictment of that case."

"That must be right, I guess."

"And after the government and the defense rested, did you come to my chambers to discuss the case?"

Darius nodded. "Yes, I did."

"And after our discussion, did you return to the courtroom?"

Perspiration beaded down Darius's face. He wiped his brow with the sleeve of his sweatshirt. "Yes."

"When you walked through the courtroom, did you find anything?"

Darius sat, nonresponsive.

"Let me be more specific. Did you find something under the prosecution's table?"

Darius wiped his hand across his lips.

"Son, I asked you. Did you find something under the prosecution's table?"

Darius slumped in the witness chair.

Don't break on me now. Carlton stepped toward him. "I realize you're only seventeen and this is difficult for you. You're under a lot of pressure. Just answer the question honestly."

"Don't approach the witness unless I instruct you that you may," Judge Peterson said.

"Sorry, your honor. He's my son and it's difficult to see him struggle like—"

"Dad, when will things go back to normal?" Daruis pleaded.

Carlton swallowed. He hadn't expected that. "They may never return to normal. With time, I hope we can all heal. Let's get back to the trial from last June that I was asking you about. The one involving the weapons charges."

Darius nodded.

"Son, you know you have to verbally answer."

"Yes, sir. The trial last June. I was there." Darius sat erect suddenly, as if he'd come out of his stupor. *Good.*

"And after our discussion in my chambers, you returned to the courtroom?"

"Yes, sir. I did."

"And what did you find there?"

A tear ran down Darius's face.

Carlton placed his hands on his hips. "I know this is difficult for you, son. What did you find?"

Darius rubbed more tears from his eyes.

Carlton's nostrils flared and he waved his arms in front of him. "Come on, boy. Did you find a pistol under the table?"

Jeffreys stood. "Your honor, the government objects. The defense is leading the witness. Because it's the defendant's son, I've let it go until now, but I've reached my limit."

Carlton pointed at Jeffreys. "This is my witness. I'll ask whatever question I want, when I want."

"We object again, your honor, leading the witness."

Peterson nodded. "Judge Carlton, I realize this is a very difficult situation. I'm willing to give you some leeway, but you need to resolve this one way or the other."

"Then I'll make a motion to treat him as a hostile witness," Carlton said.

Judge Peterson flinched. "This is your son, Judge Carlton. Are you sure you want to do that?"

"He's leaving me no choice." Carlton threw Darius a sharp look. "He knows what he has to say."

Judge Peterson sighed. "Son, I don't want to have to rule that you're a hostile witness regarding your father's defense. Please answer his question."

Carlton glared at Darius as his son's gaze turned from the judge to him. "You heard Judge Peterson. He ordered you to answer."

Darius looked down.

"I'll repeat the question. Did you find a pistol under the prosecution table?"

Darius brought a trembling hand to his forehead. "What kind of man do you want me to be?"

Carlton snapped, "Judge, I demand you rule my son a hostile witness."

"Your son doesn't look well. Maybe we should recess and he can return to the stand after lunch."

"He's fully capable of continuing." Carlton jerked his head toward the prosecution table. "Rule him a hostile witness so I can ask him leading questions without the damn government objecting."

"Judge Carlton, I caution you to settle down before you find yourself in contempt." Judge Peterson clasped his hands under his chin and turned to Darius. "Son, do you know what it means if I rule as your father has asked me to?"

Darius nodded. "Yes."

Judge Peterson stared at Carlton, then looked at the prosecutors. "Any objections from the government?"

"No, your honor," Jeffreys said.

Judge Peterson sighed heavily. "You may treat your son as a hostile witness. Go ahead, Judge Carlton."

Gloria's voice carried across the courtroom. "I don't believe this."

Carlton turned briefly to stare at her. Then he smiled and returned his focus to Darius. "Referring to the trial in June 2004, did you find a Beretta semi-auto pistol under the prosecution table?"

Darius lowered his head again, gazing at the floor. Then he slowly looked up. "No, I didn't find any pistol."

Carlton pounded the podium. "Your Honor, this witness is lying. Instruct him of the penalties under perjury and advise him that he must tell the truth."

Judge Peterson leaned toward Darius. "I realize this is a difficult place for you to be in. You need to tell the truth, son."

"The truth? What is the truth? I used to be proud of myself. I got good grades and I was looking forward to a basketball scholarship." Darius pointed at his father. "I wanted to follow in his footsteps and go to law school."

"You can still do that, son. You can do that." Carlton waved a hand at Darius. "You can be like me!"

"Like you? What a joke. Now…now I'm a fucking junkie." Darius took a deep breath. "*He* wanted me to kill that dope dealer…McElroy. That's the truth!" He lowered his head again and started sobbing.

Shocked murmurs erupted from the spectators in the rear of the courtroom. Carlton's hands trembled as he raised his voice over the clamor. "He's a junkie. He admits it. You can't trust a junkie. They'll say anything. That's what the government wants him to say."

Jeffreys jumped from his seat. "Your honor, my office has had no contact with this witness."

"This is what you did to me…to Adsila, and to Mom," Darius blurted out. "How can you live with yourself?"

Peterson pounded his gavel and called for order. As the spectators subsided, Carlton returned to the defense table and collapsed in his chair. "Judge, you've got to rule this a mistrial! The witness is lying."

Peterson frowned. "That's no grounds for a mistrial."

Jeffreys rose from the prosecution table. "Your honor, if the defense has no other witnesses, I have a motion."

Judge Peterson looked at Carlton. "Do you have any other witnesses?"

Carlton shook his head. "No, not a damn witness worth anything."

"Then let's give both sides the weekend to prepare closing arguments. Since Monday is Martin Luther King Day, we'll start Tuesday, January eighteenth at 10:00 sharp."

Jeffreys cleared his throat. "Your honor, as the case currently stands, the government feels the likelihood of conviction is highly probable. Because the defendant is facing a potential sentence of ten years for attempting to kill or harm a witness, in violation of Title 18, section 1512, we deem him a flight risk and a threat to society. Therefore, we feel Judge Carlton should be remanded to the custody of the Federal Correction Center until Tuesday, and subsequently — if your verdict is guilty — until sentencing."

Judge Peterson slowly nodded. "So ordered. Marshals, place the defendant in custody and take him to the lockup."

As the marshals approached her husband, Gloria hurried to the gates separating the audience area from the rest of the courtroom. She met Darius there and they watched as the handcuffs were slapped on Judge Carlton's wrists. His shoulders slumped and he bowed his head as he was led into the holding cell. The door slammed behind him.

Gloria grabbed Darius's hand and pulled him into the hallway. "I'm so proud of you, that you had the strength to tell the truth. I know you're hurting now. But in the end, you'll be a better man because you fought your way through this. I love you, and I'll be with you and help you any way I can. Let's go home."

Darius didn't move. "Mom, I'm scared. Scared what's going to happen to me."

"What do you mean, honey?"
"I don't know." He squeezed her hand. She squeezed back. They headed down the corridor toward the exit. Both of them were uncertain what the future would hold.

CHAPTER 40

Carlton/Nighthawk Residence, Bronzeville
Friday, January 14, 2005
1:30 p.m.

DARIUS FOLLOWED GLORIA AS THEY walked to the parking garage south of the Dirksen Federal Courthouse. On the way they passed the twenty-eight-story triangular shaped Metropolitan Correctional Center on Van Buren and Clark.

Darius pointed at the building. "Is that where Dad will be?"

"Yes," Gloria answered.

"Do you think he's in there already?"

"No, it'll be several hours before he's transported. They have a bus that takes all the prisoners from the marshals to MCC."

"Will they feed him?"

Gloria thought, *I hope it's baloney sandwiches,* but said, "They actually have decent food."

"What happens Tuesday?"

"The government gives their closing argument first, then your father gives his, and the government will give a rebuttal to whatever case your father makes in his defense."

Darius swallowed. "Does he have a defense?"

"He didn't present one, but he doesn't have to. So, he'll probably argue that the government didn't prove their case beyond a reasonable doubt."

Darius stopped and bent over, hands on his knees, and dry heaved. "I was his defense and I screwed it up."

"No, your father screwed it up." Struggling to keep calm, she laid her hand on Darius's shoulder. "Honey, are you okay?"

Darius stood, nodding. "Yeah, I'm all right, just a nervous stomach."

"You told the truth. You did the right thing. Your father never should have asked you to lie for him. It would have ruined your life." She bit back the rest of it—*I could kill him for what he's done to you*—and guided him toward the garage. "Let's go home."

"Can I visit him?" Darius asked.

"I don't think that's a good idea. He's got to work on his closing argument. He'll probably spend the entire weekend doing that." *Given the circumstances, he might not be that happy to see you.*

Darius shook his head. "The prosecutor said he could get ten years. I'll be almost thirty when he gets out. Will I be able to visit him at all? Do you think he'd let me? It would've been better to lie. Should I tell the judge I lied on the stand?"

He sounded so young, his voice so raw it made her hurt inside. "No, you can't do that. You'd be implicating yourself and committing perjury. I know you feel you let your father down. But you didn't. It wasn't your fault. He put himself in this predicament."

Gloria badged the guard at the garage entrance, and they climbed the stairs to the second floor and headed to the Blazer. "Is it okay if I lay down in the back seat, Mom?" Darius asked. "I didn't sleep too much the last couple of nights. A lot of people were going through withdrawal at the rehab center, moaning and groaning, and with Dad on my mind…" He shook his head.

His mention of withdrawal brought back the memory of how he'd looked in the courtroom earlier. "Sure, honey. I'll wake you when we get home." *I wonder what he was on when he testified and who gave it to him?*

Darius opened the rear door and climbed into the back seat. "This is the same SUV you hid me in the night you shot McElroy."

Gloria bit her lip. *At least Robert didn't bring that up during Darius's testimony.* "Yeah, it is."

He lay down without another word. Gloria tilted the rearview mirror so she could keep an eye on him.

It was early Friday afternoon, but traffic was already heavy going out of the Loop. Darius appeared to be sleeping, or maybe in a stupor. Gloria choked down her worries and drove. At 2:00, she pulled into their garage. She leaned into the back seat and shook her son's leg. "Honey, wake up. We're home."

Darius shook his head, clearly too groggy to talk. He searched blindly for the door handle, then finally grasped it, pulled it down, and leaned his shoulder into the door. He stepped out and shut the door by pushing it with his hip.

Gloria looked into his eyes and saw a vacant stare. She watched him lumber up the gangway to the back door of the house. He waited there, his back to her, shoulders slumped and head bowed. He looked awful, full of pain and anguish.

Gloria stepped up to the door, unlocked it, and pushed it open. Darius stepped in front of her and dropped his coat and hoodie on the floor. She bent over to pick them up and noticed how thin he was. His tee-shirt and sweats hung on his bony body. He looked like he had lost fifteen pounds. "How about I make your favorite chicken parmesan for supper, honey?"

He headed for the stairs without responding. Gloria repeated her offer.

"Sure," he said faintly.

She watched him go upstairs and listened as his bedroom door creaked shut. Her shoulders sagged and she raised her hands to her face as tears streamed down her cheeks. *That poor boy, what have we done to him?*

⬦

A couple of hours later, Adsila came home from school. Gloria hadn't wanted her exposed to what might happen in the courtroom, which would have been difficult for Adsila to handle. They sat in the living room and she filled Adsila in on the day's events in the trial and her father's incarceration.

"I don't care about Dad anymore!" Adsila glared at Gloria. "How could he do that to Darius?"

"Shush. You'll wake your brother. He's upstairs, asleep. He didn't sleep well in rehab."

Rage filled Adsila's face. "I hope Dad goes to jail. I don't care if they ever let him out. I don't care if I ever see him again."

"Adsila, don't. Your father made a terrible mistake, and if he's found guilty, he'll pay the price. And don't let Darius hear you talking like that. This has been extremely hard on him."

Adsila took deep breaths, her chest expanding and contracting. A vein pulsated in her forehead. She looked angry enough to explode.

Gloria had to get the girl's mind off her brother and father. "I promised Darius we'd make him chicken parmesan for supper. There's chicken in the fridge. Help me make the sauce. He likes yours better than mine."

"What's going to happen to Darius now?"

"I've got to get him back in rehab. I don't know if the center will take him back. They figure if you leave once, the risk is too high that you'll leave again. They don't want to have someone they can't count on to finish the full twenty-eight days. Maybe because he had to testify, they'll let him back in."

Adsila shook her head. "I can't believe Darius got hooked on heroin. How did that happen?"

Gloria could guess. *I'll deal with Marvin after I take care of Darius.* "I'm not sure, honey."

"I'm going to change clothes. It'll be so good to have him home." Adsila sounded calmer now, thank God. Gloria watched her as she climbed the stairs to her bedroom.

She joined Gloria in the kitchen moments later, wearing jeans, a maroon Harvard sweatshirt, and tennis shoes. "Mom, where's your saucepan?"

Gloria gestured at the dish drainer. Adsila grabbed a cutting board and a knife, and started chopping onions, parsley, and garlic. She dropped the mixture into the saucepan, then poured in a can of crushed tomatoes, along with a generous slug of chianti she sipped when Gloria wasn't looking. "Don't be watching over my shoulder. This is my secret recipe. I learned it from Mama Barone at her pizza restaurant." She stirred the sauce, and the aroma of browning garlic filled the kitchen. "Now we let it simmer for an hour. This'll be good. Darius will love it."

In the meantime, Gloria worked on the chicken, slicing it, dipping it in beaten egg and breadcrumbs. The energy of working together made the two of them feel like a family again. She hoped that somehow, they could survive what they were going through.

***

It took Darius all the energy he could muster to push himself up to a seated position and roll his legs over the edge of the mattress, his feet on the floor. His body felt tired and weak. His mind was exhausted. He pressed his bony arms against the mattress and stood. He trembled as he crossed his room and settled in his desk chair.

He took fifteen minutes to write a note to his father. Again and again, he crumpled it up in his large bony hands and threw it in the wastebasket. Finally, the note was as right as it could be. He left it on the center of his desk. Then he stood, leaned on the arms of the chair, and rolled it to the center of the room.

He went to his closet and selected a black cloth belt. He slid his hand up and down the belt, feeling the smooth fabric and admiring the shiny gold buckle. "This will work."

He wrapped the belt tightly around his neck, locking the prong in the frame. The belt loop squeezed his neck, and there was a gurgling sound when he tried to clear his throat.

Darius stumbled to the chair and braced his hands on the arms as he climbed into it, balancing himself in an upright position. The chair slid and he tumbled into its seat, rolling across the floor. It took several attempts, but he finally managed to balance himself on the chair, tie the end of the belt to the stem of the light fixture, and kick the chair away.

Sudden panic made him twist his body violently. In this twilight moment, saliva dribbled from his mouth. His tongue protruded from between his lips. His feet stretched toward the chair, but it was inches out of reach. His fingers clawed at his neck as he tried to loosen the belt. He felt the light fixture giving way as he blacked out.

Gloria added the final touch to the sauce, sprinkling cilantro into the pan. A loud crash came from upstairs. She and Adsila looked at each other and then charged out of the kitchen and up to Darius's bedroom. Gloria shoved the door open. Darius was on the floor, a belt around his neck, the other end tied to a fallen light fixture that lay next to his shoulder. His desk chair was inches from his feet.

Gloria hurried forward. "Adsila, call 911."

She heard her daughter running downstairs for a phone as she shoved the chair away. It banged against the wall. She dropped to the floor next to Darius and grasped at the belt, but it was too tight. She lurched upright and hurried to his desk, found a pair of scissors, returned to where he lay and squeezed the blade between his neck and the belt. It took all her hand strength to cut through the cloth. She tugged the belt from his neck, tossing the black cloth and the light fixture away. Scratches on his neck, fresh and livid, caught her eye. "Oh baby, I know you didn't mean to do this." She listened for his breathing, heard the faint in-and-out. She grabbed his wrist and felt a pulse, weak but unmistakable.

"Come on, Darius, stay with me!" She couldn't cry yet, *wouldn't* cry yet. *My sweet baby. I'm so sorry I didn't see the anguish you were going through, testifying against your father. Damn him to hell.*

Adsila entered the bedroom. Gloria glanced up. Adsila blinked tears from her eyes as she stared at her fallen brother. Words gushed from her mouth: "What can I do?"

"He's breathing and has a pulse. We have to wait for the paramedics. Go downstairs so you can let them in!"

Adsila rushed back down the stairs. Gloria rested her hand on Darius's wrist. "Oh, my God. Darius. Don't leave me."

Finally, she heard footfalls pounding up the stairs. "We'll take it from here," someone said. Dazed, Gloria turned toward the speaker—a slender woman in a bulky fireman's coat with a red paramedic's patch on her shoulder, two yellow stripes around each sleeve and matching stripes at the base of the pants. Her name tag spelled *Arroyo*. She and her partner, Youngman, took charge. "What's his name?" Arroyo asked.

"Darius," Gloria said.

Arroyo knelt over him. "Darius, can you hear me?"

His eyes slowly opened and he mumbled, "Yes."

"Good. It's important that you don't move. You might have injured your neck and we don't want to make it worse. Do you understand?"

He whispered *yes* again.

Gloria sat back on her haunches while the paramedics worked, checking her son's heartbeat and blood pressure and then gently raising his neck and slipping a cervical collar on it to prevent possible injury. "You're doing good, Darius," Arroyo murmured. "I'm going to put an oxygen mask on you now. Then we're going to get you on a gurney and take you to the hospital. They'll take x-rays there to make sure you're okay."

Gloria moved toward Adsila, who stood just inside the bedroom door. They watched Arroyo settle an oxygen mask over Darius's mouth and nose, while Youngman and another paramedic brought the gurney in. They gently lifted him and strapped him onto it. Gloria slipped her arm around Adsila's shoulders.

"We're taking him to Mercy," Arroyo said. "You know where that is?"

"Yes. We'll be there right away."

The paramedics took Darius down to the ambulance. Gloria exhaled, feeling like it was the first breath she had taken in the last thirty minutes. Her gaze fell on Darius's desk. A sheet of paper lay on it. A suicide note? *I don't want Adsila to see this.* "Grab your coat, honey. I'll meet you downstairs."

Adsila left the bedroom. Gloria went to Darius's desk and read the note, a hand pressed to her mouth as she absorbed the words. *Oh, my God…*

Anger swept through her along with pain. She snatched up the note and strode out of the room.

CHAPTER 41

Mercy Hospital
Chicago, IL
Friday-Sunday, January 14-16, 2005

GLORIA FOCUSED HER GAZE ON Darius, strapped in his bed in a deep sleep after a heavy dose of lithium. She listened to the beeping of the heart monitor, looked at the tubes running into his arms, the cannula in his nose, the bandages covering the scratches on his neck. *My poor baby.*

Her eyes drifted to Adsila, asleep next to her in the hospital recliner, huddled under the blanket they shared. She patted Adsila's leg. "Honey, it's 10:30. Why don't you catch a cab and go home? I'll stay the night and you can come back in the morning."

Adsila yawned. "If you stay, I stay."

"Neither one of us will get a decent night's sleep if we have to share this recliner. Go home and sleep in. We've had a tough day. We both need the rest."

"Okay." Adsila got up and walked over to Darius. She kissed him on the forehead. "My sweet brother. I love you." Then she returned to Gloria. "I love you, Mom," Adsila said as she tucked the blanket around her mother.

"I love you too, baby. Goodnight."

Adsila slipped into her parka with the fur hood and left.

Gloria listened to the silence a while, broken only by the beeping of the monitor, until her eyes grew heavy and she eventually fell into a tossing, restless sleep.

At seven a.m. on Saturday, the doctor came in. His arrival woke Gloria, who stirred and sat up. She briefly shut her eyes, realizing her nightmare was reality.

His nametag read *Dr. Akash*, she saw when she opened her eyes again. "Doctor, how is he?"

"He's doing as well as could be expected. You're probably not surprised to know that his blood workup showed traces of 6-acetylmorphine, which is a metabolite of heroin."

She sighed. "No, I'm not."

"He was admitted to the regular ward rather than the psych ward because we were concerned about potential injuries to his neck and spinal cord." The doctor glanced at Darius's arm—specifically, his wrist, bound to the bed to prevent him from doing any harm to himself. "We should keep him here for three more days. Once he's stabilized, he needs to be transferred to an in-house facility with a drug rehab program where they can also monitor his physical injuries and do some cognitive behavioral therapy."

Gloria wrinkled her forehead. "What's cognitive behavioral therapy?"

"It's a process that involves the brain relearning. I can give you literature on that."

"Do you know any facilities that offer it?"

"There aren't many. The best option might be to keep Darius here for now, even if it has to be the psych ward."

"Whatever's best for my son."

After the doctor left, Gloria went to Darius's bedside and stroked his forehead. "Baby, I don't know if you can hear me. On Tuesday morning I'm going to give your father your note. Let him see what he's done to you."

CHAPTER 42

Courtroom 2502
Dirksen Federal Building
Tuesday, January 18, 2005
8:50 a.m.

GLORIA PEERED THROUGH THE GLASS in the courtroom doors, waiting for her husband to be escorted from the lockup. Ten minutes later, the marshals brought Carlton into the empty courtroom, uncuffed him, and had him sit at the defense table. He started paging through a yellow legal pad. She assumed he was reviewing his notes for his closing argument.

Gloria pushed the door open. She controlled her walk into the courtroom, not wanting to alarm the marshals. In her hand was the one-page note Darius had written. The marshals hadn't taken good care of Robert's suit. It was one of his favorites, a dark blue Italian-tailor made that looked like it had spent the weekend lying in the bottom of someone's closet.

Gloria gritted her teeth and approached the marshals. "Can I have a minute with him?"

The senior marshal looked at her and rubbed his chin. "Didn't you testify against him?"

"Yes, I did. I'm his wife."

He gave a slow, disbelieving shake of his head. "Are you armed?"

She opened her suit coat, revealing just her belt with no weapon. "No. I'm aware only marshals can be armed in a courtroom."

The marshal nodded. "All right."

Gloria took another couple of steps, until she stood at her husband's right shoulder.

He glanced up and grimaced. "What the hell do you want?"

"I came to give you something," she said.

"Can you believe what they did to my suit? It's fucking embarrassing to appear in court like this." He shook his head. "When this is over and I'm back on the bench, you can be sure no defendant will ever have to go through this again." He waved an arm, motioning for her to go away. "I need to focus on my closing."

Rage flared, but she kept her voice low. "Your son attempted suicide Friday night—"

Carlton's nostrils flared. "What's this? Some ploy to try to throw me off?"

Gloria's heart pounded. "You arrogant S.O.B. Do you think I would lie about that? Darius tried to hang himself in his bedroom. He's extremely depressed and he's on heroin."

He turned away from her, focusing on his legal pad. "Thanks for letting me know."

Gloria leaned over and slammed Darius's note on top of the legal pad. Without even looking at it, or her, he pushed it aside.

Gloria dragged the note in front of him again. "Recognize the handwriting? You ass."

Carlton read the note.

> *Dad, I'm sorry I couldn't come through for you. I know I failed you. I'm ashamed of myself. I've disappointed a lot of people, not only you, but Mom and Adsila too. I feel like I'm on a roller coaster, and the valleys keep getting deeper and deeper. It's such a lonely ride and I've come to dread every day. Now I can finally put an end to the pain.*
> *Goodbye,*
> *Darius*

Carlton rubbed his temples. "Oh, my God. Why would he do this? I never—"

"It's on you, Robert," Gloria snapped. "It's on you that your son almost killed himself. I hope you get the maximum sentence for what you did to Darius." She grabbed the note, turned away and barreled to the rear of the courtroom, where she took a seat in the last row.

Carlton pressed his lips together. He remembered Darius asking him, "What kind of man do you want me to be?"

He slowly tilted his head side-to-side and pulled down the knot of his silver tie. He loosened his collar, lowered his chin to his chest, and stared at his feet.

The prosecution team rolled their trial carts in. They all took seats at their table except for Jeffreys, who gazed at Carlton with a puzzled look on his face.

Judge Peterson entered, and the court officer declared court in session.

Peterson seated himself in his tall black leather chair. "Are we ready for closing arguments?"

"Yes, your honor," Jeffreys said.

Carlton remained seated.

Peterson eyed him. "Judge Carlton, are you ready to proceed with your closing argument?"

Carlton didn't budge.

"Judge Carlton?"

Still seated, Carlton crushed his legal notes in his hands. "It won't be necessary."

Peterson frowned. "What do you mean?"

Carlton mumbled Darius's question to himself: "What kind of man do you want me to be." Then he met the judge's eyes. "I'm pleading guilty." He raised his hands to his face, hiding the tears.

Judge Peterson blinked and shook his head. "Did I hear you right? You're changing your plea to guilty?"

Carlton stared at his feet and nodded.

Peterson spread his hands, palms up. "I need a verbal response."

Carlton ripped his tie off and threw it on the table. "Yes, dammit. I'm guilty. Guilty of a lot of things."

Judge Peterson folded his hands in front of him and leaned toward Carlton. "I've never heard of anyone pleading guilty at the end of a trial."

Carlton's voice wavered. "You have now. I don't intend to change my plea again. I'm guilty."

Peterson's gaze drifted to Jeffreys, who looked stunned. "Any comment from the government?"

Jeffreys drew a breath. "No, your honor. We feel we've proved our case beyond a reasonable doubt and are willing to accept Judge Carlton's guilty plea. This is a cold plea, and we have not offered any inducement to him to change it."

"So noted." The judge flipped through his calendar. "We'll set March eleventh for sentencing. Until then, Judge Carlton, you'll be at the MCC. Marshals, you may escort him out of the courtroom."

The marshals moved in and handcuffed Carlton. He stumbled as he looked over his shoulder for Gloria. The last he saw of her, she was rushing out of the courtroom as the marshals took him to the lockup.

***

Gloria watched Darius swing his legs over the edge of the hospital bed. She grasped his hand. "Dr. Akash said you don't have any physical injuries. I've found a place in St. Charles I'd like to take you to. They have an excellent reputation, and I think they can help you."

Darius teetered off the bed and inhaled. "You don't have to beat around the bush. You mean a rehab clinic? I know I need it, Mom. I appreciate all you're doing for me. I'm sorry for all the pain I've caused you and everyone else."

It was 11:30 in the morning by the time they checked out of Mercy. A light but steady snow was falling. Gloria drove her personal car, a Jeep Wrangler. She hadn't wanted to take Robert's Lexus, in case Darius found it a reminder of the trial.

They headed west on the Eisenhower Expressway. It was an hour's drive to the rehab clinic. "I talked to one of the counselors, Carl Heinze," she said. "He's been doing this kind of work for fifteen years. He seemed genuine and he's helped a lot of people."

Darius was trembling. "I know it's not going to be easy. I promise I'll stay as long as I have to."

Gloria gazed at him. "How're you feeling?"

He folded his hands together to control the shaking. "Been better. I'm achy all over."

She licked her lips with cautious hope. "It'll take a while before you feel better. It'll be a month before I can see you again. They figure that's the best, so you can focus on getting healthy."

"Does Dad know about this…about the clinic?"

"No. I didn't tell him…I haven't talked to him. I don't really know when I will, or if I will. That's something we'll have to wait and see about." She knew it wasn't the time to tell Darius that his father pled guilty after all, let alone why. She would keep that secret until the time was right; forever, if need be. "There are some questions I have to ask you."

"About what?"

"About Marvin."

Darius frowned. "How do you know about him?"

"It's my job to know. I might be able to protect you, but you must tell me everything."

Darius grabbed the CD briefcase from between the seats, picked out *The Best of The O'Jays*. His hand shook as he attempted to slide it into the player. "Do you mind?"

"No, I don't mind."

Darius shoved the CD in and the song "Back Stabbers" started playing. "This is one of my favorites."

"Mine, too. Tell me about you and Marvin."

Darius rubbed his forehead. "I'm sick. It's worse than anything I've ever had."

"I know you don't feel well, but we don't have time to waste. We only have this hour or so before I drop you off at the clinic." She paused, then said, "You don't have to talk about the drugs yet. Start with how you connected with him. Then tell me about the other things."

Darius shrugged. "There's a lot to tell." He swallowed hard. "How can I—"

Gloria tightened her grip on the wheel. "Just do it, Darius!"

Darius shook his head. "He was like a father to me. He knew I was smart, trusted me to do things for him."

"Damn it, Darius! He wasn't a father to you." Her nostrils flared. "He's like your father, though. They both used you. They didn't care about you!"

Darius bowed his head and stared at the floor of the car.

She made an effort to gentle her tone. "You have a choice to make. Continue on the path you're on, and die, or you can change your behavior and choose to live. Make the right choice. Tell me about Marvin, *now*."

Darius shifted his gaze to look straight out at the road. His hands curled into fists and then released. "Me and Shorty, we used to handle the mixing houses for him. You know, apartments in the Robert

Taylor projects where women broke down kilos of heroin into dime bags."

Gloria shook her head. *Jesus Christ.* "Did you use your cell phone to talk with Marvin or Shorty?"

"A few times. Then Marvin got us burner phones. We'd use them for a week or so. Then he'd get us new phones."

"Why did you get involved?" She wanted to question him more deeply, but their hour's drive was running down, and she decided it was better for now not to know. *At least they used burner phones. Those calls can't be traced back to Darius.* She'd have to figure out what to do about any earlier calls he'd made. "Never mind. Go on, what else did you do with Marvin?"

"One time he took me to meet this Mexican guy that he bought heroin from. We met in a warehouse around Blue Island and 18th Street. Marvin and the guy argued over the price. He brought fifty grand with him, but the Mexican wanted sixty. He gave Marvin the kilo after Marvin promised to make up the difference. The next time, Marvin sent me to give the Mexican $60,000 for a kilo, but I didn't make it."

Gloria frowned. "What happened?"

"Some cop stopped me. Before he pulled me over, I grabbed a couple handfuls of cash from the top of the bag and threw it on the floor of the car. The cop stuck a gun in my face. I thought he was going to kill me. He took all the cash that was left in the bag."

"My God, Darius, didn't you realize how dangerous this game is?"

Darius shook his head. "I don't know what I was thinking, but I never did that again."

"Who was the cop?"

"I don't know. Marvin said his name once, but I don't remember it. He was a white cop. I know there was a Black cop Marvin was paying off. Don't remember his name, either."

"What happened to the cash you threw on the floor?"

Darius swallowed. "You're going to be pissed at me. I gave it to Adsila to hold. As far as I know, she still has it. I'm sorry, Mom." He shook his head. "I should have never got her involved."

Gloria slammed her fist against the steering wheel. "God damn. How could you do that to your sister?"

"She doesn't know where the money came from. I told her it was cash I got from an AAU basketball coach and she couldn't tell anyone because it could affect my college eligibility."

Gloria couldn't believe how adept he had become at lying. "Anything else?"

"Just one more thing. Marvin had me and Shorty rip off some Nigerian people on the North Side. We gave Marvin all the cash."

She'd been waiting for that confession since they started this conversation, but it still hurt to hear. The memory of seeing Darius run across the street with a garbage bag full of DEA street money would haunt her forever. They were closing in on the rehab center now, and she felt glad this journey was over. She didn't know how much more she could take.

She turned into a driveway and drove up to the main entrance. The rehab center was a modern single-story white building bordered by tall junipers, their branches covered with snow. The O'Jays CD was playing "Family Reunion" as she parked the jeep near the entrance to the center. "That's a good song for us to end with. I'll look forward to picking you up in a month."

"Me too, Mom."

"I'll go in with you. Mr. Heinze is expecting us."

They entered the lobby, Darius carrying the suitcase Gloria had packed for him. There was a fireplace in the reception area, and the aroma of burning wood filled the air as flames crackled across the logs. A middle-aged woman wearing the nametag *Mrs. Green* greeted them from the lobby desk.

Gloria approached her. "Hello, Mrs. Green. We have an appointment with Mr. Heinze. My son, Darius Carlton, is checking in."

"I'll give him a call."

In a few minutes Mr. Heinze walked into the reception area. He was slender and a couple of inches shorter than Darius, wearing a navy shirt and blue jeans. He appeared to be in his forties and his green eyes shone through his horn-rimmed glasses, which gave him the look of a college professor.

He shook Darius's hand. "Nice to meet you, Darius. Come with me. I'll show you to your room."

Gloria kissed her son on the cheek. "I love you. You can beat this. See you in a month, honey."

Darius glanced over his shoulder at her as Heinze escorted him down the hallway. He looked like a scared little boy, and Gloria could not recall ever having a greater sense of foreboding.

* * *

It was 1:45 by the time Gloria got back to the IRS office. She saw Lauren in with Stephens, reviewing Uka Kafi's subpoenaed bank records. She hung her navy pea coat over the back of her chair and headed into Stephens's office to join them. "What have we got?"

"You won't believe this. It's a gold mine," Lauren said. "Over the last two years they've deposited more than ten million dollars in cash, including our undercover funds, into three corporate accounts. They actually incorporated front companies. The account holders and corporate officers are Kunta Tama, Zubari Zalan, and Tofil Chinwe. I assume those last two guys are the other men who were in Kafi's office."

"That's great evidence," Gloria said. "In what amounts were the deposits made?"

"There's only one individual deposit over $10,000 made to any account, but there are deposits made on a single day to all three accounts that total in excess of $10,000."

"That shows their knowledge of how to evade currency transaction reporting requirements," Stephens said.

Gloria took a seat. "How are our funds sent back to our undercover account?"

"They were wired from the three corporate accounts," Lauren said. She showed Gloria a bank wire. "Get this. The other cash deposits are all wired to the biggest luxury car dealership in Nigeria. We've contacted Interpol. They have allegations that this dealership launders money by issuing checks to drug dealers, and also gives them cars."

Gloria nodded. "Let's start preparing search warrants." *For Darius's sake, I've got to finish Uka's case before the FBI indicts Marvin. Might need the S.O.B. as a witness against the cops and he would be forced to tell them about Darius.*

CHAPTER 43

CID-IRS Office
Kluczynski Federal Building
Tuesday, January 18, 2005
2:00 p.m.

GLORIA RUSHED TOWARD HER DESK, with Lauren following close behind. "We need to write the affidavit for probable cause for the search warrants regarding Uka's business. You said the three men who work for her are all officers of the front businesses the cash went through? You'll need to get—"

"I know." Lauren held up the file containing the bank records and her analysis. "I'll get copies of the articles of incorporation to prove it."

Gloria sat at her desk. "All right. I'll draft the section of the affidavit on Uka's business account. We'll see if any cash went into it. Can you work up the section on the bank accounts for the three men from her office? That'll show their knowledge and intent."

Lauren took a deep breath and exhaled. "I already started it. You should know by now that I have some initiative."

Before Gloria could come up with a response, Lauren gave her the bank file and spreadsheet analyzing all the deposits, outgoing checks, and bank wires drawn on the accounts for Uka's Auto

Insurance plus Uka Kafi's personal checking and savings accounts. "I'm still working on the other three. Kunta Tama does business as Tama Auto Sales, Zubari Zalan as Nick's Towing Services, and Tofil Chinwe as American Tires."

Gloria leaned back. "Good. Run them through TECS and—"

Lauren headed to her desk. "Jesus, Gloria, this isn't my first rodeo. I've got it. What's going on with you?"

Gloria lowered her head. "I'm sorry, Lauren. I know you're on top of things. I'm glad you're my partner. It's just…everything." *I don't know when the FBI might move on Marvin. I've got to get this done before they do.* "It's going to be a late night till we finish the affidavit. We'll take it to the U.S. Attorney tomorrow. Once they approve it, we'll get the search warrants. We've plenty of probable cause. There shouldn't be any problem." She pulled her cell phone out of her pocket and slid the ring switch to silent. *No interruptions until I have the affidavit completed and approved.*

An hour later, Lauren had a handful of printouts to show Gloria. "You'll like this. Customs intercepted another package mailed to Uka Kafi's business. It contained three fraudulent passports in the names of Adebayo Emem, Keita Balogun, and Bankole Abara. The photo in each passport is Kunta Tama from Uka's office."

Gloria shook her head. "I wonder how many passports got through, and what they were smuggling in and out of the country. Contact Customs to get copies of the passports; they'll make useful supporting exhibits to show the prosecutors and the magistrate. Any other goodies?"

"Checked TECS. There were no 8300s filed with us regarding cash expenditures over $10,000, but the bank did prepare a suspicious activity report based on the amounts and consistency of the cash deposits."

"Glad to see the bank was playing it straight. It shouldn't be a hassle to get a bank officer to testify about the records. Even though they had all this cash running through the accounts, the banker will look like a hero on the stand."

Lauren returned to her desk. Gloria called Adsila and left a message. "Hi, honey. I'm going to be working late tonight, putting an affidavit together. I'm not sure what time I'll be home. There's plenty of food in the refrigerator, or you can order out if you want. Love you." She ended the call, wondering, *why I am always leaving my kids to do this job?*

Gloria worked steadily on her part of the affidavit as others in the office around her finished up for the day. Edwards left, with a nod at Lauren, but Lauren only gave him a distracted wave, and he looked disgruntled as he walked out. Stephens told them, "Have a good night," and departed the office half an hour later. Then it was only Lauren and Gloria, still working away. "Uka's been doing this for going on four years," Gloria murmured. "One hundred forty thousand in cash deposits starting in late 2001, more than twice as much in the first six months of 2002."

"She started branching out after that," Lauren said. "The three accounts held by Tama, Zalan, and Chinwe were all opened in mid-June of 2002. Cash deposits totaled…" She scanned the paperwork in front of her. "Almost eight million through 2004, plus $500,000 so far in 2005. That includes the undercover payments we made to Uka."

"So altogether, we're talking nearly ten million." Gloria let out a low whistle. "And most of that went to—what's the name of the car dealership in Nigeria again, the one on Interpol's radar?"

"A-1 Luxury Auto Sales, in Lagos. Interpol says they launder drug proceeds by withdrawing cash, writing checks, and selling luxury vehicles to people involved in heroin trafficking."

Gloria shook her head. "This was bigger than we anticipated."

"That's not all," Lauren added. "From the accounts maintained by Tama, Zalan, and Chinwe, checks were written payable to Uka's Auto Insurance totaling $500,000—her fees for laundering the funds.

The balance of $90,000 stayed in the accounts held by Tama, Zalan, and Chinwe or were used pay their personal expenses."

All good data, all useful for their purposes. By the time Gloria was satisfied with the affidavit, it was closing in on midnight. She closed her computer and nodded at Lauren. It was time to go home. They left the office and walked down to the parking garage. "We did good, partner," Gloria said. "See you tomorrow."

Gloria got in the Blazer and fastened her seat belt, then checked her phone. A text had come in from the FBI, Agent Adamczyk, at 4:00. As she read it, her fragile calm evaporated. *We're arresting Marvin Bailey tomorrow morning. I'd like to flip this guy and make him my informant.*

CHAPTER 44

Wednesday, January 19, 2005
1:30 a.m.

THE ONLY THING GLORIA COULD think of was to talk to Marvin. She couldn't fall asleep so she texted him and he called back a few minutes later.

"Marvin thinks it way past your bedtime."

In the background, she heard Alicia Keyes and Usher singing "My Boo", the clinking of glasses, and the undercurrent of a bar crowd. "I need to talk to you," Gloria demanded.

"Tomorrow works. Say, after lunch? It's going to be a late night." She heard a woman's voice and high-pitched laughter. "Not now, honey. Marvin's just got to wrap up this call and then I'm all yours, baby."

Gloria white-knuckled her phone. "No. It's got to be now!"

"I got something going on. What's so big it can't wait?"

"If we don't meet right away," her voice tightened, "there might not be any tomorrow for you!"

"What you mean?" Marvin's voice dropped to a whisper. "Somebody lookin' to take me out?"

Gloria exhaled. "Something like that. We've got to meet now. Where can we meet?"

"Why the fuck somebody want to shoot me? Everything's going good."

"Tell me where we can meet."

"Got to be someplace safe. Someplace I don't ever go." Marvin lowered his voice some more until it was barely audible. "So, if we see somebody that don't look right you can kill 'em like you did McElroy."

"How do you know about that?"

"Marvin knows things. Word gets around."

She wiped her palm down her jeans. "Yeah. I'll protect you." She knew there might be other consequences for Marvin.

"How about the parking lot by that beach over on 63rd. Nobody be there this time of year, with the fucking weather. I'll be driving an old Honda. Gimme twenty minutes."

"Don't be late."

She headed for Lake Shore Drive, then turned south. She wasn't sure what the next twenty minutes of her life held, but she knew she would do what had to be done.

Gloria exited east onto 63rd Street and headed toward the lake. In the distance she saw a lone car parked, a Honda, the motor running and exhaust fumes escaping into the night air. She parked behind it, then quickly checked the magazine of her Sig Sauer. It was fully loaded. She pulled back the slide, chambered a round, and topped off the magazine. Gloria had killed before; she could do it again if she had to. She slid the Sig into her right coat pocket.

Marvin got out of the Honda and entered Gloria's black SUV. Words left his mouth as he yanked the door shut. "What's this shit about? Who wants Marvin *dead*?" He pulled a Ruger stainless semi-auto from his waistband and waved it around. "Let 'em come. I'll kill any motherfucker before they get close."

"It's not like that." Gloria tightened her grip on the Sig.

"I can protect myself. You don't have to kill no one for me. Just tell me who's lookin' for me and I'll take care of them."

He's got the drop on me. Gloria pulled the Sig's hammer back.

"Dammit. Who wants to do Marvin in?"

"Give me the pistol." Gloria wondered how many seconds she had left before she had to make a decision. "You're a convicted felon. You get busted with that Ruger, you're looking at five years."

"What're you, crazy? First you tell me somebody wants me dead and then you want me to give up my protection."

"It's not like that. Give me the fucking pistol." She leaned back in her seat, her body turned so the Sig in her coat pocket pointed toward Marvin.

Marvin lowered the Ruger to his lap. "What the fuck is going on?"

"The FBI is going to arrest you tomorrow morning––no, not tomorrow, this morning."

"What the fuck."

Gloria held out her free hand and he placed the Ruger in it. She shoved the pistol in her left pocket, keeping a finger on the trigger. She released her grip on her Sig and eased her right hand onto her lap.

"You didn't hear this from me. They'll be knocking on your door in a few hours to arrest you."

Marvin's eyes bulged. "Arrest me?"

"Let's walk." Gloria stepped out of the Blazer. *He's got to promise not to talk to anyone about Darius. Can I trust him?*

Marvin stepped out of the SUV. "What are they going to bust me for?"

"Don't bullshit me. You know for twhat."

They walked toward the beach. The north wind barreled down the lake. Eight-foot waves crashed onto the shore. Gloria raised the collar of her navy pea coat. "When they come for you, don't say a word to anyone. Understand? You'll get an attorney and I'll go to bat for you. I'll tell the prosecutor about your years as my CI, everything you've done for me. All the cases we owe to your cooperation."

"Fuck." They walked side by side. He turned his head to face Gloria. "Marvin get out of town. Go to Podunk, Mississippi. They'll never find me."

"It doesn't matter where you go. They'll find you. They always do. Could be tomorrow, next month, next year or whenever. Is that how you want to live? Spend the rest of your life looking over your shoulder?"

"Marvin will disappear like a ghost."

"Yeah? Then, when they find you, you'll get the max. By the time you get out you'll be an old man. Maybe even die in prison. When you're inside, things happen, you know." She could feel beads of sweat on her forehead. There was a pause in the conversation. The Ruger was still in her pocket. She tightened her grip on it and pulled the hammer back. He had to believe her, agree to do things her way, or else—

"You'll talk me up good?"

Her finger stayed on the trigger of Marvin's pistol. "I'll do everything I can. On one condition." She pressed her lips together in a grimace. *This is all for you, Darius.*

"What's that?"

"You can't tell anyone about Darius. You do that and I'll talk you up good. I'll make you sound like an angel. Tell them how you helped people in the projects get food and meds."

Marvin hung his head. "I didn't know about you and him 'til a few days ago. If I knew Darius was your boy, it never would have been like that."

"So, you'll do it my way? You'll never mention Darius to the FBI, prosecutors, or anyone else?" Gloria swallowed, waiting for his response.

Marvin shook his head. "I'd never talk on him. He's my boy."

She exhaled. "It won't be easy. They'll try to force you to talk about everything. They'll tell you your cooperation has to be one hundred percent or nothing."

"No. Marvin promises you he'll never talk on Darius. I can tell 'em about the cops I was paying off. The Feds like to do cops."

Gloria remembered Darius telling her about the police officer that ripped him off for Marvin's cash. She knew Marvin was right. The FBI would eventually bust the police officers and they would tell the FBI about stealing Marvin's money. And who they took it from!

Gloria stopped and turned toward Marvin. He stood three feet away. *Can I do this?* She paused for a moment. Doubts about whether she could believe Marvin or if she could kill him entered her mind, but if he gave up the crooked cops, he would implicate Darius in his drug business. Could she risk the story of an irate informant turning on her?

She knew what had to be done. She pulled out the Ruger in her left hand. "I'm sorry, Marvin."

"No!" Marvin lunged for her, pushing her hand up.

She jerked the trigger. The bullet exploded, rattling her ears. The bright flash from the muzzle caused her pupils to contract. The shot sailed over Marvin's left shoulder.

Gloria fell backward onto the ground. She pulled back the Ruger, fixing both hands on it so he couldn't take it from her. Her Sig fell out of her pocket. Marvin straddled her. He encased both her hands in his. She was losing the battle for the Ruger. Her vision was still blurred by the muzzle flash. Marvin's eyes darted to her Sig. He moved his left hand off hers and reached for it.

She yanked off a second round. Her eyes slammed shut as the sound of the blast reverberated in her ears. This time the shot flew over his right shoulder.

Marvin grabbed the Sig and pointed it at Gloria's head.

She pushed her arms straight ahead and pulled off one more round. The flash temporarily blinded her and the blast hammered her ears.

Marvin fell on top of her. She rolled him off her and stumbled onto her feet, stuffed the Ruger in her pocket, and rubbed her eyes. Slowly, she regained her focus and saw the bullet hole in the center of his forehead, and the blood circling his head from the exit wound.

The crash of the waves on the shore sounded oddly muffled, an aftereffect of the gunshots. "Damn it, Marvin, you gave me no choice." She reached into her pocket, yanked out her gloves, and wiped her fingerprints off the Ruger. Then she slipped the gloves on, grabbed the pistol by the barrel, and heaved it into the lake. She stared out at the dark water, shivering in the cold. *God, I didn't want this to happen. But it was the only way Darius could be safe.*

She moved away, and then remembered Marvin's cell phone. She returned to his body, pulled his jacket up, and tugged the phone out of his pants pocket. She threw it into the lake after the Ruger and watched the rough waters consume it. Then she got back in the Blazer and drove off.

She knew there was gun residue and probably Marvin's blood on her coat. She pulled over briefly at a construction site, threw her coat in a dumpster, and headed home with the cost of one more person on her soul.

CHAPTER 45

CID-IRS Office
Kluczynski Federal Building
Wednesday, January 19, 2005
10:00 a.m.

GLORIA AND LAUREN SAT IN Stephens's office as he went through the affidavit for the search warrant for Uka's business and those of her three associates. He shook his head, and Gloria caught Lauren's eye. *I know this is damn good; don't tell me he wants changes!* If he wanted them, he could do it himself. Even though she knew any changes would fall on her.

Stephens looked up, meeting Gloria's gaze. "Gloria, you look really tired."

"I'm sorry. What'd you say?" She took a hard, obvious swallow. "I didn't get much sleep. Always happens the night before we execute a search warrant." *Execute...a bad play on words*, she thought.

"I know you're going to be busy after you do the search, then going through the seized evidence and interviewing the subjects if they talk, but try to get some rest. You've got to take care of yourself."

Gloria nodded, rubbing the back of her neck. She wondered if she'd been speaking louder than normal. With her hearing still muffled from the shots she'd fired at Marvin, it was hard to tell.

Stephens was still talking. She listened, but missed some of the words. "This is textbook…excellent job putting this together overnight…example at the training center for all the rookie agents." He signed off on the approval line. "Go meet with the prosecutor."

Only when Lauren rose from her seat did Gloria realize the meeting was over. *Yeah, textbook,* Gloria thought. *The FBI's probably looking for Marvin right now. How much time before they find him?* She kept her worry from showing as she stood. "Great. Thanks, Tom. We appreciate it."

Lauren nodded. Gloria added, "I want you to know, Lauren wrote the section of the affidavit regarding Uka's associates." A small thing, but she owed her partner that, especially after the tension between them during the past few weeks. She wondered when Lauren would start asking where Marvin was.

"I'm impressed, Lauren," Stephens said. "You did a nice job. I'll note that in your next evaluation."

"Thanks, Tom. I did a lot of writing in college. Even wrote a novel. A coming-of-age story about a college girl."

Stephens smiled. "I didn't know that."

Gloria glanced at her partner. "Let's go. We have to get Tunney's approval before we take the affidavit to the duty magistrate."

They stopped by their desks to get their coats. Gloria had worn her ski jacket today. She wondered if anyone had found her navy pea coat in the dumpster. Maybe a homeless person. She shrugged into the ski jacket while Lauren put on her Kenneth Cole double-breasted tan coat, and they headed across Dearborn Street to the U.S. Attorney's office.

"You finally got rid of that old navy coat," Lauren said. "That jacket looks so much better."

Gloria nodded as she holstered her Sig. Every time she gripped her pistol from now on, would she think of her struggle with Marvin just a few hours ago? The explosions of the three shots. Their effect on her hearing and vision, and the weight of his body collapsing on her. It would become a nightmare she would live again and again.

Tunney's office was crammed with a dozen cardboard boxes containing evidence for several trials he was preparing for. Among them were a multi-defendant drug case on a West Side gang, a political corruption investigation of an alderman, and an indictment of several Chicago policemen for ripping off drug dealers. His phone pressed to his ear, he nodded at Gloria and Lauren as they entered. He gestured at the boxes on the chairs, motioning the women to shift them onto the floor so they could sit.

Gloria cut her eyes toward several boxes marked *United States of America v. Henson*. She knew Henson was a cop that ripped cash from drug dealers just like the one who stole Marvin's cash from Darius. She veered away from the boxes, hoping there would never be one containing a file marked *Darius Carlton*.

"No, I'm not going to agree to a plea with only six months' incarceration," Tunney said, most likely to a defense attorney on the other end of the line. "He over-billed Medicare by more than a million dollars." He paused, as if listening to the defense attorney's argument. "Your client should've thought about jail time when he was living in his mansion in Lake Forest and driving his Ferrari to his yacht." Tunney laughed without humor. "I'm thinking more like ten years."

Her partial deafness was clearing; she'd heard every word of that. Another pause. "Well, send me the letters about all the charity work he's done, but as far as I'm concerned, if he didn't perform all these kind acts until he was indicted it won't do him any good." Tunney hung up the phone and faced them. "Can't believe these greedy jerks. They live high on the hog and then once they're caught, they want to be portrayed as model citizens. What's up?"

"We've got the search warrant affidavit for the undercover money-laundering case involving Uka Kafi and her associates," Gloria said, handing the document to Tunney.

He paged through it several times, then glanced at the agents. "This looks good to me." Gloria brought a shaky hand to her ear. Tunney noticed and frowned in concern. "Gloria, you look beat. Take a break. I know you're the senior agent, but if you don't mind, I think it might be a good experience for Lauren to sign off as the affiant." He drummed his fingers on the top of his desk. "We might have another issue. Iruka Nnamdi is the duty magistrate today. I've never been in front of her before. She's only been on the bench about a month, and she worked for the American Civil Liberties Union for several years. She could be a liberal wild card."

Gloria exhaled. She didn't really care and in fact was relieved that she could shed some of the responsibility. "Sure, not a problem. One less thing for me to do." And one step away from making an official statement on record about where she was when she shot Marvin.

She drew in a fresh breath. "There's something you need to know. The FBI's going to arrest our informant, Marvin Bailey, on drug charges soon. They may have done so already," she said, even though she knew it would never happen.

Lauren jerked back in her chair. "When did you find that out?"

Gloria remained silent.

Tunney nodded. "So, you think we should try to get the warrant now rather than wait?"

"I think so." Gloria switched her cell phone to silent mode as they got up and left. She didn't want to be interrupted by a call or a text from the FBI that they couldn't find Marvin.

The three of them took the elevator to the twentieth floor and into Magistrate Nnamdi's office. Tunney introduced himself and the two women to the secretary and explained why they were there.

"Let me see if the magistrate is available." The secretary picked up her phone and spoke quietly into it. A moment later she said, "Okay, I'll send them in."

The magistrate's office resembled Uka's. African artifacts dotted the room—onyx statues of elephants, lions, and antelopes—and paintings of native men and women decorated the walls. On the desk was a photo of an older couple with several children in African garb. Gloria guessed it was Nnamdi's family.

The magistrate entered the office through a door behind her desk. Tall and slender, she had dark skin and wore a dress that reminded Gloria of Uka's green and gold outfit. "Good afternoon," she said, her voice deep and cool as she sat in a large black leather chair behind a massive mahogany desk. "How may I help you?"

Tunney stepped forward. "Your honor, we would like to present an affidavit for a search warrant and arrest warrants regarding an undercover IRS investigation of a money launderer, Uka Kafi, and her associates."

"May I see it?"

Tunney handed it to her. She read it three times, frowning.

Lauren crossed her arms over her chest. She glanced at Gloria, as if searching for support if this didn't go well.

Finally, the magistrate looked at them. "I'm sorry—"

Perspiration broke out across Lauren's forehead.

"It troubles me…that my people have such disregard for the laws of their new country. Which agent is the affiant?"

Lauren stepped forward.

"Please raise your hand."

Lauren did so.

"Do you swear that this affidavit is true and correct?"

"I do."

The magistrate nodded and laid the affidavit on the desktop. "Sign here, and I will authorize the search and related arrest warrants."

Lauren signed the document and the magistrate followed suit. "Be careful and stay safe."

"Thank you, your honor," Tunney said.

Gloria's phone vibrated. She pulled it out and looked at the screen. A text message from FBI agent Adamczyk, the one she'd been expecting: *We can't find Marvin Bailey. Do you have any idea where he might be?*

Her stomach roiled as she tucked the phone away. *You'll find him eventually. I just hope it's a long time before you do.*

CHAPTER 46

Carlton/Nighthawk Residence, Bronzeville
Friday, January 21, 2005

GLORIA'S ALARM CLOCK BUZZED AT 4:30 a.m. She shook the blur of sleep from her eyes and raised her head off the pillow. She stared at the clock and then slapped it, silencing the alarm. She hadn't slept well the few nights after shooting Marvin. God, she was so tired. Her thoughts kept careening around the question: Did she commit murder, or was it self-defense?

For the first time in a day and a half, her hearing and vision seemed normal, although she could still hear the shots that killed Marvin over and over in her mind.

She remembered the expression on his face changing in seconds from the initial fear of looking down the barrel of the Ruger, to his flaring nostrils as he gained control of her hands, and his desperate effort to wrestle the gun from her before she fired the fatal shot.

She swung her legs over the bedside, breathed deep, and stretched her arms over her head. Uka's associates would be armed; they'd bought guns right after Darius and his accomplice committed the robbery. Though she was not one to pray, she did so now, hoping no one would get hurt. As the undercover agent, she would not be part of the entry team at the most dangerous point, when they gained access to the insurance office.

Gloria slipped on her jeans, a shirt, and boots. She pulled open the drawer to her nightstand and lifted out her Sig Sauer. She checked her magazine, topped it off with one more round, slammed it back in, pulled back the slide, and chambered a round. As she holstered the Sig, she knew she would never forget the early hours of Wednesday morning and the outcome with Marvin.

She went to Adsila's bedroom. Her daughter was still asleep, an angelic expression on her face. Gloria leaned over and kissed her forehead. Adsila stirred and opened her eyes. She smiled at first, then blinked in apparent confusion. "Mom, where're you going?"

"I told you yesterday, honey. We're doing the search warrant this morning."

She saw Adsila eyeing the Sig. Adsila grasped her hand. "Please be careful."

"Always, honey. Don't worry, I'm not on the entry team. Just there to answer any questions and give moral support."

"Can't you get a promotion to supervisor? A nice safe desk job."

"Baby, that would be the worst thing for me and even worse for the agents who would work for me. I've got to go. I didn't mean to wake you. Go back to sleep." She pulled the covers up around Adsila's neck. "I love you."

"Mom, when will Darius come home?"

Gloria swallowed. It hurt more than she'd anticipated to be separated from her son that she loved so much. Her children defined who and what she was, and even though she had Adsila, she felt lost without Darius. "I don't know, honey. Soon, I hope. Try to get some sleep."

IRS Office
4000 N. Kedzie
Chicago, IL
Friday, January 21, 2005
6:00 a.m.

The agents from Tom Stephens's group met for the pre-raid briefing at the IRS north area office, the closest to Uka's Auto Insurance. They wore dark blue raid caps and jackets with the emblem of their badge on the front. Printed on the rear in large gold letters were the words *Federal Agent*. At this hour, aside from them, the IRS office was empty.

Tom Stephens sat at the head of a long table, watching the twelve agents as they sipped coffee and snacked on donuts he had bought. Gloria felt his gaze on her. She heard the nervous laughter that preceded every warrant executed. Whether they would admit it or not, in the back of each agent's mind was the possibility of violence.

Gloria's fear was twofold. First, the agents knew that this morning they would be crashing into a place where armed people could react out of fear for their lives. Any one of the agents might have to defend himself and shoot someone. The agents were trained to stop a person from harming anyone else. Although no one would ever admit it in court, that meant shoot to kill.

Even worse, what if one of the agents was shot? She hoped it wouldn't happen. There was always the conversation about having the will to survive. *If one of the agents was shot, could they consciously grasp that?*

She watched Stephens rise from his chair, but her mind was elsewhere.

"All right, everyone, pay attention," he said. "We know from Gloria's last contact that at a minimum, the three men in Uka's workplace are armed, and there may be weapons in her office in the rear of the business. Make sure you all wear your body armor. The most important thing is that everyone goes home tonight. As is our policy, the undercover agent will not participate in the raid, so Gloria is out. We don't want to heighten the intensity any more than necessary. Wilson and Silver are set up on Uka's condominium. Once Uka leaves, they'll radio us." He turned to Gloria. "Why don't you go over the physical layout of the office?"

Gloria scarcely heard him. She was reliving her struggle with Marvin. He was straddled over her, grasping her hands. Trying for the Ruger.

Stephens cocked his head. "Gloria, the layout."

Gloria's mind danced past Marvin and she saw Darius, running across Clark Street with a garbage bag full of cash, stolen from Uka Kafi on Marvin's orders. Marvin wasn't a threat anymore, but would her son ever be free from danger, or from his drug addiction?

She looked at Stephens. His hand extended toward her. How long had she zoned out? "Yeah. Of course." She stood and moved to a whiteboard with a diagram of the interior of Uka's Auto Insurance drawn on it. "Tama, Zalan, and Chinwe are usually at their desks in the front of the office, though last time I was there with my CI," she hesitated, "Zalan was guarding the front door. All three men carried pistols. That doesn't mean they don't have weapons in their desks as well. When you enter the office, two of you will be assigned to each individual. Cuff them, pat them down, seize their weapons, and then search their desks. Look for weapons first and documents second. Any questions so far?"

Agent Martinez, short and slim but stronger than he looked, spoke up. "Who's teaming up with who?"

"We'll make it easy. Count off one through six. Agents one and two get Tama, agents three and four get Zalan, agents five and six get Chinwe. The rest of you, assist in the office search as needed."

With something concrete to focus on, Gloria felt steadier. She watched the agents count down. "Pettigrew and Walker, you have Zalan. He was the self-appointed head of security the last time I was there. He's a muscular guy and may be difficult to deal with."

Pettigrew laughed. He was built like a grizzly bear. "A chance to put my years as a defensive tackle to use."

"Who's arresting Uka?" Agent Johnson asked.

Gloria pointed at Lauren. "She's got Uka. Lauren will team up with Sanchez, and she'll pat Uka down." She sat down in her chair again and swiveled it to gaze at all the agents. "Everyone should've read the affidavit for the search warrant. We're looking for bank records from the three entities incorporated under the names of the men in the office, and from Uka's business account. Of course, any related notes, letters, other documents, and computers are also covered in the search warrant. When in doubt, seize it.

"One more thing. If we're lucky, we'll find a large amount of cash, and there may be a safe on the premises. I never saw one, but they deposited almost ten million in cash into their various bank accounts over the past few years. They had to store it somewhere beforehand. Finally, don't forget that Customs seized fraudulent passports, so there may be more under various names."

Stephens added, "Lauren Ashberry has been on this case since day one, so she'll be the raid leader. Gloria and I will stay here, so if there are any questions, raise us on the radio. Johnson, you and Martinez head out in the surveillance van. Uka's office usually doesn't open until 9:00 a.m. If there's earlier activity, call us on the radio. We'll be on station three. Any questions?"

No more questions were raised, and the agents reported to their vehicles and their assigned positions.

Johnson and Martinez set up at 6:45 on the west side of Clark Street a half-block south of Uka's office, and called in their location. By 8:00 Lauren and the remaining agents were positioned in the vicinity of Uka's business.

Gloria headed to the ladies' room, seeking a private moment. The washroom was empty. She texted Adamczyk, the FBI agent. *I'm executing a search warrant, will be tied up for a few days.*

A few minutes later, his reply came: *Good luck. Haven't found Marvin yet. But we will.*

Gloria's fingers fumbled over the keyboard. *I'm sure of it.* She sent the text and headed back to the meeting room.

◆

At 8:40, Agent Silver radioed, "The subject has left her residence, driving a black Mercedes." He confirmed the license plate number.

8:48, Agent Johnson: "Just saw Tama get off a CTA bus. He's waiting at the door of the office. Uka doesn't let him have a key."

8:52, Pettigrew: "Zalan just parked south of the office in a Chevy." He rattled off the license plate number. Gloria scrawled it down. "Chinwe came with him. They're waiting for Uka out front."

8:58, Johnson: "Black Mercedes parked in front of the business. Uka's heading for the front door." A few more seconds went by. Then, "They're in."

◆

At 9:02, Lauren banged on the door of Uka's Auto Insurance. "Federal agents! We have a search warrant!" She opened the door just as several shots crashed through it and the storefront window. The barrage sprayed over Lauren's shoulder. Johnson cried out and fell onto the sidewalk.

Another agent rushed up. "I got him. Go!" Lauren, Martinez, and Pettigrew crouched down and entered the building, seeking cover behind the first row of desks. They fired multiple rounds at Zalan, who loomed seven feet away. His body twisted and turned as each shot hit and a red explosion erupted from his chest. He toppled backward onto his desk. They ceased fire. For a moment, an eerie silence filled the office.

The remaining agents swarmed into Uka's business, guns drawn. "Raise your hands, and don't move," Lauren bellowed. Then she screamed into her radio: "Johnson's hit. Call for an ambulance!"

Stephens replied: "Gimme a report. What's going on?"

"We shot Zalan. He's down. Stand by."

The other two men, Tama and Chinwe, stood frozen in place. Uka dashed into her office.

Kennedy stood over Zalan. Blood gushed from entrance wounds ranging from his face to his chest. Agent Walker felt for Zalan's pulse. "Zalan's gone. DOA."

Kennedy picked up Zalan's Browning semi-auto.

Martinez grabbed Tama near the file cabinets. He pleaded, "I got a pistol. I didn't shoot it. I didn't want to have it. She made me." Martinez yanked up his shirt and grabbed the .22 caliber Taurus semi-auto out of his waistband. Pettigrew patted Tama down and cuffed him. Chinwe raised his hands, begging not to be hurt. Agent Harden tugged the Colt .38 revolver from Chinwe's waistband while Radinsky cuffed and searched him.

Lauren and Sanchez hustled after Uka. The woman stood behind her desk, palms resting on the onyx top. "Put your hands up," Lauren ordered, pointing her Sig Sauer at Uka.

Uka stayed still. "What's the meaning of this?"

Lauren strode over, holstering her Sig. She grabbed Uka's right wrist, slapped a cuff on it, and twisted it behind the woman's back. Then she brought Uka's left hand close and cuffed it.

"You're hurting me!" Uka shouted.

Lauren twisted her around so they faced each other. "You're under arrest for laundering drug proceeds."

"I don't know what you're talking about," Uka sneered.

"Of course not. Before you say anything else, I have to read you your rights." Lauren removed the rights card from her credentials and read Uka the Miranda warning. "Do you understand?"

Jaw clenched, Uka bowed her head and nodded.

"You could be looking at twenty years. You want to sit down and talk with me?" Lauren asked.

Uka sat, scowling. "Attorney."

"No problem." Lauren patted her down. The woman had no weapons on her. "We're going to search your office." She moved Uka's chair into the center of the room, out of reach of anything. "You sit here for a while and think about your future. Twenty years in a federal pen."

Things had stabilized in the outer room. The arrest teams were hauling Tama and Chinwe out the door, heading for separate cars that would take each of Uka's employees to the U.S. Marshals' office in the federal building for processing. Paramedics took Johnson to the hospital for treatment of a shoulder wound and zipped Zalan's corpse into a body bag. The remaining agents continued searching the front area. At Lauren's instruction, Agent Harding came into Uka's office and made a video to show its pre-search condition. "Do a second one after we're finished," Lauren said, and the agent nodded.

Lauren and Sanchez emptied the contents of Uka's desk drawers into evidence boxes, marking the boxes with the location of each drawer. Lauren pointed at a credenza against the wall. "Jorge, check that out."

Sanchez went over to it. "Nothing in here," he said a few minutes later. "Just travel brochures from Nigeria."

Lauren glanced at the credenza. "It's on coasters. See if you can move it away from the wall."

"Sure." He pushed it, and it easily slid away.

Uka stomped her foot. "Fuck."

Lauren laughed. Not a wall safe behind the credenza, like she'd figured — a floor safe instead. "Uka, you have a decision to make. You can give us the combination, or we'll have to break the safe open."

Uka shook her head. "You open it and they'll kill me."

Lauren approached her with open arms. "Well, then talk to me."

Uka's nostrils flared. "What are you going to do, protect me? Ha. I'm a dead woman, and you'll be, too. I'll put a curse on you."

"Yeah, sure. Give me the combination for the safe," Lauren ordered. "I'm going to get it open even if I have to bust it, but the usual way is easier on your premises."

Uka took a deep breath and exhaled. "You will dread the day you ever stepped into my office." Reluctantly, she recited the combination.

Sanchez bent over the safe and opened it, then whistled. "There's got to be a million bucks in here. And there's a ledger." He pulled the book out of the safe and paged through it. "Lauren, this is a gold mine. Names and dates of people that gave her money. Gloria won't believe this."

"Gloria," Uka mumbled.

Lauren glared at Sanchez. Too late, he realized his mistake. He pursed his lips and lowered his head.

Uka spat on the floor. "Gloria and Marvin. I remember Marvin feared the power of my curse—the yellow eyes. I could see his terror."

Lauren leaned in, her face a scant inch from Uka's. "Listen, bitch. Anything happens to Gloria or Marvin, you're in deep shit."

Uka laughed. "People get sick. Don't they?"

Lauren straightened and faced Sanchez. "Pull the cash out and stack it on the credenza." She turned back to glare at Uka. "I want her to see it there. Let her see, and think about what kind of serious trouble she's in."

They piled the cash on top of the credenza. Lauren went through three bundles. They were mostly singles, fives, tens, twenties, and fifties, and each bundle totaled less than $10,000. "That's pretty smart. Each one of these is ready to be deposited, and less than ten grand means no currency transaction reports. We'll take these to the office to get an accurate count, but I'd guess there's at least $800,000 here. You're right, Uka. You're going to be in a hell of a lot of trouble with whoever gave you all this cash."

Not giving the woman a chance to reply, Lauren called out to Harding. "We need you to video the credenza, the safe, the ledger, and the cash. It's too much to count by hand. We'll take it to the office and run it through the money counter. Let's wrap this up."

She stepped into the outer room and beckoned to agents Silver and Wilson. "Take Uka Kafi to the marshals."

They strode into the back office and yanked Uka out of her chair. "You'll regret this day forever!" Uka spat out.

Lauren felt her glare but wouldn't back down. "I don't believe in your voodoo shit. Get her out of here."

CHAPTER 47

Carlton/Nighthawk Residence, Bronzeville
Saturday, January 22, 2005
Noon

GLORIA WAS IN HER KITCHEN, the paper in front of her and a cup of coffee she'd barely touched by her elbow, when her cell phone rang. She looked at the caller ID. The number was FBI agent Adamczyk's. She hesitated, anticipating the reason for his call, but knew it was inevitable. She might as well answer. "Nighthawk, CID."

"Gloria, it's Joe. I've got some bad news. The CPD found Marvin."

She wasn't sure what to say, but knew she had to play it coy. "CPD? What…what do you mean?"

"Marvin's dead. He was found at the 63rd Street beach, shot once in the head."

"Oh, my God." Her hand holding the phone trembled, like she was reliving the experience. Somehow, she managed to reply, "I don't believe it."

"I'm sorry to lay this on you. You knew him better than anyone else. Do you have any idea who might have wanted him out of the way?"

Gloria took a moment to gather her thoughts. "Violence is the nature of the drug business, Joe. There're the usual suspects—his source, competitors, dirty cops." She stumbled slightly as she went on, careful not to say too much. "I've got to admit, he pulled the wool over my eyes. I didn't suspect him of still being a dealer. I thought he was out, but he could find information for me because he'd been in the business for so long." She wet her lips and waited a second. "This undercover money laundering investigation was the first time he did anything you'd consider deep cover for me. I can't think of any suspects."

Adamczyk sighed. "That's the way it is with some of these CIs, you just can't trust them."

"Who found Marvin?" Gloria had to know.

"Some jogger yesterday morning. He made an anonymous call to the CPD. They picked up the body, found his ID in his wallet. We'd put out a BOLO, and CPD contacted us. He had $500 in cash on him, so it obviously wasn't a robbery."

"Sure sounds like a setup."

"Our forensic guys went out right away. They found three shell casings from a 9mm, but he was shot just once. Only Marvin's fingerprints were on the shell casings, so it seems like he struggled with the shooter. Whoever it was got hold of his gun and killed him."

Her mouth felt dry. "Did you find the gun?"

"No. The shooter must have taken it and Marvin's cell phone. The wallet was the only thing Marvin had in his possession. Forensics did find some fabric strands in the snow that were different from the coat Marvin was wearing. Could have been from the shooter. We'll see what pans out."

She wondered if the fabric strands were from her navy pea coat. "Thanks for contacting me, Joe. Sorry it ended this way. I know you were hoping to flip him."

"No problem, Gloria. I'll keep you up to date on any developments." Adamczyk paused, then continued with more animation. "What about the defendant in the search warrant you just executed? Anything there, you think?"

Gloria splayed her free hand across her chest. "Uka did threaten me and Marvin during an undercover meeting. She said she was going to put a curse on us. Something about yellow eyes. She never mentioned shooting us."

"You never know."

He'd handed her a diversion, but only if she went deeper into her lie. "Now that I think about it, someone involved with Uka and her business could have been responsible. When my partner arrested Uka, she said the people she laundered the money for would kill her if she cooperated."

"We'll see if we can identify her associates." Adamczyk sounded eager now. "Think about what leads you have and let me know."

Swiftly, Gloria replayed her past responses to Adamczyk in her mind. Best keep it short rather than risk making a mistake. "I will, Joe. Talk to you later."

Her thumb moved toward the hangup button. "Hold on," he said. She heard him shuffling through some papers. "Here's something. You ever heard of a Beatrice Moore? She claimed Marvin's body from the morgue for the funeral."

Gloria paused. "No, doesn't ring a bell." Then it flashed into her mind. When she was surveilling Darius, trying to learn where he was living, the red Mustang that picked him up from school was registered to Moore.

"I checked with the Secretary of State's office and ran Moore through DMV," Adamczyk went on. "She's seventy years old and had three vehicles registered under her name—a Cadillac, a Honda, and a Mustang. She might have been a nominee for Marvin. I think it would be worthwhile to interview her. See what she knows about Marvin's associates…or enemies."

What if she knows something about Darius's involvement with Marvin? "That's a good idea, Joe. I'll interview her as soon as we finish going through the documents we seized."

"Better to do it ASAP, while she's still grieving. If you can't break away from the records, I'll get it done."

God, no. "A day or two more won't make much difference. I can get free by then." She had to push him back, interview Moore on her own.

"I think I'll get out there tomorrow morning. I'll let you know if she has anything interesting to say."

"Hold on." Gloria paused, racking her brains for an alternative. There wasn't one. "Okay, tomorrow morning. I'll join you. It'll do me good to get away from all these docs for an hour."

"Great. Being contacted by an IRS agent and an FBI agent should rattle her, if she has anything to hide," Adamczyk said.

Gloria closed her eyes and leaned back in her chair. "I'll meet you at the Federal Building garage at nine."

"Sounds good. See you then."

Gloria ended the call. She crossed her arms and let out a sigh, unsure if it was relief or anxiety. Then she picked up her phone again and hit a number on speed dial.

Lauren answered. "I've got some terrible news," Gloria said. "The FBI found Marvin. He's dead." She gave her partner the full details from Adamczyk.

"Oh, my God. I'm sorry, Gloria. I know you had a long relationship with him. This must be hard to take, on top of everything else."

"Yeah. My life is like a bad dream right now." *If Lauren only knew the truth. But I can never trust anyone with that.*

"I never thought…" Lauren said.

"You never thought what?"

"Never mind."

"No, tell me. You never thought what?"

"All this death. It happened so fast. First Zalan at the insurance office, and now Marvin."

The jolt of fear subsided. "You'll probably never experience this again. Ninety-nine percent of agents never have to deal with a shooting incident in their entire career."

"I hope not."

"Could you do me a favor?"

"Sure, anything."

"Could you call Stephens and let him know? I just don't feel like talking to him right now."

"I can understand that. I'll do it right away."

"Thanks, Lauren." Gloria ended the call. The events of the past few days had brought the reality of all the deaths in her life to the forefront. It started with the Oklahoma City bombing in 1995. She was supposed to take her mother to a new childcare job at the Murrah Federal Building, but Gloria overslept, so her father drove instead. Gloria remembered the sight of her father's pickup truck, sticking out from the debris. The guilt never left her.

In 2004 in Iraq, she'd killed several insurgents during an attack on the way to Baghdad International Airport. Her lover, James Abbott, died in that ambush. A month later, she'd aborted his child. Not long after that, she'd shot Spencer McElroy before he could kill her son. It was ruled a good shoot. And now Marvin. *How would they rule that, if people knew?*

Gloria rested her head in her hands. She still couldn't make up her own mind. On the one hand, pre-meditated murder—she'd met with Marvin intending to kill him if necessary to protect Darius. But Marvin had tried to wrestle the Ruger pistol away from her, and then grabbed Gloria's Sig and pointed it at her head. She wished she could go back and change what happened, but knew she couldn't.

Some of the deaths were angels and some were devils but they all remained on her conscience. She needed to get away from all this death, put an end to her experiences with violence. Gloria needed a way to create a safe haven, not only for herself but for her children.

CHAPTER 48

Monday, January 24, 2005
9:00 a.m.

GLORIA HEADED SOUTH FROM HER office in the Dirksen building down Federal Street toward the federal garage. She saw a fresh snow had been cleared away as she passed the Metropolitan Correctional Center. She thought of her soon to be ex-husband, Robert Carlton, who was currently an inmate there. *The day Robert's sentenced and moved out of there will be a good one, especially for Darius. His father won't be able to play the guilt card, so he won't be tempted to visit his father in jail.*

As she approached the garage, she saw a man wearing a gray overcoat with a blue suit underneath. He was tall and slender, clean-shaven, with the look of a marathoner, and about her age. His blue eyes had an intense look. "You must be Joe," she said as she reached him.

"And you're Gloria," Adamczyk said, flashing his ID.

Gloria pulled out her own credentials. "This is me. My car or yours?"

"Mine's being serviced."

"Okay. Second floor, black SUV." Gloria took the lead heading up the stairs. They got into her G ride and headed out of the garage, then southbound on the Dan Ryan Expressway. She gave the FBI agent a sidelong glance as she tried to slow her breathing. Adamczyk would be interviewing a witness with her, to develop leads to solve Marvin Bailey's murder. *How's that going to work out?* She exhaled. "So, how do you want to play this?"

"He was your informant, so I don't mind being the cover agent if you want to take the lead," Adamczyk said.

Good. "That works for me."

Traffic heading south on the Dan Ryan was light. The northbound traffic into the city was heavy, almost bumper to bumper. "Chicago amazes me. It's rush hour traffic twenty-four hours a day," Gloria said.

"I'm from Chicago originally, was stationed in Virginia for ten years. Been back about a year now. Almost used to it."

Gloria's brow furrowed. "If you're free to tell me, what kind of a case did you have on Marvin?"

"Not much, I'm afraid."

She hadn't expected that answer. She cocked her head. "What do you mean?"

Adamczyk shrugged. "We had this Mexican that we got a couple of buys into. Good dope. Heroin. We flipped him and had him tape a telephone conversation with Marvin. Our guy was supposed to sell him two kilos of Mexican mud."

Gloria's eyes narrowed. "Supposed to?"

"Yeah. We had the indictment on Marvin already, so we thought we might as well go ahead and see if we could flip him. The day before our Mexican guy was supposed to do the deal, the Mexican ended up dead. A single head shot." Adamczyk sighed. "Without him, our case on Marvin went to hell."

Gloria fought to understand what she was hearing. "Are you telling me you were just confronting Marvin? That the possibility of pressing charges was remote at best?"

"I guess that's what I'm saying. The U.S. Attorney would never move forward on a one-on-one where our CI is dead."

Gloria's stomach roiled and she turned away from Adamczyk. *Why didn't I press him on the case earlier?*

She kept driving, focusing on the road to calm herself. Fifteen minutes later, she pulled into the parking space next to the sign marked 3904 South Building. The same place she'd parked the day she followed Darius in the red Mustang. Three spots away was a yellow Cadillac, sitting on milk crates. Its tires, wheels, and license plates gone.

Gloria pointed at the car. "That was Marvin's. I guess the word is out that he's gone. It doesn't take long."

Adamczyk nodded and unbuttoned his suit coat, giving him easy access to his semi-auto.

"Just to let you know, the odds are there'll be gangbangers at the entrance," Gloria said. "They won't give us any trouble, but they'll probably shout out FIVE-O, FIVE-O to let their homies know the cops are here."

"Got it. I've heard it before."

They exited the vehicle and tramped through ankle-deep dirty snow. Unlike downtown, city services hadn't cleared it. Gloria led the way around the building. As they approached the front entrance, chants of "FIVE-O, FIVE-O," rang out.

"Just as predicted. What floor did you say her apartment was on?" Gloria asked.

"Tenth. Unit 1018."

Gloria shook her head. "It's usually not a good idea to take the elevators, but ten floors are too many to hike up."

Adamczyk nodded. "We should be safe. I think we're early enough to beat the project rush hour. But we don't want to risk being easy targets when the elevator doors open."

They passed the gangbangers on guard and entered the building. Already there were people milling about in the lobby, but it was mostly older residents. They stepped into an elevator. Right before the doors closed, one of the bangers who'd been at the front doors jogged up and entered. A teenage boy in baggy jeans, Air Jordans, and a Bulls sweatshirt.

Gloria assumed he was there to see what floor they were headed to, so she beat him to the punch. "What floor would you like?"

He said nothing at first, looking her up and down. "I'll take…seven." He folded his arms and stared at Gloria and Adamczyk.

"We're heading to nine," she said, and pressed both buttons.

The elevator doors opened at seven and he hustled out. When it stopped again at nine, Gloria and Adamczyk stepped off. They hurried into the nearest stairwell and rushed up to the tenth floor. As they exited into the hallway, they heard the door down on the ninth floor slam shut. "Okay, he should be busy checking the apartments on nine. Let's go talk to Beatrice," Gloria said.

They headed to Unit 1018 and knocked on the door. A sweet voice responded, "Who's there?"

"Ms. Moore, my name is Gloria Nighthawk. I'm here with Joe Adamczyk. We're federal agents, and we would like to ask you a few questions."

"About what?"

"How about if you let us in, and then we'll give you the details."

They waited a few seconds. Gloria spoke again. "Ms. Moore, are you there?"

"Can you hold your badge up to the peephole?"

"Yes, ma'am." Gloria did as requested, and they heard a series of deadbolt locks click. An older woman opened the door. She wore a housecoat in a floral print. Her dark skin was smooth, her silver hair in a short afro.

She gave them a pleasant smile. "Come in, please."

"Thank you, ma'am." They entered the apartment. The creak of the stairwell door to the tenth-floor hallway reached Gloria's ears as Ms. Moore closed the apartment door behind them.

"Please, sit down. Would you like some tea?" Ms. Moore said.

Gloria and Adamczyk declined her offer. Beatrice Moore seated herself in a tall chair with a pattern of small roses and a doily over the back. The two agents sat opposite her, on a French-style sofa with a quilted back and curved wooden legs. "Your apartment is lovely." Gloria eyed a large screen TV on the wall. *Has to be a gift from Marvin.*

"Thank you. I've been here a long time." Beatrice Moore waved her hand. "Many, many years."

Gloria nodded in acknowledgment. "We're here to ask you about Marvin Bailey. How did you come to know Marvin?"

Sadness crossed Beatrice's face. "I met Marvin about five, maybe six years ago. As time went on, I got to know him quite well. He wasn't a CHA employee, but if you needed something done, he was the man to see. I was complaining to the workers that the kids were getting a little rowdy in the hallway, playing loud music and such, but it didn't do any good. One day, when I went to the office to complain again, Marvin was there. I explained my situation to him. He said he'd take care of things. After that, it was as quiet as a church mouse in the hall." Beatrice smiled. "I don't know how he made it happen, but the next time I was at the office, I saw him there and I thanked him. He was such a gentleman."

Gloria waited for her to expand on her answers, but she didn't volunteer any details. *I need to ask for them, or Adamczyk might think I'm avoiding that.* "What other favors did he do for you?"

"If I was ever short for the rent, he would help me. You know, a few hundred here and there. Not much. My Social Security usually is enough to live off. He'd ask if I had groceries, or needed anything. That's all."

"Did he ever ask you to do anything in return?"

"Every once and a while he would ask me to sign some papers. I was happy to do that."

"What kind of papers?"

She rested her chin in her palm and thought for a moment. "I'm sorry, I just don't recall. I didn't pay close attention. I don't know what they were exactly."

"Do you think they might have had something to do with cars?"

"I wish I could help you, but I just don't know. I would scribble my name where he told me. Sometimes, he would stay for a sandwich, and we'd chat. Mostly he'd be on his way, though."

Adamczyk leaned forward. "This might refresh your memory, ma'am. Did any of the documents you signed mention cars? Like a Mustang, a Cadillac, or a Honda?"

Beatrice pulled a white handkerchief from her sleeve and twisted it in her hands. "I really don't know what they were for." She looked down as if ashamed for her lack of curiosity.

Gloria stood. She'd heard enough, and it was clear they'd get no further. Hopefully, Adamczyk was satisfied. Beatrice Moore knew nothing of Marvin's illegal activities. Darius was safe. For a moment, she allowed herself to feel relief. "I think we're done. Thank you for your time, Ms. Moore."

Adamczyk stayed seated. "I have one more question. When Marvin visited you, did he come with anyone else?"

Gloria sank back into her seat, waiting for the answer.

Beatrice raised a hand to her mouth. "Let me think. There were some young boys. One was short, little on the heavy side. The other tall, like you, Mr. Adamczyk. He dressed a little cleaner than the other boys that are usually in the building."

"Do you know their names?" Adamczyk asked.

Gloria felt the muscles in her neck tighten. *Adamczyk and Darius are about the same height.*

"I don't think Marvin ever introduced them," Beatrice said.

Adamczyk stood. "Okay, I guess we're done."

Those were the words Gloria desperately needed to hear. She rose again and moved from the sofa toward the door.

"Wait. I'm sorry. One more question." Adamczyk held up a finger. "Ms. Moore, you signed a release to take custody of Marvin's body from the morgue. Did someone tell you to do that?"

Gloria stopped, one hand on her hip. *Come on now, let's go.*

A tear rolled down Beatrice's cheek. She sniffled and wiped it away with her handkerchief. "Marvin did. A week or so ago, he came to my apartment. He told me he wasn't feeling well. He didn't mention an illness, but said just in case something happened, he'd made arrangements at a funeral parlor. He asked me to take care of things."

Adamczyk's jaw dropped, and he gave Gloria a befuddled look. Gloria ran a shaking hand through her hair. Had Marvin guessed she was going to kill him?

Beatrice rose and opened the door for them. "You're such nice people. Sorry I couldn't have helped you more. Have a good day."

She was either innocent or playing coy, Gloria thought. They nodded at her and left Beatrice's apartment. Gloria heard the locks click shut behind them. They walked in silence toward the elevator. It was open, and loitering by it was the gangbanger who'd followed them up. Gloria grabbed him by his Bulls sweatshirt and pulled him into the elevator. "You like to ride in this thing so much, you can come with us."

The doors closed, and Adamczyk pushed the kid against the wall. "What's your name, tough guy?"

He smirked. "Michael Jordan."

"You think you're a smartass." Adamczyk went through the banger's pockets, pulling them inside out until he found a wallet. "Huh. His name *is* Michael Jordan. Well, that's good to know. You're going to be in my report. We ever hear of you harassing Ms. Moore, your next residence will be a federal pen." Adamczyk cocked his head. His eyes narrowed. "You know about Marvin Bailey?"

Jordan shrugged. "You mean him being dead. Everybody knows that."

Gloria shoved her hands into her pockets, squeezing her fingers into her palms. *If he knew Marvin, he might have known Darius.*

"How well did you know Marvin?" the FBI agent asked, as if he'd read her mind.

"Didn't know him. Just knew about him."

"Fine. How'd you know *about* him?"

"People talk."

"You know any tall boys that hung around Marvin?"

"Just one."

Gloria's face tensed, her elbows tight against her sides.

Jordan looked at Adamczyk. "He about your size but…"

Gloria held her breath.

Adamczyk interrupted. "But what?"

Jordan waved his hands. "Chill man, you ain't cool. That tall boy is dead, too. I don't know nothing about it. Just word on the street that some homie shot him, just like Marvin."

"You know who shot Marvin?"

The gangbanger shook his head. "Na."

The elevator stopped on the ground floor and the doors opened. Gloria uncurled her fists. The three of them stepped out into the regular crowd in the foyer. Rap music was blasting. Adamczyk looked at Jordan and smiled. "Thanks for your cooperation. We'll be in touch."

The two agents left the building. Adamczyk caught Gloria's eye. "Marvin knew someone was coming for him. Sounds like we're getting close."

She glanced at him. "Could be just a matter of time." She looked away, as if toward her Blazer, and swallowed.

CHAPTER 49

U.S. Attorney's Office
Dirksen Federal Building
Tuesday, January 25, 2005
10:00 a.m.

BEFORE THE ARRAIGNMENTS OF UKA Kafi and her associates, Gloria and Lauren met with Phil Tunney. They sat in the prosecutor's office, which wasn't much larger than a jail cell, and was still jammed with boxes containing evidence for his next two trials plus three grand jury investigations.

Gloria scooched to the edge of her seat. She remembered someone saying once, *if you tell a lie long enough, you start believing it.* So far, for her, that wasn't the case. Here and now, she could stick to the truth. "Let me bring you up to date, Phil. The FBI recently indicted our informant, Marvin Bailey, on drug charges. They couldn't locate him and put out a BOLO. CPD found his dead body a few days ago. A single shot to the head."

Tunney leaned back in his chair. "I've got two questions for you. What's left of our case? Was Uka implicated in the informant's death?"

Gloria glanced at Lauren, then returned her gaze to Tunney. "We still have a good case against Uka Kafi. My undercover transcripts with her where I advised her that my cash was from heroin proceeds. The bank records, which reflect millions in cash deposits prior to our contacts, and the results of our search warrants. Lauren seized over $800,000 in cash from a hidden floor safe during the raid. The major problem might be probable cause for the search warrant. Marvin Bailey was responsible for the initial groundwork identifying Uka Kafi."

Tunney clicked his ballpoint pen, "I think we can overcome any motions fighting the probable cause. What about my second question? Were Uka or any of her associates implicated in Bailey's death?"

Gloria fought down a swirl of emotions, mainly fear and regret. She knew this was something she would have to deal with again when she was testifying, and especially in cross-examination. *I'll have to be strong to continue the ruse.* "So far, we've no evidence she was involved in any way in the shooting. We'll continue looking into that."

Tunney clicked his pen once more and slid it into the pocket of his crisp white shirt. "The coincidence of his death and Uka's case can't be denied, but I doubt the judge will allow us to bring it up at trial if we have no evidence implicating her one way or another."

Lauren raised her eyebrows. "She threatened me with a curse when we executed the search warrants. Gloria too, during the undercover meeting."

Tunney looked at Gloria. "A curse? You're kidding me."

Reluctantly, Gloria shook her head. She didn't want to talk about anything more to do with Marvin, wished Lauren hadn't mentioned the meeting. "It's true. She threatened me and Marvin both, telling us it would be lethal and our eyes would turn yellow. Marvin was visibly shaken up."

Tunney shook his head. "I'm not going to get into any of that at the arraignment. If we develop solid evidence regarding your informant's murder, we can always supersede the indictment." He peered more closely at the two of them. "Yellow eyes, huh? I don't see any yellow. You guys look okay. You are, aren't you?"

Gloria shrugged. "I think so."

"I feel fine," Lauren said.

Tunney stood. "All right, then. Let's head up to court."

They went to Courtroom 1905 and sat in the first row of benches behind the prosecution table. Judge Gomez was middle-aged and stocky, with a medium complexion that made him look tanned and healthy. He was already hearing motions filed by several attorneys in a massive class action suit against a banker who had defrauded several hundred investors in a Ponzi scheme, and the judge was visibly losing his patience trying to keep the attorneys from talking over each other.

Judge Gomez pointed a finger at one of the attorneys. "Mr. Shroeder, I've advised you on numerous occasions to let the opposing attorneys complete their arguments without interruption. If you continue, I'll have no choice but to fine you, and I mean a substantial amount. If that doesn't work, I'll find you in contempt of court and you can spend a few days at MCC. Am I clear?"

Shroeder pursed his lips and nodded. "Yes, your honor. I apologize. I just want to make sure my client gets fair treatment."

The judge pointed his finger down. Shroeder got the message and sat at the defense table. He looked rebellious and mumbled a few unintelligible words.

"Did you say something?" the judge snapped. Shroeder nervously shook his head and looked down at the tabletop.

"All right, we have all the motions filed. I'll review them and make a final ruling on..." Gomez glanced at his calendar. "February seventh. See you gentlemen then."

The attorneys cleared the courtroom. Tunney moved to the prosecutor's table. Gloria and Lauren remained seated in the first row of benches behind him. Tunney leaned toward them and whispered, "We're definitely not mentioning anything about yellow eyes or a curse. I don't want Judge Gomez pissed at me for wasting his time with frivolous allegations."

A few minutes later, marshals herded Uka Kafi, Kunta Tama, and Tala Chinwe into the courtroom. The three defendants wore orange jumpsuits and were handcuffed. Their attorneys followed them in. Gloria recognized James Winston, one of the top Black criminal defense attorneys in Chicago. A former corporate counsel for the city, he was now taking advantage of his political contacts and reeling in top money. He was tall, sophisticated, and carried himself well in the courtroom. The other two attorneys were public defenders.

"Good afternoon, your honor. James Winston for Miss Kafi." Winston's voice boomed through the courtroom like a preacher giving a sermon.

The public defenders introduced themselves and confirmed they were representing Uka's associates. Then it was Tunney's turn. He stood and moved confidently to the podium. "Phillip Tunney for the government."

The judge leafed through the charging documents. "It looks like we have an undercover investigation by the IRS, alleging the defendants laundered funds that were purported to be the proceeds of heroin trafficking. Do we need to read the charges?"

Winston brushed a hair off his thousand-dollar suit. "Not for me, your honor. I would appreciate it if you would allow the marshals to remove the defendants' handcuffs for the time being. I don't think they're a flight risk from your honor's courtroom."

Judge Gomez looked at the defendants. "All right. Marshals, remove the handcuffs for this session. They will be cuffed again after this proceeding is over."

Winston thanked the judge. The cuffs came off, and Uka and the others massaged their wrists. Winston looked at his client and then at the judge again. "About Miss Uka's bond —"

Tunney braced his hands on the podium. "I don't believe a bond is appropriate for these defendants."

The judge gave Tunney a long look. Tunney got the message: *Don't interrupt defense counsel.* "Mr. Tunney, since Mr. Winston doesn't require a reading of the charges, can you give me the facts supporting your position?"

Tunney exhaled. He could tell the judge was leaning his way. "Your honor, these three individuals have committed serious offenses." He went through the details of the money laundering, including the large amount of cash found in Uka Kafi's hidden safe. "In addition, U.S. Customs intercepted several packages mailed from Nigeria to Miss Kafi's business that contained fraudulent U.S. passports, all with Mr. Tama's photograph but listing different aliases, and other passports for unknown individuals. Miss Kafi also made threatening remarks to the undercover agent, her informant, and the agent executing the search warrant for Miss Kafi's insurance office."

Judge Gomez looked at Winston and shrugged. "Are you going to argue for a bond?"

"Your honor. Miss Kafi has had a difficult life. She has overcome many obstacles. She has lost both of her parents and is a single mother of an eight-year-old girl. She has no other relatives living in the area. It would be an undue hardship on her and her daughter for her to be incarcerated during the trial. Electronic monitoring would be a reasonable compromise."

The judge lifted his chin and thrust his shoulders back. "Given the situation, bond is set at $500,000 for Miss Uka and $100,000 for her associates, with each defendant required to wear an electronic ankle bracelet." He banged his gavel, signaling the end of the preliminary proceedings.

On their way out, Uka gave Gloria and Lauren a menacing stare.

Gloria wondered, *what will she think when she hears about Marvin? Will she fear being charged with his murder?*

CHAPTER 50

Downtown Chicago
Tuesday, January 25, 2005
11:30 a.m.

GLORIA AND LAUREN STEPPED OUT of the Dirksen Federal Building. Gloria paused and looked at her partner. "I'm going for a walk. I'll meet you back in the office."

Lauren cocked her head. "Would you like some company?"

"Thanks, but I just need time to clear my head. I can do that better on my own. It's been a hell of year with Robert pleading guilty, Darius going into rehab, and Marvin dying." She cleared her throat. Her abortion and Jim Abbott's murder came to mind, but she thought it better not to mention them. "I need some alone time, to think things through."

"Sure, no problem. If you want to meet for a drink later, give me a call."

Gloria nodded. Watching Lauren hustle across Dearborn Street and into the Kluczynski Federal Building, she thought, *where would I be without her? Thank God she's in my life.*

The sky was gray and the temperature around freezing. The damp cold seeped into her bones. She pulled the collar of her ski jacket up around her neck and started walking north into a chilling wind.

The streets started to fill with people heading out for lunch. She turned east on Monroe and headed toward Michigan Avenue, a path that protected her from the north wind until she got to the intersections on State Street and Wabash where the wind tunneled through the passages. On Wabash, the El squealed on its tracks above her. She stopped at Michigan Avenue just as it started raining. "I've to get out of this damn weather," she mumbled. The Art Institute was on the east side of Michigan Avenue, and she headed toward it.

Once inside, Gloria went to the gallery devoted to the French Impressionists and found a spot on the bench facing a series of Gustave Caillebotte's paintings. *I've got to spend more time here, escape from things at least temporarily.*

She took off her jacket and laid it on the bench. The painting in front of her captured a chilly overcast street filled with pedestrians wearing heavy overcoats and holding open umbrellas. She whispered the title: " 'Paris Street; Rainy Day'. God, I can't get away from the darkness in my life."

It dawned on her that her husband's sentencing was scheduled for March 11, four days after Uka Kafi's trial started on March 7. *That'll be a memorable week. My husband goes to prison and we try to present a case with a dead informant. If Winston puts any of the defendants on the stand, they can say anything they want — like, Marvin threatened them.*

She felt mixed emotions about Marvin's death. He'd gone from informant to a friend of sorts, then to foe for a while. Was it self-defense or murder, at least in her mind? *With him out of the picture, Darius will be free.* Unless other people could incriminate Darius, but she didn't think that would happen. *Did I let my relationship with Marvin cloud my judgment? What am I always trying to prove? Or maybe I'm just searching for an explanation about my relationships that's eluded me all my life.* A sigh escaped her. *Maybe it's time to move on to something else.*

A man sat next to her on the bench. Rainwater dripped off his black overcoat and started puddling on the seat. She moved to her left, giving him more room. He edged closer to her. She glanced at him. His coat was nice, but it was drenched, and his salt and pepper hair looked windblown and disheveled. There were crow's feet at the corners of his eyes.

He pulled a handkerchief from his pocket and wiped moisture off the back of his neck. "The rain really started coming down hard."

She nodded and stared straight ahead at the painting. *I have to be seated next to a talker, just when I wanted this time to myself.*

"The weather in that painting is almost as bad as it is outside," he said.

Gloria moved to the far end of the bench.

"Thanks, I was kind of sitting on the edge." He moved closer to her again. "That's more comfortable."

She turned toward him. "Look, I don't mean to be rude, but I came here for some quiet time. I've got a lot of thinking to do." *It really must be pouring out there. This guy's a mess.* She laughed.

"You laughing at me?" He grinned and pushed his fingers through his damp hair.

"Isn't that a line from a Joe Pesci movie?" she said, then remembered she didn't want to get into a conversation.

"Yeah, *Goodfellas,*" he said.

Gloria exhaled and glanced away from him, folding her arms across her chest.

"Look, I don't mean to pry, but you're Agent Nighthawk, aren't you?" he asked.

She jerked away from him and frowned. "How do you know who I am?"

"I was in the gallery at Judge Carlton's trial. I saw you on the stand. Must have been difficult to testify against your husband?"

"Yeah. Why the hell were you there?"

"I had a meeting at the U.S. Attorney's office. I saw the docket sheet with Judge Carlton's name on it and came to watch the trial. I didn't know you'd be testifying."

"Are you an attorney?"

He laughed. "No, that's something I never wanted to be."

"Well, my husband and I won't be married much longer." She shook her head. "Why am I telling you this? It's none of your business." She grabbed her jacket, ready to leave.

"You're right. It's none of my business. I just know how difficult those personal situations can get. I…I've been there."

"Really? I doubt that."

He reached into the inside pocket of his suit coat and came up with a business card holder, slid out a card, and handed it to Gloria.

She read the card. *Scott Garity Investigations, Retired Federal Agent.*

"My phone number is on the card," he said. "If you're thinking of pulling the plug on your job any time soon, give me a call. I've got a lot of work and can always use a good investigator. Hope I didn't upset you." Garity stood and headed out of the gallery.

She watched him go, his card still in her hand.

CHAPTER 51

Courtroom 1905
Dirksen Federal Building
Monday, March 7, 2005

GLORIA AND LAUREN HAD SPENT the last month preparing for Uka's trial, scrutinizing reams of paperwork that involved reviewing all the memorandums of interviews with Marvin Bailey, memorandums of surveillance, chain of custody for the evidence seized during the search warrant executed on Uka Kafi's business, tapes of the undercover meetings with Uka, records received from United States Customs and the Drug Enforcement Agency, currency transaction reports, records of bank accounts belonging to Uka and her three associates, and the analysis of those records. They had to make sure everything accurately reflected the results of their investigation, because there's nothing worse than being impeached by your own evidence.

Now they sat at the prosecution table with Assistant U.S. Attorneys Phillip Tunney and his second chair, Cheryl Boston. Gloria leaned over and whispered to Lauren. "This is Cheryl's first major trial. She's spent the last year preparing preliminary motions and warrants for cases assigned to other prosecutors. I hope she's up for this."

"She was a graduate of Morehouse State, majoring in political science. That's one of the best Black schools in the country," Lauren replied. "She was a jock too, a top sprinter on the track team. She graduated from Yale Law School and was an author for the *Yale Law Journal*. She's smart and smooth. I like Cheryl."

The defense attorneys were led by James Winston, representing Uka Kafi, and public defender Morris Greenspan, who represented Kunta Tama. Tofil Chinwe was cooperating and would be testifying as a witness for the government. Hearing the case was Judge Jorge Gomez. In pre-trial motions, it had been agreed that no mention was to be made of the murder of Marvin Bailey unless the government had evidence implicating Uka or an associate in his murder. A similar ruling regarding the shooting death of Zubari Zalan had been made because the nature of that evidence would be more prejudicial than probative.

By mid-afternoon they had picked the jury. The judge glanced at his watch; it was 2:45. "I think it would be a good idea to leave opening arguments for the morning, giving all parties a chance for a fresh start at 9:30 tomorrow. We will commence with the opening statements by the attorneys for the government, and then the defense attorneys. Is everyone in agreement with that?"

All the attorneys and the jury were happy with the judge's decision.

Courtroom 1905
Tuesday, March 8, 2005
9:30 a.m.e

Judge Gomez stood up from his seat behind the bench when a court security officer brought the jury in. There was a rumble in the courtroom as everyone followed the judge's lead, and then sat down again after the jury was seated.

The gallery in the courtroom consisted of newspaper and TV reporters, law students, and courtroom buffs, retired men and women who attended the trials. The retired folks even published a paper after each trial, summarizing points of interest and evaluating the performance of prosecutors, defense attorneys, and agents.

"Good morning, ladies and gentlemen of the jury," Judge Gomez said. "Today we will be starting the trial of Uka Kafi and Kunta Tama, who are charged with several counts of laundering money alleged to be the proceeds of heroin trafficking. The prosecutors and defense counsel will make opening statements. Those statements are not to be considered as evidence by you. They are only the opinions of the attorneys, describing what they expect the evidence to show. Is that clear?"

The jurors nodded that they understood.

"Good. I will rule what evidence is admissible and what is not admissible. If I rule that certain evidence is not admissible, you must not consider it in your deliberations. In this case, there are tape recordings and memorandums of interviews from a government informant by the name of Marvin Bailey. You will hear his name during this trial. Mr. Bailey is not available to testify, but I have ruled that testimony regarding his actions, testimony about him, and tape recordings from which you will hear him speak may be admissible. I will make specific rulings as to which parts of them are admissible based on the law. You must decide what weight to give the credibility of his testimony. Is this clear?"

The jury members indicated it was.

"All right, I believe we're ready. The government will go first. Mr. Tunney, you may proceed."

Phillip Tunney stood. He wore a red silk tie over a crisp white shirt. He buttoned his dark gray suit coat and proceeded to the podium. "Good morning, ladies, and gentlemen. Seated with me at the prosecution table to my left is Assistant U. S. Attorney Cheryl Boston, and to my right with their backs toward you are IRS Special Agents Lauren Ashberry and Gloria Nighthawk. It is our responsibility to represent the U.S. government in this case, which involves an undercover IRS investigation into a money laundering operation." He paused, walked across the courtroom, halted three feet in front of the defense table, and pointed defiantly at Uka Kafi. "Headed by this woman."

She scowled at Tunney. Winston placed his hand over hers as if to comfort her.

Tunney returned to the podium. "The evidence we will introduce is overwhelming. The defendants are charged with violating Title 18, Section 1956 and Title 31, Section 5326 of the U.S. Criminal Code. That is the legal description and it may sound complicated, but when you hear the evidence, you will agree we have proven the allegations.

"I'll keep my opening statement short. In this case, there are three elements we must prove. First, that the defendants were predisposed to commit this crime. Second, that they structured the deposits in certain bank accounts to avoid having the financial institution prepare currency transaction reports. And finally, that the defendants knew the cash they received was from an illegal source.

"Uka and her associates deposited approximately ten million dollars in cash. Now, common sense tells you that a small neighborhood auto insurance company does not generate over ten million dollars in cash business within a mere few years. But Uka Kafi was smart. She knew she had to conceal her interest in this cash. She didn't use her own personal or business accounts. Instead, she opened accounts in the names of three men that worked in her office, and used their purported businesses as fronts. If you are not familiar with the term 'fronts,' that means these businesses had few or no legitimate transactions and were used for the purpose of laundering money. By that, I mean the monies deposited were from illegal sources, and when such funds are withdrawn, the parties involved hope the monies appear legitimate and can be spent or deposited into other bank accounts. Use your common sense based on your life experience. Imagine in your mind what ten million in cash would look like."

Tunney shifted his weight slightly. "Tofil Chinwe was charged in the original indictment. He has pled guilty and is cooperating with the government. He will testify that the three businesses in question were set up as fronts per Uka Kafi's instructions, and that all the cash deposited to these accounts was given by her to Chinwe, Zalan, and Tama.

"The bank records for these accounts reflect that during the period prior to the undercover operation, all the deposits were wired to an automobile dealership in Nigeria, except for certain checks made payable to Uka Kafi. The proceeds delivered to Kafi from the undercover operation were deposited into these same three accounts, and wired to a government undercover bank account in the Bahamas.

"You will hear tapes where the informant Marvin Bailey and undercover agent Gloria Nighthawk tell Uka Kafi that Agent Nighthawk is in the heroin business. You will hear much more than that, and after hearing the evidence, you will make the decision. I'm sure it will be guilty beyond a reasonable doubt. Thank you." Tunney returned to the prosecution table and sat.

The judge nodded to Winston and Greenspan. "The floor is yours."

Winston stood. He wore a tailor-made black pinstripe suit with a silver tie and a matching pocket square over a light gray shirt. "Your honor, since these cases are so tightly knitted together, the defense team has decided that I will make the sole opening statement."

"Is that acceptable to Miss Kafi and Mr. Tama?" Judge Gomez asked.

They both responded, "Yes, your honor."

"Very well." Judge Gomez sat back. "You may begin, Mr. Winston."

Winston moved to the podium without any notes in hand. "Good morning, ladies and gentlemen. It is my honor to represent Uka Kafi and speak for Kunta Tama. I'm afraid I won't be as short as Mr. Tunney was because I have a lot to tell you about Miss Kafi and only a few days for you to get to know her. Miss Kafi was eight years old when she migrated to the U.S. with her mother and father, who were both doctors in Nigeria. It wasn't easy for them. Even though her parents were well educated, their degrees weren't honored in our country. Her mother cleaned other people's homes and her father ended up as a postal worker. It was a price they were willing to pay to bring up their daughter in this land of the free. They stressed education in their home, and Uka graduated from the University of Illinois right here in Chicago with a degree in business. Unfortunately, her parents never saw their daughter graduate. Her father was killed on his mail route by a drunken driver when she was only thirteen, and her mother died from cancer one year before Uka received her diploma."

Winston paused, went to the defense table, and laid his arm around Uka's shoulders. She buried her head against his chest. "I'm sorry to put you through this," he said, clearly enough to be heard throughout the courtroom, "but the jury must know the whole story." He straightened, picked up a glass of water from the table, and returned to the podium.

"After graduation, Uka got a job working for a local insurance company in the Nigerian neighborhood on the North Side around Lawrence Avenue. She wanted to aid her fellow countrymen. Over the years, she has returned to Nigeria on humanitarian trips representing various nongovernment organizations that supply doctors, medical supplies, and food to her native land. In fact, she spent so much time in Nigeria, she was made a high priestess in the Yoruba religion." Extra warmth shaded his voice. "Uka is also the loving mother of a beautiful eight-year-old girl. Unfortunately, she is a single parent. She has brought her daughter along on many of her trips to Nigeria because Uka wanted her to become familiar with her heritage."

Winston paused. When he resumed, the warmth was gone. "You have heard Mr. Tunney mention ten million dollars in deposits prior to the undercover investigation as proof of her predisposition to commit the crime of money laundering. But you haven't heard that there will not be testimony from the government regarding the source of those funds. That's because the government *has* no testimony regarding the source of funds prior to the undercover meetings. The truth is that those monies were given to her by Nigerians who wanted to help people in their home country, and were used to finance the operations of the nongovernmental organizations Miss Kafi represented.

"Another problem with the undercover investigation is that numerous meetings with the informant Marvin Bailey were not recorded. We don't even know if these meetings were documented. What was said in them? Did the informant threaten Miss Kafi or any of her associates? Did he intimidate them into accepting the cash from the undercover special agent? As jurors, you must question undercover investigations because they lead to all sorts of unusual events. You will hear some of those events described during this trial. What was the motivation of the undercover agent? Was she looking for a promotion? What kind of agreement did Marvin Bailey have with the government? Desperate men do desperate things.

"The final issue we must deal with is entrapment. If the cash deposited prior to the undercover investigation isn't proof that Uka and her associates were predisposed to launder drug proceeds, then the government has failed a necessary element of proving its case, and Uka Kafi and Kunta Tama must be acquitted." Winston nodded, as if to emphasize the point. "Thank you, ladies and gentlemen of the jury. I look forward to presenting this case to you."

Judge Gomez looked at the jury. A first-generation American, he appeared thoughtful and sympathetic. "Ladies and gentlemen of the jury, you have heard the opening arguments. I caution you once again that these statements by attorneys are not evidence, but only what they hope to prove in this case. It's 10:30. Let's take a fifteen-minute break and then we'll start hearing the evidence. The government will call their first witness when we resume at 10:45."

The court clerk said, "All rise," as the jurors left the courtroom.

"I hope the judge doesn't fall for that hardship and Goody-Two stuff," Gloria mumbled to Lauren.

Tunney turned to face them. "Is that bull about the nongovernmental organizations true?"

Lauren shrugged. Tunney motioned for Gloria to move closer. She slid toward him. "He was your informant! Did he ever say anything to you about the NGOs?"

Gloria shook her head.

Fifteen minutes later, the judge and jury were seated again. Judge Gomez looked at Tunney. "Call you first witness."

Tunney stood at the prosecution table. "The government calls Special Agent Lauren Ashberry."

Lauren stood. She felt her heart pounding. This was her first time testifying. She stepped up onto the witness stand and steadied her hands on the railing in front of her. She knew she looked good—professional, competent—in her tailored gray suit. She remembered what Gloria had told her: "Answer the questions as simply as possible and look at the jury when you do."

She was sworn in. The beginning was easy. The background questions—education, training, two years on the job. Then the questions began requiring longer answers and explanations. Tunney asked, "Did you prepare the government exhibit Bank Account One, analyzing incoming deposits and outgoing transfers for the bank accounts maintained for Uka Kafi's business and the accounts for the front businesses maintained under the names of Tama Auto Sales, Zalan's Towing Service, and Chinwe's American Tire?"

"Yes." Lauren's eyes drifted to the jury. She noticed a couple of the older female jurors focused on her. *That's a good thing, I hope. Maybe they like me...hopefully they don't think I'm too young and inexperienced.*

Tunney interrupted her thought process. "What do those exhibits reflect?"

Lauren tried to remember. *Look at the jury.* "They list each deposit made to all four accounts, the transfers and checks out of the accounts, and are summarized by year.

Tunney requested, and got, the judge's permission to enter the exhibit and publish it to the jury. He slid copies of the deposit tickets onto an overhead projector, so the documents appeared on a screen to the left of the judge's bench and were visible to the judge, the jury, the defense, and the prosecution. "Are these three copies of deposit tickets to checking accounts titled Tama's Auto Sales, Zalan's Towing Service, and Chinwe's American Tires included in in the exhibit we just introduced?"

Lauren nodded and said they were.

Tunney went on. "Let's examine these deposit tickets and see how they fit into the defendants' scheme. They are all on the same date — Monday, September fifteenth, 2003 — for cash deposits in amounts of $3,000, $5,000 and another $5,000, totaling $13,000. Title 31, Section 5326 requires banks to send currency transaction reports to the IRS anytime they have a financial transaction of more than $10,000 cash in one day. In your expert opinion, Agent Ashberry, why would someone break up $13,000 into these smaller amounts?"

Lauren answered smoothly, sure of her ground. "Breaking down same-day deposits in this manner is a common way money launderers attempt to have banks avoid preparing currency transaction reports. It's referred to as a structuring violation."

"During your analysis of these three accounts, approximately how many similar same-day deposits of more than $10,000 in cash did you find?"

"There are hundreds of such deposits. The total amount of them is over $1,400,000."

"Now, you were the raid leader when the search warrant was executed on Uka Kafi's insurance business, on January twenty-first, 2005?"

Lauren pushed her long blonde hair over her shoulder. "That's correct."

"What did you find there?"

"We found bank records for all the accounts you previously mentioned, but more importantly, we located a floor safe in Uka Kafi's office hidden underneath a credenza. The safe contained over $800,000 in cash, wrapped in bundles varying in amounts from $3,000 to $5,000 and a coded ledger reflecting the receipt of the cash."

"Why are the amounts of those bundles so important?" Tunney asked.

"Because they match the dollar amounts listed on the hundreds of deposits I previously testified to, which were structured so the bank would not prepare currency transaction reports," Lauren said.

Tunney and Lauren spent the next hour going over many of the one hundred structured deposits, until Tunney saw some of the jurors yawning. "I only have two more questions to ask you," he said. "You testified that prior to the undercover investigation, approximately ten million in cash was deposited to the three accounts maintained by Uka's associates: Zalan, Tama, and Chinwe. What happened to those monies?"

"Approximately $70,000 to $80,000 remained in the respective accounts or were checks issued to Zalan, Chinwe and Tama. Checks were written to Uka Kafi totaling $500,000 and the balance was wired to Nigerian Luxury Auto Sales."

Tunney braced his hands on his hips. "Do you know what a nongovernmental organization is?"

"Yes. They're commonly referred to as NGOs, and usually they're charitable organizations. They're not affiliated with any government entity."

"As far as you know, Nigerian Luxury Auto Sales is not an NGO?"

Lauren faced the jury. "No."

"As far as you know, Nigerian Luxury Auto Sales had nothing to do with sending doctors, medical supplies, food or any other items to Nigeria?"

"No."

Tunney stepped back from the podium and returned to the prosecution table. "I have no further questions for this witness at this time, but I reserve the right to call her back later."

Judge Gomez cleared his throat. "It's 1:15. Let's break for lunch and we'll resume with the cross-examination of Agent Ashberry when we return."

At 2:15, the judge welcomed the jury back. Lauren returned to the witness chair. "Miss Ashberry, I remind you that you are still under oath. Mr. Winston, the witness is yours."

Winston stood, straightened the sleeves of his suit coat, and walked to the podium. He slammed his notebook on it, as if hoping to unnerve Lauren. "So, two years on the job. I guess you're an up-and-comer."

Tunney stood. "Your honor, I object. First, it's not a question and second, it's argumentative."

Judge Gomez clenched his jaw. "Mr. Winston, not in my courtroom."

"Yes, your honor. I was just making the point that to give such an inexperienced agent so much authority can lead to mistakes and a lack of good judgement."

The judge crossed his arms and leaned back in his chair, "Save it for your closing arguments. In the meantime, ask appropriate questions of witnesses."

Winston nodded acknowledgement, then turned his gaze on Lauren again. "Were you present for every interview involving Marvin Bailey?"

Lauren folded her hands in front of her. Winston made her nervous, but damned if she'd show it. "Special Agent Nighthawk had a relationship with Marvin prior to me becoming an agent. So in response to your question, no."

"Is that how you referred to him, as Marvin?"

She nodded. "Yes."

"So, you're kind of friends?"

She shook her head. "No, he was an informant. That was our relationship."

Winston went on for the next hour, hitting Lauren with a barrage of questions. "Was each interview documented by a memorandum? Do you know if confidential informant Bailey had any contact with Uka Kafi or any of her associates that you or undercover Agent Nighthawk were not aware of? Were there times when Agent Nighthawk was the only agent with Marvin Bailey? Do you know what they talked about? Were you the raid leader when the search warrant was executed on Uka Kafi's auto insurance business? Did you threaten Uka Kafi during the execution of the search warrant?"

Lauren answered each question, trying to focus on the jury. Then he asked one she wasn't expecting. "Didn't you tell Uka you didn't believe in her religion?"

Lauren's face reddened. "That's a misstatement. She claimed that because she was a high priestess in the Yoruba religion, she could put a curse on Marvin, Gloria, and me. It's the curse I said I didn't believe in, not her religious faith."

"Just a few more questions, Agent Ashberry. As far as you know, is Nigerian Luxury Auto Sales a nongovernmental organization?"

Lauren pursed her lips. "Not to my knowledge. Actually, the first time I heard it *was* a nongovernmental organization was in your opening statement."

Winston mimicked Tunney, placing his hands on his hips. "So, in fact, you're saying you don't know either way. Is that correct?"

Lauren crossed her arms over her chest. "Yes."

"And you also don't know that they didn't have anything to do with sending doctors, medical supplies, food or any other items to Nigeria?"

"No. I don't know that."

Winston puffed out his chest. "Within minutes after delivery of the $100,000 in undercover funds to Uka, she was robbed of it at gunpoint. Was this part of the investigation?"

Lauren pressed her lips together. "No."

"Later that same day, Agent Nighthawk returned with the $100,000 and gave it to Uka again. How did Agent Nighthawk get hold of the funds to give them back?"

"Marvin gave her the cash," Lauren said.

"Surely, you investigated how super informant Marvin Bailey got his hands on the money?"

"No."

Winston stepped alongside the podium so the jury could see his exasperation and extended his arms, palms up. "Did anyone from the government investigate who initially stole the $100,000 in undercover funds from Uka?"

Lauren answered calmly. "I don't believe so. The only one who knew was Marvin, and he was not available."

Winston nodded. "Interesting. No further questions at this time."

Lauren kept her head lowered as she left the witness stand and walked to the prosecution table. She'd answered as best she could, but she felt as though she had let her team down. She sat next to Gloria, feeling like she should apologize, but said nothing.

Gloria scooted toward her and whispered, "You did well. As good as anyone could do. You always win some points and lose some. That's just the way it goes."

"Next witness," Judge Gomez called out.

Tunney stood, but remained at the prosecution table. "The government calls Tofil Chinwe." Beside him, Assistant U.S. Attorney Cheryl Boston rose and proceeded to the podium with a leather folder containing her notes.

The door to the courtside lockup opened and two U.S. Marshals escorted Chinwe in. He wore a prisoner's orange jumpsuit that hung large on his slender frame, and spoke with a heavy Nigerian accent when he was sworn in by the clerk. Before he answered any questions, he asked for a glass of "wata." Boston went to the prosecution table and poured him some water. "Your honor, may I approach the witness?" The judge waved her on.

Chinwe accepted the glass and took a sip. He responded to the prosecutor's questions without hesitation. He met Uka Kafi in 2002, and she offered him a job at her insurance company. It involved running errands for her, including making cash deposits to the bank for an account titled American Tire. Yes, this was an account set up by Uka Kafi. The other men working for Miss Kafi, Zubari Zalan and Kunte Tama, did the same thing. No, he was not familiar with the names of those accounts. They all received the cash from Miss Kafi, usually in bundles ranging from $3,000 to $5,000. Various men would come to her business and meet privately with her. He was never introduced to them, but assumed they were the source of the cash. In January 2005, the insurance company was raided and they were all arrested by the IRS. He agreed to cooperate with the government because he suspected that what they had been doing was wrong.

AUSA Boston closed her folder. "No further questions for this witness." She resumed her place at the prosecution table.

The public defender, Morris Greenspan, conferred with Winston and wrote a few notes on his tablet. He wore a brown off the rack three-piece suit with a matching bow tie. He rose and went to the podium. "Mr. Chinwe, nice choice of clothing," Greenspan said.

Tunney stood. "I object, argumentative."

The judge exhaled. "That's not appropriate, Mr. Greenspan."

"Sorry, your honor." Greenspan perused his notes, then began firing questions at Chinwe "What has the government promised you in connection with your testimony?"

"Nothing," Chinwe said.

"You realize that at some time after this trial the government will sentence you. You will go to jail and ultimately be deported back to Nigeria?"

Chinwe shrugged. "Whatever happens, happens."

Greenspan thumped his fingers on the podium and looked over his shoulder at Winston. Winston waved at him as if urging him to go on. "You were present when the robbers took the $100,000. Can you identify them?"

"No, they wore masks when they came in and flashed their guns. I dropped behind my desk."

"Did you see their car?"

Chinwe shook his head. "No."

Greenspan briefly looked at Winston again and shrugged. "One more question. Why're you cooperating?"

Chinwe raised his chin. "'Cause what I did was wrong. What I'm saying is the truth."

Greenspan paged rapidly through his notes, then shook his head. "No further questions." He walked back to the defense table, looking like a beaten puppy.

The marshals returned Chinwe to the lockup.

Judge Gomez said, "It's 4:00. Let's take a fifteen-minute break."

Everyone stood as the jury exited. Tunney leaned forward, grinning at his team. "Chinwe said exactly what needed to be said by a witness. I love it."

At 4:15, court was back in session. Tunney stood. "Your honor, considering the late hour, I think the most efficient use of the court's time would be to read stipulations to the jury and begin with actual testimony first thing tomorrow."

The judge looked at Winston, who nodded. "That's fine. It will give us overnight to prepare for Agent Nighthawk."

CHAPTER 52

Courtroom 1905
Dirksen Federal Building
Wednesday, March 9, 2005
9:30 a.m.

EVERY SEAT IN THE COURTROOM was taken. The tension was heavy. Everyone waited for the diminutive undercover agent to face cross-examination by one of the most seasoned defense attorneys in Chicago, James Winston.

Gloria waited at the prosecution table for the judge and jury to enter the courtroom. She was absorbed in thought, wondering how many hours she would be on the witness stand and how she would respond to even Tunney's questions. She felt jittery and looked around to see if anyone had noticed. Her direct testimony at some point would require her to conceal the truth to protect her son, and herself for killing Marvin Bailey. Gloria had tried to put Bailey's death out of her mind, but it wasn't possible. Even now, the vision of Marvin straddling her and reaching for her Sig flashed through her mind. She could almost hear the shots fired. She knew Winston would dig even deeper and harder with attacks on her credibility during cross-examination, which could result in an acquittal. Even worse would be if she broke down under the pressure. What effect might it have on her life, not just today, but in the future? That could be the worst part of it, the future.

The next thing she heard was Tunney. "The government calls Special Agent Gloria Nighthawk." Tunney nodded at her, waiting for Gloria to approach the witness stand.

Gloria rose and marched to the stand like she had many times before, but she knew this time would not be the same. Her heart raced and she wondered whether she could hide her anxiety from everyone in the courtroom. She placed her hand on the Bible and was sworn in. When the clerk got to *do you swear to tell the truth and the whole truth, so help you God*, she thought, *do I really?* Her verbal response was, "I do."

Tunney began with the usual background questions. How long have you been an agent? How many awards have you received? What has been the nature of your assignments? Then he cleared his throat. "Who was Marvin Bailey?"

He was going straight at the most vulnerable part of the government's case to show they had nothing to hide. In a steady voice, Gloria responded, "My informant."

"What was the nature of your relationship with him?"

"He had worked for me for about five years, giving me information on people involved in narcotics trafficking."

"At some point, did your relationship with him change?"

"Yes. Marvin brought me allegations regarding Uka Kafi. Marvin put me into the case. His friend Babatunde Okoye knew Miss Kafi. He initially advised Baba that I was a heroin dealer, that he was delivering duffel bags full of cash from my drug operations to my banker, and that my banker went missing, so I needed someone else to launder my money."

Tunney opened his palms upward. "Was any of that true? Or was it all a ruse to give Marvin Bailey credibility in the eyes of Uka Kafi?"

"The latter. A ruse."

"Is this the way an investigation normally runs?"

"No, but it seemed like a good cover story, so we ran with it."

For the next hour, Tunney put a series of memos and transcripts of telephone calls and undercover meetings on the projector, their dates ranging from December 8, 2004, through January 7, 2005. He reminded the jury that Special Agent Ashberry had previously testified regarding these documents, and Gloria corroborated Lauren's direct testimony.

Tunney took a deep breath. "Now I want to direct your attention to the memos and transcripts of January eleventh, 2005. What transpired on that date?"

Gloria's hands tightened in her lap. "At approximately 2:30 p.m. Marvin Bailey and I went to Uka Kafi's office with $100,000 in cash contained in two green plastic garbage bags. It was money the DEA loaned us from a seizure they made. Street money, mostly fives, tens, and twenties, like a dope dealer might have. The recording device I used was a special set of eyeglasses.

"We entered and were greeted by Kunta Tama. There were two other men in the office area. None of the men appeared to be armed. I advised Tama that my associate, Marvin Bailey, had previously met with Miss Uka and that we would like to meet with her now. Tama went to her office briefly, and upon returning, told us she was busy. I asked him to try a second time. He did, and we were allowed to meet with her. Tama, Uka Kafi, Marvin Bailey, and I were present for this meeting. Uka instructed Tama to pat us down for weapons and listening devices, which he did. He found nothing, of course.

"I explained to Miss Kafi our reason for coming. I told her my partner had closed our Swiss account and opened a new account in the Bahamas, something we regularly did for security reasons, and that if she had attempted to send the $15,000 Marvin previously gave her, it would not have gone through. She advised me that she had not moved our funds yet. I gave her the new account information."

"And then?"

"I said I hoped our relationship could be long and mutually profitable. Uka replied that she doesn't do business with people she doesn't know. I told her our situation was a little different, since Baba and Marvin had known each other for over five years, I'd known Marvin for many years, and she had already accepted $15,000 of my money from him."

"What do you think she meant when she said she doesn't 'do business' with people she doesn't know?"

"That she laundered money for people she knew personally," Gloria said.

Winston rose from his seat at the defense table. "Objection, your honor! I don't think it's appropriate for this agent to interpret the meaning of Miss Uka's statements. She's twisting them to make them fit the government's case."

Judge Gomez turned toward him. "Overruled. You can argue that in your closing, but the witness's conclusion is not an unreasonable one to make."

Winston sat down, banging his fist on the table. The judge gave him a long look.

"What happened next?" Tunney asked.

Gloria drew a breath. "Marvin placed the garbage bags on Miss Kafi's desk. I told her the contents represented the proceeds from the weekend, and that every weekend's take was about the same. Right then, my glasses started humming, a sign they needed to reboot. The tech agent had told me this might happen, and also that the humming would not be noticeable to others in the room. I took them off and folded in the earpieces, as I had been instructed, and placed the glasses on Uka Kafi's desk. Unfortunately, nothing after that point was recorded."

"Because the device was rebooting?"

"Yes."

Tunney nodded. "Please tell the court what transpired, to the best of your recollection."

"Uka said the amount of money was good. We shook hands across her desk." Gloria fidgeted in her chair. "She told me she would launder the $100,000 at a seven percent commission and it would take about a week. I gave her my business card with an undercover cell number on it in case she needed to contact me. Uka said she was looking forward to a long and successful relationship, and she would notify us when the money was laundered. At that point, Marvin and I left her office. It was approximately 3 p.m. We drove off in Marvin's car and met Agent Ashberry a few blocks away. Marvin then left in his own vehicle."

Gloria paused to collect herself. Tunney was waiting for her to continue. She tried to focus, to keep thoughts of Darius at bay. "At approximately 3:15, I realized I had left the glasses in Uka's office. Agent Ashberry drove me back and dropped me off about a block away, and I walked toward Uka's business." She hesitated. In her mind's eye she could see Darius and another boy dashing across the street with the garbage bags full of drug money. She felt perspiration running from her armpits, and glanced down at the floor before continuing. "When I got there, I knew something was wrong. The glass door was cracked, and Uka and her associates were upset. Uka told me two men in ski masks robbed them of the cash and fired shots into the rear wall. She demanded to know if I was trying to get her killed. Uka went to her office and retrieved my glasses.

"I knew I had to fix the situation. I told her this had never happened to me before, that I would find out how and why the robbery occurred, and I would come see her when I got my money back. At that time, I didn't know whether to believe Uka Kafi, because I thought she might have ripped us off."

"How did Uka respond?"

"She said it was going to cost me ten percent to launder the money now."

Winston shifted in his chair as if about to object, but kept silent. Tunney motioned for Gloria to continue. Now that she was past the worst of it, her words came more freely. "When I returned to the car, I asked Agent Ashberry if she saw anything. She said that from her vantage point she hadn't seen anyone enter or leave Uka's business." Gloria left out that Lauren had been on her cell phone. *That's the least I can do.*

"Did Marvin call you later?" Tunney asked.

"Yes, at approximately 4:40. Marvin said he had the bags with all the cash that was stolen. I should have asked him how he got the money back, but I didn't. My immediate concern was keeping the Uka Kafi investigation alive." Gloria moistened her lips. "There was a tape recorder in Agent Ashberry's car. I used it to record my next call to Uka's office. Tama answered. I told him everything had been resolved, that I had recovered the $100,000 and would return with it in about thirty minutes. After that, Ashberry and I met Marvin. I got into his car and verified all the cash was there.

"About 5: 15 p.m., Marvin and I arrived at Uka's business. I put the glasses on, activating the recording device. A few minutes later we entered the premises." Gloria scooted up in her seat. "At our initial meeting, none of Uka's associates appeared to be armed, but this time one of them had a firearm clearly visible and the others had pistols tucked under their shirts. Uka didn't look happy to see us, especially Marvin."

"Then what happened?"

"I told her Marvin was not the problem. That the problem had been resolved. Uka again agreed to launder the $100,000 at a ten percent commission. I said yes to that, and we left."

Tunney nodded. "When was the last time you reached out to Marvin?"

Gloria didn't recall if anyone had subpoenaed her or Marvin's phone records. If they had been subpoenaed, her world could crumble on cross-examination. She drew a deep breath. She had to get this part of her testimony exactly right, keep her answers vague enough that the jury might blame Uka or one of the other defendants for Marvin's absence. "I was busy with this case, going over the undercover transcripts to make sure they were accurate. I tried periodically to get in touch with Marvin to find out how he got the drug cash back, but we kept playing phone tag. To the best of my recollection, the last time I texted or called him was January nineteenth, 2005. I never heard back from him."

Tunney looked at the jury. "One last question. Were the undercover payments of $15,000 and $100,000 made to Uka Kafi deposited to the government's undercover account?"

"Yes, they were," Gloria said.

Tunney closed his folder of notes, and looked at the judge. "No further questions."

Judge Gomez nodded. "Let's take a fifteen-minute break. Mr. Winston can begin his cross-examination when we resume."

Winston looked dapper, as usual. He wore a tailor-made three-piece light gray suit with a red silk tie, a matching pocket square, a crisp white shirt and shiny black loafers. Before he strode up to the podium, he leaned over and whispered something to Uka.

Gloria watched him like a hawk. The only words she made out, from the way he mouthed them were *agent…hiding…something.*

Winston marched up to the podium, brimming with confidence. He carried a yellow legal pad. "Good afternoon, Agent Nighthawk."

"Good afternoon." Gloria knew that was the last friendly gesture Winston would make.

He tilted his head, his eyes fixed on hers. "When was your last contact with Uka Kafi? Was it January twenty-first, 2005, the day you executed the search warrant?"

Winston knew perfectly well otherwise. Gloria kept her expression neutral. "I didn't execute the warrant. As the undercover contact, I wasn't on that team. My last contact with Uka Kafi occurred on January eleventh, 2005."

"Of course." Winston glanced briefly at his legal pad. "But the last time you reached out to Marvin Bailey was January nineteenth? You had no contact with your informant since that day?"

Gloria took a deep breath. "That's correct."

"When was that last contact? Morning, afternoon, evening?"

If Winston has the cell phone records, this could be the end. Somehow, she managed to answer. "I don't recall exactly. As I said earlier, I've had a lot to keep track of with this case."

Winston turned and looked at Tunney. "I don't recall getting copies of any phone or text records in discovery?"

Just for a heartbeat, Gloria closed her eyes.

Tunney glanced at Lauren, who was responsible for organizing the discovery materials. She shook her head and raised her hands, palms up. Tunney stood and responded to Winston. "We turned over everything in our possession."

Winston shrugged. "Unusual, that those particular items weren't included." Tunney opened his mouth as if to object, but Winston raised a hand and returned his focus to Gloria. "I want to clarify something for the jury. Your response was a little vague regarding the absence of Mr. Bailey during this trial. Some jurors may think Miss Uka or one of her associates had something to do with Marvin Bailey not being available to testify." Winston raised his voice. "That is not the case. Am I correct?"

Gloria kept her cool on the surface, but on the inside she felt like she was losing it. "That's correct. There's no evidence that Miss Kafi or any of her associates had anything to do with Marvin Bailey's absence from this trial."

"Good. I'm glad we all agree on that fact. Now, was every telephone call and meeting, undercover or otherwise, with your friend Marvin documented?"

"He was not my friend. He was my informant."

Winston's eyebrows rose. "Well, you and Agent Ashberry did refer to and address him as Marvin, not as Mr. Bailey. Isn't that true?"

"It is. I've known him for five years." *And now he's dead.* Gloria steadied herself against a pang of guilt. "To the best of my knowledge, every contact with Marvin Bailey was documented, except for calls made solely for the purpose of setting up a meeting."

"Do you know if Marvin ever threatened Miss Uka or any of her associates?"

Her answer was guarded. "There is no evidence of any threats on any of the recorded conversations."

"But you don't know if Marvin talked to Miss Uka or anyone else outside of your investigation?"

Gloria's gaze went from juror to juror, and she shook her head. "I told Marvin not to have any contact with Uka or anyone else involved in the case. I can't say if he disobeyed that or he didn't."

"You know Marvin talked to his friend Baba before he ever mentioned Miss Uka to you."

"Yes, that was the only contact he made outside of my direction."

Winston folded his arms across his chest. "You mean that you know of?"

"Yes."

Winston took a step toward Gloria and pointed his finger at her. "Agent Nighthawk, do you really expect the jury to believe this hogwash that your informant Bailey had nothing to do with the theft of the $100,000? When he brought it to Miss Uka at your direction in the first place, and he restored it to you for a second try almost immediately after the robbery took place?"

Gloria stood her ground. "Yes. I do." Her head was spinning. Winston was getting uncomfortably close to the truth.

Winston waved his hands in the air. "Oh, come on now. Isn't it true that you knew who was involved in the theft of the $100,000 from Uka?"

Gloria lowered her head and braced herself on the railing at the front of the witness stand.

Tunney rose swiftly from his seat at the prosecution table. "I object. This is an outrageous claim not supported by any evidence, and it affects the credibility of Agent Nighthawk, who has an unblemished reputation."

Judge Gomez stared Winston down. "Sustained. The jury is instructed to disregard that last question." He scowled at the defense attorney. "I caution you to limit your cross-examination to subject matter that has been raised in the government's direct examination. Do you understand?"

Winston kept a poker face. "Yes, your honor." He returned his attention to Gloria. "Now, getting back to your undercover role. What name did you use as a supposed big-time heroin dealer?"

"Gloria Nightingale."

Winston smiled. "Sneaky. Close to your real name in case someone recognized you."

Gloria raised her eyebrows. "I don't believe that's a question."

Winston shook his head and returned to the defense table. "Your honor, I have no further questions for this witness. This run-amuck investigation was controlled by a missing informant who is conveniently unavailable to testify and be cross-examined."

Judge Gomez glanced toward Tunney. "Does the government want to redirect on Miss Nighthawk?"

Tunney said, "No, your honor. The government rests."

Relief washed over Gloria. Her secret, and her son, were safe. But she knew she would be haunted for the rest of her life by the killing of Marvin Bailey.

Judge Gomez dismissed her and she returned to her seat at the prosecution table. Gomez looked over at the defense. "Any motions?"

Winston caught Greenspan's eye. The public defender shook his head. "Not at this time," Winston answered.

The jury was escorted out of the courtroom. Once they were gone, Winston stood. "Your honor, the government has not proven their case beyond a reasonable doubt. I move for a directed verdict of acquittal for Uka Kafi and Kunta Tama."

The judge picked up his pen and tapped his calendar. "The law states that I must consider all the evidence in the light most favorable to the prosecution. Therefore, despite certain weaknesses in the government's case, I must deny your motion. Closing arguments will begin at 1:30 this afternoon. Until then, court is adjourned."

CHAPTER 53

Courtroom 1905
Dirksen Federal Building
Wednesday March 9, 2005
1:30 p.m.

T HE JURY REENTERED THE COURTROOM, and everyone stood until the jury was seated.

Judge Gomez addressed them. "Ladies and gentlemen of the jury, the defense and the prosecutors have rested their cases. By law, Miss Kafi and Mr. Tama are presumed innocent, so the defense is not required to present any evidence or call any witnesses. The government has the burden of proving that Miss Kafi, Mr. Tama, or both are guilty beyond a reasonable doubt.

"You, the members of the jury, are the triers of fact. Which means it is your job to sort through the evidence introduced during this trial, including the credibility of witnesses, the admissibility of certain types of evidence, and the weight given to each piece. It is my responsibility to deal with questions of law, which means I decide how the law applies to a given set of facts. To find either Miss Kafi or Mr. Tama guilty, your decision must be unanimous. That means all twelve of you must agree on the verdict."

The judge then described the elements of the crime of money laundering, followed by instructions on deliberations and how to ask questions of the court. "We will now start the closing arguments," he said, finally. "Is the prosecution ready?"

Tunney stood. "Yes, your honor. My co-counsel, Miss Boston, will commence."

Cheryl Boston approached the podium and opened her folder. For the next ninety minutes she talked about the $800,000 found in the hidden floor safe, reviewed the analysis of the three front accounts' bank records, and played the tape recordings of the undercover meetings between Gloria, Marvin Bailey, Uka Kafi and Kunta Tama, highlighting the transcripts on the overhead projector. She finished by thanking the jury for their attention, closed her folder, and returned to her seat at the prosecution table.

The judge nodded at Winston. The defense attorney rose and thanked the jury for their time, and then went on for an hour claiming the government had entrapped Uka Kafi and Kunta Tama when Agent Nighthawk flashed substantial amounts of cash in front of them. "In two transactions, for a total of $115,000. Who could refuse that much money?" he exclaimed, raising his arms. "The government has never produced an ounce of evidence that the funds deposited to the accounts of Kunta Tama, Zubari Zalan, and Tofil Chinwe, prior to those transactions, came from any specific unlawful activity."

He spent the next half hour ranting about Marvin Bailey, the government's missing witness. Partway through this performance, he turned from the jury and sneered at Gloria. "What secrets lie under the government's case? How could someone like Agent Nighthawk, with all her years of experience and awards, fail to ask her informant how he got his dirty hands on the $100,000 that two other, unknown men allegedly stole from Uka Kafi's business premises shortly after Mr. Bailey's departure? Doesn't that make you wonder what was really going on here? You can't let them get away with this!" Winston slapped his hand on the podium. "You must find Uka Kafi and Kunta

Tama innocent!" He turned from the podium with a disgusted look on his face and resumed his seat at the defense table.

Judge Gomez looked at the prosecutors. "Mr. Tunney, the floor is yours for rebuttal."

Tunney stood, buttoned his navy suit coat, and proceeded to the podium. "Ladies and gentlemen of the jury, let's get back to what the evidence in this case *has* proved beyond a reasonable doubt. When you do that, there is only one conclusion you can reach." He turned and pointed at the defendants. "Uka Kafi and Kunta Tama believed that the cash they received from Agent Nighthawk and her informant, Marvin Bailey, was generated from a heroin ring. *That's the specific unlawful activity the law requires.* You heard the tape recordings from the undercover meetings. Mr. Winston claims these defendants were not predisposed to launder drug money before the undercover operation. Where do you think the $800,000 in the floor safe came from? If it were legitimate money, why would Uka Kafi hide it? If you recall, those bills were all fives, tens, and twenties. The same denominations commonly known as 'street money' and generated from *real* drug rings, the same as the purported drug profits from Agent Nighthawk. There was no entrapment. Kunta Tama counted the number of bundles of cash in the bags brought by Agent Nighthawk and her informant. Uka Kafi demanded a ten percent fee for laundering the drug money. You heard her. Those were their words.

"Now, if you were to believe Mr. Winston, there was some kind of conspiracy between Agent Nighthawk and Marvin Bailey. But if that were so, we wouldn't be here today because that $100,000 would not be included in the evidence for this case. If Marvin Bailey was involved in the theft of the cash he himself carried through Uka Kafi's door, why would he return that cash to Agent Nighthawk so she could complete the undercover transaction? No one was trying to get away with anything. Agent Nighthawk was simply doing her job."

Tunney paused to let that sink in, then thanked the jury and returned to his seat.

Judge Gomez swiveled his chair to face the jury. He spent the next several minutes reading through the twenty pages of instructions and then looked at his watch. "It's 4:30. The officer will escort you to the jury room to begin deliberations. If you don't have a verdict by 6 p.m., we will resume tomorrow morning at 9:30. Don't feel that you must reach a verdict this evening. Take your time to go through all the evidence you need to."

After the jury left the courtroom, Gomez looked at the attorneys. "Any items that need to be discussed before we adjourn for the day?"

Tunney rose. "Your honor, Miss Uka and Mr. Kunta have had access to false passports, and they may have access to substantial amounts of cash of which we are not aware. We believe they are flight risks." He looked over his shoulder as four beefy U.S. Marshals entered the courtroom. "We believe they should not be released on their own recognizance."

Winston shot upright. "That's ridiculous. Our clients have both shown up every day for trial. What more could you ask of them?"

Judge Gomez raised his hand for Winston to be quiet. "I appreciate that they came for trial each day. However, things are different now pending a verdict that could result in a lengthy period of incarceration. If acquitted, they'll only be incarcerated for a day or two." He signaled to the marshals. "Take them to the lockup."

Winston whispered a few words to Uka, then shoved his legal pads into his briefcase and slammed it shut. The marshals handcuffed Uka Kafi and Kunta Tama and escorted them through the side door of the courtroom.

Winston gave Gloria a hard stare as he hustled out of the courtroom. Tunney's eyes followed Winston's exit. The AUSA had a smirk on his face.

Lauren smiled at Gloria, then noticed Gloria's trembling hands folded in her lap.

CHAPTER 54

Courtroom 1905
Dirksen Federal Building
Thursday, March 10, 2005
10:30 a.m.

LATE THURSDAY MORNING, THEY WERE all summoned back to the courtroom. Gloria knew what that meant. The jury had a verdict.

Seated with the rest of the prosecution team, Gloria could feel the daggers thrown her way from Uka Kafi's eyes. Apparently, James Winston had been able to get Uka's green and gold Nigerian dress cleaned and pressed. She looked resplendent in it as she glared at Gloria. Tama wore his wrinkled African garb from the day before. He sat with his head down and his shoulders slumped.

Gloria stared back at Kafi. *Try to put your curse on me. It won't happen.*

"All rise," the court security officer intoned as the jury entered. There was a rumble in the courtroom as everyone present came to their feet and then sat when the jury did.

Judge Gomez addressed the foreperson, a well-dressed middle-aged woman. "I understand you have arrived at a verdict."

The woman stood. She held a few slips of paper. "Yes, your honor, we have."

"Please give your verdict forms to the court security officer." She gave the papers to the officer, who gave them to the judge. Gomez inspected them and gave them back to the officer, who returned them to the foreperson.

"You may read your verdict," the judge said.

"Guilty on all counts for Uka Kafi, and guilty on all counts for Kunta Tama," the foreperson announced.

Winston shook his head and brought his hand to his mouth. Kafi slammed her fist on the table. Tama shook his head and a tear rolled down his cheek.

Everyone at the prosecution table remained stoic, saving their celebration for the privacy of their office. Gloria let out a long breath she hadn't been aware of holding. *I'm one step closer to the end of a long journey, one I would never wish upon anyone. My lover is dead and so is our child. My marriage is a failure, my son is an addict, and I murdered Marvin Bailey, likely for nothing.* She clenched her hands together, gripping one finger as if twisting an absent wedding ring. *My world is crumbling. I need to find a way out.*

Courtroom 2502
Friday, March 11, 2005

Darius Carlton slouched behind two tall men in the last row of benches. He was three weeks out of rehab and wanted to see his father on this sad day, the day of sentencing, because he knew it could be a long time before they saw each other again.

His mother had asked him not to come to court today. She'd told him she wouldn't be there. That was enough reason for Darius to show up.

He looked over at the prosecution table. His mother's partner, Lauren Ashberry, was seated there along with the U.S. Attorneys,

Todd Jeffreys and Phillip Tunney, and two FBI agents. The side door from the lockup opened, and he watched as two U.S. Marshals escorted his father into the courtroom. They removed his handcuffs and stood next to him at the podium as if they thought he were going to flee. In place of his usual tailor-made suits, Robert Carlton wore a baggy orange jumpsuit. Darius's father had always held his head high. Not today. Today he was a broken man, his head bowed.

"Do you have anything to say?" Judge Peterson asked him.

Carlton raised his head. "No, let's get this over."

The judge cleared his throat. "I have considered your years of service as an assistant U.S. attorney and federal judge. They do not compensate for the deeds you were convicted of and pled guilty to. Threatening a federal witness is a serious offense. God knows what you would have done if your wife, in her capacity as a federal agent, had not shot and killed him. I sentence you to ten years' incarceration." He shook his head. "Take him away."

Darius thought, *I've lived through that night a hundred times. My father wanted me to kill Spencer McElroy. Expected me to be his savior and lie in court for him. I don't know if I can ever forgive him.*

He watched the marshals cuff his father, grab him by his elbow, and escort him back to the lockup.

Darius buried his face in his hands to hide his tears.

CHAPTER 55

Harry's Bar
Wells and Van Buren, Chicago, IL
Friday, March 11, 2005
6:00 p.m.

IT WAS THE USUAL CROWD at Harry's, one of the safest places in the Loop to have a few drinks on a Friday night. The bar was elbow to elbow with armed federal agents, in addition to a few plainclothes Chicago police officers assigned to DEA and ATF and a collection of badge honeys. The jukebox played classic rock from the Stones, Beatles, and the Four Seasons, along with rhythm and blues from the Temptations and Smokey Robinson. On the television over the bar, the Bulls were jumping all over the Bucks.

Gloria sat at a table with Lauren, Jeffreys and Tunney, and the FBI agents, Fanelli and Axelrod, as they shared celebratory drinks. The jury had returned guilty verdicts for Uka Kafi and her associate, and Gloria's husband had been sentenced to ten years in a federal penitentiary. Everyone kindly left the subject of Robert Carlton's sentence off the table.

"How much time are you going to ask for Uka and Tama?" asked Lauren.

Jeffreys took a sip from his frosty mug of Miller Lite. "We'll go for the max, but realistically I think Uka will get five years, Tama three and Chinwe one because of his cooperation. None of them are U.S. citizens, so they'll be deported back to Nigeria after they complete their sentences."

Fanelli raised another scotch and water. "Send 'em back. Don't need them in our country. I heard they have schools where they teach 'em how to steal mail and sell stolen credit cards. Send 'em back!"

Gloria glanced at Lauren and then at Fanelli. "You going to be all right driving home?"

"Got my chauffeur. Ain't that right?" Fanelli tapped Axelrod on the shoulder.

"Wish I could stay longer, but I've got to get home to my kids." Gloria drained the last of her beer and stood. She'd managed to play along with the collective good mood, but she wasn't feeling it. "Congratulations to everyone. We did good." *When will I start believing that?*

Lauren drained her Corona, toasted them with the empty beer bottle, and stepped away from the table. "I'm heading home, too. Until next time. See you guys." She lifted her briefcase.

Fanelli blinked at them. "Come on, stay for one more. It's on me. When we're working on cases, we get wrapped up in our egos and say things that shouldn't be said. No hard feelings, huh?"

"Thanks, Tony, but I really need to get home." Gloria waved, and then she and Lauren walked out the door into the damp chill of a late winter night. Gloria pulled the collar of her ski jacket up around her neck and Lauren fitted a stocking cap over her head. Gloria glanced at Lauren's briefcase. "Don't tell me you're taking work home. You just finished a trial. Chill out for a weekend."

Lauren grinned. "This *is* me chilling out."

They walked side by side down Van Buren, heading to the federal garage. "You got fifteen minutes?" Gloria asked. "I'd like to talk to you about something."

"I've got plenty of time. I'm just not one to hang around Harry's." Lauren laughed, "Not likely to meet the love of my life there."

"Can't argue with that." Gloria gave her partner a long look, knowing she had to tell Lauren what was going on in her own life. Some of it, anyway. She hoped she could find the right words. She gave Lauren a side hug. "When we started working together…" A bemused smile crossed Gloria's face. "I didn't see it lasting too long. But I was wrong. You turned into someone special—a good friend and a *damn* good partner."

Lauren placed a hand on her heart. "You and me, we're a good team. I've been fortunate to work with you. I couldn't have gotten those experiences with anyone else." She shook her head, remembering. "Iraq, that asshole Nestor."

Gloria stiffened, reliving that moment when she'd jammed the barrel of her Sig Sauer into Nestor's forehead. She could almost feel her finger squeezing the trigger. "I would've killed him if it wasn't for you."

Lauren swallowed. "Nah, I don't think so. I mean, I understand how you were so charged up with the thought of avenging Jim Abbott's…murder. But you realized you had more important things to do—taking care of Darius and Adsila."

"There's a Starbucks on Clark and Adams. Why don't we stop there?" Gloria asked.

"Sure."

They headed into the coffee shop. It was empty, and the barista gave them a look like he'd like to close in fifteen minutes. Gloria ignored it and ordered a black coffee, Lauren a caramel macchiato. She laughed at their coffee choices. "In some ways we're still as different as day and night."

Gloria pointed a finger at her. "Yeah, I'm like the street cop and you—you belong in the ivory tower with the title 'Chief' before your name."

"Don't even say that!" They took their coffees and found themselves a clean table. "Now tell me about Darius and Adsila."

"They mean so much to me," Gloria said softly. "Darius is doing good. I'm so proud of him. I think he's going to make it through this tough chapter in his life. He'll have to go to summer school to get his diploma because he skipped too many days hiding from his father and messing with Marvin. He plans to apply to Kennedy-King in the fall. He's studying hard, working out every day, and playing ball. He wants to try out for the Kennedy-King basketball team."

"That's great. And how's Adsila doing?"

Gloria beamed as she took a sip of her coffee. "Adsila's so bright. She has her heart set on an Ivy League school. She and Darius have grown even closer. She watches over him like she's his mother. Her love for him is strong. They study together every night."

Lauren swallowed and glanced down at the table. As she raised her eyes to meet Gloria's again, Gloria knew what the next question was. "Did you tell them about their father's sentence?"

Gloria nodded. "We've talked about it, and they knew it was going to be around ten years. Darius was in therapy during rehab, and we've been seeing a family therapist since his release, which has helped a lot. I went to the first couple of meetings with them, but now it's just the kids. They seem to be in a good place. They've really focused on their schoolwork and social activities."

Lauren shook her head. "I can't say for certain. I think Darius was at the sentencing today. There was a young man seated in the last row of benches, trying hard not to be seen."

Gloria shook her head. "Damn it. I asked him not to go!"

Lauren glanced away again. "I'll never forget the change in Robert during his trial. In the beginning, he was so arrogant. But the day he pled guilty, the S.O.B. acted like a broken man."

Gloria's jaw clenched. "Seeing your son's suicide note will do that to you. Robert's out of my life. Our divorce will be final in a couple of weeks."

Lauren's eyes widened. "Suicide note?"

Gloria nodded. "Darius tried to hang himself. I found the note he'd written to his father. I took that note to the courtroom and showed it to him." She shook her head. "He thought it was bullshit and I was playing him. He shoved it to the side without even looking at it. So I told him to look at the handwriting. He recognized it and went ashen. That's when I knew the trial was over."

"Oh, my God. Did Jeffreys know about Darius?"

"Yes, I told him. Not about the note, though. I took it back when I left the courtroom. I have it in a special place in case I ever need it again."

"What do you mean? Why would you?"

"If Robert tries to come back into our lives. I'll know the time and place is right." Gloria leaned forward, resting her weight on her forearms. "This past year, I felt like I was caught in a spiderweb. I kept twisting and turning to get free of all the problems, but I only got stuck deeper and tighter."

Lauren reached across the table and laid her hands over Gloria's. "Your life will change now that you're through all this."

Gloria swallowed a lump in her throat before continuing. "Lauren, I need to make a clean break. I know in my heart that now is the time to do it."

Lauren frowned. "Do what?"

Gloria looked down at the table and then at Lauren. She almost lacked the courage to tell her. "I filed my retirement papers. I'm leaving."

Lauren gaped at her. "No…no, you can't. I need my partner! And you're too young. You can work for another five or six years and get a lot better pension."

"No, my time has come. It's the best thing for me to do." She managed a small smile. "I even have a job offer."

"What? You loved being an agent. Nothing will compare with that."

"I don't know if it was love. More like it was a need I had to fill. Now I have to change my priorities and be a real mother for Darius and

Adsila. Can I do that if I don't leave? I don't know. I can't take the chance."

Lauren pulled her hands away and tightened them into fists. "I've got to be selfish. What about me, Gloria? Who'll I have to work with?"

"You? Come on. You'll have a new chapter in your career. You're one of the best agents the service has. You can hand-pick your next partner. There's no limit for you. You can become whatever you want."

Lauren's expression remained glum. "So, what's this new job?"

"I'm not sure about it. I'm not even sure if it's for me. I'm going to take at least a month off, maybe more, and just be there for my kids. Then I'll figure out the job situation."

Lauren took a deep breath. "I've got something for you," She opened her briefcase and took out an envelope.

Gloria squinted at it. "What's that?"

Lauren pushed it across the table. "It's the records that were subpoenaed from the telephone company for Uka's trial. I got them this afternoon. A day after the trial ended."

Gloria's face froze. These records would show she'd paged Marvin at 1:30 in the morning, not long before he was killed. "What're you going to do with them?"

"This." Lauren got up from the table and grabbed the envelope. She walked out of the Starbucks and Gloria followed. They headed down Clark Street to Van Buren. Lauren turned right and headed down an alley, toward a homeless man standing by a fire burning in a 55-gallon drum. Sparks from it flew into the night air. A scarf wrapped around the man's head covered a worn stocking cap. His ski jacket was threadbare at the elbows.

The man gave them a glance, then went back to staring at the blaze. Lauren's eyes teared and she sighed as she threw the envelope into the fire. It burst into flames. "I know you must go. But I can't imagine going to work and not seeing you at your desk, knowing you won't be there for me."

THE END